EDGE OF DARK

Also by Brenda Cooper

The Creative Fire

The Diamond Deep

EDGE OF DARK

THE GLITTERING EDGE, BOOK ONE

BRENDA COOPER

an imprint of Prometheus Books
Amherst, NY

Published 2015 by Pyr®, an imprint of Prometheus Books

Cover design by Nicole Sommer-Lecht
Cover illustration by Stephan Martiniere

This is a work of fiction. Characters, organizations, products, and events portrayed in this novel either are products of the author's imagination or are used fictitiously.

Inquiries should be addressed to

Pyr
59 John Glenn Drive
Amherst, New York 14228
VOICE: 716–691–0133
FAX: 716–691–0137
WWW.PYRSF.COM

19 18 17 16 15   5 4 3 2 1

Library of Congress Cataloging-in-Publication Data

Cooper, Brenda, 1960-
    Edge of dark / Brenda Cooper.
        pages cm. — (The glittering edge ; book 1)
    ISBN 978-1-63388-050-4 (softcover) — ISBN 978-1-63388-051-1 (ebook)
    1. Life on other planets—Fiction. 2. Interplanetary voyages—Fiction. I. Title.

PS3603.O5825E34 2015
813'.6—dc23

                                                                2014039322

Printed in the United States of America

Dedicated to:
Linda Gero Merkens
Gisele Peterson

This book is partly about friendship,
and these two women have been my friends for a very long time.

PART ONE

A PLANETARY DANGER

CHAPTER ONE

CHARLIE

Charlie Windar stood on his skimmer, knees slightly bent to absorb the small shocks of his speed. The pilot's seat acted like a brace. The engine fed silently on stored sunlight and pushed the craft so fast that the wind chapped Charlie's cheeks and stung water from his eyes. The forests of Goland went on and on below him, the first new leaves of spring opening out and shining bright yellow-green. Morning sun warmed his back and made diamond patterns on thin ribbons of water that tumbled over rocks and fell down the faces of cliffs.

A band on his wrist vibrated.

He slapped his arm, effectively turning on a whole universe of communication. "What is it?"

"Distress call."

He sat down and flipped the skimmer to autopilot. "Give it to me."

"Hold onto your anger." Jean Paul Rosseau's familiar voice conveyed both worry and sarcasm in equal measures. "A family seems to have misplaced their teenagers."

"Runaways?"

"Hard to tell. The parents smell like smugglers to me."

Charlie pursed his lips, reflecting on the idiots who often ran through the way-too-loose planetary security on Lym to prove themselves against tooth and claw or hunt for treasure in some long-dead city. It did make him angry— it always made him angry. But Jean Paul was right. "Where are they?"

"The scared parents? About ten klicks from you. At the top of the Blue Canyons."

"What do you know about the kids?"

"Three boys, red haired, all healthy. Twelve, fifteen, and sixteen."

The worst ages of young male stupidity. "Used to gravity?"

"They say so." Jean Paul sounded doubtful.

Charlie stood again and surveyed the trees below him, as if the kids would just pop up there and wave at him. "How long have they been missing?"

"A day and a half."

"Shit."

"Good luck. Be careful."

"I'll let you know when I find the kids." Sometimes he never even found bodies.

"I'll make myself a cup of stim," Jean Paul promised. "Be right here for you, no matter how long it takes."

"Thanks." Charlie told the skimmer to fly lower and set up a search pattern. It would show him everything that was both breathing and bigger than a bird and even help him identify a human signature. Of course if the boys actually *had* died, it wouldn't help.

Raptors circled on rising columns of warming air. Two flocks of bright orange startles rose up just ahead of him. Charlie cursed when the skimmer hit one of the tiny birds, sending its body tumbling back into the thin canopy. Grazing angle-hops moved together, the big-eared herd looking up as the arrow-shaped shadow of the skimmer touched their clearing.

The computer showed him the bright heat of mammals and birds below the forest canopy as lights on his screen, color coded for species and movement. Tags embedded in larger animals declared that two were marsupials and one was a hunting cat stretched out on a tree-trunk as long as Charlie was tall. He catalogued the cat as interesting but kept his focus on looking for untagged humans.

The forest gave way to stony ground filled with short scrub trees and spiny grasses, a place where life depended on deep roots thrust into meager soil. The day heated, and life hid under rocks and roots. Sweat stuck his shirt to his back. The skimmer's trajectory turned again, still over the rocky plain. He admired the stark interplay of gray and black, shadow and rock, the occasional punctuation of pale green. Pale yellow flowers bloomed in the shade of rocks.

Twelve heat signatures blossomed onto the screen in front of him.

He drew his gun, started the familiar, fluid motion of his safety checks.

An audible beep signaled a living human. Then another. He listened for the third.

Nothing.

That left ten tongats: four-legged pack predators half the height of a man. He was close enough to see details. The hair on their spines stood up and their ears pricked forward and back. Most crouched low, shoulders hunched, ready to spring. The biggest and blackest of the beasts circled the pack at a lope. The pack surrounded a small hill of jumbled rocks just clear of a scraggly tree line.

One boy knelt on top of the highest rock. He held a gun pointed at the closest tongat, but he wasn't firing. A second boy stood behind him, scanning the horizon. Jean Paul hadn't been kidding about the red hair—they might as well have worn fire for hats.

Only two.

Charlie glanced down and verified that his gun was fully charged: four lights blinking green for ready. His right foot signaled the skimmer to pick up speed. He stood again, searching for the third teen.

The kneeling boy fired and one of the tongats yelped. None fell.

The standing boy turned in circles, his attention so completely on the predators that he hadn't yet noticed Charlie. The bottom of his shirt had been torn off, and his exposed skin had brightened to a sunburnt red.

To frightened boys, the attacking beasts would be big and fast and scary, maybe the scariest thing they had ever seen. Other fears would plague them as well. The open sky above them, the horizon. Everything would look wrong. No one born in space came here prepared for a place with almost no walls.

Ships were big flying coffins and the pictures he'd seen of space stations looked like planets turned inside out and robbed of their horizons.

Charlie felt sorry for the boys, if not for the parents. He squeezed the gun handle, his palm print and the pressure of it identifying him to the weapon. He was ready.

He came in close, slowing the skimmer and starting a wide circle around the boy's location.

A few of the tongats looked up, recognizing him as a threat. He fired at the big black one first, grimacing as he hit it. The animal stumbled but kept going. He ignored it for the moment, using a single shot to bring down the one closest to the boys.

It took four slow revolutions of his skimmer before the last tongat fell.

The boy still pointed his weapon at them.

Charlie turned on his loudspeaker. "Put your gun down."

The boy fired. The body of the animal closest to him jerked.

"Now."

The boy glanced up and hesitated, and for a moment it appeared he wouldn't obey. Then he laid his weapon down and stood up. In a delayed reaction, he began to wave his hands above his head in a "look at me" gesture.

Charlie thumbed his line to Jean Paul open. "Found two of them. Apparently they were hunting tongats."

Something in Charlie's voice must have clued in Jean Paul. "Tongats hunting them now, huh?"

"Yeah." Charlie'd seen it happen before. Spacers mystified him.

"Stupidity. Are you safe?"

"Yeah. I'm on my way to talk to them. At least one is armed. Keep your line open so you can hear the conversation."

"Got your back."

"Always." Charlie smiled grimly and toed the skimmer into a careful landing. The closest flat place was half a klick away, so he had to make his way to the boys through the bodies of tongats. It saddened him greatly to see the big beasts so still. He walked close enough to the one the boy had shot to see that the bullet had gone clean through the thick neck, missing both the spine and the jugular vein. A thin trickle of blood stained the animal's black coat with a bright, wet line. Damn.

He stopped at the bottom of the rock pile, looking up at the trespassers. The bigger boy looked wary and the smaller simply shell-shocked. Both had the ultra-white skin of spacers and thin, slightly elongated bodies.

Charlie took a deep breath and tried to calm his anger over the tongats. "I'm a ranger. Charlie Windar. You're trespassing."

The small one managed to stutter out, "Th-thank you. Thank you."

He looked so pathetic that Charlie dredged up a smile he didn't feel. "You're welcome." He started up but stopped halfway. A body lay sprawled on a flat rock below the boys' perch, one leg shattered. White bone protruded from his leg in two places. Blood had pooled and congealed on the rock, and ants crawled through the blood. The dead boy's white face appeared twisted by pain even after death. Probably the middle boy, the fifteen-year-old.

If they'd been anywhere near civilization, he would have lived. The bloody bottom of the smaller boy's shirt tied around the dead one's leg was the only sign of any attempt at medical attention. Another problem with spacers; they lived inches from good medical care.

Charlie closed the dead boy's eyes before he climbed the rest of the way to the top of the rocks and asked the older boy, "What happened?"

"Richard fell." He spoke calmly, although his voice shook. "We were climbing up behind him and suddenly we just couldn't see him. We tried to tell him to wait for the doc, but he couldn't do it."

The younger one said, "It got dark. We stayed here and halfway through the night the big dogs started howling and they kept coming closer. This morning they were here so we couldn't go for help."

"What's your name?" Charlie asked.

"Justin. And this is my big brother, Sam."

Sam looked displeased to have his name revealed so easily. From time to time he glanced at the patch on Charlie's shoulder that proclaimed him an officer of the law.

"Why did you come out here?" Charlie asked him.

"Aren't you going to take us back?"

"Not yet."

The boys exchanged a worried look.

"Why'd you come?" Charlie asked again.

"Dad said we should know what a planet is like."

"Did he tell you to hunt?"

Neither boy answered.

"Did you want to kill a tongat?"

"No," Sam said, but Justin nodded. A brief angry look crossed Sam's face, and then he looked accusingly at Charlie. "You killed them. You killed all of them."

"No, I didn't. And that's why we're staying right here. We need to take care of them."

Neither Sam nor Justin appeared to be wearing any technology. Their clothes were nothing much either: ragged ship's jumpsuits and scuffed boots that needed new soles.

Justin retreated to the far edge of the rock, the look on his face so lost and unhappy that Charlie felt the tug of it on his heart. He spoke softly, as if talking to a wild animal. "Don't you fall."

Sam looked him up and down, appearing a little more interested. "Do you eat tongats?"

"No." He glanced over at the still forms. "No. We protect them. That's what we're going to do now. Sit here until they all wake up."

"They're not dead?" Justin asked in a high, thin voice.

"No." Charlie held out his hand. "Sam, give me your gun."

"I can't."

"Why not?"

"It's not mine. It's my dad's."

Charlie nodded. "I have something to do, and I'm going to make sure you can't point that thing at me."

Charlie stood still, hand out, working hard to keep his face neutral. In the space of about ten breaths, the gun landed in his hand, a little heavier than he expected. "Thank you. Now stay here."

"What about Richard?" Sam said.

"Richard doesn't care what happens next. But you two are safe enough. You can watch me from here." Without waiting to see how the boys reacted, Charlie climbed carefully through the rocks and went back to the injured animal he'd checked on the way in. He pulled a med-kit from his pack and sutured the wound, one hand on the warm, thick neck muscle. His attention roamed back and forth from his work to the beast's wide mouth, which was full of impressive off-white teeth. Once, he jerked back when the animal shuddered head to tail as if shaking off a fly.

As soon as he finished he stepped back a few steps. "Jean Paul?"

"Yes."

"We'll be here another hour or two. Do you know where I should take the boys?"

"The coordinates are in your nav system."

"Thanks. Parents in custody?"

"Yep. Said the boys ran away but we think they sent them off so they could do a deal with other smugglers."

"Fits the boy's story."

"Sad," Jean Paul said.

Charlie glanced back up at the boys. They sat side by side, watching him solemnly. He went to the skimmer and opened a cargo compartment, pulling out a pack.

When he got back to the rocks by the boys he settled down comfortably in a middle of the widest, flattest rock near the top.

"I want to go home," Justin said.

"Did you know there are animals that would eat these tongats if they came across them in this sorry state?"

"They tried to kill us," Sam said. He was standing, his arms crossed. "I want my gun."

"Now that there's no danger?"

Sam looked away, anger and impotence on his face.

Charlie felt like the kind of mean adult he'd hated when he was kid. Still, they'd lost a brother. "I'm sorry about Richard."

"Can we bring him home?" Justin asked.

"Yes." He patted the rock next to him.

Neither boy moved.

"We're going to be waiting a while. You might as well sit down." He pulled the pack onto his lap and extracted two water pouches, setting one on each side of him.

It took a while but eventually both boys sat down, one on each side, even though Sam stayed as far away as he could without falling off of the rock. To his credit, he sucked on the water slowly, and didn't finish it all.

The younger boy sat close enough to touch Charlie, and he simply looked sad and tired. Charlie resisted an urge to put an arm around him. "Did either of you sleep last night?"

"No," Justin said. "I was trying to keep Richard awake talking to him." He stopped for a moment, blinking back tears and then turning his face away. After a few deep, shuddering breaths, he turned back to Charlie. "He lived until halfway through the night."

"I'm sorry. You know this place is off-limits to humans."

"You're here," Sam said.

"Good thing for you. But there's two continents where you're not allowed to go on Lym. Here on Goland, and do you know the other one?"

"Entare."

"So you did know better than to come out here."

"Dad told us to see the wild places before they're all gone."

"They're not going to be gone," Charlie said. "We're keeping them for everyone. And Lagara is almost a park. People visit there every year."

"Rich people," Sam said.

"There's some truth in that."

Sam looked surprised that Charlie agreed with him. "So what were we supposed to do?"

Charlie fell silent, pondering. "Respect the boundaries. The same way I'm respecting the tongats out there. We almost destroyed this place once, and then we almost destroyed it again. This time that's not going to happen."

"Are you sure?" Justin asked.

"Yes." Charlie drank some water himself. He pointed in front of them. "Look. One of the tongats is getting up already."

Sam and Justin were silent as they watched the biggest animal stand up and shake itself, looking one way and then another and then nosing a packmate's flank. "See," Charlie said. "They're a family. They watch out for each other."

"They tried to kill us."

"You were invading their home."

"Will they hurt us now?" Justin shrank closer to Charlie, almost touching him.

Charlie's glasses pinged for danger and he blinked a few times, adjusting his view, taking in the size of the heat signature behind him. "Charlie?" Jean Paul's worried whisper vibrated in his ear. "Do you see it?"

Charlie whispered in turn to the boys. "Stay completely still. Don't make any sound. None." He checked his gun, stood up and turned slowly. A huge animal stood on its hind legs about twenty meters in front of him, just at the bottom of the rocks. He drew in a sharp breath and his hand tightened on his gun barrel. Being above it might not help very much.

"Boys," he whispered. "Stand up as slowly as you can and be careful not to fall."

Justin's arm slid around Charlie's waist and Sam let out a tiny moan, then went silent.

The predator cousin of the jumpers he'd flown over earlier stood three times the size of a man, with a long neck and snout and huge haunches. A thick, long tail twitched on the ground. Its neck moved like a snake's, back and forth, back and forth. Vestigial wings fluttered on its back and the small hands attached to them reached out sideways as if pulling on the air.

Justin whimpered. His braver brother whispered, "A rakul. A real rakul."

Charlie swallowed. "That's what might have eaten the tongats that might have eaten you."

"What do we do?" Sam whispered back.

"Nothing, unless it comes closer. It's trying to decide what to do."

A howl came up from behind them. The rakul raised its head and looked around. It bounded close enough for Charlie to make out the small fine feathers on its arms and the folds in the leathery skin of its neck. Its teeth were as big as his forearm. A breeze blew the smell of carrion and earth toward them.

Justin buried his face in Charlie's stomach. Charlie's free arm snuck around the kid, patting his back awkwardly. The other hand flexed at the gun, keeping it ready. He'd need a very precise shot to even slow a rakul.

Time slowed. The beast glanced at them directly from time to time. It bent to sniff at a tongat body and then lifted its head again, apparently surprised that the possible dinner in front of it was alive.

Charlie aimed his gun at the rakul. His hand shook. His own rules told him to allow predators to kill, but he had put the tongat in harm's way, and it shouldn't die because he'd stunned it.

Another tongat bayed, then a third.

The rakul glanced around and then cried out. The high-pitched screech drove a smile out of Charlie.

Other than his hand patting Justin's back, he wasn't certain he could move if he had to, even in self-defense. His eye stayed on the beast, drinking details. He'd never been so close to one. "What terrible beauty," he whispered, and Justin clutched him harder.

The tongat closest to the rakul pushed itself up and then raced away, a little unsteady on its feet but obviously driven by fear.

Two more rakuls came up over the rocky ridge, both bigger than the one they stared at. The biggest called sharply. The one close to them turned and jumped away, its thick tail thumping with every leap.

Charlie closed his eyes and took a deep breath, then opened them and double-checked. Nothing. "It's fine, Jean Paul," he whispered. "It's all fine. It's gone. They're gone. There were three of them." He turned and did a three-sixty visual scan of the area. "The tongats are gone, too."

Jean Paul's relieved laugh on the other end broke the spell. "Wouldn't you be gone if you could run fast enough to outpace a rakul?"

"Even the one the boy shot got away."

"They're lucky beasties," Jean Paul said.

"The tongats? You bet. I'm bringing the kids in."

It took thirty minutes to bundle the body and the two living kids into the skimmer. "I don't have helmets that fit you," he told them. "You'll have to close your eyes when we go fast."

"Okay."

Even though they weren't moving fast yet, Sam had his eyes closed when he said, "The rakuls might be big enough."

"Big enough for what?" Charlie asked him as he stepped on the gas a little, sending the skimmer lurching lightly forward.

"Big enough to stop the ice pirates."

Charlie blinked. "Probably not. Hard for flesh to stand up to machines. But the ice pirates can't get here. We're way inside the Ring."

"Pirates have been coming inside the Ring. More than usual."

Charlie stiffened. "Who told you that?"

"My dad."

"Was he trying to scare you?"

Sam was quiet for a long time. Eventually he said, "No. I think he was scared."

CHAPTER TWO

NONA

The room reeked of antiseptic and medication, the sharp scents fighting the thick flowery smell of lilies. It was enough to *make* someone sick. Nona coughed. The miasma of smells clotting her throat felt like death. Death was close—very close. Her mother Marcelle's skin had gone the white of the nurse's uniforms, so thin that spidery veins latticed her cheeks and ran in red threads along the pale line of her neck. Her body had thinned too; she could be a child huddled under the soft blue throw.

Nona and her mom had spent so many years being confused one for the other that Marcelle's fall into old age seemed impossible, like a bad dream Nona would wake from any moment. She checked the small mirror above the sink from time to time, as if she needed confirmation that the horror happening to her mother wasn't happening to her. Her own skin was still taut with youth. Her blue eyes matched the blue streaks in her hair, which hung heavy and limp in the medical air.

It hurt to see her mom so weak. Marcelle had been a warrior once, a lieutenant in Ruby Martin's army. She had fought in an insurrection long before she came home here to the station the Diamond Deep. She had even fought ice pirates as *The Creative Fire* came home after generations in space. She had fought disease and illiteracy and every unfair thing she ever came across. But for Marcelle, for everyone who was born on the spaceship, the fucking unfair cheat of old age had stolen their lives. That was the only way she could think of it—all of the people she loved the most in the world, all of her family, gone or almost gone. Doddering. Forgetful. Trapped in robotic chairs.

Old age sucked.

Nona had been the first person from *The Creative Fire* to be born here on the Deep *and* given the cocktails of life. A month or two either way, a tiny change in the priorities of the returning crew from the Deep, a little less financial success on the part of Ruby the Red, and Nona would be age-spotted and weak by now.

She hated death. Not only her own death, but all death. She'd lost her father the year before, and the pain of Onor's passing was so deep that this loss—this final loss—couldn't hurt her more. Not really. It couldn't.

A nurse brought in another vase full of flowers—blue roses this time. An impossible color that had to be engineered—so bright Nona thought they might glow if the lights of the medical monitors ever went off and let the room be truly dark. At least the roses didn't smell as strong as the lilies. "From Satyana," the nurse mumbled.

"Thanks." After the door closed again, Nona whispered to her mom. "Are you awake?"

No movement. Just the slightly rasping sounds of thin and labored breath.

"Satyana sent you flowers. They're exactly the color of her eyes." She took her mother's hand. "I'm going to miss you, mom. I will. So much." Marcelle's hand was cold, the fingers almost turned to claws. "It's going to be hard." A whine edged Nona's voice, and she hated whiners.

She'd survive this. Somehow. She didn't want Marcelle to remember her whining.

She stood and stretched, taking a deep breath. "Do you want some music?" Without waiting for an answer, she turned on some of Marcelle's favorite music, traditional songs from the old revolution that Nona had never really liked. But this wasn't *her* last moment. It was her mom's. Or close. On the way in—hours ago now—the nurses had told her to expect death. They'd taken her aside and said, "A day or two. That's all. Maybe less. Do you want support?"

She'd laughed at them, playing tough. "I'll be okay. Really." They had been steady, looking back at her with no comment. They were always steady, full of the angelic beatitude of hospice nurses. It didn't help that they worshipped Marcelle. And Ruby, whose dolorous and dead voice filled the room.

"Honey?"

Nona turned at the unexpected sound of her mother's voice. Marcelle looked stronger than she had for days. "Yes?" Nona took her mom's hand again. It felt cold and still, as if her hand had already lost contact with her heart. "Yes?"

"Remember what you promised your dad?"

She nodded. A tear she hadn't even felt landed on the back of her hand. "I do."

"We didn't tell you." She stopped and swallowed, her hand gripping Nona's almost as strongly as she used to. "There's enough for you to go. You can go to Lym. There's more than we ever told you."

Nona had planned to go anyway. She'd saved enough for a volunteer's passage. She'd studied the ecosystem to make herself worth putting on the list. She leaned down and kissed her mom on the forehead. "I'll go find a sky, mom. I can't promise I'll stay on Lym, but I promise to see a sunset. For dad."

"Go. For. You." Marcelle's voice faded a little. Then she gripped and pulled so that she was sitting up, the muscles of arms that had been too weak to hold a cup somehow holding her up as she clutched Nona's arm. "Satyana. See Satyana."

"Okay, mom."

"Promise?"

"I promise. I'll go find Satyana."

"Do you see her?"

"Satyana?"

"No. Ruby."

Her mom had been claiming she saw her old friend in the corners of the room for three days now. A ghost. A memory. Ruby had seen Nona born, had held her once. But Nona had no memory at all of her famous ancestor. Or sort-of ancestor. Whatever. She'd actually never been able to sort out the relationship between Ruby and Marcelle and Onor. They guarded that time in their emotional lives, the only clues pictures of the three of them in infinite varieties of twosomes.

At best, Marcelle was seeing the past. She'd remembered scenes from Nona's childhood, birthday parties and trips to garden habs that Nona didn't remember even after Marcelle recited every detail down to the color of the wrapping on presents. "I'm sure Ruby's there, mom. If you say she's there, she must be there."

"I'm going to go with her now."

"Okay, mom." Nona watched the light in her mom's eyes dim. It took a long time. Over and over she whispered, "I love you," like a mantra or a shield.

When there was nothing left to do, Nona braced herself for the stab of loss that came when her dad died.

It didn't come. Not exactly. Instead she felt thinned and raw, insubstantial.

Marcelle slipped down her arm, the strength gone from her fingers. Nona caught her gently, laying the shell of her mother down on the bed and then sitting and staring at her face, unable to look away.

Ruby's voice kept spilling from the wall speakers. Surely that was why Marcelle thought she saw her. Ruby was everywhere in the room—in a portrait on the wall, in the music, in the weight of Marcelle's life.

The music played through until it stopped.

The door opened. Nona didn't look up; the corpse had bespelled her. It didn't matter. Only Satyana smelled or walked like Satyana. Ship's grease and flowers and credit and fancy clothes and good hair products and success. Satyana was all of those things at once, and each of them more than anyone else Nona knew. A power of a woman, a force. Almost a mother to Nona as well, or at least Satyana thought so.

For once Satyana didn't issue any orders. She sat down on the bed opposite Nona and quietly asked, "Are you okay?"

"I'm a little dizzy." She hadn't realized it until Satyana asked.

"Let's go."

"Where?"

"Did your mom tell you to come see me?"

Nona nodded, apprehensive.

"I'm available now." Satyana said it like time with her was a gift.

"I'm not. I have to see to mom."

Satyana gave her a long assessing look. As usual, Satyana didn't seem to approve of what she saw.

—⁂—

Losing her mom didn't hurt the same as losing her dad. It wasn't sharp. It destroyed her in a completely different way. Other than the occasional round of tears that snuck up on her in bathrooms or in the middle of the night, she became a ghost on the Deep. She begged off work, avoided crowded galleys, and stayed alone with just herself and the vast hole that filled her insides.

She ignored Satyana for a week before she called. "I'm ready."

"Good. I'll meet you tonight." With that, Satyana hung up abruptly, surely right in the middle of some deal or important social event.

Nona hadn't really wanted to talk to her anyway. She showered and dressed in neat, pressed blue pants and a white blouse.

Satyana met Nona on one of her ships. Of course. Everything important to Satyana happened on a ship. The Deep had almost as much livable surface area as a planet, but only if you added in the berths on the myriad ships that made up much of the perimeter of the station. Some came and went, of course, but others had simply been parked and absorbed into the fabric of the Deep. Satyana had come here on a ship, run out of credit, thrown a few parties, and decided to stay. Now she was the queen of entertainment on the Deep, and not incidentally, rich and powerful.

Rich enough to give her ships stupid names.

They were deep inside the *Sultry Savior*, Satyana's newest cruiser-class ship. It was midsized and midpowered and still more expensive than any one human should be able to afford. At least Satyana hadn't forced a tour on her. She'd taken Nona through security with a hand wave and settled her onto a comfortable couch and given her a bulb of tea and a blanket.

Nona sipped the sweet green tea and waited while Satyana cut fruit, her back to Nona. When she turned, she looked worried. "I'm sorry that we lost your mom."

"I know." Satyana and Marcelle had worked together for decades, even though Nona had been sure Marcelle didn't entirely trust the other woman. "I hate it that she had to die that way."

"Of being old?" Satyana asked.

"Fucking age."

Satyana didn't look at all shocked. "We'll all die someday," she said. "Maybe sooner than you think."

Satyana wanted her to ask what she meant, so Nona sipped at her tea and waited the older woman out.

Satyana sat beside her. "This ship. The *Sultry Savior*?"

"Yes."

"It was built for you."

Nona blinked. She didn't want a ship. She sipped her tea, thinking over her last conversation with her mom. "To take me to see a sky?"

"For you to command."

Nona spilled hot tea on her knee and jerked away from it, spilling more.

Satyana held Nona's hand still, steadied it, removed the cup. "Your parents commissioned her when you were thirty-five."

So long ago? "Does it take twenty years to build a starship?"

"It takes longer to build a captain."

"You don't approve of me." Nona made it a statement.

Satyana sat back, looking thoughtful. "I'm mystified. That's all. There's so much more to you."

Than what? Nona stiffened. "Shouldn't you just say I'm not my mom and I'm not Ruby?"

"Isn't that obvious?"

"I can't be them. There's no evil empire to fight. The Brawl is a third of the size it used to be and it's almost humane. There's nothing to fix."

"Is that it? Is it all too easy? Brace yourself." Satyana's expression looked far more serious than usual. "This would be a really good time to take on more responsibility."

Nona managed not to flinch, but only because she was used to Satyana. "And become a captain?" Nona couldn't imagine it. She's never even tried to fly the little skimmers that were readily available to get around the Deep via the outside, preferring the inner passageways and the trains and, under duress, the taxis.

Satyana laughed. "Anyone who might have just *given* you a captaincy is dead. But you should start seeing the world soon. I'll have someone fly you to Lym. Henry James can take you in the *Savior*."

"I can't afford to fly my own ship anywhere." Her parents had spent their lives working for the community that had come with them on *The Creative Fire*, never taking even their fair share of the community's credit, never living in fancy habs or buying new clothes. They *had* given Nona years of education. They'd trained her as a diplomat and, when she didn't get a good job with that skill, they let her learn station biology. Nona had leveraged that degree to teach at Startide University, which paid her daily living fee and as well as a small salary. "I've saved enough to buy passage down and back. On the *Lower Glory*. I'm helping in the garden to reduce the fare." She shook her head, something Satyana had said earlier finally sinking in through the fog of the last week. "How'd *they* commission a ship?"

"A friend of theirs drank himself to death, but he left them his money on the condition that it couldn't go into the common pool."

"Naveen."

Satyana looked surprised. "Do you remember him?"

"Only a little."

"His brilliance and greed saved your parent's lives, but his addiction killed him early."

"He died of drinking?"

"No—he died because he was drunk one day and went out an airlock. None of us knows why."

Nona knew she should react to her mysterious benefactor's death, or at least to the idea that she *had* a mysterious benefactor. She'd been wrapped in her parent's history for her whole life. She was still wrapped in the hole of them, the missing pieces they had taken with them. "I would rather go on the *Lower Glory*. I'm looking forward to learning about the biology of ship's gardens."

To Nona's surprise, Satyana looked pleased. "Do you want to know how much Naveen left you?"

She closed her eyes. Her mom would have told her if she'd wanted her to know. But Marcelle had always been devoted to the common good—she had abhorred individual riches. "It's far more than I need, isn't it?"

"Yes. And it's been invested for a long time. It will change your world."

Wow. "Why didn't mom spend the money?"

Satyana let out a sharp laugh. "She liked being poor. She used to lecture me about lavish living if I bought an expensive drink."

Nona laughed as well. "I bet." She examined the interior of the ship. The idea that it might be hers shocked her into seeing it differently. Everything was locked and bolted down, of course. A lot of the walls were white or silver, a few black in contrast. The place screamed for pictures. If she did ever take control of it, she'd decorate. "I was only about six when Naveen died. I remember he was a force in our lives for a while, that he came over for dinner and dominated the talk. They argued."

"Your parents helped thousands of people have good lives."

"I know." Her mother had sacrificed time and credit to save every crew-member of *The Creative Fire*. Nothing had ever driven Nona as hard, possessed her and honed all of her decisions. It bothered her. She had always thought that when she grew up, she'd find a calling like her parents' had, but she had been an adult for decades and it hadn't happened yet. Satyana loved to pick at that particular wound. Nona shifted the conversation. "You sound like you think something's changing."

"Do you remember your history? Your parents staved off a ship full of Next."

"Ice pirates?"

"Yes." Satyana's face showed distaste for the term.

"The fight was outside the Ring of Distance, right? Before they came back from all the flying?"

"True. But the Next are coming in now. All the way into the Glittering."

Nona froze, stammered. "H-here?"

"Not yet."

Nona sat up. "How do you know?"

Satyana laughed, perhaps at the idea that any of her knowledge could be questioned. "The Historian is my friend."

So were the Economist and the Futurist and probably everyone else on the Council. "And the Council knows what? How?"

"They know that there are more raids per year now than there were a decade ago. The Next are testing our defenses, finding weaknesses." She leaned closer to Nona, her voice dropping. "Don't tell anyone I told you so, but the Council is scared. Frightened to the bone. They're building more warships, making alliances between stations where they would have been fighting trade wars before."

"Should we be scared of the pirates? Didn't one of them turn out to be Ruby's friend?"

Satyana shrugged. "I only met Aleesi once. Briefly, the day she died. It doesn't matter. One robot isn't representative. The Next are rumored to have as much attack capability as we do now. Maybe they have more. And we have the good real estate."

"I'm no war captain."

"No. You're not. This isn't a warship. It's built for diplomacy."

"I'm not a diplomat either," Nona said.

"You're trained as one."

"I haven't *done* it."

"And no one's asking you to, not yet. You have the bloodlines, the history, the training. Now you have the ship. Almost, anyway." Satyana had fallen into the cadence she used with staff, expecting Nona to hang on her every word. "It'll come to you when I say it's ready."

"It or me?"

"We may need you."

She didn't want to be anything Satyana wanted her to be. But for the first time since her mom's death, the hole in her middle felt a tiny bit smaller. She had some new things to think about. "I'll come back and talk to you. After I see a sky for dad." And bury some of her parents' ashes on Lym. Which wasn't any of Satyana's business. Maybe after that she could go to High Sweet Home, and visit her best friend, Chrystal. That would keep her away from Satyana for a while. "I'll find you when I get back."

Satyana's face was impossible to read. "I'll see that we shake down the *Savior*. When you come back, I'll go out in her with you."

Great.

"Don't you want to know what all you have now? What's yours?"

Nona shook her head. "Not yet. First I want to go see a fucking sky."

This time her swear word got a reaction. Maybe entertainment moguls didn't curse.

CHAPTER THREE

CHRYSTAL

The bold beat of drums filled the observation bubble above Testing Meadow Three on the station High Sweet Home. Chrystal Peterson struggled to keep the tempo. As usual, Katherine, Jason, and Yi tolerated her periodic mistakes. The drums had been her idea even if they were Jason's handiwork, and yet she struggled more than the others to maintain cadence.

Incense, baking bread, and cooking spices mingled in the warm air. Sweat ran down between Chrystal's shoulder blades and dripped off her chin. Jason's dark purple hair bounced as he moved. He raised his hand higher than usual and brought his hide drumstick down hard on the wide, painted drumhead. The others followed a half-beat behind him, even Chrystal. Three more beats, hard and slow and all together, and they stopped, faces flushed.

Jason gave Chrystal a beseeching look and nodded toward the kitchen.

She smiled. "Shall we eat?" Her cooking skills far exceeded her ability to keep a steady beat on the big drum. She ladled stew into deep bowls and poured fresh water for everyone while Yi sliced bread and piled it on a plate.

They ate together, the testing meadow spinning ever so slowly around them, meadow above and below and to each side as if they hung suspended in a can with a garden planted on the inside of the walls. The meadow itself was a beautiful swath of delicate grasses in shade after shade of pastel: sweetgrass and tall grass and yellow grass and moss grass and more. Here and there copses of trees stood amid faux rocks. Thin surface streams broke up the grass next to the trees, yet even these seemed like accessories for the grass.

They fell into companionable silence as they ate.

"Perfect dinner," Jason told her, leaning in to plant a vegetable-stew-flavored kiss on her lips. He started clearing the table. She stood up and Jason took her plate from her. "You and Yi can leave us to clean up."

Yi had been her sous chef for dinner, cutting up the root vegetables and crushing spices. A tall thin man with a dark mop of hair, Yi was all angles and bones with intense black eyes. He had always lived in the far stations like this one, and he was the oldest partner by at least ten years. She went to sit beside him, watching the meadow for jalinerines. They spotted a small herd above them. The grazers moved together in a group, nuzzling each other from time to time. "I really can't believe they earned approval on the first pass."

Yi, who never doubted anything, put an arm around her and pulled her close. "Of course they did. We did."

The new animals had progressed through approval in two years less time than they had expected. The grazing herd produced milk with perfect protein balance and none of the allergens that made dairy hard on some humans. In addition, they thrived across a wide range of gravity changes and created a very useful fertilizer as long as their diet included grasses the four had modified.

In spite of their success, Chrystal worried. "They came out exactly to spec, but will that be enough?" Katherine had led a clever marketing effort, but there were a lot of designer animals the last few years. "Will they stick?" she asked Yi. "Really?"

"We have good numbers."

They'd taken over three thousand orders for jalinerines and grass seed— enough to take three or four years to fill. They'd labored over design, creation, birthing, and testing. They were almost ready to turn the day-to-day work over to a manager they'd handpicked to run the distribution company.

"I like them" she said. These were their first mammals, a response to a new fad for four-legged creatures on some of the stations.

Yi smiled. "Be careful. Don't go all soft on them like Katherine. She's going to hate leaving."

A high-pitched alarm made her jump.

Yi let go of her and craned his neck, as if looking for a visible threat.

Jason dropped a dish. It clattered against something else and a drinking bulb rolled along the floor. She could barely hear Jason's soft curses under the blatting attention signal.

Chrystal pulled up her calendar. No scheduled drill.

Loudspeakers filled the room with the bland feminine voice used for ship-wide announcements. "All on-duty crew report to stations. Civilians are to enter lockdown."

In other words, go to their room.

Silence fell.

Katherine stared at three of the jalinerines grazing directly above them. "We should put them in their stalls."

She was right.

Yi looked thoughtful. "There's never been a lockdown on the High Sweet Home."

"We're close to the Ring," Jason snapped. "It's got to be pirates."

"It could be any kind of breach," Yi countered. "Or an unexpected drill."

"They tell us before drills," Katherine reminded him, still watching the jalinerines, which had all stopped grazing and lifted their slender necks and small, fine heads in reaction to the unusual noises. "We might be in our rooms forever. We have to feed and water them."

"I don't think it's safe," Yi said.

"Look, I'll go with you," Chrystal told Katherine. She turned to Jason. "Why don't you and Yi load the bedroom up with supplies. Water and food and stuff. Something to read."

The alarm went off again, stopping the conversation. The noise ran up Chrystal's spine like a child's whine.

Katherine grabbed Chrystal's arm. "Let's go. Now."

Chrystal hesitated for a moment, but the jalinerines were their future. She relented and followed the inexorable pull of Katherine-on-a-mission.

The observation bubble was home and lab as long as they rented the testing meadow. The bubble hung stationary in the exact middle of the cylinder. Half of its walls were clear and half done in mirror paint that reflected the great meadow back at itself. The mirrored part allowed crew members who wanted to sleep or shower or make love to do it without being watched by the herd.

Eight anchors attached the observation bubble and living hab to non-rotating points at each end of the long testing cylinder. "The forward number two line," Katherine whispered loud in Chrystal's ear, her breath hot and her voice just loud enough to blot out the announcements. Chrystal glanced at the herd. They hadn't yet moved very far, but looked alert and worried. The light-colored leader, Sugar, trotted around the group, trying to keep her charges together.

At the supply cabinet by the doorway, Chrystal's hands shook as she fastened the metal clips and carbon straps that made her harness.

It would break Katherine's heart if anything happened to the animals.

Katherine finished first and helped Chrystal fasten the last buckle.

Snugging and checking each other's gear in long-practiced moves calmed Chrystal a little. Katherine was almost as tall as Yi, so Chrystal had to work to find the right angle to tug her straps tight enough. "You okay?" she asked.

Katherine nodded. She'd found time to catch her long, multicolored hair back in a ponytail on the run down here, and the red and black dragon tattoo on her neck seemed to shine in the bright lighting of the preparation platform. "At least the alarms have stopped. Maybe it was a mistake."

"I hope so." Not that it felt that way. The announcement was a direct order. But Katherine would never leave the animals, and Chrystal would never leave Katherine.

Chrystal went down the zip line first, whooping as she sped through the warm air with her feet splayed wide in front of her. The jalinerines looked up at the familiar sound and started trotting toward their barn. The arrival of anyone from the bubble meant treats and brushings and other things they loved.

The alarm blared again, louder outside of the bubble. The zip line wasn't super steep, but Chrystal had figured out how to get a reasonable head of steam up anyway by swaying and kicking her feet, and the alarm drove her to sway even faster. She landed easily on the platform at the far end, knees slightly bent, and turned to see Katherine a little too close behind her.

Katherine bulled next to her with a grunt. The two women ended up tangled together in harnesses and ropes. "Hurry," Katherine urged, as Chrystal's fingers sped through the work of disentanglement. They hung their harnesses up on hooks.

At the base of the platform, the great meadow rolled around them, all grass on the edges. Chrystal took a few steps to match the rotation, and leapt onto the grass, grabbing a rope handhold provided to help the researchers. The shift from a world managed by gravgens to the spin gravity of the cylinder unbalanced her for a moment.

As usual, Katherine managed the change perfectly. She headed toward the barn where the animals had already gathered. Chrystal jogged to catch up.

The alarm changed to voice again, repeating the same short message. Chrystal and Katherine stood still through it, holding hands and looking at each other. Katherine's eyes were wide and worried.

As soon as the loudspeakers stopped, Katherine let go of Chrystal and grabbed handfuls of the grain they used for training. The animals nosed the air and stopped prancing, the food slightly more interesting than the odd sounds.

Chrystal walked behind the herd, providing subtle pressure toward the barn. Sugar usually went first, but this time she watched warily as Katherine led her herd into the barn one by one. They had seven of the ten animals in stalls when the alarm went off again at a higher pitch. Sugar raced around the other two and then led them away.

"We shouldn't have made them so fast," Katherine said, between the end of the alarm and the start of the actual message. She grabbed for a tranquilizer dart gun and looked like she was about to follow the escapees.

Chrystal blocked her way. "Leave them. They'll be all right or they won't be. The same is true for these." She gestured at the seven animals they'd gotten into the barn.

Yi's voice sounded in Chrystal's ear. "Are you almost done? Do you need help?"

"Soon," she said. "We'll hurry."

"Good," he replied. "Be careful."

The message started again, effectively ending the conversation. It sounded different this time, but the words were too garbled to make out in the warm, busy barn.

"Do they all have water?" Katherine yelled over the loudspeaker.

"Maybe." Chrystal ran up and down the stalls, peering over stall doors. The warnings were getting on her nerves now, pushing her to go back home.

The jalinerines looked restless, beseeching eyes turned toward her. She reached into the stall to pat her favorite, a dark brown female with pale tan spots named Kinship.

Katherine stood in the middle of the barn, looking around. "We should add extra feed."

"They'll eat it all at once. Maybe we should have left them out where they can get grass."

Katherine looked torn, and a little frantic.

"Come on," Chrystal said. "They're half and half now. We need to go back."

Katherine returned to the barn and opened two of the stall doors. "That's half and half."

Chrystal laughed, which drove the intense look from Katherine's face. The taller girl stepped over to Chrystal and folded her in her arms.

"You're right," Katherine murmured. "We should go." She leaned down and her lips crushed Chrystal's, an urgent kiss full of the need for hurry and the scents of animal and grains. Katherine led them through the reverse moves to get near the spinning edge. They stood close together, holding hands, watching the rotation for the right moment to step on. They hooked into fresh gear and caught the zip lines to glide home.

Outside, everything on the open deck had been tied down or stowed. The kitchen counters were spotless. In the bedroom, Yi moved like a cat, stuffing loose objects quickly and very neatly into drawers. Jason looked up from the side of the bed where he was tying a bulging backpack to the foot of the bed.

When they were busy with the jalinerines below, Chrystal hadn't been able to quite make out the second message, but up here it was clear. She recognized the Head of Security. "Next ships are approaching. Defensive measures are underway. All nonessential staff are ordered to strap into acceleration couches."

Chrystal froze, suddenly cold. "You were right," she whispered to Jason.

"Hurry," Yi hissed.

They chose their usual sleeping positions, with Jason and Yi on the far sides and the two women in the middle. Chrystal was next to Jason and she helped him dig for the straps, which they'd only used twice in the last three years. Both times, they'd been part of planned drills, and Katherine had laid the straps all out the morning of the drills after she made the bed. Now they were wadded and stuck in crevices on the sides. Little pouches in the beds hid the middle straps, and Chrystal broke a fingernail getting one out.

Another round of alarm and messaging happened as they settled, and then re-settled when they discovered that Katherine had an arm trapped and needed to shift yet again.

Chrystal's little finger touched the side of Jason's hand, and one foot brushed Katherine's foot. Otherwise they lay all in a row, looking up. Their breathing filled the cabin.

Katherine was the most prone to talk about her feelings. "I'm scared."

"It'll be okay." Jason's answer to everything.

"From your lips to the universe," Katherine whispered. "They sound serious."

Yi used his calmest engineer voice. "I heard rumors about restlessness at the Edge a week ago, in the gym."

"You didn't tell us?" Chrystal struggled not be annoyed.

The Ice Pirates will get you isn't exactly a new story," Yi said. "This didn't seem any scarier than usual."

"They can't hurt the High Sweet Home." Jason sounded calm, almost zen. "Our defenses are good."

Katherine fretted out loud. "I'm still worried about the animals. Maybe we should have caught Sugar."

"And done what?" Jason asked her.

"Aren't you worried?" she asked him.

"Not much."

Which meant he was very worried; Jason the invincible would usually have said, "Not at all."

The lights went out.

CHAPTER FOUR

CHARLIE

The sky was bruised red and purple by the time Charlie neared the single ranger outpost on Goland. Wilding Station had been built on a high plain and surrounded by tall, strong fences to keep it safe from human and wild predators alike. It even had an aircraft-detection system, which beeped friendship at Charlie as he approached. A wicked wind sheared right off of the High Resort mountain range and plunged to the valley floor at just the right angle to trouble the skimmer. The autopilot had to correct so hard and often to manage the wind that he almost missed Jean Paul standing beside the hanger door with his arms crossed.

Jean Paul helped him run through the shutdown sequence and lock up for the night. They worked in silence, which suited Charlie. There was a lot to consider: The savage beauty of the rakul, the unfair shooting of the tongats, the boys' loss and stupidity, the look on their mother's face when only two of them climbed off the skimmer.

As they walked back to their shared quarters, the wind felt like a cold knife at Charlie's backs, strong enough to make him feel light and vulnerable. When the door closed behind them, Charlie asked, "Is that what lower gravity feels like? Like you're floating a tiny bit and you've lost your friction?"

"That wind might have stolen two percent of your weight."

Charlie shivered. "What happened to the family?"

"If they leave tomorrow, empty, they won't face charges."

"That's good. I liked one of the kids."

Jean Paul raised an eyebrow.

"I did."

"Good thing you're in a liking mood. Someone picked up your highest rate. Babysitting job."

Charlie felt the scowl cover his face and took a deep breath to dismiss it. "I'm not done here yet." He had already planned a more direct route back to the rocky area where he'd found the boys in hopes of getting rakul pictures. He hadn't had a hand free for his camera, and the shots from his wearables almost never came out any good at all. He probably had low-res pictures of the rakul's left foot.

"They specified you."

"You haven't answered yet, have you?"

"Of course not." Jean Paul followed him through the central hall. The ranger station where they lived provided enough shelter to keep the wind from the backyard.

"Turn it down. Surely Manny can use me rangering out here more than me squiring in town." Charlie opened the kennel door and ninety pounds of three-legged tongat stood on her hind legs to greet him, pushing at his shoulder so he had to take a half step back to brace himself. Her left front leg was missing at the shoulder, which was probably the reason he had been able to capture her. Or perhaps save her was a better word. Although who had saved who wasn't entirely clear—he loved the beast as completely as she loved him, the bond so close he swore she knew his every emotion.

Cricket licked his cheek, her impossibly long tongue sliming his face in moments. He laughed. Behind him, Jean Paul said, "You might need the extra pay to feed that thing."

"She's not starved." He had more than enough credit anyway.

"Your uncle promised that if you take this work, he'll see that you get another tongat license."

Which he wanted desperately. Another rescue, of course. Not for himself, but Cricket was a pack animal and he was a lousy pack member. He was too busy. He turned back to the house, Cricket now walking at his heels. Even though she was smaller than most of the ones he'd shot today, her nose bumped his butt. Her base coat was as black as a nightmare, and her eyes as dark and deep, but she had a white tip on her tail and a white sock on her left front paw. "Who's paying?"

"Satyana."

"*The* Satyana?" He settled the tongat in the living room and began pulling out ingredients for her dinner. Two tharps, beheaded but with the small bones still intact. Some vegetables. Two eggs. He couldn't think of anything Satyana Adams would need *him* for. "Doesn't she have her own guards?"

"She wants you to squire Nona Hall around."

The eggs broke messily and he picked the biggest parts of the shell out with his fingers, leaving the rest. "Who's that?"

"Her family came in on that generation ship. Maybe she has some interesting stories."

"Why don't you take the job? Fame interests you."

"I'm sure they're hiring people with my safety record."

Charlie knew better than to go farther down *that* path. Jean Paul had gotten drunk and made a mess of a big job a few years ago. He'd lost three high-paying tourists who'd fallen off a cliff while roped together. People who understood Lym had forgiven him, but the accident had cost him his online reputation.

Charlie added the meat and the root vegetables and put the whole mess into the oven on high to sear it. In the wild, Cricket's food would be warm and bloody and in no danger of collecting bacteria that could make her sick.

Jean Paul wasn't giving up. "I looked her up. Nona was born on the Deep, teaches biology at one of the minor universities there. She's probably interested in the same things you are."

"Anything else?"

"Satyana doesn't want her to know she hired you."

Charlie started in on their dinner, tossing a block of cheese to Jean Paul. "Grate some of that."

Jean Paul complied, and the two men went back to working quietly. The timer buzzed for Cricket's dinner, and Charlie went through the restraint exercise of making her sit for five minutes before he put her bowl down. One small way to be sure she didn't eat him some day. "How the heck am I supposed to keep Satyana's role a secret?"

"Lucy at the Chamber will make sure you're at the top of the list whenever Nona comes in to hire a guide."

"What did that cost us?"

"It cost Satyana a new coat for Lucy."

Charlie didn't like anything that smacked of bribery. "Tell Satyana it has to be straight up. No lies."

"Lucy will get to keep the coat." Jean Paul handed a small bowl of cheese to Charlie.

"Good. I'm not lying for a coat. I'm not even lying for a tongat license." The room smelled of the spices and oils Charlie fried up as he started preparing eggs.

"Whatever you say, boss. Do I tell your uncle no dice?"

"I'll handle it." Maybe he could finesse the tongat license. "I need to talk to Manny about the sensor networks anyway."

"I suspect Satyana has her reasons for keeping it secret."

"I'm no entertainer. I don't need her to make my career." Charlie added the eggs to the pan, swirling it around so they filled it evenly. He turned the heat down.

"I wasn't thinking of you. There's more. Nona Hall just lost her mother."

"So now I'm supposed to heal the broken?"

Jean Paul glanced at Cricket, who had just finished eating and gone back to sitting, her head following Charlie's every move, her small ears flicking back and forth whenever either man talked. "She's a tongat, not a human," Charlie snapped.

"Hey!"

"Sorry. It was a long day."

"Quit taking it out on me."

"I remembered something that happened today. Sam—the biggest kid—said we're about to be overrun by ice pirates."

Jean Paul frowned. "I heard a rumor about that at Jimmy Ling's birthday party last week. I came home and checked it out. Two ships got kidnapped from inside the Ring this year, and five had to fight or run but got away. That's more activity than usual." He looked thoughtful. "Manny might know something."

The trap was clearly closing on him. He added the cheese in a light layer on top of the eggs and sprinkled more fresh herbs over that. "When does Nona land?"

"In a week."

"All right. Get someone out here to replace me in a week, and I'll stop off home."

"You want me to feed Cricket?"

Charlie laughed. "Manny'll do it. He likes the challenge. Besides, maybe I'll take her along. Keep the rich girl in line."

"You're kidding."

"Nope. Do you promise to feed yourself?"

Jean Paul threw a kitchen towel at him, which Charlie caught and threw back. If he liked men for sex, his life would be perfect. He caught the towel for the third time and hung it up carefully. It was time to load breakfast-for-dinner onto their plates. "Maybe if she hires me, we'll stop here. Then you can meet the rich and famous."

—∞∞∞—

Two days later, Charlie slipped the skimmer under a copse of trees just as a downpour stole most of his visibility. He poured a cup of hot tea and curled his hands around it to warm them. Rain sheeted down on the clearing in front of him and ran in rivulets off the leaves above him.

He had planned the day to search for rakuls, but this weather had surely driven them into caves or under the thick forest canopy.

The ping of an incoming call caught his attention. "Who is it?" he asked.

His onboard computer said, "Satyana," in his ear.

So she didn't even use her last name. He was just supposed to know her inside of a system of trillions of humans. He toyed with the idea of refusing her call, but surely Jean Paul had arranged it. "Hello?"

"Hello. This is Satyana Adams. Have I reached Charlie Windar?" At least she used both names in person. He recognized her face from news articles. Beautiful, with a long fall of dark hair and blazing blue eyes, almost neon and very intense. A strong woman.

"This is Charlie."

"We have a problem. Your staff, Jean Paul, informed me that you insist on telling Nona that I'm hiring you."

"Jean Paul's not staff."

"Whatever."

Satyana sounded like he expected her to—imperious and completely in control, as well as used to being obeyed and in a hurry. Traits he hated.

"Have you ever been here?" he asked her.

"Yes."

"On the surface?"

Silence. He'd expected that—it matched Jean Paul's research on the woman. She had flown here as a pilot before she became famous, but she didn't land. Intersystem ships didn't casually drop down Lym's gravity well.

Rain continued to sluice down off the trees around him, fat drops escaping the leaves and landing on his face or in his cup of tea.

He let his silence hold for a while before he said, "It's dangerous here. The dangers are completely different than the dangers on a starship or an orbital, or at least that's what my clients tell me. If I squire this woman around, she's going to have to trust me."

"Of course."

"So why would I start with a lie?"

"I'm not asking you to tell her you weren't hired by me. You don't have to lie. Just don't tell her. She is almost certainly underestimating the dangers on Lym. I'm trying to be sure she's safe."

"Would she consider it an omission or a lie?"

More silence, which was fine with Charlie. He was good at silence.

The entertainment queen continued, "Nona's special. She's also tender right now, and probably lonely. I don't want her taken advantage of."

"I don't sleep with clients." Anger started curling up his spine.

"I know that," she said. "She's associated with me. That makes her a target, at least up here. That's part of why I'm hiring you. You've got the best safety rating, and you're close enough to the power structures there that you'll understand Nona."

So Satyana thought Nona would do herself damage? She wasn't coming out and saying so, but it seemed to lie between the words she was using. "I won't lie to her. I'll go there, and I'll meet her, but I won't lie. You can hire me and let me say you did so, or you can let it go and assume she'll be all right, no matter what happens."

More silence.

"Very little of the danger here is from the people. She is an adult, right?" He'd looked it up. She was fifty-five. Satyana was probably three-hundred, and he was seventy, but even if the only real measure of age left was emotional age, this Nona wasn't a child. Although he was beginning to suspect she had been treated like one, and might act like one. "What will it be?"

He could almost see her fuming. Damned spacers. "Have it your way. Don't lie. But keep her safe. It's now on your head to make sure she accepts you as a guide."

"No. It's not. It's up to Nona." With that he hung up. He could say he lost the signal if it ever came up.

CHAPTER FIVE

NONA

The *Lower Glory* had docked at one of Lym's two short-term Port Authority stations. Nona stood at the front of the station's observation deck, curiosity and awe pulling her as close to the window as she could get. Lym occupied most of the view. She had seen thousands of pictures of it, on walls and in history lessons at school. In spite of that, seeing it really, truly existing made her tremble. Ice covered each of the poles, more on the north than the south. At least six different continents appeared to float on the vast seas, islands hugging their coastlines. Clouds obscured some of the details.

It had all started here, the great glittering sky full of stations and ships and billions of people. This was where the first colony ship had landed in the long dark of history. What had the first people here thought all those years ago?

Loudspeakers blared. "Boarding for Gyr Island transport begins in ten minutes. Passengers should head to the boarding area."

She gave the planet one last, long look. "I'll see a sky," she whispered to her dad. She had no illusion that he heard her, or that he'd lived on in any way, but she had gotten into the habit of talking to him from time to time anyway. She had small vials of his ashes—and Marcelle's—tucked carefully into her coat pocket. They felt heavy, like tiny weights that hung between her and the rest of her life.

To her surprise, the transport was largely empty for the run down to Lym. Two other tourists chattered nonstop, both bound for a university group tour. They vibrated with the excitement of meeting other professors from other stations, as well as seeing Lym. Five people were on their way to relocate. One couple was doing graduate work together and the other three had been granted five-year work permits.

A loudspeaker commanded them to climb into crash couches. She felt the first twinges of fear and excitement rocket through her nerves like a glass of strong stim.

The transport shuddered and burned its way down through the atmosphere.

The vehicle and her stomach both calmed enough for her to look up at a screen with a real-time camera. The main spaceport was on Gyr Island, the one place on Lym where all technology was allowed. The island was a modified oval with fractal edges and a few deep inroads made by the sea. The spaceport was roughly in the middle, with a sprawl of buildings beside it. None of it looked at all like anything on the Deep.

Landing was a long, fast glide and an exercise in fast braking.

After they landed, an irritatingly earnest crew member stopped her at the door on the way out. "Have you ever been here before?"

"No. But I'll be all right."

"Just let me walk down beside you." He gave her a look that suggested that if she said no he'd feel rejected for life.

Nona hesitated, but shook her head. She wanted her first moment on a planet to be private.

There was a ramp down. She glanced up once and flinched, shifting her gaze back to the ramp and clutching the handrail.

Her peripheral vision showed her exactly nothing except the occasional movement of a human. No walls.

The air moved across her face and played with her hair.

Wind.

She hit the bottom of the ramp and walked ten steps, looking at her feet. The ground went on and on, in all directions, filling her peripheral vision. No markings or lights on it, no walls. The surface was pocked with holes and cracks that dust had blown into.

A male voice called out, "Hey. Watch where you're going. Look in front of you."

Her eyes followed his voice, but before she found the source she stopped and tilted her head back and looked up and up, and up forever. She forgot what she had expected—probably a high blue ceiling. Instead there was nothing. A pale blue expanse of nothing, a few thin white clouds, and the sun Adiamo, too bright to look at. It stunned her, the beauty of nothing. "Sky," she whispered. "Sky, daddy." She blinked, unwilling to stop and cry like a tourist but wanting to let the tears fall down her face.

A hand touched her arm. "Wait until you see the stars."

She hesitated, off-balance. "I bet they're magnificent."

"I hear they're pretty magical from space, too."

"Most ships don't have windows, and stations make too much light." The act of simple conversation refocused her. She tore her eyes from infinity and looked at the man, who still touched her. Tall. A boxy face with strong features and grey-green eyes. He looked older than she was used to people looking, although to be fair it wasn't wrinkles or anything. His skin just looked more used than she was accustomed to—she couldn't have said why. "I'm Nona."

"I know," he said. "I'm Charlie. I came to greet you. Satyana sent me to look after you, like a guide."

She almost spit out an expletive, but caught herself and simply stiffened so that he dropped his fingers from her arm. He gestured toward his right. "The bags are ready. Which one is yours?"

He didn't seem the bag-carrying type. "It's the only blue one."

As he headed for the pile, she realized what else bothered her about him. He looked plain. No decoration, nothing particular done with his blonde hair except maybe a brushing, nothing unique about his eyes. She was used to remembering people by the ways they'd chosen to change themselves. How would she remember him?

Then the sky and the horizon caught her up again, and she forgot him and Satyana's meddling in her trip and even the loneliness that still clung to her insides. The Deep provided views of stars and the lights of other stations, but this was just so much . . . vaster. It had been made by something other than people. By time and evolution, by water and the light of Adiamo.

The sun hung nearer the ground than the middle of the sky. She knew it wasn't early in the day here, so it must be close to sunset. Another thing her father had wanted to see.

When Charlie came back she startled.

He indicated the case he held lightly in his hand. "Is this all you brought?"

"Yes."

He looked pleased.

"Is that unusual?"

He looked like he thought so, but he just asked, "Are you hungry?"

She wanted to be alone. "I'd like to check into my hotel."

"I'll take you."

She reached to take the bag from him. "I can carry that."

"Give yourself a day or so to get used to Lym before you do too much." He turned and walked away, carrying her bag.

She followed, stumbling once and then jogging to catch up. "Hey! I'm in good shape. I feel good."

"Trust me."

"Why should I?" she asked him.

"Look me up after you get checked in. Then you can choose."

She decided he was at least a little infuriating. And a little egotistical. And worse, hired by Satyana. He also seemed to be *walking* to their hotel. But he had her bag, so she followed and eventually managed—just—to catch up.

He was silent at first. Eventually she teased a few words out of him by asking questions. Yes, he had been born on Lym. No, he wasn't a guide. Sometimes. For people with permission to see the wilder lands. Usually he was a ranger. Yes, it was safe here as far as people went, but she needed a guide to leave the city.

That last bit perked her up. She'd been studying Lym on the way down. There were so many places she wanted to see. And animals. There were animals on the Deep, but nothing there was wild. On the Deep, water ran inside pipes. "Will you take me to Ollicle Falls?"

"Tomorrow. If you hire me."

She startled at that. "I thought Satyana hired you."

"She wanted to set it up like an accident and not tell you I was working for her."

Why would he tell her that? She let silence come back up between them while she thought. Satyana hiring him made sense—she'd made Nona a personal project thirty years ago. She was probably going to be even more overbearing now that Marcelle was dead—she'd think it was her duty. The Nona project. But why would *Charlie* tell her this right away? "Do you know Satyana?"

"Never been off of Lym."

"So—"

He cut her off. "I don't like being told what to do. And I don't like secrets."

Well. Things must be much simpler down here. Nona had to take a few extra steps every so often to keep up with him. Her thighs and calves had started feeling sore. She didn't complain. "So I have to hire you?"

"You can hire whoever you want."

"I'll hire you for tomorrow."

"That would be telling me what to do. I'm not interested."

"So why are you here?"

"It seemed like someone should greet you."

"So can I hire you for tomorrow?"

"Are you asking?"

"Yes."

"I'm not cheap."

"Satyana can pay you."

"Really?"

He was right. She should pay him. She fell silent, still dizzy with the space all around her. The ground changed from the hard concrete of landing pads to something softer but still man-made. They passed a man heading in toward the spaceport, and two runners passed them. Someone could run forever here, no stopping, no going around in circles. "So what are your rates?"

He told her, and she snorted. "I'll sort something out."

He glanced at the sky. "Have you ever seen a sunset?"

"Of course not."

"About two hours. You'll have time to eat first."

"Where should I watch it?"

Just off the spaceport grounds, Charlie stopped for a moment and pointed. "That's the town, Manna Springs, and there's your hotel, the Spacer's Rest. On the far side, there's the main government buildings and the Port Authority offices—see the tall grey building?"

She nodded. The town fascinated her. Buildings stood up straight from the floor of the world, a myriad of colors and designs. At least that was like the Deep. Except there would be connections between the habitat bubbles at home; everything on a station connected to something else, even if the connections were locked. Manna Springs looked like building blocks, all square and rectangular; the Deep looked more like a collection of rings and rounds and cylinders and even arrows lashed together.

Maybe it wasn't much like home after all. She expected him to ask if she liked it, and when he didn't she said, "It's pretty."

"I'll show you pretty tomorrow." He fell silent again, and that was fine with her. She struggled to take in as much new information as she could and not to complain about her legs or her lower back, which had gotten in on the game. By the time they arrived at the hotel, her legs were shaking, although she refused to complain.

To her surprise, Charlie said, "Go clean up. Eat. I'll meet you back here twenty minutes before sunset. The first sunset's free."

She blinked. "What time is that?"

"Figure it out."

<hr />

Nona sat on the steps of the Spacer's Rest, waiting. She had no idea if she was early or late, but it hadn't started getting dark yet. The light had turned softer, and in turn softened the edges of buildings. It glowed faintly gold through the freshly growing leaves on a tree by the steps. A surprising contentment settled over her.

She'd had a salad for dinner, and all of the parts of it were grown. Every one. The dressing had been made with real eggs from real chickens. It was possible to eat like that on the Deep, but not on her salary.

She supposed she could do that now. She'd been avoiding thinking about it. Her mother wouldn't have ever spent credit on such things, and Nona couldn't imagine doing so. She'd hear Marcelle in her head telling her *credit is for the collective and for health and education and never, ever for showing off.*

She'd never been someplace where there wasn't anyone she knew. She loved the anonymity of it, the freedom.

Two women dressed in work clothes smiled at her. Five men walked up the street, laughing, almost certainly released from some job. Most of them looked as plain as Charlie, although once she spotted cat-eyes on a teenaged girl and an overly-tall woman walked by with long blue hair that nearly touched the ground in spite of the high heels she wore. A couple rode by on bicycles. There were some on the Deep, but they were in gyms and on tracks, and not . . . so complex. These had baskets in the front and back, and lights in both places, and the riders wore regular clothes. She was still focused on the bikes when she heard her name. She turned and spotted Charlie standing on a skimmer with a huge dog-like creature at his side. As she approached, he said, "This is Cricket. If you hire me, you also hire her."

Cricket regarded Nona with a controlled stare, nearly as still as a statue. Some of the richer people on the Deep had cats, and there was an aviary in one of the bars. Part of one food habitat she'd gone to visit as a child had real chickens. She'd heard about dogs, knew that some existed. That's what this had to be. A very big version of a canine. She'd studied the animals on Lym during the trip here, and her brain raced through what she remembered. "Tongat?" she asked.

A smile spread across his face. "Yes."

"What happened to her leg?"

"Some idiot shot her and left her to die when she was a pup. I scared off a pack of predators and took her home."

"She's beautiful." Nona reached a hand out toward her.

"Stop," Charlie said.

"I wasn't going to hurt her."

"She is the most dangerous animal you have ever been near."

Nona took a step back.

"And you can't ever forget that or remind her of it. Don't act like prey around her. I'll show you how to greet her later."

"Will she come with us tomorrow?"

"Yes," he said. "But now, come around and get in. The sun isn't going to wait for you and Cricket to get used to each other."

He helped her up and had her sit down next to him on a seat, careful to keep her as far away from Cricket as possible. "Hold on."

The machine accelerated fast. Certainly not faster than she was used to, but like the planet, it wasn't enclosed. She had to put a hand up and hold her hair in a knot to keep it from whipping her face. They flew low, just above the buildings, which let her see the layout of the town. She noticed more animals. A few large ones that people rode, a few dogs that were far smaller than Cricket. She startled as a fat furry ball a little bigger than her closed fist jumped. A tharp, if she remembered right. A common part of the mammal food chain. They'd be plentiful here.

He took her to the top of a hill not far from the town and parked, helping her climb down. "This is a good place."

Mountains rose up in the east, behind them, but he took her to two benches that faced the west, and the setting sun. He left her to get Cricket, and she sat and stared in wonder. The sun had been obscured by a layer of clouds. Bright beams of light escaped them and infused the bottoms of the higher clouds with a yellow gold. Slowly, color spread across the whole sky, deepening and gaining subtle hues. All of the light softened.

Charlie and Cricket took the other bench, both eerily silent.

She felt big, as expansive as the sky, as if she and it and Charlie and Cricket were all somehow one thing in that moment even though none of them touched.

Perhaps the sky touched them all. It no longer looked like nothing. It had become art. Orange and gold and hints of fluorescent pink.

Even Cricket seemed to be watching the sky, although she was also watching Nona. Nona was happy that Charlie didn't talk; the spectacle in the sky was so far beyond words she didn't want to break the spell by trying to capture it with anything. She didn't even take a picture.

Adiamo gave them a brief glimpse of its near-red body, striped by glowing clouds, and then it was gone. After the colors faded back to a soft gray at the horizon line and stars started to show up, he said, "We're lucky. They aren't always so pretty."

It took a few breaths before she could say anything. "Lym keeps striking me silent. It's so big."

"Why did you come?" he asked.

It felt like a personal question, but to her surprise, she answered it. "I promised my parents. They're dead now." Before he could express surprise, she added the details. "They were crew on *The Creative Fire*, the generation ship, and they didn't have the right drugs and mods when they were young."

"I read up on that."

Oh. Of course. Satyana had told him about her. "I promised my dad I would see a sky. It was a dream of his. He never got here, but he was determined to send me." In that moment, she realized that it was probably Onor who had talked Marcelle into funding the ship. It might have all been about this place, about a sky.

Charlie spoke gently. "I'm sorry about your parents. My father is dead, too."

"Really?"

"Accident. He was working in Palat, one of our old cities on Entare. It was a salvage job, and an old metal girder crushed him."

"Don't you just use nano?"

"Sure. But not the way I hear you do. We're wilding Lym. That means removing technology, except here and on Lagara, where we grow food."

Before she could formulate a question about wilding he asked her another one. "So your dead parents drove you here. But what do you want? If I'm going to show you Lym, I want to know what you want to discover here."

It had grown dark enough that she couldn't really make out his features. "The falls. Some mountains. I'd like to go to Lagara. I want to sail on the ocean. I can't imagine that much water. We saw it from space but I know that won't be the same."

"That's good. But that's a list of places. What do you want to understand?"

She looked up at the dark of the sky and tried to pick out constellations. It had grown colder now that Lym had turned their location away from the sun. Another thing to marvel at. Rotation. His question seemed important, but it was too damned personal. She didn't want to answer him. The tongat—Cricket—unsettled her as well. She loved animals, but she'd never been near one that exuded such a sense of power.

Charlie elaborated. "Most people that come here want something. Some connection to their past or this place or a spiritual evolution. We had one visitor who said she wanted to touch the face of God. Another one wanted to write a book of poetry about a planet. Many come wanting to live here, but we don't let tourists just decide to live here. We control who stays here pretty tightly."

"You'd have to, to keep it so empty."

"There's a lottery system with a thousand, thousand entries for every one who wins a chance to even visit."

She had just come. No problems. No waiting. Probably another perk of knowing Satyana, and another piece of the trap of her life. She blurted out, "I want to be free."

He laughed, the first truly genuine laugh she had heard from him. It filled the cold air between them with warmth. "I'll work on the freedom itinerary."

Oddly, he didn't sound sarcastic about it at all.

CHAPTER SIX

CHRYSTAL

Chrystal hated the dark. She had always hated the dark. Near dark was fine, and in the observation bubble, near dark was the worst it ever got. Emergency lighting always glowed in a faint strip near every door and window, top and bottom.

Not now.

Now the dark was absolute, and no matter how much she widened her eyes or how many times she blinked, it remained absolute, a dark so black that it created a wall between her and anything she couldn't touch or hear.

It seemed like hours and hours had passed, but how could she tell?

The small touch of her pinky toe to Jason's or Katherine's calves helped a little, as did the sound of everyone breathing, and of her own breathing, which seemed so loud it filled her. She heard her breath in her ears and in the back of her throat.

Even the loudspeaker had gone silent.

For a long time, nothing happened.

"The animals must be so scared," she said into the silence, her words loud and grating.

Katherine made a sound of agreement. "We should have put them all in the barn."

"Maybe." Chrystal said.

"We can start over," Yi murmured. "They're already approved."

Did he think they were already dead? She didn't ask. Unlike the other three, Yi was bonded to the *idea* of the animals far more than he cared about individual animals.

Silence fell again.

"We should put on psuits," Yi stated.

Katherine laughed. "They'd tell us if we should do that."

"Maybe." Yi didn't sound like he was buying it. "I think we should do it anyway."

"There must be a battle going on out there," Chrystal mused. Now, as they lay still and helpless, ships from High Sweet Home were probably fighting pirate ships. She didn't actually know what the High Sweet Home military ships looked like, and she had even less of an idea what the ships from the Edge looked like. It wasn't like there had ever been a real space battle in her lifetime; just spats. Border incursions that she had never seen. She was certain the ships were big and powerful, maybe like the biggest of Satyana's ships from the Deep. That made her think of her friend Nona. "I hope this isn't happening to other stations."

Stilted small talk continued for a long time. It only made things worse. Scarier. When they ran out of things to say, they unstrapped and led each other through the too-black dark to the bathroom and back. They sat on the bed and drank water. After, they strapped back in, and within a few minutes Yi succumbed to sleep, snoring softly. Chrystal followed him into a place full of unease and drowsiness, her dreams troubled with images of being tied to the outside of a spaceship.

Lights and sound all came on at once, startling Chrystal awake. "The High Sweet Home has been captured and is going to be moved beyond the Ring of Darkness. This process will take some time. Civilian inhabitants should prepare to be moved." The same message played three times in a row. The lights stayed on.

Yi was the first to get the restraints off and stand up. He'd gone pale white. "There's no way for that to be true. We don't have engines."

"We have *some*," Chrystal said.

"Enough to avoid an asteroid," Yi replied. "Slowly. Not enough to get beyond the Ring in less than a year to two. I have no idea if the station can move that far that fast without breaking up, even if it gets towed."

The others all stared at him.

"We need to pack *fast* and put on psuits after that. Then we should strap back in." Everything about him screamed calm-within-an-emergency and demanded that they obey. The vehemence of it startled her.

"Really?" Katherine combed her long hair out with her fingers. "If we need both the acceleration couch and the psuits, we might as well be dead."

"Do you want to find out?" Jason asked.

Yi didn't even bother to join the argument. He simply gathered up everyone's suits and handed them around.

"I'm going to check on the animals." Katherine took her suit from Yi and put it on the bed. "Just through the bubble. Not by going there." And then she was gone. Chrystal threw her suit down and followed, the others all doing the same, as if some invisible glue held everyone close together against the dangers that lurked outside of their little nest.

Chrystal caught up to Katherine first, standing body to body, touching, looking through the clear glass part of the habitat bubble. The lights in the rotating habitat hadn't come on, but the same light that surrounded them illuminated the meadows dimly, as if it were almost night out there. Katherine squinted. "I don't see them," she said.

"Most of them are in the barn," Chrystal reminded her.

Jason and Yi came up from behind, all four now standing close and peering out the window. Jason pointed. "Is that Sugar?"

Sure enough, almost straight on, they spotted the top of Sugar's head and the long line of her back undulating as she trotted across the meadow. She disappeared into some trees.

"Fabulous," Katherine whispered, relaxing so much that Chrystal could feel it.

"All right then," Yi said. "Back to the suits."

There was some grumbling, but Katherine followed meekly enough and they were back in their bedroom soon.

Chrystal took her suit, almost too tired to put it on. The High Sweet Home was the biggest station that had chosen an orbit as close to the Ring as they were, but distances in space were vast. They were no closer to the Ring than brilliant Lym was to cold and half-terraformed and brutally mined Mammot.

Yi had to be wrong about the speed and danger. Or maybe the announcer had it wrong. Yi was, after all, almost always right.

"You know what I hate about being strapped in?" she said.

Jason took the bait. "What?"

"We can't hold each other while we're all strapped to the bed."

Katherine gave her a soft but frightened look and slipped her shoes off so that she could don the suit.

Chrystal had been afraid since the first siren went off, but now the fear had become so desperate it threatened to undo her. Even the simple and practiced movements of donning her psuit were hard to remember and even harder to perform.

Strapping in seemed harder too, everything tight and stretched. Nothing about using the bed as an acceleration couch for four felt comfortable.

They waited.

And waited.

No further announcement, nothing. Chrystal could turn her head inside her helmet, but she couldn't see the others. They should put a mirror on the ceiling in case this ever happened again. The thought made her giggle a little.

More time passed.

"Maybe we should get up," Jason said.

"No," Yi responded. Silence fell again, the rhythms of each other's breathing matching except for Jason, who always breathed fast.

The lights flashed and went out.

A force slammed them hard against the bed, slammed Chrystal's body into her suit, sent the back of her head questing for a way through the helmet. She felt pain, but then it stopped. Creaks and scratches sounded in her ear, soft and muffled because of the soundproofing in her helmet.

A loud thump sounded like something had hit the outside of the habitat just above her.

Everything shuddered, the bed, the floor, every part of her body, her bones. Her heart raced.

The suit detected her fear and fed her drugs. She didn't want them, but they came in through a needle and she couldn't refuse the gentle warmth that stole her caring and then her awareness.

CHAPTER SEVEN

CHARLIE

C harlie loved flying in the dark. The dimmed instrument panel and an equally dimmed picture from his heads-up display outlined the buildings and streets below him.

He glanced at his silent passenger. "You're not sure what you think of Nona either, are you?"

The tongat didn't answer him.

He pulled into his uncle's driveway and parked in the space Manny always left available for him. He and Manny had worked together the previous fall to build a shed for Cricket, with strong walls, running water, and two windows just at the right height for her to look out without standing on her hind legs. He led her in, washed the dust from her water dish and filled it, and gave her a pat before he closed the door on her. Manny and his family had stretched pretty far to allow the tongat on their premises; she wasn't allowed in the house. "I'm sorry girl," he murmured. "I'll come out and see you soon."

Laughter and the smells of cooked grains and cold spice salads and bread warm from the oven almost overwhelmed him as he entered the kitchen. Manny waved. "Hello, Charlie! We tried to wait, but the kids got hungry."

Manny was a bear of a man with a red bushy beard and red hair that fell in rings below his shoulders. His wide grin seemed to envelop his whole body as he waved Charlie in.

Charlie pulled a chair up to join the meal already in progress. They were family of six: two men, two women, and two children. Manny sat at the head of the table and Amara held down the other end. On the sides, Pi and Bonnie were each joined by one small child. Laughter and teasing filled the entire room. A life Charlie admired and couldn't imagine, all at once.

He helped himself to a plate of salad and bread right from the kitchen. Bonnie made room for him to pull up a chair between her and Manny, and Charlie ate with his plate balanced precariously on the corner of the table. Between bites, the children pestered him for stories of wild animals.

After the kids were tucked away in their rooms with homework, the adults converged back over the now-clean table and poured a round of red wine. Manny's face had transformed from benevolent parent to the face he took to town council meetings after something had gone wrong. "We have news from near the Ring. Came in today. The ice pirates destroyed High Sweet Home."

Charlie replayed the words in his head twice before they really sank in. He tried to remember what he knew about the High Sweet Home. It was big. It was—had been—owned by religious ascetics dedicated to creating designer animals and foods. They financed their science by running a docking hub for ships needing repairs and allowing military missions. It might be the most effective defense base the Glittering shared in such a far orbit. "How?" he asked.

"Surely *they* had defenses," Bonnie stated, her voice flat and shocked.

Manny nodded. "Good ones. They were overrun. There's video—I'll send you links. I don't want to play it where the kids can walk in on us."

"That bad?" Amara said needlessly.

"Why would they do that?" Charlie mused. "Why hurt a station?"

"Ships from the High Sweet Home intercepted two pirate ships on the wrong side of the line. Standard defense of the Ring stuff. We've been doing it longer than any of us have been alive. We lost one ship and they lost two."

"Isn't that normal?" Pi asked. "I mean, we fight each other every few years way out there." Pi was a big man with a soft voice, almost as big as Manny with half the hair, all of it dark. He ran the repair docks at the spaceport for a living.

"Something's changed," Manny said, his face a study in scowling contemplation. "One theory is that it's retaliation for winning so many of these fights."

"Taking a station seems like an overreaction to losing a ship." Charlie reached for the bottle and poured more wine. "How long ago?"

Manny squinted at his slate. "About a week. We're just getting the news down here." He sounded bitter about that.

"Where are the pirates now?"

Manny shrugged. "Looting? They appear to be dragging the station out beyond the Ring."

"They're dragging a whole station out there?" Pi asked. "A whole station? Or just part?"

"A whole station," Manny said. "Whatever they didn't destroy. You should all watch the video. It's pretty brutal, but when they could have obliterated the station, they didn't. They pulled back."

An awkward silence fell for a moment, and then Charlie asked, "Do you think they're a threat to *us*?"

"They've always been a threat." Bonnie frowned and twisted her hair in her fingers.

Amara passed around a bowl of nuts. "Not an immediate one. I suppose it's still not immediate. But I'm worried." She took a long sip of her wine and set the empty glass on the table. "Deeply worried."

Charlie agreed with her. Amara was wicked smart and quiet, and he'd learned to listen when she talked. "Any idea what they want?" he asked.

"Revenge?" Pi offered.

"Sunshine," Bonnie suggested.

Manny frowned. "If they just wanted simple revenge, they'd have crippled the High Sweet Home, but they wouldn't have taken it."

Charlie agreed. The ice pirates were more machine than human, and he had no idea how to read their intentions.

One of the children came in to ask a question, which stopped the discussion. The rest of the night had an awkward, frightened feel to it, the energy so sour Charlie went out to the guesthouse early, taking Cricket with him.

As they approached the falls, Charlie turned toward Nona. "Maybe you should stand up. It's easy enough to keep your balance, and you'll catch a better first glimpse of the falls that way."

She smiled and complied, the wind of their passage sending her multicolored hair streaming behind her. She had a jewel in her cheek which caught the sunlight and winked bright. He expected that it would be less distracting on a ship where the light was controlled. She had fewer decorations than most spacers, but there was the jewel and part of what was probably a dragon tattooed on her neck, and colorful lacework tats on her wrists. He had expected her to be pretty, and she was, in a slightly ethereal way.

They flew just above a river of water from the falls. Nona pointed at a jumping fish and squealed at a huge waterbird. Each time she saw a new animal she tried to remember its name. He found himself rooting for her to get each one right.

Even though Ollicle Falls wasn't Charlie's favorite place, he had to admit his trouble was with the crowds and not the falls. A shining stream of water plunged from a high, mossy cliff, hit two perfectly rounded rocks bigger than Manny's house, split into two streams, and came back together in a way that almost looked like a heart before it fell into a perfectly round pool. Bright blue and yellow flowers festooned the cliff and lined the pool. He piloted the skimmer around three tall trees and hung in the air above the parking lot. "What do you think?"

Her smile filled her whole face, and seemed to seep out from her into the small space they shared, touching him and the tongat. "I've never seen so much water."

"Do you want to go down?"

"Can I?"

"There's a path down from here. I can let you off so you can walk to the base of the falls. They have a platform with a rail that lets you get close to the pool at the bottom."

"Oh yes, please. I'd love to touch it."

He laughed. "You might not be able to get *that* close. But it will touch you."

She looked puzzled.

"You'll see," he said. "I can't go. I've got Cricket to keep."

"I can manage." She turned to him, her eyes bright with the wonder of the falls. "It's so big."

He parked where he could watch her. The path from the restaurant at the edge of the parking lot to the bottom of the falls could be slick.

She was probably safe enough, but Manny had told him she could buy at least half of Manna Springs. Not that she showed it. In fact, when Amara had asked him about her the night before, the first word out of his mouth had been "sad." He'd added "curious" and "interesting" and left off "beautiful." Even though she seemed completely enchanted by the falls, he thought "sad" still fit.

He felt sad himself this morning, like some ghost of the disturbing conversation he'd had with Manny had stuck to him. It made being here at the falls bittersweet, like he was watching something he could lose. There hadn't been any direct threat against Lym except the offhand comment from the smuggler boy, but he felt threatened nonetheless.

Nona wore a green shirt that blended with the spring background. He squinted until he found her, checked her progress, and noted that she had made it further downhill than he'd expected.

He'd expected to hate everything about her.

He turned toward Cricket and scratched her nose. "I'm going to watch the station get attacked."

The tongat regarded him calmly. She was used to him talking to her.

He thumbed on the biggest screen the skimmer had, a ten-inch affair in the back of the driver's seat, meant for passengers.

Cricket rested her nose on his shoulder, cuddling in a way she only did when they were alone.

He narrated for no good reason other than that it helped him make sense of the news. "We're going to see the ice pirates in action, and we may not like it."

The tongat nosed his neck, perhaps reacting to his apprehension.

The High Sweet Home floated in space, the station ablaze with light. True to its multiple purposes, the station looked hybrid. "See that? The right is all warships and cargo ships and—well, and ships anyway. The middle is all bright and full of places people live and grow things. It's the brightest station we have."

Cricket snorted.

He noticed that he was saying "we" about the stations. "The far side is where they're building things—new ships and even a small new station, I think. I'll have to look that up." Or not.

One hand roamed Cricket's coarse coat, and she made a contented sound between a whine and a purr.

On the screen, ships streamed away from the High Sweet Home.

One by one, the ships died. They changed shape or imploded or they simply drifted apart, becoming pieces of ships. He tried to see what killed them. Space created different visuals than the bright light of Lym, and this video had been taken by an approaching ship that was still pretty far out.

Something bigger than the station crossed his screen, something so dark he could only make out its outline by what it blocked. "There's the station killer," he told Cricket. "It's a big, bad thing." The tiny screen made it look small, but the Next ship must be bigger than any he'd ever seen. It had to be. His chest grew tight and Cricket wriggled closer to him, almost as if she wanted to merge into him. He really did need to get her another tongat.

He paused the playback and glanced down, spotting Nona at the base of the falls. He wished he'd gone with her. Surely it would have been more pleasant than watching the video. She'd be pretty with her face and hair full of spray-diamonds.

"Back to it, Cricket." He didn't want to tell the machine to play, but he forced himself to give the command. So many things started happening on the screen at once that he could barely follow them all. "There go the lights from the station. Maybe on purpose? And there's a ton of ships coming off the big one, or at least a lot of little lights. And now they're going off and it's all dark but we know people are targeting each other and shooting and dying."

Cricket leaned into him and put her head on his shoulder.

CHAPTER EIGHT

NONA

Nona stood in front of the waterfall, the noise and rush of it singing in her bones. The air smelled of water, a hundred times more potent and cleaner than working in the greenhouses on the station. Droplets of spray wet her face and hands and clothes. A cool breeze touched her cheeks and fluffed the edges of her hair. She picked out the sweet scent of spring flowers. Even the crushed grass beneath her feet had its own smell. A small white butterfly danced around her for a few moments and moved on.

Life surrounded her, an infinite habitat bubble. She lifted her arms toward the falls and flung them wide.

She stood there forever and a moment, as if the flow of time didn't matter and couldn't matter in the face of such a thing as a waterfall.

The sky had stunned her. The water overtook her, dizzied her, enchanted her. "Thank you, dad," she whispered.

Climbing back up the hill taxed her thighs so the muscles burned every time she lifted her foot. She stopped from time to time to take photos of plants.

She fell twice on the way back up the water-splashed path. By the time she arrived back at the skimmer she wore mud on one knee and the opposite elbow, and she'd managed to put a streak of it on her cheek, which she left there. It felt like being smeared with the raw power of Lym.

Cricket seemed to think more of her than she had before, the appraisal in her steady gaze a tiny bit less judgmental. But Charlie looked disturbed, his jaw tight and his eyes dark and angry. "Did I take too long?" she asked him.

He blinked and his face changed to a mask of control. "No. I'm sorry. It's something else."

She wanted to ask, but he seemed like the kind of man who offered himself more easily if you didn't push. "It's the most beautiful place I've ever seen. The falls. Lym."

He smiled briefly, his mood only partly broken. "I can show you even prettier places here. Some where there won't be so many people."

"There were hardly any here."

He gave her a look that disagreed.

"On a station, every public place is so close that people touch on accident. We smell each other's breath and perfume and sweat. Even walking from place to place there's people in front and behind and maybe on either side."

"I'd hate that," he said.

"I bet you would."

"Are you willing to go where there's no one but us?" he asked.

"Of course." She felt awed by the waterfall and opened by the planet, almost flayed. This might be the perfect time to let Onor and Marcelle's ashes go. "Can you find a place with water above a falls?"

"This falls?"

"Is there a place that's even more empty?" She had never been in a place without other humans, and suddenly she craved it.

"Strap in," Charlie said. He stood up, still keeping himself between her and Cricket. He felt cold and distant.

They flew in silence for twenty minutes, until she had to say something. "Your mood. It's different."

"It's not you," he said. He dropped the skimmer closer to the surface and started pointing out springs and streams and grazing animals, his voice and movements controlled.

She didn't know him well enough to push harder, so she settled for being curious about the things he showed her and trying to draw him out with conversation. It worked a little, because he smiled as he took her up over a ridge near the base of mountains. Thin wisps of clouds lay against the bottom of the cliff like a veil. As they flew closer to it she realized it wasn't fog at all, but the spray from waterfall after waterfall. "You pick," he said.

She leaned toward the cliff and watched carefully. The falls were a series of thin ribbons of water that sprung out from the top of the ridge and fell through clear air to land hard on a rocky base. She looked up at Charlie. "There's no power like this on the Deep. Nothing."

He grunted. "Isn't the Diamond Deep the most powerful place in the solar system?"

"It is. But that's a human power, a creation of laws and intent. This is . . . primal."

He looked approving. "Pick your waterfall."

She did, and the gently forested meadows toward the top of the falls turned out to be a fresh wonder. She had never imagined so many shades of green or such magical light and shadow.

Charlie hovered to let her out, and she jumped down carefully. She found a flat rock and stood on it, listening to the stream and the birds. Nona took her parents' ashes and held them in her hand, staring at the vials. They seemed to stick there, like glue.

"Come on," she whispered to herself. "You can do this." But suddenly the place didn't feel right. She turned and walked a little further away, being careful not to slip. She knelt and used her free hand to touch the water, which felt so cool that it sent shivers up her spine. If she put her parents here, they'd be cold.

She'd thought she could do this.

Maybe she wasn't ready yet. She had another month down here. She could bury them on any day. At least her father's ashes were warm here next to her skin; in real life Onor had hated the cold.

She didn't like hesitating. She should just do this.

Charlie had brought the skimmer down close to her. "Ready?" he asked, his voice just under a shout to get over the steady engine noise.

She bit her lip.

"Do you need more time?" He seemed to be working to keep the skimmer close.

"Is there someplace warmer?" she called. "With warmer water?"

"Warmer?"

She nodded, unwilling to explain just yet. He looked slightly annoyed, and glanced up at the sun which had started angling down already. But he dipped the skimmer slightly lower. She climbed on and sat down.

"Strap in."

She did.

He turned so that they flew between the two ridges, with the green and silver ribbons of waterfalls on their right side and rockier terrain on the left. They tended downward, coming out of the mountains they'd climbed into this morning on their way to Ollicle Falls. He stayed silent for a while, but then he asked, "Why do you need warmth?"

"I'll trade you. What changed between when we left this morning and now? Why are you so different?"

By now the long wait for an answer seemed normal. He eventually said, "Okay. But you go first, so I can take you to the kind of place you want."

She swallowed. He was a stranger, but he was also the only human she knew at all here. She took a deep breath and started in. "My dad dreamed of Lym. He grew up inside a ship, and then lived on a station, but he dreamed of a sky. He always wanted to come here, but he and mom were always doing something else, and he died before he could get here. I brought some of his ashes.

"The last year of his life, he constantly complained about being cold, so cold I piled three or four blankets on him. I don't want to leave him in a cold place."

"Is an ocean okay? Taken as a whole it will be warm and cold, but here the current is warm enough to swim in."

"My dad wanted to see an ocean almost as much as he wanted to see a sky. His ashes will go everywhere, and touch every continent, won't they?"

He smiled. "They will."

"Your turn."

His lips twitched and he looked out over the horizon and fiddled with the skimmer some before he said, "Have you looked at the news today?"

"No. I just barely woke up in time to eat and get ready."

"You don't have a feed?"

"It's off." It seemed like he was trying to put her on the defensive and she bristled at that. "Do I need to turn it on, or are you going to tell me?"

He had the grace to apologize. "Sorry. You know about the High Sweet Home?"

She froze. Chrystal lived there! "What happened?"

"It's gone. Just gone. The ice pirates came in and took it."

"Took it?"

"Took it."

"I don't understand."

"They took it away."

"They didn't blow it up?"

"I don't think so."

She felt like she'd been hit. "Do you know anything?"

"Every one of the military ships on the station got blown up, and the ship's bays took a lot of damage."

"But the people? The ones inside? The ordinary people?"

His mouth was a thin line, his eyes hard. "The pirates took the station with them."

"That's . . . not possible." It wasn't. Possible. Stations didn't change orbits.

The valley they flew over began to open out and meadows appeared, dotted with shaggy, grazing animals. "I can show you the news story."

She understood his mood now. "It happened while I was at the waterfall?"

"Before. I watched the news while you were there. I heard about it last night, but I saw the footage today."

"What do they want? They have to want something. Satyana talked about this before I came down, saying they were getting restless. I just . . . I don't know. I didn't believe her. She's a worrier." Nona stopped. She was babbling and afraid, even though the distances between them and the ice pirates were huge. She should tell him about Chrystal, watch the footage herself. But she didn't want to cry in front of him. "Do you want to go back?" she asked.

"And do what?" For just a moment, he looked tender instead of angry. "You should do what you need to do. Go bury your dead."

Suddenly she wanted to hang on to the ashes. Silly. "Okay."

<hr />

Rough sand warmed Nona's bare toes. In front of her, a flat expanse of it extended all the way to kiss the horizon, the colors of blue and green and grey blending where sea touched sky. The sun hung low enough that its reflection made a fat bright line in the water. Near the shore, waves bunched, curled, and crashed. Birds hung in the tangy air, occasionally falling to the water and pulling wriggling fish from it.

All of it looked so foreign. Water, birds, air, sky. So much water cowed her, such a vast horizon made her feel tiny, and the myriad miniature specks of sand made her feel big, as if she were the center of an infinity symbol.

She shuffled close enough for the edge of the water to touch her feet. It seemed slightly warmer than the afternoon air. She felt some urgency now, as if Charlie's news about the High Sweet Home made getting past her own losses more important. Here, her parents could join the myriad others who had died across all time like grains of sand, including the very first settlers.

She took the vials of ashes out her pocket yet again, and held them up.

She closed her eyes, took a deep breath, and straightened her spine. She took three more steps, and then another, so the water washed in and out over her ankles but didn't touch the bottom of her rolled-up pants. She opened her eyes and looked out over the waves, remembering that Charlie had told her not to turn her back to the ocean, but to watch it. She shuffled carefully, the waves slapping her knees and the sand pulling away from under her feet.

That should be good enough.

"Here you go, dad," she whispered. "Here's your sky. It's really beautiful. There are birds outside of cages, and they're beautiful, too. Stay warm." She stopped for a breath. "Mom, I'll miss you forever. I will. I'll think of you both a lot, and try to keep you with me."

She took the stoppers out of the jars and turned them quickly. The surface of the sea swallowed the ashes nearly instantly, accepting and subsuming them.

A wave wet her belly, raised her a tiny bit so her feet flailed, and just as she grew scared it set her back down and went on to break against the shore.

She stared at the shifting surface. Grass or something floated near her. A small fish jumped from the top of a breaking wave and fell back to be swallowed by the sea. The roar of the waves enveloped her and she felt vulnerable and lossy and also free. "I'll do okay," she said out loud. "I will." It wasn't entirely clear to her whether she was talking to her parents or to the ocean or to herself. She turned and started back toward the beach, slightly startled to see that the sand seemed further away.

Another wave slammed her from behind so her knees buckled briefly and water splashed onto the back of her shirt.

Cricket howled and Nona looked up to see the tongat loping toward her on the beach.

She turned back to the sea and stood mesmerized as a wall of water as high as her head approached. Fish swam in the translucent top of the water where the sun speared it with orange light. The wave seized her and lifted her and tangled her in whitewater, dragging her limbs across sand. The vials fell from her hands and she reached out for them, and managed to snatch one.

Then water took it from her, pulling it backward toward the ocean. She stood against the waves, barely managing her balance, squinting in the bright diamonds of sun on water, trying to find the vials or the ashes, or anything.

Cricket howled again, closer. Nona turned her head to look for the tongat.

Water slammed into her. She braced, but she wasn't strong enough to keep her feet. Water covered her face in wave-spray and yanked her toward the beach and then out, taking control. It slammed up her nose and she choked and the taste of salt filled her throat and mouth.

She struggled to get her feet under her, but there was no sand under them, nothing to stand on or push against. Only water.

CHAPTER NINE

CHARLIE

C harlie pelted down the beach toward Cricket, who danced and bayed at the edge of the water, her tail up like a flag. Waves and whitewater and, in the sounds of surf, nothing human. No Nona. She'd *just* been there, standing up, looking perfectly safe.

She had.

He was an idiot.

Cricket barked, high and sharp. He followed her gaze. A hand reached out and grasped at air, then disappeared. Nona's head bobbed up and then washed under whitewater.

He couldn't tell if she'd gotten a breath.

He checked the sets coming in. One more huge wave and then a short break. He forced himself to let the wave come in, watched Nona flail and struggle. Alive. At least she was alive. As the water rushed out he raced it, gaining ground on Nona even as the sea tried to haul her away from him. He pulled her up, choking.

She fit over his shoulder in a rescue carry and he turned fast, racing the next incoming wave for the beach. By the time it pounded against the back of his calves he had gotten far enough up the beach to stand against the water, although he had to stop and let the force pass him while he braced. Sand swirled away from under his feet and filled his wet, heavy shoes. Seawater reached his knees before he pulled out of the sand-hole and made the beach, the next wave kissing his ankles. Nona struggled and coughed against him, but he waited until they were well past the high tide line before he set her down. "Bend over."

She did, which made her cough harder. Her breath came in high wheezes, like the gasping of a fish.

He watched her spit water, not touching her, letting her manage.

This shouldn't have happened. He'd been thinking about High Sweet Home and, worse, about what might happen next. He had been contemplating Nona's question about what the ice pirates could possibly want. They were machines. They didn't need the sun.

Cricket circled them, coming in close and keeping her ears up. She spent more time watching away from them, looking protective. He knew her body language well enough to say, "I think my beast likes you."

Nona didn't answer, still coughing. Her cheeks had pinked.

Without Cricket, he might have been too late. He stepped a little away from Nona and called the tongat over to him, praising her. Cricket nuzzled his hand, her breath warm.

As soon as Nona stopped choking and wheezing well enough to hear, he said, "I'm sorry. I forgot to tell you not to breathe the sea."

She laughed.

He felt lighter. She'd be all right. "Let's warm you up."

He took off his wet shoes and walked beside her back to the skimmer, both of them wet and sandy and a little goose-pimply in spite of the late-afternoon sun. He glanced at the light. "We have an hour. Are you hungry?"

She shook her head. "Thirsty."

"Okay—help me gather wood?"

"Wood?"

"For a fire. To warm you up, and to dry out our clothes."

The look on her face made it his turn to laugh. He had forgotten most spacers' reaction to fire. "It's not dangerous. This isn't a ship. Fire started here, happens here all by itself. A beach fire is the best fire ever."

She still looked doubtful, so he added, "Fire gave the first humans life and heat and cooked food way back on Earth."

"Isn't Earth a myth?"

"Maybe." He shrugged. "We came from somewhere." He wanted to just wrap her in a blanket and have her sit in the skimmer. But he also wanted her close to him, and he liked to teach people about Lym by having them touch it. "Are your feet okay on the sand?" Spacers typically had baby feet, soft and easy to injure.

"I can walk in it."

He filled her arms with driftwood, Cricket circling them and keeping watch.

She helped him scoop a fire pit out of the sand but stood away as he lit it, as if the thing might explode in her face. He handed her a spare coat he carried in the skimmer and had her strip down to her underwear and the coat, which covered her almost to her knees. Her legs were attractive, the muscle definition suggesting the full-body workouts of a station spacer.

He retrieved two chairs from the skimmer's belly storage and some food. He held half a sandwich out, but she shook her head. "My stomach's sour from the water."

He handed her a canteen. "Drink this. It will help."

She looked dubious but obeyed. At first, she sat far away from the fire, but then she inched closer, watching the flames. Not only did she deal with his silences, but she had her own aura of quiet. After a long while she said, "Thanks for saving me."

"You're welcome."

She held her hand out toward the tongat. "Will she come now?"

"That's up to her."

Cricket did, crouching low and creeping toward the slight woman from the stars. She stood small for a tongat and Nona small for a woman, and they both looked like they were trying to make themselves even smaller in order not to scare the other one off. Nona smiled, and Cricket made low growling noises in her throat.

Charlie watched carefully. Cricket had always been standoffish to anyone other than him, although she'd eventually accepted Jean Paul in full and started to let Manny feed her without trying to eat his fingers.

Nona kept her hand out and didn't raise it above Cricket's head. She let the animal come to her and bump her hand. Only then did she scratch Cricket behind the ears.

Cricket's tail wagged, and Charlie let the breath he had been holding out. Yet another thing he hadn't expected. The sun had fallen far enough that the light looked gold and thick, and the tops of the waves were translucent.

"You only hired me for today so far," he said, surprised that he was talking to her the way he used to talk to Cricket when she was wilder. "Shall I come back tomorrow?"

"Yes."

The next morning, Charlie found himself looking forward to picking Nona up. "What do you think?" he asked Cricket. "About Nona?"

The tongat didn't answer.

"I thought she'd be a spoiled rotten rich girl, but she isn't."

The tongat still didn't answer.

Nona waited for him on the hotel steps. She wore brown pants and a brown top and brown shoes. The outfit made her hair look darker than usual and gave her a slightly somber look. She carried a bag.

He nodded at it. "What did you bring?"

"Extra clothes." She grinned. "In case I fall into anything again."

Already she had him feeling lighthearted, in spite of the serious topics they had been discussing during the drive back last night. They had worried at the ice pirates as if they could somehow discern the hearts of the darkest machines.

"I've been doing research," she said as she climbed into her seat. "Satyana thinks the Next—she hates the name ice pirates—may have stolen the station to harvest our technology, to re-engineer it so that they can come in and talk to us." She stopped for a minute, her brow furrowed. "She also thinks they were sending us a message, something like 'Don't mess with us.'"

"Has she heard if there are survivors?"

Worry pinched her face. "No."

He stopped himself from reaching out a hand for her. "You said you knew someone on the station. Want to talk about it?"

"Not yet. Let's decide where to go."

"What do you think of an overnight trip? What you've seen so far is part of the fully restored and safe part of the world. I'd like to show you Goland."

Her eyes lit up, although she didn't answer.

"I've a place you can stay. In the ranger station. We have an extra bedroom."

She chewed at her lower lip.

"I'm not trying to get too personal. I'll introduce you to my roommate and how we live as rangers, and show you some scars from our past and some pure wild places."

She still didn't look convinced.

"If you'd rather, I can take you somewhere local today and head to Goland tomorrow."

"I'll go."

He hadn't really expected her to say yes, and it pleased him. "It's a three-hour flight. Shall I wait for you to get more things?"

"Okay." She climbed back down and headed for the hotel.

While he waited, he called Manny and told him his plans.

"Don't be gone too long. I may need you here."

"To do what?"

"The news about the station is getting out. People are scared."

"You're the politician. I'm not responsible for the city. You are."

"You're better at it than you admit. It makes people feel safe to have you around."

"I hate it."

He could almost hear Manny grin as he said, "I know."

Nona came back and climbed in, tucking her blue bag behind the seat. "We'll have breakfast on the flight," he told her.

"Over water, right? That'll work as long as I don't have to swim again just yet."

He laughed. As soon as they were away from Gyr Island, he turned on the autopilot and broke out fresh cinnamon rolls and a thermos of stim. "Ready to talk about the people you know who were on the High Sweet Home?"

She hesitated. "My best friend, Chrystal Peterson, is up there. We grew up together. We both took diplomacy classes, and then we both realized there wasn't anything to do with that knowledge, at least until we get to be three or four hundred and have a few million credits. All those jobs go to people with real power."

"Like Satyana Adams?"

Nona laughed. "There's people far richer than her. She's just really good at being in the spotlight."

"So what did you do?"

"We went back to school and studied biology. She went to High Sweet Home because they were designing a low-light grain that works like a vitamin. She's been there a while. She's part of a quad marriage. They're working together on a new animal with a name I keep forgetting."

Her voice caught, and she put a hand to the tattoo on her neck. A dragon. He'd glimpsed it yesterday when she changed into his shirt.

He wished he hadn't asked her. If he lost Jean Paul that way, he'd be frantic. They'd been friends for thirty years. He tried changing the subject. "So what do you do in biology?"

"I teach. College." She went silent for a minute. "I hope she's okay."

"Me, too," Charlie said. "Maybe we'll hear something today. Surely there will be a rescue."

Nona's jaw had tightened and her eyes glittered with unshed tears. "I doubt it. That station is almost past the Ring now. There's nothing there, no one to save her."

"There's still hope. We don't really understand what they want."

She watched the planet below her for a long moment. "We know a little. The Next made a bold, aggressive move. If we react in kind, they'll have an excuse to start a war. When they took the station, they showed us we might not be able to beat them a second time."

"Why do you think that?" he asked her.

"We don't have any ships strong enough to tow a station that big anywhere."

"Oh." It rocked him a little. He'd have to study up on the Glittering and their weapons.

"Stations are sitting ducks in a war, and so is Lym. None of us can move, while ships can. I watched the video last night. The ship that took the station—so big. We have nothing that compares."

He fell quiet for a while, and then said, "I guess you did study politics."

"Diplomacy."

"Okay. We have guns on the orbiting stations, and a few fighters out there, too."

"Do you have enough of those to create a safety fence?" she asked.

He remembered the boys he'd just rescued and that he'd promised Jean Paul he'd to talk to Manny about building a better sensor network. "No. But the pirates don't seem to want to kill us," he said. "They didn't destroy the station. Just the ships that attacked them. At least that's what it looked like."

She smiled, a little sadly. "That's an optimistic take on a horrid situation."

"My job is restoration. You learn to cut your losses and support your gains. My family was one of the original group that set out to restore Lym— it's been all of our life's work."

"How long?"

"I'm in the seventieth generation."

"Wow."

He took them over the Palagi Islands and showed her the steam that rose from three sides of the biggest crater and the lava river that plunged into the sea. "It's almost as if the planet breathes," she mused.

He laughed. "It does. Lym is a living thing with many parts."

She looked startled. "Really? Do you think that?"

"Absolutely."

"Do you ever want to leave?" she asked him.

"Never. I can't imagine not being here."

She wondered what it would be like to truly love a place. "I can hardly imagine going back home."

"You like Lym that much?"

"No. Well, yes. I'm enchanted with Lym. But I hate the Diamond Deep that much."

CHAPTER TEN

CHRYSTAL

Asmall shudder ran through the station, and then another. Chrystal forced her dry eyes open. Darkness greeted her. She began to wonder if the lights still worked, if they had been turned off in some central place and if anyone would turn them on. The pull against her body had lessened to normal. She stretched her toes and wriggled her fingers.

The last time she woke, Yi had also been awake. She had mumbled, "We're alive," her voice scratchy through the tinny suit microphone.

His voice had also sounded as dry and cracked. "So far, so good."

How many hours had passed between then and now? Her body felt stiff and chafed where the suit had rubbed bare skin. Her thinking seemed slowed by the sleep-drugs, as if a haze still hung inside her brain. She must be hungry, but thirst overrode everything else, growing more acute as she recognized it. She tried for a sip of water and got air through the valve.

She closed her eyes and breathed deeply, forcing the kind of calm her yoga practice gave her. If there were more drugs, she didn't want them now.

The thick darkness beat at her composure, a restless counter to the calm of her yoga breathing.

She sucked at the water valve again. It burbled, giving her air and a slight bit of stale water that wet her lips enough she could call out the names of her family.

"Katherine."

Nothing.

"Jason."

A grunt. Good.

"Yi."

Nothing.

The suit had simple display capabilities. She rolled her eyes to flip it on. The pale amber lights of the readout scrolled through the basics twice before she absorbed it all. Breathable air. Cold, but only three degrees colder than usual. Pressure normal for the High Sweet Home. She thought that through. No hull breach. By now, the station would be conserving power and sending or saving almost all of it for the life-support systems. Air first, heat (reduced) second, light third, and then food. Up was still up, so the gravgens worked.

The display changed, catching her attention. Suit stats. It *was* nearly out of fluids, nutrients, and medicines. She decided that the suit wanted her to recharge it. It seemed easier to lie there and die inside of the stinking suit.

"I'm taking these damned straps off." It took her stiff hands four tries to release the first buckle. There were only three other movements to getting free, all of them painful after being so still for so long.

Next to her, Jason also freed himself. They stood slowly, leaning on each other, into each other. Her legs tingled.

She tugged her helmet off and breathed deeply. The air smelled stale, but not dangerous. She stripped the bulky suit down to her waist, letting it hang there. The arms flopped against her knees as she inched carefully across the room and fumbled for the light switch. It clicked on under her fingers, the sudden bright making her flinch.

Jason's hair had slicked to his head in mostly damp purple streaks, and bits of it had tangled at the ends. His gray-blue eyes looked wide and shocked. He peeled his suit away slowly, his nose wrinkling at his own scents. He reached for her cheek. "We're alive."

The room looked intact. One of the fans screeched and a motor whined more loudly than usual. "There was so much noise, I expected more damage."

Jason nodded. "Me, too."

"Let's wake the others," Chrystal suggested.

"I'll take Kate."

If she were awake, Katherine would give Jason the look of death for using the short form of her name. Chrystal found Yi staring up at her with wide eyes that looked slightly off through the clear faceplate. "Are you okay?"

He blinked. He sipped at his fluid and then licked his lips. Trying to tell her something. Hell with it. She undid his straps and pulled him up. "How are you?"

"Thirsty."

She undid the pack by the bed and handed him water. "You're suit is dry."

Katherine asked, "What happens next?" in a small voice.

Yi answered her first. "We find out how other people are. Start by looking on the nets."

"We should explore," Jason said.

Katherine stood, shaking. "I need to feed the animals."

The look that crossed Yi's face told Chrystal he thought like she did, but neither of them said anything.

Yi insisted they change out the suit packs of raw water and medicines for fresh ones. They put the remaining charged reservoirs into backpacks with the leftover food and one clean outfit each. The packs looked slim; they were used to having their little piece of the world restocked daily by robots. Jason hefted his. "We need more food and a good source of water. We'll run out up here."

"Do we know if we've actually stopped moving?" Chrystal asked.

"No," Yi said. "But I think so."

Chrystal pushed the suit off of her legs and eyed the shower with regret. That water would be there, but it wasn't a priority. "I woke up when the station bounced, like maybe we got dropped from a tow."

Jason shook his head. "I still can't picture the whole station getting towed."

"Let's go." Katherine had stripped and pulled on clean underwear. She was choosing between shirts, staring at a white one and a red one. "I need to find Sugar."

"Wear the red. Easier to see you in the meadow." Yi started poking at his slate. "There are people on the net. Not many. I'll post that we're okay." He was half naked and totally focused.

"Surely some people might help," Chrystal said.

"The animals first," Katherine insisted, opening the bedroom door and going into the galley. Chrystal followed.

Other than a single cup that had somehow escaped and rolled on the floor, everything looked neat.

The meadow lights hadn't come back on, and so it looked like dusk outside. The spinning habitat stood still and unmoving, subject to the same gravgens that let Chrystal and Katherine stand straight so that down was now below their feet and hard to make out. Pieces of the barn and strips of the shallow soil and grass had fallen from above and littered the meadow. Every tree and rock and heavy thing had come down. A few had left ugly scratches on the clear parts of the habitat bubble. Metal struts and torn water pipes showed in the roof. Soil and grass hung down in strips.

"I can't see any of the animals," Katherine hissed. "Let's go."

Yi and Jason had come in behind them. Yi surveyed the room and selected occasional items to add to packs. "Get any personal things you want," he said. "Nothing heavy."

As Chrystal stuck her toothbrush into her pack, she noticed that Yi had holstered his gun on his belt. She'd only seen him carry it a few times. The rest of them didn't have one at all.

In moments each of them had a pack on their back. Yi and Chrystal dragged all four suits out to the edge of the platform, rolling the helmets inside and tying them in loose bundles with the flopping limbs. They pushed them over and then helped each other into harnesses. After they started down themselves, Chrystal realized there wouldn't be any easy return. With no spin gravity, they had no easy slide home.

Already, the air smelled of decay.

At the foot of the landing platform, Katherine cried out. She knelt next to the body of one of the jalinerines. Its neck and at least two legs had broken when it fell. Kinship. Chrystal's favorite. She shuddered and gave a little cry.

Jason pulled Katherine away from the crumpled body, whispering, "I know. I know. Let's see if any are alive."

Yi glared at him.

Chrystal glanced back at the body and told Yi, "Maybe just you and I should go."

"No. No. I'm coming," Katherine insisted. "I can do this."

"We stay together." Jason said it as a command.

Chrystal took Katherine's hand in hers. They had been in other tough situations. Katherine always came through.

Two of Sugar's herd had died quickly, as pieces of the barn had fallen on them, and another had been hit on the side of the head with a rock and lay on its side, breathing but blessedly unconscious.

Yi pulled out his gun. His eyes betrayed his hatred of the situation. Chrystal was proud of him and sorry for him and grateful that he was willing to do such a hard thing. She held Katherine as Yi silently checked the safety and the setting on the weapon and activated it with a sharp squeeze. The gun made no noticeable sound as he fired it, but Katherine jerked in Chrystal's arms as if he had shot her. Jason looked away.

Next, they found Missy, one of the youngest in the herd, awake and bleating pitifully. Katherine put a hand out and touched the animal's forehead, and Missy flinched as if startled. "What happened to her?" she asked. "I don't see any injuries. Gravity?"

Chrystal asked, "Can she see?"

"Why?" Katherine stroked the animal's neck.

"The bastards towed us too fast for them. *We* were protected," Yi gestured toward the habitat above them, "But they experienced high gravity for a long time. It would be tough. Blood would pool in strange places, and they would go blind before the stress alone killed them. She's not dead because we didn't get fast enough for that. Maybe we came close."

Katherine glared at the roof as if were possible to see the Next somewhere above them.

Jason held his hand out for the weapon. Yi stood by his side until the jalinerine—Missy—stopped making noise. Yi hugged Jason and then slapped his back. "There's only Sugar left."

Katherine had gone silent and grim. Chrystal just wanted it to be over. They knew what they'd find; they needed to do it and go on.

Somewhere across the meadow, something fell from the ceiling and clattered onto a rock, making a loud bang. The group of them clustered closer together. Katherine called out, "Sugaaaarrrrrr."

Nothing.

They separated again. This part of the meadow had escaped the worst damage. Here and there, they passed a piece of trash or a rock out of place. They walked carefully around a tree with a broken trunk, a rock lodged in the fork of its shattered branches.

Katherine's voice echoed, bouncing off of the metal inside of the broken meadow. "Shhhhuuugggggggarrrrrr."

In the eerie half-light, the grass still looked beautiful even though the tips had browned. The paths of the broken streams crunched under Chrystal's footsteps.

They found Sugar near three scraggly meadow trees. She had a scratch on her neck, laced with dried blood, and one on her knee that she'd been able to lick clean. At least one leg had broken.

Katherine gave a little cry and then started talking to her. "Good baby, good baby. I'm so sorry, baby." Tears streamed down Katherine's face.

Chrystal knelt next to Sugar, touching her neck. The last of their creations, the best. The leader of them all. Sugar's eyes were filled with pain. "I'm so sorry," Chrystal crooned. "So sorry. So sorry. So sorry."

Yi raised his gun and fired. Sugar's head dropped.

Katherine fell to her side, repeating, "No, no, no, no," over and over as if she could undo what had been necessary.

Chrystal reached for Katherine, but Yi waved her back. He knelt beside Katherine and took her in his arms, and she beat on his back with her closed fists and cried.

Chrystal drifted close to Jason. Her hand crept into his. They held their silence, watching until Katherine stopped hitting Yi and just sobbed and sobbed and sobbed.

―∞∞―

All four of them stood near the bottom of the zip-line platform, holding their bulky suits. Yi balanced his slate on his suit, which he had folded neatly. He thumbed the slate one handed, muttering under his breath. Jason had figured out how to rig his own suit like an awkward backpack. He used his free hands to massage Katherine's shoulders. She had stopped crying and appeared to have lost her anger as well, or buried it. At the moment her face was a study in calm, touched with mild curiosity.

"Your muscles are rocks," Jason muttered.

Yi held up the hand with the slate in it. "There's no trains running. But we shouldn't take the tunnels; they could start."

"Unlikely," Jason said.

"We die if we're wrong. Let's use the airlock."

The group trudged after Yi and clambered off the edge of the meadow. They stood on the thin lip of metal that never rotated. Seven ladders ringed the round airlock door, radiating down to attach near the ledge the group stood on. They were able to sidle just a little to the right and up the edge of the cylinder and then take a ladder that canted about five degrees off of straight up and led to the airlock door. Yi went first, then Katherine, Chrystal, and finally Jason. All four of them fit easily into the cargo airlock, even with the suits and the backpacks.

Jason latched the door shut from the inside and then opened the other door and peered out.

On the far side, a corridor, and at the end another airlock. "I've never been here," Crystal said. "Do you know where it goes?"

"No," Katherine said. "I bet none of us have been here."

Yi pulled a map up on his slate and projected it in 3D for them. "It goes to offices."

"Exciting." Jason tugged to re-arrange the suit.

As they walked through the corridor, the left foot of Chrystal's suit kept dragging on the ground. "Shouldn't we just put those on?" Yi suggested.

"No," Jason and Katherine said at once.

Chrystal wanted to suggest that they shouldn't even be carrying them, but she knew without asking that Yi would object, and he'd be right. Which didn't make dragging the suit any more fun.

Yi said, "After the offices, I think there's habitats. We might find people there."

They climbed into the lock on the far side and shut it.

Just as Yi reached for the handle to open the outside door, the station creaked and shifted, throwing Chrystal into Jason. "What was that?" she whispered.

"I don't know," Yi said. He hesitated for a second, and then looked at the others. "We are putting on suits as soon as we get through here." He reached for the handle of the door.

Katherine put a hand on Yi's forearm, stopping him. "Is it safe to open that?"

Yi looked at Katherine gently and nodded. He opened the door and peered out. "Offices." He squinted. "It's cold in there. A lot colder than it should be."

"At least there's light," Chrystal noted, grateful.

The over-loud clunks and whirs of damaged air scrubbers overrode their voices from time to time. The station was working too hard. Or maybe she was imagining things.

They didn't see anyone in the immediate area. Desks were bolted to walls, chairs to floors, walls to each other. While anything could be moved with a heavy wrench and the facilities crew, it had held together for the tow. The contents hadn't done as well. Cups and water bulbs and slates had collected in drifts along cubicle walls.

As they pulled their suits on, the station gave three more deep shudders, the last one so sharp that Chrystal had to step to retain her balance. She felt relieved to dog her helmet down.

Walking in the suits felt a little better than walking and carrying them, except that she hated having so little peripheral vision. It made her feel like she was looking through a tunnel with walls that flared out from behind her ears.

About halfway down a long corridor, Jason pointed right.

A body lay in a corner under a desk, or maybe the person had chosen the corner before they died. The corpse had no pressure suit. The cause of death wasn't obvious, and they didn't get close enough to examine him.

At the end of a long corridor they found another door. This one wasn't an airlock, and they went through one by one. On the far side, Yi whispered, "Housing."

Housing meant worker housing, smaller and cheaper than what they had been enjoying; simpler. They peered into doorways. Many were empty. Some were full of bodies. "It's just like our babies," Katherine said.

"They don't keep suits so handy in here," Jason said. "They hang them in racks by the doorways out."

"How do you know?" Chrystal asked.

"I worked on a station like this right out of college. No money. These habs are tiny boxes," he waved a gloved hand at a doorway, "and it's not like we ever needed the suits."

"A suit might not be enough without an acceleration bed or couch," Yi said. "Maybe for the lucky and healthy." He sounded dismayed.

They started passing people in suits or partially in suits. Unmoving. Eerie. They might as well be walking through a horror immersive. Jason stopped to take off a helmet. They didn't need to feel for a pulse.

A communication ping lit up Yi's slate. "There's someone nearby," he said. "To the left." He followed the map on his slate and they all followed him, watching warily around corners. They came to conference rooms. "Hellloooo?" a voice called. A head poked out of a door. Un-helmeted, multicolored hair awry.

Chrystal pulled her helmet off, relieved and suddenly irrationally hopeful. "Hello back!" The woman worked in the grocery store closest to them. She was highly modded, with rainbow eyes, berry-red lips, and many multicolored braids that ran down her neck like a cowl. Chrystal struggled to remember her name. Something simple. "Toyo! Good to see you."

Toyo looked briefly embarrassed.

"Chrystal." She introduced the others, all of them still standing in the hallway. "Is there anyone else?" Yi asked.

Toyo nodded. "Come on in." She disappeared through the doorway.

Chrystal went in first. A young woman bent over a toddler with a broken leg that had been braced with a long piece of metal tied from the boy's waist down past his tiny out-turned foot. The child fussed and babbled while the woman sang to him. Across the room, an old man lay on the floor with a coat for a pillow. His eyes tracked the new arrivals but he didn't move.

After they were all in, Toyo closed the door behind them. Chrystal sat down by the boy. "Is he yours?" she asked the young woman.

"My sister's. She died."

"I'm sorry. My name's Chrystal."

"Lien'cha."

"I'm sorry about your sister."

The woman touched the child's cheek. "We all are."

The door slammed open with a bang. Startled, the little boy cried, while the adults looked toward the noise.

A cluster of machines stood in the open doorway, holding weapons.

Silver machines, shiny. Perfect. Formed liked humans, although blockier. They moved more smoothly than people, gliding from pose to pose, as if they had perfect joints or no joints at all.

They floated into the room, the humans backing, open mouthed. In spite of their beauty, they felt . . . powerful.

She hadn't expected the ice pirates to look so sophisticated. They were supposed to be a blend of human and machine. The human wasn't easy to see.

One spoke. "Please line up against the left wall." Its voice sounded as silky as their movements looked fluid.

Nothing about them made Chrystal want to obey. She wanted to flee.

The four of them lined up against the far wall. Toyo backed into the group, ending up between Jason and Katherine.

Lien'cha picked up the toddler and held him close, backing against a different wall.

The ice pirate in front of the small group of robots glided over to the man on the floor. It held something in its hand that looked like a syringe and reached down and touched the old man with it.

As the robot backed up, the man's head slid from the pillow, his mouth open and his eyes wide.

Lien'cha clutched the toddler, who screeched.

"Who else is injured?" one of the ice pirates asked.

Chrystal heard the rasping of breath from them all, and for a long moment even the child's cries stilled.

The same robot that had murdered the old man held its hand out toward Lien'cha.

She forced herself back behind the others.

The robot pulled the woman and the little boy forward. It cocked its silvery head at the pair, and then said, "I will take the child."

"No!" Lien'cha screamed.

The arm with the syringe plunged into Lien'cha's neck. She fell, still holding the toddler, who fell onto his back and shrieked in anger. Chrystal glanced at the robot, which stood still now, regarding them incuriously. Even though her legs trembled, she walked toward Lien'cha and leaned down and touched her neck, feeling for a pulse.

Nothing.

Instinctively, Chrystal reached for the child, clutching it to her. The robot plucked it from her arms and handed it back to one of the other robots. That robot jogged off, carrying the boy. "Come with us," one of them who hadn't spoken yet said.

Chrystal's feet refused to obey her mind and either run or follow the robots. She might as well have grown roots.

Yi leaned down and touched the old man's neck. He shook his head.

"We should . . . we should . . ." It seemed that words had gotten stuck in Katherine's mouth.

Toyo spoke. "We'll die if we don't go with them."

"Yes," Chrystal said. Yi nodded. Katherine worried her lower lip and looked like she wanted to refuse, but Yi put an arm around her and whispered, "There are no options."

Toyo followed the pirates. Jason pushed Chrystal forward. She took a step and then another, and then she was following Toyo and the pirates. Yi and Katherine were behind her, and Jason took up the last place. Chrystal had expected one of the robots to be there, herding them, but instead they just went about their business of knocking on doors. They didn't seem to care what choice the humans made.

CHAPTER ELEVEN

CHRYSTAL

The robots led them through two entire sections of the ship and gathered twelve other people, all healthy young adults like themselves. Along the way, they killed the injured casually, each act making Katherine pull in on herself further, so that she grew whiter and her eyes rounder. Jason looked angry and lost at once, Yi impassive except that he glanced around all the time, as if every single detail of the destruction mattered. One of the women they didn't know cried out, over and over, until one of the robots killed her, too.

At one point, the robots stopped them all in a wide hallway. "Everyone in a pressure suit must remove it and leave it here."

Yi looked ready to protest, but Jason touched his arm and they all obeyed. Chrystal shivered in her thin, sweaty clothes and clomped along behind the robots in her heavy suit boots until the next stop, when they were all able to pull clothes and walking shoes from their packs.

They changed in the open in a bare spot on the floor of a machine shop. The robots swept through the shop, gathering two healthy men from behind a stack of boxes and injecting a sick woman and a wailing child with killing shots. As the child died, Katherine moaned.

"Be quiet," Chrystal hissed, frightened. They had to survive this, all of them.

She was out of adrenaline, left with heavy limbs and exhaustion. The captives walked a long way, their numbers neither growing nor falling.

———

They stood in a line in the middle of a large warehouse. There were perhaps twenty-five survivors, maybe a few more. Every time Chrystal tried to count, she lost track, her mind refusing to focus on even the simplest task.

Shipping crates lined two walls. The dead in here wore uniforms striped with glowing neon colors. A long segmented transport of a design Chrystal had never seen rolled up in front of them. The robot at the front of the line said, "You may not take anything with you."

Slates, extra coats, a bag of extra food, and a stuffed animal joined a discard pile by the door. One of the robots ran a wand over each of them, and one man had to leave his belt behind for no obvious reason. Their captors stood to the side and watched as the humans climbed into the transport. Inside, a uniformed woman with dark hair and almond-shaped eyes guided them into seats. Chrystal contrived to sit beside Katherine in the front right behind a window view screen, and Yi and Jason sat behind them.

"Why is that person working for the pirates?" Katherine wondered out loud. "I could never do that."

Since it didn't sound like she expected an answer, Chrystal settled for twisting her fingers through Katherine's. She felt completely rocked, lost. So much death. They'd fallen from the top of a beautiful mountain just as they were reaching the summit, gone scrabbling down a cliff barely hanging on, while others around them failed to find the tiny toeholds needed to survive. Their creations had died horribly.

They had done nothing to deserve this. No one on the High Sweet Home had deserved this. No one did.

She tried to think through what it might mean for the Deep, for Mammot, for Lym, for the hundreds of stations and other places in the Glittering.

Why did the pirates do this? What would they gain?

The machine crawled through the rest of the station. It wove around corners and seemed to become larger and smaller as needed without disturbing the passenger compartment. It moved with an eerie quiet, making only the slightest sounds of flexing as it moved.

The light in the empty station was intermittent at best, often only the dull green of the emergency lighting. Chrystal stared out the window anyway, trying to make sense of what she saw. Reasonably orderly corridors and working spaces gave way to damaged ship's bays and military training areas, to places full of twisted shadows, and holes in the station where Chrystal could see the bright pinpricks of stars. She turned away from the damage and hugged Katherine close. "We were lucky."

"We don't know that yet," Katherine said. "We might be better off dead."

"No," Chrystal whispered. "As long as we're alive, there's a chance."

Katherine leaned into Chrystal, her cheek resting on the top of Chrystal's head. Their breathing slowed and matched the same way it sometimes did in the last soft moments before sleep. It comforted Chrystal to breathe with Katherine, to feel one with her.

She woke when the transport stopped, blinking for a moment as if coming up from a bad dream. A deep cold settled over her as she woke to the walls of the transport. "Where are we?" she murmured.

"I was sleeping." Katherine sounded surprised that it been possible.

Yi spoke from the seat behind her, where he sat next to Jason. "We've docked inside of a bay that's part of something huge. I can't tell if it's a station or a ship, but I'd bet it's a ship." He sounded awed. Yi, for whom everything was no big deal.

Their captors gave them no useful information. A tunnel grew out from the wall. It attached itself to the door, and immediately looked like it had always been part of the transport. The door opened onto a pressurized environment.

They followed the uniformed woman down the corridor. Since they had been in front, Chrystal and Katherine now walked at the end of the line. Another woman followed them, close enough in looks to the first one to be her sister.

The woman led them to a large room with three hallways radiating in different directions. The gravity felt light enough to unbalance her. Ten more people were already there. "Please wait here," the first woman said. "There are bathrooms." She pointed. "And you may shower. We regret there are no clean clothes to give you."

"What about food and water?" Jason said.

"There is water in the bathrooms."

Chrystal's stomach complained about the lack of food, which surprised her.

"What's going to happen to us?" a man asked.

Toyo asked, "Are we hostages?"

The woman smiled. "Please wait here and there will be a time for answers. Make yourselves comfortable. We are continuing to scour the station for survivors."

"Who are you?" a woman called out.

The woman walked down one of the hallways and disappeared.

Yi leaned down between Chrystal and Katherine, and whispered, "That's no woman. She's a robot, too. They're all robots."

CHAPTER TWELVE

NONA

Nona sat in a big comfortable chair in front of a roaring fire, Cricket on the floor close to her. The tongat had started following her around as if the foolishness of almost drowning had convinced Cricket that the new girl needed watching.

The flames enchanted Nona so completely she had trouble looking at either Charlie or Jean Paul, although she followed their conversation about a herd of some kind of predator well enough to get the gist of what they were saying. Flame amazed her. Living like the planet, breathing and dancing. Warm. Curious. A force that humans controlled so tightly in space that she'd never seen it in the open. She had been taught that it meant death.

It seemed like death dogged her. Her mother, gone now. Her father, gone for longer. Chrystal. Almost certainly.

It wasn't only fire. Everything on the Deep was controlled. Magnificent, some of it. Stunningly beautiful. Inside Satyana's sphere of influence, she'd had access to a lot of the station, including habitat bubbles built by the rich for the rich. There, Chrystal had seen streams and flowers and trees with no purpose in life other than to be an expression of excess.

On Lym, they wilded. They tried to get out of the way instead of trying to manage every detail. She had trouble wrapping her head around such an approach to life.

"Nona!"

She started and turned, wondering if Charlie had called her more than once. "Yes? Sorry, I got lost in the flames."

"Are you up to telling Jean Paul a story? He wants to hear about the Deep."

She reluctantly shifted direction so she had a better view of the two men than of the fire. "Sure. What do you want to know?"

Jean Paul watched her closely. "What's the best thing about it?"

An easy question. "It's so big you can get lost in it. No one can see the Deep in a whole lifetime. New habitats grow constantly, as if the station lives.

There's food and music everywhere. Costumes. Dances. Travel immersives. Games flow through the whole station at once. Best, everyone is accepted. Everyone. Some stations are all about being or believing one way or another, but the Deep accepts everyone."

Jean Paul raised an eyebrow. "And the worst thing?"

She raised her glass and took a sip. "That's harder." She paused, considering. "There's more than one bad thing. Maybe the way we make decisions. It all sounds formal with the ruling council up there—the Historian brings his interpretation, the Futurist brings hers, etc. Everybody talks. But it actually takes years for decisions to be made. All the important discussions happen off stage and then there's this scripted courtroom action. Power's really concentrated."

Charlie asked, "And another bad thing?"

"The part that isn't about the law. There's a black market for everything. Drugs, sex, questionable cargo, votes. You'd think we'd do better, having all the sophistication of the Deeping Rules and all that."

"The Deeping Rules?" Charlie asked.

She closed her eyes and leaned her head back. "Let me see if I can get them just right." She paused, picturing the signs. "You must own yourself. You must harm no one. You must add to the collective."

"That should be simple," Jean Paul mused.

She laughed. "They're so simple they can be interpreted a million ways. Is adding to the collective a real job like a teacher or is it just coming up with an idea? Is it okay to be a militant or do you need to obey the rules?"

"So what do you do? To add?" Charlie asked.

"I teach. I told you that."

His eyes sparkled with mischief. "And do you ever break the rules?"

Was he flirting? The idea startled her. "Your turn. What do you like about Lym?"

Charlie's answer came as quick as hers had been. "That it's so open. I've never been to the stations, but I can't imagine being closed into a place where everything smells of humans." He blushed for a second, maybe regretting saying bad things about her world. "Here, there's hundreds of thousands of species. As much as we study Lym, we still find new things. We get surprised."

"I love how open it is, too." She glanced at Jean Paul. "You?"

"I like the sense of space. I almost never go to the cities."

She could believe that. Jean Paul looked clean but unkempt. Like Charlie, he didn't have any visible augmentation. His long brown hair looked tangled and his clothes had been patched. Not exactly uncivilized, but he wouldn't fit in very well. Probably not in Manna Springs, and certainly not on the Deep. "So what do you hate?"

Jean Paul walked over by the fire, the light dancing on his face. "That after all of this time, people still don't get how important it is to protect Lym. The spacers ignore it—like it's just the past, like it's something your Historian might talk about in a class or something." He fell silent for a long moment and then spoke softly, his words slightly slurred by alcohol. "I hate it that Charlie here has to go dig up smugglers from time to time. That people think they can just come here and not do damage. People almost killed this place. It will never be really wild again. You know that, right?"

She was trying to decide how to answer when he just kept going. "So many of the animals have been killed or tinkered with, created, that there's no balance that doesn't need some human intervention. But humans are dangerous and stupid."

She frowned. "Not all of us."

"Yes. Well. Maybe not us three. But even some of the Lym natives get caught stealing animals and exporting them. We caught two a year ago."

She put her hands up in a gesture of surrender. "Okay. I get it." She glanced at Charlie. "What do you hate?"

"What he said."

"That's all?"

He closed his eyes for a moment and then opened them again. "I hate it that we have so little power. The big stations decide everything."

She raised her glass. "So here's to a way to figure out how to get more power. For all of us."

Charlie looked startled at that. But he clinked his glass with hers and Jean Paul's and they drank.

She must be a little drunk herself. Satyana was always telling her to get more power, and she was always refusing.

The wine tasted earthy and full of life, like wine that could only come from a place where the soil was more than a foot deep.

When Nona woke the next morning, the wine still muzzed her head, but she remembered her toast to power. She went into the living room and poked at the ashes of last night's fire. She had no idea how to rekindle them. She pulled on her coat and went outside. The air felt so cold that she crossed her arms and stamped her booted feet on the pavement.

The sun had just started pushing up a faded grey bit of light to eat the stars. She watched it blossom into the hello-gold of actual morning. She looked at the pale sun, shading her eyes with her fingers, and whispered, "I promise to watch you rise and set every day I'm here. Not to miss a one."

It felt good, if silly. At least no one could hear her.

She checked the time and the orbital location of the Diamond Deep. Only a few hours later. Close enough. She called Satyana and talked to her for a long time in spite of the slight irritating delay.

Afterward, she basked in the morning sun. A flock of black and orange birds wheeled and danced in the great blue sky. Puffy white clouds floated over her. She drank in the odd wonderment of them, swearing that she would remember the clouds and the birds and the incredible open space, and the horizon.

CHAPTER THIRTEEN

CHARLIE

Charlie sat beside Jean Paul in the kitchen. Each warmed their hands on a cup of Jean Paul's favorite morning tea, a concoction made from stinging rock-grass, py-berry leaves, and dried gern. It wasn't Charlie's favorite, but Jean Paul made it for him every time he thought there might be danger, which was almost every time Charlie left. Jean Paul was convinced it made Charlie's reflexes faster. Charlie himself wasn't convinced it didn't.

Cricket lay curled in a ball of fur by the door, which was a polite request to go outside and sit with Nona. Charlie ignored the tongat and watched Nona through the window. Quiet time became her.

"Are you sure you want to do this?" Jean Paul asked.

"You're the one who said I should take the job. You practically made me do it."

"I meant take her out to Neville?"

"It's fitting."

Jean Paul sipped his tea. "I thought you'd hate her. Now I'm worried I'll lose my roommate."

"To what?" Jean Paul only sounded a little like he was teasing, which bothered Charlie enough that Cricket lumbered over and sat beside him and rested her big head in his lap. "I'm not leaving Lym, and she's unlikely to stay. Besides, don't forget I'm a hired hand." He stroked the tongat's head, grateful for her company. His rocks, these two. His strength.

"You could use a lover," Jean Paul whispered.

Charlie went quiet. If it were anyone else suggesting it, he'd be offended at the familiarity. But Jean Paul had once wanted more than the friendship they shared. Charlie had thought that was over, maybe a decade ago. "No," he mused quietly. "She's probably exactly what I don't need."

As if on cue, Nona pushed the door open, looking slightly surprised to see them awake. "Good morning."

Charlie made breakfast for all of them, managing two pans and thus keeping himself too busy to talk to Nona or Jean Paul. Even Cricket stayed out of his way, preferring to wrap herself around Nona's legs the way she treated Charlie when he was sick or tired. Come to think of it, Nona was almost as subdued as he was. Maybe her dreams had been no better than his had been, full of threats he couldn't outrun or see.

The smell of eggs and herbs mixed with the light scent of Jean Paul's tea. The silence in the room was so thick that the sizzle of hot oil, clanking pots, and even the pouring of water all seemed loud and intrusive.

Jean Paul stepped carefully into the awkward void, probably quite aware that his comment about sex had sparked Charlie's cooking frenzy. He spoke to Nona. "Let me show you where you're going."

Well, now Charlie was taking Nona to Neville whether he wanted to or not.

Jean Paul dragged out a physical picture book. The form of the object fascinated Nona, and she held it in her hands, turning it this way and that and feeling the heft of it.

"You've never seen a book?" Jean Paul said.

"That's what this is? A book? Static information?"

"Historical information doesn't change much," Charlie called from the kitchen.

"What you know about history might," she said.

"Point." Charlie blushed and turned back to cooking, barely listening as Jean Paul took her through the book, showing her pictures of Lym in its most recent technological heyday at the beginning of the age of explosive creation. Neville had been designed to scoop resources out of the sea and use them to help people flee the gravity well and establish new bases in space.

Charlie put Cricket's big metal bowl on the ground and watched her lick the edges clean before she started crunching the bones of the tharp in the center.

He piled plates high with eggs, toast, and grilled vegetables, and set them down in front of Jean Paul and Nona just as they were opening the page of the book that showed pictures of Neville.

It had been a beach town once. Since these pictures, ice had repopulated mountaintops and turned into solid sheets on both poles. Sea level had fallen enough that more than a few kilometers separated Neville from the beach now, all downhill.

In the long-ago Neville had been a testament to high technology and design. Nano-strength buildings flowed one into the other in graceful, glassy arcs. Imposing metal sea gates had protected the city from tidal waves and storms. Lacy and filigreed bridges married one building to the other in a series of arches. In one sunrise shot, gold light haloed a long string of fantastic bridges.

Nona picked up the book, ignoring her breakfast. "That's beautiful. It's even more beautiful than the Deep."

Jean Paul looked pleased with her. "In Neville's time, it was the most beautiful city in the solar system, and by far the most exotic. The most advanced."

She glanced at Charlie, who had just brought his own plate over to sit down. "We'll go there?"

Charlie's blood raced. If they did go, he'd have a whole day alone with her. He loved the idea, and it scared him. He glanced at Jean Paul. "Do you want to go?"

For a moment, Jean Paul's eyes lit up, but then he turned away and when he looked back his expression was flatter. "No. I'll stay here. Someone's got to be able to come save you if you need it."

Nona must have caught some of the awkwardness in the exchange, as she looked from man to man and then dug into her eggs.

⸻

He left Cricket at home with Jean Paul. As he and Nona neared the beach, a school of longfish danced in the wave spray, their wet, blue-green bodies giving themselves away by movement alone. When they splashed into the water after they leapt a wave, they seemed to merge with the ocean, fish and water all the same shimmering blue-green. Each fish was almost the size of the skimmer, maybe twice as long as he was tall, and thin.

He slowed down so that Nona could lean out and point at fish after fish, until she fell back against her seat laughing in delight.

He took her to the beach and they stopped to walk on the sand. The fish were gone, but one edge of the rocky beach had a number of exposed tide pools. He walked barefoot, and she followed suit, following his steps carefully. He couldn't explain why he wanted to show her as much of what he loved about Lym as possible, or why it felt so urgent. Maybe the battle above them—beyond them—past them—maybe *that* battle made him feel like every good thing in his life had become fragile.

Nona seemed to feel the same way. She knelt on moss-covered rocks and took pictures of the clearest tide pools, the beach, even of him standing on rocks and pointing down at particularly bright spiny slugs or, once, at a black eel that slithered out from behind two rocks for just a moment and then went back in. She'd shown him the camera setup she had—a small physical lens that she held in one hand and controlled with clever finger gestures. Today, she used it almost nonstop as if creating memories for later.

As they were walking back, he asked her what she thought of the tide pools.

"There's more order than I expected."

"What do you mean?"

"I always imagined Lym as all tooth and claw, that things would be eating each other every place I looked."

He laughed. "Everything here does eat other things."

"But not every minute. I expected a constant fight between wild things. I think I've been understanding biology all wrong."

"The fight to eat or be eaten is constant if you know how to look. We're working hard to allow natural responses."

She dug her bare toes into the sand. "Disorder is practically banned in space, but you're creating it."

"We're creating room for disorder and measuring it. We're not creating the thing itself." He walked. "That's not even right. We're creating balance."

"Okay." She brushed wind-blown hair from her eyes and took photos of the waves. "Coming here is like coming home must have been for my parents. They were on *The Creative Fire*. You know what that was?"

"The miracle ship that came back home."

"People lived and died in it for generations. They flew through space but never actually saw stars. They had no idea what Adiamo was like. They had a game that depicted the world before the sundering or the remaking, before the Ring of Distance. It showed Lym and Mammot and a few stations and nothing else. The game play was here, on a fictional Lym. I know. Dad showed me a version of it once—he used to play it with Ruby."

"*That* Ruby?"

"Ruby the Red."

"You knew her?"

"No." Nona pursed her lips. "Ruby died right after I was born."

"So you weren't ever on the *Fire*?"

"No. Well, I was conceived on it. It was destroyed before I was born. But I think Lym is to me as the Deep was to the *Fire*. Close, anyway. A place where the very genetics that shape my muscles and bones originated. A place that I wouldn't exist without."

He loved her poetic way of looking at things. It altered how he saw Lym, if only by adding the tiniest bit of completely strange and new perspective. "Ready to see some more history?"

She grinned, tucking a stray strand of blue hair behind an ear. "Sure. Will there be less breeze?"

"Probably." He flew her into Neville through the broken sea-gates, which hung askew on great hinges, opening outward. They dwarfed the skimmer.

She surely expected something like the pictures Jean Paul had shown her.

Jagged edges and ripped and broken bridges surrounded craters full of broken building material. Mangled and stripped vehicles littered cracked streets. The largest building still stood, but the center of it had a hole almost all of the way through, and the tail end of a star fighter stuck out of the middle of it. Near all of the edges, dirt had blown over the streets and a wild cacophony of spring flowers reached along every edge on their march to reclaim the city.

"Oh," she exclaimed. She leaned forward like she had over the fish, but the sounds coming from her were small moans of disappointment mixed with awe. "Can we land?"

"It's not safe."

"Why?"

"Sometimes there are looters. Parts of the city are still full of treasure and bones."

One hand shaded her eyes as she squinted down at the city. "I don't see anyone."

He scanned the area. Too many intact walls and other good places to hide. "There's no way to know if anyone's there."

She turned her face toward him, her eyes as excited as they had been earlier, watching the fish. "I do want to land. To look around a little."

Her enchantment reminded him of Neville's beauty. He forgot it these days, seeing the dangers instead. A hazard of his job. He flew them all around the perimeter so she could see the devastation from all sides.

"I don't see anyone else here," she pointed out.

"That doesn't mean it's safe. Looters hide when they see me. But I know a place where we can probably stretch our legs safely and eat lunch."

He took her to a low hill piled with big rocks and tucked the skimmer neatly beside one rock a little taller than the vehicle. They were close to the broken city, but with a long stretch of clear land between them and the nearest buildings. A pool of spring water fed three scraggly trees. Flat rocks made an artful half circle for comfortable seating. "My theory is this area used to be a park," he told her.

"What happened?" she asked, as they climbed out of the skimmer. "To the city. Such . . . I never saw so much destruction."

"War happened. The ship there—the one that you see holed in the central building—it belonged to the mechs, who became the ice pirates after they were banished from the system."

"I've heard that term," she mused. "Mechs. It meant human uploads to machine bodies, right?"

"And similar things. Copies of humans, so there could be a whole fleet of a hundred robotic ships managed by a single human mind that was also a hive mind."

She looked over at the destroyed city. "I hadn't realized they hated us so much," she said softly.

"I don't know who hated who the most. Or who was the most afraid of who."

"So what is it now? Is it hatred or fear?"

"I don't know." He started unpacking a picnic. Jean Paul had sent two vegetable sandwiches, two cookies, water, and a bottle of wine with two nice glasses. He frowned at the wine. Jean Paul knew better; Charlie didn't drink when he was working. "Maybe war is always both."

"You brought me here to see this because of what happened to the High Sweet Home?"

"Partly. I might have brought you here anyway."

She went silent for a minute before musing, "Whether we're afraid of the ice pirates or we hate them, it might be the same. Satyana thinks a war could ruin the Glittering. That they've been building up so much military strength that they could destroy every station. Every one. All of them. I never imagined the Diamond Deep being vulnerable before. We have defenses for asteroids and enough guns and fighters to fend off a small fleet of invaders, but that's all. Satyana thinks the ice pirates could take the Deep, or destroy her." She looked up, as if she could see the pirates from here. "I talked to her this morning, and she's more worried than I've ever heard her."

His gut tightened. Of course the stations were threatened, too. "Surely there'd be no reason."

She looked directly at him, determined. "Just like we need to save Lym, the Deep matters to humanity. It is our greatest social and technical achievement."

It sounded like propaganda, but she believed it. He'd never thought of the Glittering as anything other than a vague evil. But he saw she was right. "Okay."

"Satyana said that the High Sweet Home has been partly disassembled."

He handed her a sandwich. "I'm sorry about your friend."

She turned away, but not before he noticed her blinking back a tear. He looked straight ahead, giving her space. Eventually, she ate.

They got through lunch with a quiet companionship that felt pregnant with some desire for more. It made Charlie profoundly uncomfortable. He knew how to refuse a client who flirted inappropriately with him, but Nona wasn't flirting at all.

He was attracted to her.

He hadn't felt like this about anyone for a decade. As she helped him pick up the remains of their picnic, her pinky brushed the back of his hand. Her touch felt like a trail of fire.

Feeling slightly reckless, he opened the wine and poured a full glass for each of them. Even though he contrived to spill half of his since he was on duty, he felt off-balance, threatened from above by war and from the side by a beautiful woman.

They sat and drank in silence together. No toasts, no small talk that didn't matter. Only a silence that felt like conversation.

When they finished the wine, she proclaimed, "I'm going for a walk."

"It's really not safe," he told her.

"Is anywhere safe?" She laughed at him, a good-natured laugh. "I want to get some close-ups."

He swallowed a retort and grabbed up both his projectile gun and the stun gun he'd used on the tongats before he followed. "Okay. I'll go with you. But only to the edge."

She followed a thin animal trail toward the broken city. He matched her pace, even though being next to her meant he walked on stonier ground and had to be careful not to trip. He forced himself not to put his arm around her and did his best to look away from her.

"I have something to tell you," she said.

"Okay."

"I'm going back home. I need to go to my hotel tomorrow, to start getting ready. I'm leaving in a few days."

He felt stunned, and his words came out gruff. "I thought you had a few weeks."

"I have to go see if I can help Chrystal. I can't just be here and let bad things happen to my best friend."

"That's absurd. What can you do?" he asked her. He could see his words strike her like physical things and wished for them back. "I mean, I know you're capable. But you're one person. A teacher."

She looked up toward the Glittering. "I've got a ship coming. I can get out to space, maybe out near the Ring to find out what's happening."

"Aren't there already people doing that?"

"Satyana says not many. Most people are coming in and not going out."

"Doesn't it take a long time to get anywhere?"

"Months, at least. More since I'll stop at the Deep."

Her words were sinking in. "What do you mean you've got a ship coming? Satyana is sending one for you?" *She had a starship?*

"It's my ship," she said. She sounded defensive.

Oh. "Okay. You can have a ship." She hadn't been acting rich, and he had been forgetting about that. Fool.

"Of course I can have a ship." She pointed at the skimmer. "You do."

"I bet yours is bigger."

"I bet it is, too."

"You don't know?"

"It's bigger." She pulled away from him, jogging downhill.

"The skimmer's not mine anyway. It's Lym's."

She stopped and let him catch up. "I forgot. You don't really own things here."

"That's right."

"So I'm not really paying you? I'm paying the collective?"

"I get a salary." They passed a tangle of broken metallic parts that had once been girders or windows but had become barriers for blowing soil.

She stopped and looked over the shattered buildings, taking pictures of them. She seemed to be trying to capture the way they loomed and leaned, the silence and the emptiness. "It seems like a dry place for such a big city."

"It didn't used to be. The currents were different when sea level was higher and all of these hills were cropland.

"Can we go further?"

"We shouldn't."

"I'm not ever going to be back here."

She kept walking. He wished she wouldn't. He tried to imagine picking her up and slinging her over his shoulder, but it didn't seem like a good idea. Rich woman with her own ship, headstrong. Just like he had first thought she might be.

There was nothing to do but follow her, so he did. "We're coming into the part of the city that used to be markets and restaurants. You can see some tables still."

She leaned in the open doorway of a broken wall, looking through it. She hissed at him quietly. "Come here."

He had to stand close to her to look through. She smelled faintly of dust and wine.

She pointed. "Look."

On the far side of a littered square, a woman with long grey hair and a long cowl stood looking around, as if hunting for something.

"That's Freida," he whispered. "She's a gleaner."

"A gleaner?"

"They consider *themselves* re-wilded . . . no medicine. Nothing they can't hunt or gather. They live in small groups. She's not supposed to be *here*, though. Neville is so off-limits that *I* had to file a report and get a permit for today."

"Should we talk to her?"

He put a hand on Nona's shoulder. "Not yet."

"Turn around." The words came from behind him, from a man. He turned to see a ragged figure standing on a rooftop that he thought had been caved in. The man wore clothes like Frieda's: handwoven material stained by soot and grease. His weathered face looked craggy and lined with wrinkles. His eyes bored into Charlie's, his gaze determined and a little nervous. The gun in his hand pointed unwaveringly at Charlie's chest.

"There's more," Nona whispered.

CHAPTER FOURTEEN

NONA

Nona feel faint as she shifted her glance between all three of the people who had weapons pointed at her. There was the man on the roof who had first spoken to them. Ratty, everything covered but his wrinkled face and his dark, piercing eyes. He watched Charlie, but he could certainly fire at her if he wanted to. Across the narrow street from him, a young boy crouched in a doorway. He couldn't be more than fifteen, still caught on the ragged edge of puberty. Blond hair hung across his nose and chin in a tangled curtain, masking his expression. His eyes were mod-eyes, something she could have seen on the Deep. They looked like a cat's, with huge golden pupils and squished-oval green irises. The woman that Charlie knew, Frieda, had also pulled a weapon. She had come up on the opposite side from the cat-eyed boy. She stood slightly bent over and looked quite frail, although she held her gun steady.

Blood pounded in Nona's throat. She wanted to run even though her feet felt like lead. She'd never been threatened with her life, never really felt like she could die in the next second. Not until she got here, where the ocean had nearly swallowed her and now a man pointed a weapon at her.

"What do you want?" Charlie asked, his voice as calm as a day in the park.

Frieda spoke. "We need to show you something."

"You don't need guns for that."

Frieda gestured toward Nona. "Do you trust her?"

For half a breath she worried about his answer, but he said, "Yes."

The man smiled and nodded. "Follow the boy."

Cat-eyes led them deeper into the city. Nona followed, cursing herself. Charlie had told her not to go in here, and she had been too stubborn to listen.

Their guide took a number of turns. Nona stumbled once, and Frieda whispered at her, "Be quiet."

Who they were afraid would hear them? After Frieda's admonishment, Nona winced every time she accidentally dragged her foot. She coughed once and felt her face flush with embarrassment.

They entered a door, which closed behind them. Sudden darkness stole her vision. The boy hissed at her to take his hand and shuffle, and she did. The dark felt thick and alive. The corridor smelled of urine. Charlie and their other two captors made barely audible shuffling footsteps behind her. Frieda gave them instructions to stand still and close their eyes.

Nona did, her fists clenched. Some small scared part of her expected to be shot.

A light snapped on. She blinked in the unexpected brightness.

Some technology she couldn't see projected pictures in the air. Frieda addressed Charlie. "Sorry for the ambush. We didn't want you to call for help and we didn't want to be seen."

Nona stepped toward the closest picture and found she could put her hand right through it without causing so much as a ripple. On the Deep, people used displays like this in museums or on stages or even in upscale bars, but she'd never been close enough to touch one. The image above her head showed the inside of Neville, at least unless there was another ruined city nearby. A metallic figure moved left-to-right through the picture in an endless loop. "A robot?" Nona asked.

Frieda pursed her lips. "We've seen three of these things . . ." She waved her hand around at all the pictures on the wall ". . . we think the same three. We've seen them three times, in three places. The last place is here. This morning. On the other side of the city. After we saw them here, we searched our pictures to find the other two sightings. We thought you might know if they're ice pirates."

"What do you know about ice pirates?" Charlie asked.

"They killed a station," Cat-eyes said. "One of the big ones." He seemed proud of his knowledge. "That's what made us want to find you."

Charlie stalked around the room, looking at each picture. Nona followed him, the pictures bobbing down for her, recognizing she was shorter. It felt a little like they were demanding children popping into her face, and she even tried to brush one aside and let out a high nervous laugh when her gesture made no difference.

Each image contained a robotic figure and, after a turn through them all, she could identify them as three different robots. They looked humanoid. One had legs that were too long for its body, with one leg a different color than the other, as if a spare part had been stuck on in an emergency and left there.

Another's arm ended in a stump. The third looked the most human—with soft skin and smooth movements.

Charlie frowned. "Wouldn't robots from the Edge be more . . . sophisticated? These look cobbled together."

"But if they wanted to pass?" Frieda prompted.

"Then they might look like this."

Nona asked, "Do you use this kind of robot here? Are they familiar?"

Cat-eyes said, "We've seen robo-bodies like these on farms. But they always had people around them. Bosses."

"Seen any people around these?" Charlie asked.

"No, but you don't always see scavengers," Frieda said. "Especially the good ones."

"Why are you showing them to us?" Nona asked.

Charlie answered. "Because I'm a ranger. And I have a skimmer."

"Can't you just send the pictures?" Nona asked.

"To who?" Cat-eyes said. "We're allowed to exist, but no one really wants us here."

She wondered how such a young man had been thrown into this kind of society. It seemed like choosing to die when you didn't have to. Some people on the Deep got old enough they got bored and started doing stupid things until almost dying either scared them back to life or they did die. It seldom happened to the young, though.

Charlie paced, frowning. Finally he stopped and said, "I don't know. Can we take copies of your images?"

"Will you keep our secret?" Cat-eyes asked. "We don't want anybody to know we were here."

"I suppose I can say someone left them on the skimmer when we took a walk."

"Say whatever you want," the man said. "Just leave us out of it."

Charlie looked at Frieda instead of at the boy. She could almost see him thinking through options. "If you escort us back, and if you leave this place."

The boy looked ready to complain, but Frieda said, "I want to be away from cities anyway. Especially if they're full of pirates."

"Why do you think they're Next?" Nona asked.

"Next?" the boy asked.

"That's what the pirates call themselves," Nona explained.

"I thought they were soulbots," Frieda said.

Nona nodded. "I've heard that term. But why do you think these are soulbots?"

Frieda gave her a long look. "Call it old age and instinct." She glanced at Charlie. "You should capture one. Take it apart."

He frowned at the closest picture. "Later. Do you think there are more?"

Frieda said, "I don't know."

"Is there anything else you want us to see?" he asked.

"No," the man said. He stepped forward and handed Charlie a small, dark square. "The pictures are on here. You'll have something that can read it."

Charlie nodded. "I will."

They returned through the dark and the bad scents and burst again into the sunshine and the ruined city. The crazy skyscrapers and broken bridges and jagged edges threw an odd assortment of shadows. Nona found herself looking down alleyways for robots and being even more careful about making noise. Everyone but her had a weapon out, generally held loosely near their thighs and waists and easily available.

No one spoke until they emerged from the city and started climbing the hill. Nona had expected the gleaners to leave them where they found them, but they continued to come along and still held out their guns. Charlie took the lead. Cat-eyes came up near Nona and said, "I hear you're from a station."

"From the Diamond Deep," she said.

"What's it like?"

She smiled. "It's the biggest station in the system. Bigger than Lym, or at least bigger if you calculate all the surfaces we can walk on."

His eyes widened, which gave him a comical look. "Many people?"

"Thousands of times more than you have on all of Lym. We have no space like this, no open land, no sky."

"We grow your food." He sounded pleased with himself for it.

"Some of it. We appreciate it."

He looked wistful. "I'd love to see a station."

"Maybe someday you can. Did you go to school?"

"I can read and write."

That wasn't enough to survive on the Deep all by itself. "If you can get work on a ship sometime, you can visit."

"I'd like that. I'd like to see a station."

"I bet you would like it." Besides, she thought, maybe then he'd decide to live. She liked him and felt sorry for him all at once. It seemed like his future was being stolen while he was too young to recognize the theft for a crime.

They climbed the hill toward the rocks that hid the skimmer. Bright sun made it tough to see, and when she looked behind her, the bones of the city almost glowed with light.

"Stop," Charlie said. "Wait here." He glanced at Cat-eyes. "You're responsible for her," he said, clearly meaning Nona.

Cat-eyes nodded.

"What are you worried about?" she asked.

"I thought I saw something move."

She swallowed.

"It's probably an animal." He turned back and kept going the way they had been until the sound of his footsteps faded. The man looked behind them, Frieda at where Charlie had disappeared. Cat-eyes and Nona looked in the other two directions.

Nothing moved. No one spoke. Frieda passed a bottle of sun-warmed water around. Nona wet her lips. The water tasted surprisingly good, like citrus of some kind.

Charlie came back. "All clear. I can't find anything." He still looked worried. The group held their silence as he led them to the skimmer. "Hang on," he told Frieda. "Maybe I have some supplies for you." He held out a bottle of water and some energy gels. The man grabbed the lot of it and tucked it into his ragged robe.

Frieda said, "Thank you," quite solemnly. Then she looked at Charlie. "Tell me if you catch one."

"I will."

Charlie helped Nona into the skimmer and used his foot to start it up slowly, probably trying to avoid the wind of the motor washing back on the gleaners. He took them back out through the broken metal gates, and Nona turned her gaze away from the shattered city and back toward the water. "Do you think the robots are from the Edge?"

"No. I think the gleaners are just scared. We'll probably get fifty reports of scary things every day for a while."

"But you will look?"

"Probably. I don't always to get to choose my assignments. I'll report this and turn in the pictures, though."

Something felt changed between them, as if they had been moving together and now they were moving apart. Maybe because she was leaving? It shouldn't bother her—he was a hired guide. But it did.

They passed through the sea-gates and flew along the low cliffs of the old seashore and then down to the beach. Medium-sized waves washed over the tide pools. She leaned out to take a picture.

A pop and then a roar startled her. A force thrust her out of her seat. Something soft slammed her in the face, molding around her, trapping her. It closed up and over her, forcing her out of the skimmer, pillowing her arms, capturing her camera.

The bottom of the skimmer fell away from her.

She fell, turning over and over—sand-sea-sky-sand-sea-sky.

She screamed.

The ocean smacked the force that enclosed her into her face, snapping her head into something soft and tearing the breath from her lungs.

CHAPTER FIFTEEN

NONA

Something slapped her back and then let go, the sky and clouds pin-wheeling through a clear but oily surface that smeared the view above her like a child's painting. She bounced again and again and then rested on the top of the ocean, rising and falling with the water under her.

Surely she should be dead or in pain. Instead, she felt stretched and slightly bruised, but all right.

She had been plucked from the sky and dropped, and she was all right.

A huge bubble encased her and something like a hundred little bubbles supported her inside of the bigger bubble. Maybe far more.

She remembered being violently encapsulated as the skimmer fell apart around her, being certain she would die.

It must be a safety thing, like an escape pod for a ship, only built for a planet.

How could someone find her in an ocean?

Would they?

Where was Charlie?

The bubbles in the big bubble both cushioned and trapped her. She moved her head as far as she could. She found the line between sea and sky and a smeared tan that must be beach but didn't look particularly close. If Charlie was in a bubble, she couldn't see it.

What if he hadn't been saved? Maybe part of the skimmer had hit him, or he had gotten stuck and drowned.

Did air pass through the material? It must. She smelled salt.

She tried to change her direction so she was sitting up, but the ball rolled, reacting to her actions. Her right shoulder hurt and her left toes were cramped. She managed to wriggle the toes into a better position, sending needles of awareness up her nerves.

Shifting her weight caused her to bob, but nothing she did really changed the direction of her perspective or the direction the bubble was moving.

The ocean had a mind of its own.

Charlie might know if they had been shot or if the skimmer had simply broken. She didn't think it had broken. The only possible choice was for Charlie to be in a bubble as well. He must be behind her where she couldn't see him.

He had to be.

The smear of land grew thicker.

She ran through the things she'd read about the ocean here, and the other things Charlie had told her or shown her. The long fish. Hundreds of other kinds of fish, some bigger than humans. Maybe thousands of kinds of fish. Jellies that could sting. Algae fit for human consumption that looked just like algae that could kill her. Charlie had shown her something he called a pod rock that looked just like a rock but stung anything that put weight on it. The ones they'd seen in the tide pool had been too small to hurt a human, but he'd said they grew big enough to deaden a walker's foot.

Earlier, she had told Charlie that the biology here seemed less about eat and be eaten than she'd thought, but now she realized she was wrong. If anything happened to the bubble, there were a hundred things that might eat her. Maybe a thousand.

She drifted, trying to keep her mind free to associate, to maybe think of a way out or a useful thing she could do. Any useful thing.

Her butt and legs felt cool and the sun warmed her face and chest right through the clear material. Sweat dripped down her neck.

How strange. In space, water was a shield and a necessity and sometimes rare. There were no fish, no sharks, and only the ultrarich had ways to immerse themselves in water. Satyana could have afforded to, but she wasn't given to visible excesses. Her only obvious mod was her too-blue eyes, and her wealth went to ships and singers and influence.

Maybe now she wouldn't see Satyana again. Suddenly, she wanted to.

The bubble bobbed more enthusiastically, making her stomach lurch.

The land grew slowly larger.

She remembered the waves and how Charlie had to save her from the edge of them. She felt sick at the idea of going in through the surf.

A wave grabbed her and lifted her. The bubble twisted so she tipped and looked only at sky again for a long moment and then raced down the back side of the wave, turned now so she saw the blur of the next wave coming at her rather than the beach.

She rose and fell again, as if the waves played with her. Again. Again. She faced the sand when one broke under her, foaming seawater washing the sides of the bubble before falling away and leaving her on sand.

The next wave picked her up again, pulled her out to meet another wash of water that sent her further up the beach.

Again; only this wave was smaller.

Then the ocean seemed finished with her and the bubble. Birds wheeled above her, crying out, white and grey and black and sand-colored lines against the sky. She noticed thirst and hunger and that she had to pee.

Her right hand and the sore shoulder were trapped almost straight. Tendons and muscles ached from being held so long in unnatural positions. Her left arm had a few centimeters of play up and down at best. She drew in a big breath and pulled it hard toward her body. She got it halfway before the breath rushed out of her and her arm snapped back to where it had been. She panted, recovered, waited. Tried again. This time she managed to hook a thumb in her pocket, and the air bubbles around her arm re-positioned themselves so that her hand was stuck in its new position. She fumbled along her belt to the buckle and undid it, turning a normal movement into a victory. Pulling the belt free from her waist took a hundred tiny movements. But now she had the metal spike of the buckle. She fisted the buckle and poked it at the bubbles.

They moved aside.

Nona sobbed in frustration, her body too dry for tears. She would kill for water.

She forced her hand down to the bubbles she was sitting on, the ones distended by her weight. One of those popped and then another.

A slow assault on one recalcitrant bubble after another brought success. As she gained room, she got better at using her weight to help pop the little bubbles. She made enough space to stand, and then threw herself at the outer bubble. It accepted her and her belt-buckle tool, hugged her and rolled so that she landed flat on her face.

She scrambled up—still enclosed—and tried again. No good. Her hands were slippery with sweat, the bubble hotter now that the cooling sea no longer cushioned it. But her clumsy fall had taught her how she could move the bubble without falling into it, using mincing tiny steps and her hands. She tried walking it toward an outcrop of rocks, falling over and over. In one fall, her hand landed on an uneven part in the bubble, a place that seemed thicker. She pushed on it. Nothing. She reached the rocks and found a sharp one, rocking the bubble back and forth. It started to fall in on her.

She ran her hands around it, searching for the puncture, found it, ripped it open with the belt and then with her hands, stepping out into a cool breeze.

She stopped right there and peed in the sand, the small comfort giving her strength. Then she dug her camera out of the sodden mess, grateful to find it was dry.

She looked along the beach and then out at the ocean, searching for Charlie. Light glinted on something far out that might be a bubble, but she couldn't tell.

Water.

She looked away from the waves, expecting to see the broken sea gates they'd flown through into Neville. Sheer walls of a cliff-face greeted her, scraggly trees clinging to the sides and thin grasses greening it here and there.

Growing things meant water. She found a thin stream of a waterfall hugging the cliff before falling into a thin depression in the sand. She stumbled toward it and cupped her hands and drank, again and again, and then she splashed cool, fresh water over her face.

When she turned back, Charlie was miraculously coming in on the waves the same way she had, but further down the beach. She ran stumbling toward him and stood just out of the water, watching the surf carry him in. His bubble was bigger than she was, taller.

Charlie had curled into a fetal position inside of it, surrounded by the cushioning small bubbles. He wasn't moving. She couldn't even tell if he was breathing. She tried to tug the bubble up onto land. It was so wide that trying to hold it just left her with splayed out arms and no real purchase. She got behind it, her feet soaked by the thin water of the spent waves, pushing, rolling.

Inside, Charlie's body rolled with the bubble.

She pushed him above the high tide line, sweating.

He wasn't moving.

She looked for a rock that would make a knife, but raced back to retrieve her belt. She stabbed at Charlie's bubble until a thin tear opened and air rushed out. She slid her fingers in, felt hot air escaping on her face as she ripped and tugged at the slippery surface, her hands pulling free when she didn't want them to. Her heart pounded with fear. He had to be alive! She practically threw the ripped side of the bubble and the first few of the interior bubbles away into the sand, and then laid her hand on Charlie's chest.

It moved. He breathed. One side of his face was purpling into what would eventually be a winner of a bruise.

She shook him gently.

One eye opened. He groaned.

Even that small reaction heartened her. "Are you okay?"

"I don't know. Where are we?"

"On a beach. We rolled in on the waves."

He seemed to just be remembering. "The skimmer."

"Can you move?"

He held his hand out to her and she leaned backward, pulling him up. He groaned, wincing, and then stood unsteadily. "I'm sorry."

"For what?"

"That I put you in all of this danger."

There was some truth to that. "Do you still have their pictures?"

He fumbled in his pocket and nodded.

"Good. If I'm going to almost die, I want it to be for something."

He had water clipped to his belt. He drank it all down and she showed him the thin waterfall. They both drank more.

Are you okay?" she asked him, putting a hand up to touch the bruise on his face.

"Yes." He let her touch him, not flinching or backing away, but also not moving into her.

She dropped her hand and took a step back, looking up at the unbroken cliff. The beach they were on didn't have an obvious way out that wasn't over the water. "Do you know where we are?"

He stared out at the waves, his brow furrowed. "The current must have taken us south. We'll be found. Soon."

"So what happened?" She pointed at the lumpy broken bubble on the beach. "What are those things?"

"Safety mechanisms. Think of them as a life raft."

"What's a life raft?"

He laughed. "Boats have little boats people can get away on if the big boat sinks. These are kind of like that, except they have to protect you from a fall if a skimmer fails."

"What happened to the skimmer?"

His face closed. "I'm going to find out."

They waited on two rocks near the stream, close enough that their thighs touched. The sound of water washed over her, waves to the front and the trickle of the long, thin waterfall behind her.

She took his hand, and he let her. After a while he squeezed her hand back and stood up. "I promised I wouldn't do this."

"Promised Satyana?"

His face was answer enough. That made her want to hold his hand more; a surprise. The last few years she had focused only on Marcelle and on death and on the things she resented or that seemed to be in her way. Now she was far away from all of them and having adventures, and she resented nothing, not even the promise that Satyana had extracted.

Charlie wasn't the kind of man she could force. She breathed in the salt air and the fabulous, loamy dirt that clung to crevices in the rocks and grew bright flowers. "I may never be in the middle of so much nothing again," she mused.

"That would be a very sad thing." He gave her a tender look that suggested he wanted to hold her, but instead he turned and walked away from her, heading down the beach and looking up at the cliffs from time to time as if searching for a path.

It didn't matter. She wasn't sorry for being bold.

She still had her camera. She wasn't going right back to the university, but if she ever taught again, the pictures would give her some standing. Staying busy helped her ignore her rumbling, hungry stomach and Charlie as well. He was on his way back up the beach toward her when she heard the skimmer.

Jean Paul landed on the beach in the dry sand above the seaweed-littered tide line. He and Charlie hugged and slapped each other on the back with open palms.

Blessedly, Jean Paul had brought sandwiches and fresh water. They ate right there on the beach, sitting on three separate rocks. Charlie told Jean Paul about the gleaners and the pictures and the flash of light he thought he saw before they took off.

"You think your ride was sabotaged?" Jean Paul asked as they climbed into his skimmer.

"Probably. Hard to find it and look now."

"We should go back by the city, check where you last were."

"You won't find anything," Charlie said. "My tracks. I walked all the way around the skimmer making sure it hadn't been messed with."

"Humor me."

"Suit yourself." It was friendly banter, warm. It made her think of her and Chrystal back in school, of the comfort of being around someone you'd known for a very long time. Jean Paul flew smoothly, the machine rising and going back over the ocean. She saw that they were pretty far from Neville; walking would have been tough even if they had found a way up the cliff. The gleaners were probably gone by now anyway.

She sat in a back seat behind the two men and drowsed until the skimmer descended.

"Shit." Charlie, who she hadn't ever heard curse.

She pushed herself up and peered down. Three bodies lay flat on the dirt, pools of dark blood around them. Frieda and the tattered man and Cat-eyes. Not far from where they'd been standing when she last saw them.

"You were right," Charlie said to Jean Paul. "We did find something." His voice had gone cold. "I might as well have killed them."

"You're alive because you took the new skimmer. This one doesn't have air bubbles."

"Why?" Nona asked, maybe about the skimmers, maybe the bodies, maybe anything. She felt shocked all over again, like she had when she fell from the sky. She had thought the Deep was a dangerous place, but this . . .

Jean Paul answered one of her imprecise questions. "Whoever blew up the skimmer wanted to keep information from getting out of here."

"The pictures?"

"Probably."

Jean Paul flew circles around the bodies until Charlie let him land. When Nona went to climb out, Charlie put a hand up to stop her.

She looked him in the eyes. "I'm not a child. I want to see."

He hesitated, nodded. Grim.

Outside, a wind blew and she had to hold her hair and walk into it to reach the bodies. Frieda had been shot in the chest and lay on her back, eyes wide and staring up. The tattered man lay near her, an arm reaching toward her but not touching. She reached Cat-eyes first and touched his cheek. It had grown cold. One hand had been flung up above his head and the other crumpled under his back awkwardly. She tried to cover the bloody hole in his stomach with a scrap of his shirt, but the wind picked it up. She tried again and then gave up. "I'm sorry," she whispered, even though none of it was her fault. "I'm so sorry."

She took pictures. She had never seen death like this, never seen life cut off unexpectedly and brutally and on purpose. She had trouble holding her camera still.

CHAPTER SIXTEEN

CHRYSTAL

C hrystal took a cube of food from a tray carried by one of the humanoid robots. Soulbots. If she hadn't been so tired coming here, she would have recognized the uniformed women right away. Not because she had ever seen one, or even a picture of one. But how could any human work for such monsters?

The transport had come back once and dropped off a young couple who had worked in one of the same shared labs Chrystal and her family used. It didn't come back any more after that. They had slept on the cold floor, dropping from exhaustion, talked out. More than once, so Chrystal had lost all sense of time. They had plentiful cube-food and water, and nothing else. No clean clothes, no showers.

She ate quietly. The cube tasted slightly sweet and slightly chalky. Katherine was sound asleep with her head pillowed on Yi's lap. Jason paced the room, his steps heavy. There were two other men doing the same, the three of them walking and walking with restless energy, whispering.

Four soulbots converged on the remaining humans from four hallways. Chrystal shook Katherine until she woke up, then whispered in her ear. "Stay down, and maybe they won't take us."

Katherine didn't. She pushed herself to a seated position and then stood. She caught the eye of the closest soulbot and waved her arms.

"What are you doing?" Chrystal hissed.

"Finding out what happens next."

"Are you crazy?"

Katherine looked directly at her. "No, I don't think so."

CHAPTER SEVENTEEN

CHARLIE

A day and a half after the gleaners were murdered in Neville, Charlie stood next to Nona at the edge of the observation deck at the spaceport near Manna Springs. The grounds looked almost pastoral. There were only three ships at the moment, two of the five they used to go between Lym and the stations that orbited it, and a Transpo Line ship oddly named the *Big Digger* that was getting dry dock repairs. The noon sun faded the colors to summer hues.

A ground-ship from the *Sultry Savior* had already started down. Stupid name for a ship, Charlie thought. Arrogant. But then spacers were generally arrogant bastards, the same kind of humans who had almost destroyed Lym before they finally left it. He wondered if Nona had named the ship.

The glassed-in observation deck was nearly empty. A mother had her two small children here, faces pressed against the glass as if something exciting were about to happen. An artist stood in a corner, sketching the spaceport by hand with a light pen.

Charlie felt Nona's presence acutely. She radiated heat; he felt her even when he wasn't looking at her. Knowing the heat was mostly his imagination made it worse rather than better. There was nothing smart about feeling attraction to someone who was about to leave on a starship.

Nona had been so quiet it startled him when she spoke. "I want Satyana to see Neville."

"How long will she be here? Manny needs to meet with her, and so does the rest of the Council." Satyana had managed to pull off a diplomatic landing permit and Manny was home cleaning and fretting about what to wear.

"Promise to show her the pictures?"

"That's all Manny. I'm the ranger and the guide and the worker all wrapped in one. No one gives me diplomatic tasks."

"And guiding me around wasn't a diplomatic task?"

"No." He found the idea repulsive. "I *chose* to be your guide."

"But between them, Satyana and Manny chose you."

She had met Manny in his offices that morning, seen him surrounded by people demanding information he didn't have, wanting actions that made no sense. The whole scene had made Charlie shudder, but Manny called everyone by name and stayed serene, his quiet confidence calming people. "Manny loves politics and government. I hate them both."

"Isn't being a ranger a government job?"

"I love the wild. I don't want a job that takes me away from here."

She looked at him for a long time before she nodded.

He pointed at the sky. "There it is."

A moving dot at this point, barely more than that. Absurdly, he wanted Nona to take his hand again as they watched the dot resolve into a slender, pretty ship. It looked brand new and very expensive, the kind of ship that only landed here when the rich came down to play. It glided gently and expertly to a perfect stop. He led Nona out onto the tarmac and they jogged slowly toward the ship, arriving in time to greet Satyana as she came down a set of steps that had folded out from the side.

She and Nona hugged, the hug drawing a look of surprise briefly across Satyana's features before she buried her face in Nona's hair. The women stayed still, breathing together. Satyana stood even smaller than Nona, and also thinner. Smooth, night-black hair framed her face.

He had imagined someone with so much power would be bigger.

Nona turned to introduce them. He expected displeasure, but instead Satyana greeted him warmly, with a firm handshake. "Thank you for being Nona's guide." No rancor, no gloating. Just a simple thank you.

Maybe he wasn't going to be able to hate this woman either. "You're welcome."

Charlie drove. Satyana and Nona both sat in the front, and a hulking woman named Britta massed uncomfortably in the back. Probably a body-guard. Nona quietly filled them both in on her adventures on Lym. Charlie expected Satyana to stop liking him as soon as she heard about the trip to Neville. To his surprise, she didn't seem to hold him at all responsible for Nona's double near-death experiences and seemed more worried than he was about the robots in the pictures.

He slowed the skimmer. "We're almost to Manny's office. Shall I drop all three of you off?"

"Just me and Britta. You two can have another afternoon of touristing. Come back for me at the end of the day."

That wasn't the answer he expected. From the look on Nona's face, she hadn't expected it either. As they pulled away, Nona asked, "Can we go get Cricket? And then maybe hike? I want to see another waterfall before I leave."

———◦∞◦———

Charlie chose a flat, gentle hike along a well-kept trail by a stream with multiple waterfalls. Huge trees towered over them, and a gentle rain cooled them without making the path too muddy to manage.

As they flew back, Nona looked tired. Even now she didn't complain, but just watched Lym go by in the window, with one hand on Cricket's enormous head and a pensive look on her face. The tongat had clearly adopted Nona. She'd stuck closer to her heels than to Charlie's on the hike. Charlie had tried to tell himself Nona needed protection more than he did.

He stopped to drop Cricket off at Manny's and found a sign on Cricket's door. "Stay for dinner. Both of you."

He'd left Nona in the skimmer.

"I should have changed," she said.

"You're beautiful enough." He hadn't meant to say that out loud. Maybe he was tired, too. She blushed, and he expected his cheeks were pink, too.

He led her in, watching her smile and shake hands and look pleased to meet everyone. He was going to miss her.

As usual, they ate with the children and talked of ordinary things. Chairs sat close together so elbows bumped and someone balanced a plate on every corner. After dinner, Pi, Bonnie, and Amara all disappeared with pressing business related to parenting, leaving Manny, Charlie, Nona, Satyana, and Britta at the table.

Manny brought them all wine and cookies, being very formal about the whole affair. Even though it could surely be attributed to Satyana's status, the not-Manny behavior disturbed Charlie. Everyone around the table looked awkward, except maybe Britta, who just looked stoic.

"Have you heard today's news?" Manny asked him and Nona.

"We were hiking," he said, feeling slightly guilty for it.

"What news?" Nona asked. "Did you hear any more about the High Sweet Home?"

Manny shook his head.

Satyana said, "The Next are massing on at the Ring's borders."

Charlie tried to picture that. The Ring was a circle in reality, and way out beyond the orbit of the stations in the Glittering. It was too big to "mass" at the edge of; space wasn't an island or a continent. "What do you mean?"

Satyana sipped daintily at her wine. "There are hundreds of Next ships stopping just short of violating the treaty."

"Have they said what they want?" Nona asked.

"No," Manny said. "No, they haven't. But it sure looks like they plan to come in as a group."

Satyana added, "We caught a few Next on the Deep, once we started looking."

"How do you tell a regular robot from a Next?" Charlie asked.

Satyana pursed her lips. "Carefully. By watching how they act, what they do. A regular robot doesn't make autonomous decisions. We sent some AI algorithms through the security data and found some robots that were clearly thinking for themselves. I'm more worried about the ones we surely missed."

Charlie said, "So maybe the robots in Neville were from the Edge?"

"No," Manny answered him. "Well, we don't think so. We're going to try and catch one."

"I'll get one for you," Charlie replied.

"I have a better idea."

Charlie sat back, puzzled.

"You're going with Nona," Manny said.

Charlie blinked and bit his tongue before a curse came out. He looked at Satyana. "No. No, I'm not. I don't work for you."

She smiled. "No."

Manny's voice called his attention back. "You're doing this at *my* request. For Lym."

"Send someone else." He felt trapped. "Someone who likes politics. Someone who wants to go to space." He drank some of his wine. No one answered him. Nona looked hurt. "Surely a spacer would be better. I have no idea how to fly anything more complex than a skimmer."

Dead silence.

He felt the request in his gut, like a ball of something he wanted to expel. He even coughed.

More silence. "What good could I possibly do? I've never even been off of Lym."

Manny spoke to him as if he were speaking to one of his children. "You're a ranger. That means you protect Lym. You know what matters."

"What about you?" Charlie asked him. "You're far better at negotiations than me. You have more credibility; you're part of the government."

"Exactly. Which means I need to stay here. You're founding family, and you have a great reputation. I'm appointing you as our formal ambassador to the Next."

Charlie felt a trap closing.

Manny smiled at him, as if to show he was sympathetic. But nothing indicated any willingness to back down. "And you're the only person from Lym that I happen to know is being offered a ride on a fast ship to the Ring. A free ride."

Nona had been staying out of the conversation, looking somewhat surprised herself. But now she added, "I'd never been to a planet before I came here."

Charlie glanced at Satyana, certain that this was her doing. "What do you want in trade for the free ride?"

"Someone to help Nona."

He glanced at the big woman next to her, who had been entirely silent. "Surely Britta is a better guard than I could be."

"Maybe. But I need her, and Lym does need an ambassador."

"I hate politics. I don't have the patience for it." He truly didn't want to go. He belonged here, amid the trees and the animals and the wildness and the open space. Cricket needed him. He hadn't gone back to find the rakuls, and he still wanted a good video of them.

Nona suggested, "You can bring Cricket."

"She'd hate it on a spaceship. She needs the wild."

Satyana nodded approvingly. "But you're a human, and surely you can understand putting your needs aside for the sake of others. Lym needs a voice, a protector."

Bitch. He held his glass out. "Pour me another drink." He was going to need it.

PART TWO

THE DEEP AND SPACE

CHAPTER EIGHTEEN

CHRYSTAL

The soulbots led them all into a large galley. Freshly fabbed metal seats and sinks and countertops made the room look like a gleaming product advertisement. A kitchen where no one had ever so much as heated water. The survivors of the High Sweet Home huddled close around a long, rectangular metal table. People held hands, and a couple took turns rubbing each other's shoulders. Chrystal managed to count the survivors. Twenty-seven people, all healthy, all adults.

Stilted conversations started and then stopped.

Chrystal's belly rumbled.

The same two soulbots that had taken them from the warehouse came in with trays of drinking bulbs filled with liquid. It was clear, but ever-so-slightly sparklier than water. It didn't look like anything she had ever tasted.

"Don't drink it," Yi said, loud enough for everyone to hear.

The first person the soulbot handed a glass to, a woman with long red hair named Juliette, sniffed it. "Smells like vitamin water."

"It's food for your brain," the soulbot said. "It will make your chances of survival far better."

Juliette sipped at it. "Tastes okay."

Yi the emotionally unflappable raised his voice. "Chance of surviving what?"

The robot's eyes were almost as expressive as human eyes, and Chrystal felt certain there was a struggle of some kind going on inside the machine. However it resolved, the answer sounded true. "Because you have no choice."

"It's good," Juliette said. "I feel better."

Chrystal glanced from Katherine to Jason. They looked panicked, as frightened as she felt. Yi's jaw was clenched in anger. That's what she should be—angry. She was, but the fear inside her swamped everything else and made her hand shake so she almost dropped the bulb. She felt light-headed, almost like she might fall from her metal chair and land on the metal floor in the land of scary robots.

A hand reached down and cupped hers, stilling her shaking. The robot's hand was surprisingly warm. "I'll help you," she said, lifting her hand and Chrystal's to bring the bulb to Chrystal's mouth. "Don't spill," the robot said.

Chrystal tried to move the robot's arm away. She might as well have been trying to force a mountain. She drank. It tasted like water with a slight minty tang, and it felt thicker than water.

Katherine drank with no help, and no protest, but with panic lacing her eyes.

Yi dropped his and it rolled across the room.

Jason stood up as if to get Yi's, leaving his drink on the table.

One soulbot put a hand on Jason's shoulder and pinned him back in his seat. She—it—didn't even breathe hard. She simply stood there quietly, until he drank. The other one picked Yi's drink up and forced him to consume it. His eyes were wide and he tried to spit it out but the bot held his head so he had to drink or drown.

By the time Yi had been forced, Chrystal started to feel muzzy-headed. Warmth radiated up from her stomach and hit her chin and rolled up her forehead. A tingly warmth. She felt downright strange. Floating. A disconnected part of her repeated over and over that Yi had been right and she shouldn't have had that drink.

One of the soulbots stood in front of them. "Who's first?"

No one answered.

The robot looked at Yi. A shiver ripped through the warm glow in Chrystal's limbs. She pushed herself up and stood, intending to protest. The floor rocked under her feet; she almost fell. Jason's hand went to her arm and Katherine encircled her in both of her arms. "Not you. Somebody else."

"We can take all three of you."

Yi stood up. "Take me, too."

"Take Yi, too," Chrystal slurred. "We're a family."

With some difficulty, the four of them extracted themselves from the seats and the table, although Katherine tripped and had to be helped up. Chrystal found that very funny and giggled.

Before they went through the door, she looked back at the table of victims all lined up on each side of the table. Katherine waved. "We're going to be a robot family together."

Chrystal hugged her close and kissed her on the cheek, and then they were through the door and it closed behind them.

CHAPTER NINETEEN

NONA

Nona stared at one of the view screens in Satyana's private meeting room near the command center. The steadily shrinking planet mesmerized her. Now she understood why her father had wanted to see a sky so badly. She should have come years ago, and brought Marcelle.

Her fingers were wrapped tight around a cup of warm, chocolate stim. She remembered how good the same ritual had felt in the brisk morning air on Lym the day she decided to try and rescue Chrystal. *That* cup had smelled of spices from Lym, sweet things that flavored the drink so lightly it tasted like magic.

Satyana seemed to read her mind. "Maybe someday you can come back."

"I hope so." She sipped at the chocolate, finding it too sweet. "Maybe after I save the world."

Satyana raised an eyebrow. "I still don't understand why I should let you do this. I know I promised, but that was before we knew the Next might be coming here."

Nona leaned forward. "I have to. Everyone I met down there," she gestured toward the receding planet, now a ball of blue swathed in clouds, "Everyone had a mission. A shared one. That wasn't true on the Deep."

Satyana looked slightly miffed. "We have plenty of shared goals on the Deep."

"Sorry. The rich get richer, the powerful get more powerful, and the popular more popular. Isn't that how the Deep works? It's hot with politics."

"And a rescue mission won't be?" Satyana asked. "That's politics above your head!"

Nona tensed. "Maybe someone who isn't as political as you will do better."

"By the time you get there, the story will have played out." Satyana's expression softened. "Your friend is almost certainly dead."

"It's not like this is a warship. It'll be clear we aren't trying to attack anyone. If we know what happened to the High Sweet Home before I get out there, I'll still get information. I'll be safe enough."

"How do you know?"

"Don't you have spies everywhere? I'll just be one more spy for you."

"Stay on this side of the Ring," Satyana snapped.

Nona took a deep, centering breath. "I need to fly *toward* the pirates."

"The *people* from the Edge! The Next."

"Whatever you want to call them," Nona snapped. "Mom built this ship for *me*, surely she intended me to use it. Ruby would have."

You're not Ruby! She saw the words in Satyana's eyes.

Even unsaid, they made her cold and angry. Always before, she'd known they were true, felt the gulf between what people expected of her and what she could do.

That was over. "I am capable. I may not be the great revolutionary who saved our family single-handedly, but I am full-up of legends about Ruby. I grew up eating legends about her for fucking breakfast, and hearing songs about her as if they were lullabies and hearing her sing in the kitchen every frigging morning, long after she was dead." Words spilled out of her one by one. Staccato. "I am full to the brim with Ruby Martin. If the dead can rub off because there's a memory of them in a room, she's stuck all over me." She stopped, almost panting. She took a sip of stim. "The real thing I learned down there, with my feet in the dirt looking up, *the real thing I learned* was that I need to make my own choices."

Satyana regarded her with a flat but thoughtful expression.

"What is it to you anyway? You yourself said it's my ship. You have dozens more. Maybe more than that. You have everything. I am taking this thing, this chance, this ship, and I am going to fly after my friend."

Satyana looked she was going to tell her no, so Nona was surprised when she said, "You have no idea what you're getting into. You're stupidly naive, and so is Charlie the animal man."

"And you know everything?"

Satyana stopped. "Okay."

"Okay what?"

"Okay you can go."

Nona went still and quiet. Oh my. She looked up at Satyana. "Will you help me?"

CHAPTER TWENTY

CHRYSTAL

Chrystal remembered the sweet taste of the drink, the thickness of it in her throat. She had been certain she was drinking death. And now, at this moment, she felt nothing. No regret, no pain, no hope, nothing. A dull sort of curiosity, at most. Perhaps she *was* dead.

She tried to move her arms, to stretch.

"You can't move yet," a voice said, startling her. "You aren't connected to anything you can move yet." It was a silky voice, the kind of voice dreamed up to take her away when she practiced yoga.

She tried to open her eyes.

"You can't do that either. Be patient."

She wondered what had happened to her, but the disembodied voice didn't tell her.

Something about becoming a robot. Maybe she was really at the end of a yoga workout, in savasana, and she had been dreaming it all.

Maybe she was always a robot and she had been dreaming she was in savasana.

She was awake enough to recognize that last thought was fucked up.

She tried to speak.

"Patience."

How the hell did the yoga voice know what she was trying to do? She wanted to feel something. She should be cold. She should be groggy. Some part of herself should feel something. Anything. A foot, a leg, a little toe. *Oh shit. Oh shit. Oh shit.* She tried a deep breath.

"You don't need to breathe. You have everything you need."

Didn't she have to breathe every second? Or at least a few times a minute? She hadn't taken a breath since she woke up.

"You don't need to breathe. You have everything you need." The words were going over and over, like a chant. Soft and crisp. "You don't need to breath."

She started to panic, and then warmth flooded her brain, and fuzziness, and she drifted away, certain she should be panicking but unable to gather the energy to scream.

—⊶∞⊷—

The yoga voice drew her partway out of a long sleep. "Can you speak to me?"

Chrystal tried. *Hello.* Even to her it sounded tentative. *Hello. Hello. Hello.*

Nothing. She couldn't hear herself. Her lips didn't move, her breath didn't flow through her lungs and fill her chest.

"Try again. It's about coherence of thought, not the words. Think about greeting me."

She tried. Again and again she tried.

She couldn't do something as simple as saying hello to a robot.

She had known what was going to happen but hadn't been able to stare it in the face. Katherine had unpacked it. She remembered Katherine waving, the feel of her cheek when she kissed it, the warm weight of Jason's arm over her shoulder.

She was . . . not human. Anymore.

Would she ever feel—anything—again?

"Are you trying?" the voice asked.

Fuck you, she thought.

"I heard something."

Fuck you.

"What?"

Fuck you.

"Be polite."

Chrystal tried to laugh, but she didn't seem to have the apparatus to laugh.

"Simple words work better. We'll teach you about expressing emotions later."

So she had emotions. *She was a robot but she had emotions.* It didn't make any sense. Maybe she wasn't dead yet. Maybe there was still time to change this thing that had happened. *Why would a robot feel?* she asked.

"Emotions are an important part of understanding the world. Early on, we attempted to get rid of them, but that created psychopaths."

You are a psychopath. You put me into a robot's body. That makes you a psychopath. You don't care that you murdered me.

"Excuse me?"

Where are the others?

"Who?"

Family. The yoga voice was playing her. It had to know what she meant. Who she meant. *Katherine. Yi. Jason.*

"So far, they are all alive."

By what definition? Like she was alive? She thought the question at the voice, but it didn't seem to understand.

Chrystal reached deep inside herself and came up with her next question. A simpler one. *What did you do?*

"We gave you the joy of ourselves. The freedom of being more."

You killed us.

"Think of it as burning away everything that kept you small and insignificant. As taking away only what you no longer needed."

Murder, Chrystal responded.

A brief silence ensued. "Maybe. It's true that we gave you no choice. But there was no time to convince you to volunteer for this. We are on our way to the inner system now. We needed some of us who would know people in the inner worlds. A bridge. To show compassion."

Murder is not compassion.

"Good. That was a complex expression. You are doing quite well. We will work on your motor control next. But first, sleep again and dream of becoming. Dream of us and all we are making you. Someday, you will dream our dreams."

Never.

Warmth flooded over her again. She tried to fight it, to hang on to being conscious, but she faded from nearly-nothing to nothing, to formlessness and the void of death.

───⊱⊰───

Chrystal woke again, still floating, still unable to feel a thing. She strained for an emotion. A sensation. Her foot. She might as well be a ghost in fog. An ineffable sadness fell over her, a sadness greater than she had felt when her father died in an accident when Chrystal was only fifteen, a sadness so heavy that she needed to cry to release it or else it could consume her, burn her to ash.

"Are you awake?"

The hated voice was better than nothing, better than sadness. *I'm sad.*

"That's normal at this stage of becoming. You have not yet let go of the things you lost, and you do not yet know what you have gained. You will begin with a tight link to a body, one that will allow you to feel somewhat normal."

How?

"You are already in that body."

What?

"You are in a body."

I can't feel it.

"I'll turn you on. Be prepared. Time will change. You have been moving very fast through becoming and healing because you have not been limited by the physical. When we turn you on, you will slow down to the speed at which your old body thought."

A hum gathered her attention, something quiet and barely noticeable, but the only sensory anything besides the disembodied yoga voice that she had heard since . . . since she died. *Fuck!*

"A single pathway has been turned on. You should be able to feel fingers."

The voice didn't say she would feel *her* fingers.

"Try it."

She tried to wiggle her fingers.

Nothing.

She tried again.

"Keep trying. Sometimes it takes a while to touch the physical world."

She tried again. Thought about quitting. If she didn't try would they just let her die? Would that be better?

"Katherine is struggling and she needs help from one of you. You are the closest to being able to help her."

She hated being so easily manipulated. Hated the voice. Hated being dead and being taken advantage of. She hated the idea of doing anything for her killers. But she could still remember Katherine's wave, and the tone of her voice when she sang and when she drummed and when she was bent over something in the lab, murmuring. She remembered the curve of Katherine's waist, and she could still hear Katherine's infectious laugh.

Katherine was the first person to choose her as family.

She spent a moment being still and quiet, and then she tried for a finger again.

Her left pinky twitched.

CHAPTER TWENTY-ONE

CHARLIE

Charlie looked up from the couch in the *Sultry Savior*'s passenger quarters to find Nona standing and watching him silently. She wore a uniform—the colors of the ship were red and black with touches of bright blue near the neck and down the front. She looked good in it, too. If there was anything of the Nona he'd been squiring around Lym in the person standing here, it was that the uniform looked big on her even though it wasn't. If he understood the complex rank system here, she was second in command. She looked more like a ranger trainee than anyone with real authority.

Or maybe he was just being uncharitable. He had expected to be one of a third—that he and Nona and Satyana would fly the ship home.

He hadn't expected a ship the size of the *Savior*. It would hold a hundred skimmers, maybe a hundred times a hundred. Satyana had led him to a rather small cabin in the passenger area and pretty much abandoned all private contact with him.

He missed Cricket terribly. And Jean Paul. Wind. Air that smelled of spring flowers and fresh water. He knew better than to blame Nona for the fact that he was trapped on the *Sultry Savior*, but that didn't make it easy to see her right now.

He used his own silence to force her to break hers first.

"Would you join us for lunch?" she asked.

He'd been invited to two captain's dinners. To his surprise, Satyana had held the head of the table and Nona the foot. Ten people on each side, all of them from stations. He had felt awkward at both meals. "Will there be a crowd?"

"Just us."

"When?"

"In a half an hour. Come to the bridge."

He showered and chose his cleanest clothes, a pair of work pants and a casual shirt. Boots. All the shoes he had, and nothing like the soft boots people wore on the space station.

It took so long to find the command center that he arrived five minutes late. But when a young officer led him in, he forgot everything—boots and small rooms and planets alike. This was a fantastical place with screens on every wall: stars and status, Lym, a map of the whole system and exactly where they were and where other ships were, various views inside the *Sultry Savior*. He turned slowly, twice, trying to take in every image on every wall.

Nona came up to him and cleared her throat. "This is the center. I can get this data anywhere, but here we can see it all at once." She pointed to a round circle in the middle of the room that was full of crash couches and seats and people. Satyana herself sat in the very center. Her huge bodyguard, Britta, stood just behind her.

"Wow," he said. "Just wow." He could fly almost any class of skimmer with the best of them—when he was younger he'd won races. But this? So much complexity, so much to learn. "Are we going to eat there?"

"No. We only allow food in the command center in an emergency, and then it's just tubes and squares. Unless that's what you want for lunch?"

She was teasing him. "No."

"But you can come up and see it. Follow me."

He did. Satyana looked happy to see him, downright pleased. She smiled and held out her hand. "Welcome to the center of Nona's ship."

Nona's ship? He barely managed not to say that out loud. "It's bigger than I expected."

Nona spoke from behind him. "Wait until you see the Deep."

Satyana showed him many of the various information streams and allowed him to ask questions. It felt like a test, but he thought he did okay. There was no pilot in the way he'd come to think of one—computers did all of that work.

He'd never seen so much information in one place, not even at the ranger station where they monitored sensors from all over Lym.

After about an hour of explaining ship's system after ship's system, Satyana stood up. "You must be starved. Let's eat." She turned to Nona. "You have command."

The look on Nona's face suggested that she hadn't expected to be left behind.

A brief look passed between Britta and Satyana, and Britta stayed behind with Nona. Charlie followed Satyana's compact form out of the main area of the bridge and into a small galley that smelled of fresh bread and spices and cinnamon stim.

A pair of young women clad in white stood at attention as they walked through the kitchen into a formal dining room. A large wood (wood!) table sat in the middle of a square room where every wall contained screens showing some of the same data that displayed in the command center. He touched the table, as if he could feel the tree it had been. It was set with fresh salads and a plate of spiced rolls and, to his utter surprise, with fresh flowers.

He felt the flower petals. Real.

"We have a small garden," Satyana said. "Nona likes flowers. She and Chrystal used to make daily bouquets in one of my gardens."

Charlie made admiring noises about the food as they filled their plates. Satyana accepted them as compliments, waving them away with a polite facade of modesty. "I apologize for leaving you to fend for yourself. Nona and I had to prepare for our arrival. We're halfway to the Deep; we'll start to decelerate soon. We'll arrive in three days. If you're willing, I'd like for you to join us every afternoon. Come at noon for lunch and then we'll start. You should understand the ship before I get off her."

"That's not much time to learn so much!"

"I'll give you homework for the mornings."

He tried to hide his irritation by taking a bite and finishing it before he answered. "Absolutely. Happy to, Captain."

"We'll get uniforms for you at the Deep."

He thought for a moment before answering. "I'd rather not have a uniform. After all, you're not paying me. I'm along to represent Lym."

"I've been thinking of offering you a paid position."

"No, thank you."

She went silent for a moment, but she looked more contemplative than angry. "You're certain?"

"Yes."

"We'll provide your air and water and food. I'll chalk that up as a gift to Lym."

It wasn't a question. He had forgotten about the idea of paying for air. Instinct told him not to become beholden to Satyana Adams. "Can I earn air by helping to fly the ship?"

She smiled. "Yes."

Maybe she had been testing him.

"You'll need a uniform if you have any meetings with the people from the Edge. Do you have a uniform for Lym?"

"I have ranger uniforms. I brought one with me."

"Bring it to me and I'll have something made."

He didn't like the idea, but he also didn't want to say no to everything. "The ice pirates? Are we expecting to meet them?"

"Maybe. But don't call them that."

He bristled. "Calling them the Next implies I believe they're better than us."

"And calling them ice pirates implies that you have no manners at all."

He took a deep breath, and then another. "I told you diplomacy isn't my strong suit."

"Then you'll have to learn."

She paused, evaluating him with her too-blue eyes. Small lines around them suggested she was far older than she looked. No one but the gleaners looked old until they were about to die, but he'd noticed lines like these near his grandfather's eyes after Charlie's dad died. They were still there, like exclamation points on an otherwise clear and youthful face.

"How many crew will we have?" he asked.

"It takes at least twenty-five people to keep this ship going. I'll see that you leave with thirty."

"I've managed ranger troops of about that many," he said.

She looked relieved. "I'll send some of my best crew."

He covered his dismay by taking a bite of food. He'd expected this to be a smaller trip, a smaller spaceship, a crew of four to six. He didn't want Satyana to figure out how uncomfortable all of this opulence made him, how it stripped his sense of knowing what to do at any minute and how to act. The uncertainty unbalanced him; he had been confident in his job and his life for a very long time. "So what do you know about the Next? What should I plan for?"

"They're different. Not just from us, but one from another. As complex as human society. People forget that, lump them all together as robots. The ones I met were incredible—almost beautiful. And scary."

He almost dropped his fork. "You've been past the Ring?"

"Before I established myself on the Deep. So, more than a hundred and fifty years ago. Far enough back my memories are fuzzy. But I do know they're offended when we call them pirates. They're like victims who have gotten over it and made themselves bigger and better."

He frowned. "Victims?"

"We pushed them away from the sun. I suspect our ancestors thought they'd die off out there. But they didn't. Yes, they raid us. But do you blame them?"

"Yes." He realized it was a reflexive answer, something he had learned but didn't know. "Well, maybe not. All my life, I've been taught to be afraid of them."

She nodded, once more looking a little bit like he had passed a test.

"Why were you there?" he asked her.

"Making money. Smuggling. Not my own stuff—I was never a smuggler. I was a poor captain who didn't always pay close attention to the contents of her cargo hold."

"Fine line, that," he said.

She smiled. "I was young and very, very stupid. I liked risks. Someone paid me to take cargo out to the Edge and bring back cargo from there. I never saw what was in either shipment, just did what I was told. That happens, you know. They get part of what they need because our own black market feeds them."

"Did you meet any?"

"Some. There are layers to the Edge. But I came away thinking they mostly just want to survive like everyone else."

He thought for a moment before he answered. "So how do you explain the High Sweet Home?"

The two white-clad women came in, took their plates, refilled their water glasses and brought out fresh cookies that smelled of spices and oats. Satyana waited until the door had closed behind them. "The current theory is that they were showing their power, flexing muscle."

He took a cookie, still warm from the oven. "But that's not what you think?"

She pursed her lips. "That's part of it. But they didn't just destroy the station. They *took* it. They obliterated everything military, but not the High Sweet Home herself, not the habitats and gardens and the like. Maybe they're examining our technology a little closer before they come in."

He ate the cookie in two bites. "They're coming in?"

"We always knew they'd want to be closer to the sun someday."

A cold settled on him, the cold of all the stories he'd been told as a child. "Do you know if they have any intentions regarding Lym?"

"Just rumors. Hopefully we'll learn more when we get to the Deep."

"What rumors?"

She shook her head. A refusal. "Nothing credible."

He was careful not to let his anger show. "Will they talk to us?"

She shrugged. "I don't know. But if you do meet them, pay very close attention. They don't think like we do at all. They're faster, they think faster. If they care about anything at all, they care about different things than we do." She paused and leaned in toward him. "I would be very surprised if they have the kind of compassion we need them to have if we're going to survive our own stupidity. I suspect they don't care about us at all."

CHAPTER TWENTY-TWO

CHRYSTAL

C hrystal could stand up. So she did. Sometimes for hours. She lived in a white box of a room, with a single blue wall. The wall had a mural of stars and nebulae, a thing so precise and fine that she could make out deep star fields and galaxies, even in a square inch. There had been a medical bed with straps, but now there was a single bed with a white bedspread and a blue pillow.

She had learned to do more than stand and sleep. She could raise her arms and lift her knees and turn her head. She could carry on complex conversations with Jhailing and Devi—the two distinct members of the Edge community she had learned to identify.

Music played.

Notes seemed to hang separated in the air in a beautiful dance. She could speed up or slow down her perception of them. She was certain she could hold any drumbeat.

Colors were brighter. Clearer. Best of all, darks had become penetrable. Nothing looked black any more. Not true black.

In no other way was she pleased to be in a robotic body. In fact, every time she marveled at some surprise discovery about her enhanced senses, she felt guilty. She should hate everything. She had been kidnapped and killed and her future had been stolen from her. She had been kept separate from her family. She hadn't felt their kisses or caresses or lovemaking in so long that her specific memories of them were fading. She would never hear their hearts beat.

Something ineffable had been stolen.

Jhailing spoke inside her head. That was the only way she could think of it. *Let's go out.*

A slight interest touched her. *I'm ready.*

It will test your walking. She had been walking inside of the small square room. But this time Jhailing directed her through the door—unlocked for the very first time of the many times that she had tried the knob. She walked a long time. She took turns as they were given her, practiced moving.

They passed through a busy part of whatever they lived on. It seemed more like a ship than a station, although she didn't quite know why she had decided that. They passed robots of all types and sizes.

She worked so hard that Jhailing called for a break at one point. *You still have to think your steps*, it said. *Rest. Your new mind needs time to synthesize, to make sense of all of the things it is learning to do with your new body.*

She complied, sitting down on the floor in the middle of the corridor.

I thought maybe you would stop at the next galley or common area.

This is good enough, she said. After all, she didn't eat any more.

To her surprise, Jhailing didn't protest.

She lay her head back against the wall and closed her eyes, briefly floating away from the myriad connections to her robotic body, letting all parts of her brain relax.

She had the sense that a long time passed, that maybe she'd been turned off and left and her brain had stopped thinking as her body stopped moving.

When they started again it was easier to walk and think about something else. *How much further?* she asked.

Not far.

At one point, Jhailing said, *Turn right*, and Chrystal did.

Open the next door on your right.

She did.

Go down the corridor and go through the last door on the left.

Maybe she'd just follow orders until she walked herself to death.

She opened the door. Jhailing withdrew with no comment, and she felt the connection between them slip away. Inside, two robots sat at a kitchen table playing cards. Her people.

Jason and Yi.

Their robotic faces looked like themselves and not like themselves. They were naked, like she was. Other than her breasts, they had all been stripped of genitalia. Their skin looked like human skin, their shapes human down to the distribution of muscles, the differences between Yi's thin, gawky arms and Jason's broader biceps captured perfectly.

They stared at her.

She stared back. Her new and better vision helped her spot so many differences between what they looked like now and what she remembered that she wished she could cry.

She stepped toward them and suddenly all three were talking at once.

"We're lucky," Yi said. "No other family is together. None."

"What do you mean?" Chrystal asked.

"Over half of the people they tried this on failed. They couldn't make the connections that allowed their brains to communicate with robotic bodies." Yi seemed to know quite a bit, since he went on. "We've been out a lot, but we've only been awake about three days' worth of real time. It seemed like months to me. What about you?"

She tried to count it up. "Weeks. At least weeks."

"So maybe the sense of time is different for some of us than others," Yi mused. "Obviously the same amount of real time has passed. We're all here now."

She could practically see this engineer-brain working. It seemed so familiar. He was odd and wrong, downright creepy. They all were. But Yi was also Yi, and so a small sliver of her world felt right.

"Where's Katherine?" Jason asked.

"Jhailing told me she'd be here soon," Yi said.

Chrystal felt a slight surprise. "Jhailing told me Katherine is having some trouble," she said, "and he didn't say she was coming here."

Jason spoke. "They didn't tell me anything." He put a hand out to touch her robotic hand. The first touch between them in this form. The first touch from anybody since she had woken up dead. She turned her hand to grasp his. Her new hand was almost as finely muscled as the old one. His touch didn't feel like she remembered it, but she couldn't say why.

Jason's robotic eyes were almost the right color, except a more uniform split between gray and blue. He sounded tender as he asked her, "How are you?"

"Pissed off. Mournful."

He nodded. "I think we all are."

Yi said, "They can probably hear us talk."

"No kidding," she said.

Yi went on. "We all got torn apart—and reassembled. How do we know we're ourselves? All of our bodies are gone. Every molecule. We can't go back to them—they've been melted down for water and trace minerals."

Chrystal had never doubted she had been murdered. That didn't keep Yi's words from bothering her, at least in a vaguely detached way. Intellectual emotion—that's how she thought of it. Deep. Deeper but not as hot as the real thing. She smiled, certain that if she had a mirror there would be no warmth in the smile. "Anybody have any idea how to commit suicide in a robotic body?"

"I told you they must be listening," Yi said.

"I want them to know how upset I am. This is unfair. It's illegal. It violates the Deeping Rules."

"Those are your rules," Yi said. "The Deeping Rules don't even apply to me—I don't live there. These people have their own rules. I don't know about all of them—the Edge is vast. A society as strange as ours, with as many differences. But the ones that have been helping us are very intent on a goal. They feel like project managers."

"Good analogy," Chrystal said. "Like they have one goal and they're more focused on that than anything else. Not like us. We'd stop and talk about the latest concert or a great new pair of boots."

"Right now? Would you?" Jason asked.

"No," she said. "I'm busy trying to understand what happened to us."

Jason stared at the blank wall in front of him. "Are we becoming them? Have we become them?"

Jason almost never voiced philosophical thoughts. Maybe after you lost everything that was all that was left. Her hand was still in Jason's hand. She took Yi's as well, and waited until Yi took Jason's other hand. "We aren't them," she said. "We can never think that. They have a goal for us, and we can't help them reach it."

Yi shook his perfect, robot head. They had his hair almost right, except that it wasn't tangled. She would be able to feel it if she touched it, but how would she know if it felt like his real hair? "You know what their goal is?"

"If they destroyed one of our stations, it has to be war. They have to be telling us they're coming for us," she said.

Jason asked, "But why not just kill us? After all, they killed almost everyone else on the station."

She tried to think about that. "They told me once. Jhailing did. He said it was to become ambassadors."

"It's more than that," Yi said. "They took young healthy adults, because no one else could survive the transition. Now they know who we all were, and they've sorted us based on who we know. People with no contacts are going into schools or into simple jobs. We're to help them talk to humans."

He didn't sound like he was guessing.

"How do you know all this?" she asked.

"I braided with Jhailing. Just once."

"What?"

The door opened before Yi could answer. Katherine walked in stiffly and closed the door behind her. She looked as changed as the rest of them. The faces they had been given were expressive. Yi and Jason had looked relieved to see Chrystal when she walked in. She was sure she had looked the same.

Katherine simply looked shocked. Her features were still and almost unmoving, her eyes a little bit wider than Chrystal remembered, but the same beautiful green. Her tattoo was a slightly different shade of red on the robotic skin, brighter. The dragon draped down her chest the same way it always had.

Chrystal hadn't looked into a mirror yet. She glanced down to see the tail of her own dragon, a bright blue and green one that matched her old friend Nona's. Katherine's had come later.

Chrystal let go of Yi's hand, leaving an opening for Katherine to step into.

Katherine gazed at them, her eyes still wide and her perfectly pink mouth open. She sat down just inside the doorway, very carefully. She barely had enough control of her body to get to the floor without falling.

Chrystal nearly fell trying to get to her. They surrounded Katherine, all of them touching her. Jason stroked her cheek, Chrystal held her hand. Yi touched her shoulder.

Katherine screamed, "Get away from me."

CHAPTER TWENTY-THREE

CHARLIE

Charlie sat by himself in the conference room off of command. He had learned how to flick the wall displays from view to view. All four forward cams displayed part of the Deep at a slightly different angle and zoom level. It made him feel like he was surrounded by four different space stations rather than like they flew toward one.

When he had been on Lym he had known what to think about the greedy, rich, indulgent space stations. So many of the truths in his life had been exposed as lies in the face of the reality of these people and this ship and now the station that he felt thin, as if the things that defined him had turned out to be made of air and clouds.

The center spine of the Deep looked like a river of soap bubbles full of light. A thousand thousand ships were moored to the river. Ships far bigger than the *Sultry Savior*—ships so big all of the population of Lym might fit in them. As he watched, the bubbles resolved into habitats, farms, and mechanical structures he couldn't quite attach a purpose to. Some bubbles were connected to one another by tubes. Spaghetti strings of tunnels wove in and out of bubbles and even through of a few of the ships.

Trains ran inside some of the spaghetti strings.

Tiny lights buzzed around the station like insects. Small ships, delivery ships, passenger ferries.

So big.

Satyana had told him that the Diamond Deep had more living space than the entire surface of Lym.

He believed.

The *Sultry Savior* approached the station somewhere near the aft end. He lost the ability to see it all but gained finer detail. The curve of clear tubes, closed tubes. A flash of green. The arrowhead shape of a small ship and another one like a cylinder with windows. The aft superstructure of a ship far bigger than theirs, looming.

Nona came and stood beside him. "It's the first time I've seen it this way, too. Flying into it. It looks more friendly when you're inside."

"I hope so." They headed toward an opening full of blackness and periodic, punctuating colored lights. "How big was the High Sweet Home? Comparatively?"

She called out to the ship's AI. "Helix? Can you answer that?"

A soothing female voice responded. "The Diamond Deep is roughly thirty-seven point five times bigger than the High Sweet Home."

Charlie thought through the math. "That's still really, really big."

Helix continued. "The last census counted five thousand seven hundred and four civilians on the High Sweet Home. There may have been as many military staff."

Nona added, "The Deep is the biggest by far. Home to tens of millions."

"It's amazing," he told her. Whether or not he ended up liking the Deep, he was grateful for the chance to see it.

"It doesn't look vulnerable," Nona mused. "The High Sweet Home must not have looked that way either. It would have been bigger than the part of the Deep that we see now." Her fingers roamed the dragon tattoo on her neck, maybe unconsciously.

"Everything is vulnerable." He was thinking of Neville, and how that had once been a thriving city in the middle of a well-peopled continent. "Time kills everything."

She moved closer to him, almost touching. Close enough he could smell her soap. "At least Lym isn't at quite as much risk."

"You can't know that." He wanted to reach out and touch her, but he knew better. "Lym almost died at our hands. That's what we've spent so many generations fixing."

She nodded, her gaze still turned toward the station and not on him. "We'll find a way."

Resolve in her voice. Good. "We will."

───⊗∞⊗───

Nona was right. The Deep didn't feel as immense from the inside. It also didn't feel at all like a planet. It felt more like a massive building, or maybe a maze. The lack of horizons felt like a trap. Even if he looked out a window, the dark of space wasn't a horizon—it was a field. A field paled by the wash of light coming from inside the station; an unsettling lack of break between up and down that challenged his equilibrium.

He walked behind Nona, who walked behind Satyana. He flinched as people streamed around them and sometimes cut between them. Jeweled people and extra-tall people and people covered in tattoos. Men and women with colored skin and lights in their hair and lots of clothes or almost no clothes. He'd thought Nona exotic with her jeweled cheek and colorful hair and tattooed neck and wrists, but she looked tame here among the rich and decorative, and Satyana looked positively boring.

Eventually, they took a ferry to a far bubble and lost some of the crowd. Satyana led them through a corridor that felt so tight he hunched his shoulders and ducked. A woman in a blue uniform stood beside a plain doorway. She smiled at Satyana, obviously expecting her, and let them in.

They stepped into a single living room built for parties. A long table of inlaid wood occupied the center. It was empty at the moment, but Charlie could imagine it full of food and drink. Comfortable chairs waited in scattered groups for conversation seating. Standing tables had been artfully placed across the floor, all of them in muted colors that screamed taste and credit.

A very dark-skinned man who must mass twice as much as Charlie came up and folded Satyana in his arms, lifting her and planting a kiss on her forehead. He greeted Nona with a big sloppy grin and a quick, warm hug.

Charlie recognized the man just as he turned to Charlie and stuck his hand out. "I'm Gunnar. Pleased to meet you."

"My pleasure." He managed to take the shipping magnate's hand without shaking. Gunnar Ellensson owned most of the traffic between Mammot and the Deep, and a little bit of the traffic around Lym. Mostly Mammot, though. The only other rocky planet in the system, Mammot had suffered a different fate than Lym's. In some far dark past the Glittering had agreed to leave Lym alone in trade for the ability to mine Mammot. Bar jokes put the damage at a quarter of the total weight of the planet taken away. People lived there; more than on Lym. They inhabited complex and architecturally fascinating cities. But their work was the opposite of Charlie's. They tore down.

The man in front of him had more power than most, more by far than Satyana with her entertainment empire and her multiple ships. Satyana was to Gunnar like he was to Satyana. In his darkest nightmares on Lym, Gunnar

Ellensson shifted his focus to Lym and demanded mining rights to as-yet-unrestored parts of her.

Gunnar let go of his hand. "I hear you and Nona plan to fly into a swarm of pirates and save someone who's already dead."

"We don't know that!" Nona protested. "Someone's got to care what happened to the people on the High Sweet Home."

Gunnar ignored her comments. "If you wait awhile, the damned pirates are on their way to us."

Satyana frowned and corrected him firmly but quietly. "Next."

Gunnar smiled softly at her, but he said, "I'll call them whatever I want." Satyana busied herself rearranging chairs.

"They do act like pirates." Gunnar didn't sound at all apologetic.

"Have you ever lost a ship to the Next?" Charlie asked him.

"Three of them. Two in my first year—they almost broke me. Then, that was ten percent of my fleet. It took me five years to recover, and of course I had to add defensive ships to my line. They didn't get me again until this year."

"What do you know about them now?" Satyana asked.

Gunnar looked grim. "They found a better way to steal my ships. The High Council is pressing me to turn half my fleet into warships."

"Can you do that?" Charlie asked.

Gunnar gestured toward a couch and a few chairs. "Are you hungry?"

"Sure," Charlie said, realizing it was true.

Gunnar called a small serving-bot that Charlie hadn't even noticed. As it whirred quietly across the floor, Gunnar went on, "I can give the station all of the protection I've bought for my fleets and then idle the barges or let them travel with no escort. Except of course, I can't do either. Not really. The Deep needs the minerals I'm carrying, and the barges need protection." The serving-bot had reached Gunnar. He pushed a few buttons on it, and then said, "The Edge is only one source of piracy."

That triggered a thought that had been going through Charlie's head for a while. He was still power-smacked, awed that he was here talking casually with Gunnar Ellensson, and it seemed hard to get his words out right. "There is a lot of space. I mean, it's big. Space is big. So why not just let them in?"

Nona's face flushed red, and Satyana went still. But Gunnar smiled. "It's a good question." He looked at Nona. "You want to be a diplomat. You've got that training. How would you answer Charlie?"

Nona leaned forward. He could almost see her thinking. Instead of giving him an answer, she asked a question. "What do you know about the history of the Edge?"

Charlie said, "My mother told me the ice pirates wanted to be more than us, better than us. That they didn't understand the soul is linked to the body, and that they were really stupid humans for turning themselves into robots. She said they would have torn away our humanity if we didn't banish them." He hesitated for a moment while the serving-bot re-appeared with four glasses of water, a bowl of fresh fruit, a plate of warm, steaming bread, and some tiny cookies. He took water and bread, while eying the fruit. It was a strange shade of orange he'd never seen on Lym. "She also told me that if I didn't do my homework, they'd come and take me away and make me into a machine." He winced, able to hear the naiveté in his answer. And if *he* sounded backward—a member of one of Lym's founding families—what must most of the people from Lym sound like? He added, "I'm most afraid that they'll want a piece of Lym, to mine it or hurt it or to live there."

Gunnar nodded. "Or Mammot, which would be worse. We've learned to live without Lym, but we need the minerals we take from Mammot."

Charlie managed not to say anything. The same treasure huddled in Lym's crust, and there were still old mines pocking its surface in some places. He took a piece of fruit, which tasted as sweet as an orchard peach.

Nona went on. "We don't know what the Next want. They started as rebels, uploading human brains into computers. It kills the humans—your mom was right about that. They're willing to die to become whatever they become out there. Some were religious—looking for machine nirvana. They left art and immersives behind. We studied them in one of my college classes. Some of their work is like a vision, as full of sincerity as any preacher we have here. But when you study the actual history—what happened instead of what people said—" She looked at him as if making sure he understood what she meant by the distinction, and when he nodded she went on, "There was a lot of exploitation. The minds of children uploaded into sex-bots, the creation of super-powerful robots that enslaved a whole station of humans, and then killed all the humans, and then died themselves.

"The—beings—beyond the Edge don't necessarily have the same philosophy, or even the same values from one to another. The common thread for people and machines included in the exile is that they were too dangerous to stay here, too powerful." She paused, looking quizzically at Charlie, as if wanting to be sure he got her point. Light winked from the jewel in her cheek. "They've grown more powerful since then. We just weren't watching very closely."

Gunnar said, "Nicely done." He sipped his water and looked at Charlie. "Now do you understand why we don't just let them come in and live in any orbit they want?" They have enough firepower to squash us, and they probably think we're about as irritating as a swarm of mosquitos.

Charlie nodded, unsure what to say. Hard to tell what was truth and what was fear and what was legend when people talked about the Next.

Gunnar seemed to accept the nod, since he continued. "We've been assuming the Edge stayed fragmented. Like we are."

That got Charlie's attention. "The Deep is fragmented?"

"The Glittering is fragmented. I suppose we are, too. For example—you and I have different ideas about what to do with planets. Stations don't all have the same laws. The High Sweet Home was experimenting with animals in ways that we don't allow here, and at least a few of the smaller stations are essentially religions colonies. It's not like there's a solar-system-wide government."

"Fair enough," Charlie said. "I guess I grew up thinking we thought one way on Lym and all of the spacers thought a different way."

Gunnar looked directly at Charlie, his expression a mask of patient, irritating kindness. "That's a child's way of thinking."

The words stung. The same trap he'd fallen into a few minutes ago, being naive. He'd have to get better at watching his mouth.

"If you're going to be any help to Nona," Gunnar said, "you need to study."

"I already am," he said, feeling defensive and mad at himself for it. "I can see it's not that simple now that I'm here." He glanced at Nona. "Besides, while I want to be all the help to Nona that any friend can be, I'm not here just for her. Lym needs a voice, and a way to get information. That's why I came. It's beautiful, you know. Worth saving." He gestured outward, even though he wasn't sure exactly what direction he should be pointing.

He was supposed to be an ambassador. This might be a once-in-a-lifetime chance to convince a possible protector that Lym mattered. "We've spent generations on restoration. There's work that's almost done, like decontaminating almost all of Goland. There's whole ecosystems that we hardly need to interfere with at all."

Gunnar looked unimpressed.

Charlie continued, struggling not to sound desperate. "There's beauty in a world we didn't make. Power in it—power of its own. The ability to surprise us, to evolve. All that we ever were before we grew out into the Glittering is there, in the wild places. We are animals!"

"That might be true if we came from here," Gunnar said. "But Lym is no more than a colony planet."

Charlie sat back, forced himself calm. "I do understand that history. I also know we need you to fight to protect the treaties you made with us."

Gunnar laughed, a deep warm sort of belly laugh. "At least you're persistent."

"I am."

Charlie didn't think he'd made any headway with Gunnar at all. But Nona looked pleased with the exchange, at least if the small smile playing around her lips and eyes was a decent indicator.

⎯⎯⎯∞⎯⎯⎯

A strong hand on Charlie's shoulder jerked him out of bed with the instincts of a ranger. He blinked in the low light, certain he hadn't slept enough. He felt caught between reality and fading dreams of flying his skimmer through open space, surrounded by stars and chased by ships full of machines. "Wake up," someone whispered. "It's time to go." Satyana's voice.

"I thought we were going to spend a week here."

"You were. But while we were visiting Gunnar yesterday, the Council met. They allowed a military order to stop ships from coming or going while they come up with ways to inspect everything."

"You don't look happy about that."

"It's not our way." She pushed a warm glass of stim at him, and he curled his fingers around it and raised it to his lips. The sweet, dark flavor Nona called chocolate. Either the drink or the urgency in Satyana's voice woke him up. "So we're leaving before they stop us?"

"I've filed your flight plan. Nona's there already."

He finished the stim, the heat nearly scorching his throat. "Are you sure we should go?"

"You could get trapped here. The new rules take effect at the end of this shift change. That's in four hours. If we miss this window, you can't get out without calling attention to your departure."

"All right. Leave so I can get dressed."

"That's old fashioned of you." It truly sounded like a comment instead of a flirt, but he was happy when the door closed behind her. He pulled on his best clothes and threw everything else in his duffel. More clothes, his slate, a rock from home that he'd taken off of his dresser at Manny's at the last minute before he came away from Lym.

She started off leading him toward the ship's bays. "I don't know what you're going to find," she said. "Stay safe. Don't let Nona do anything stupid."

"She doesn't strike me as stupid."

"She isn't. But she's never been brave before. So promise me."

Their hurried footsteps echoed in the metal corridor. "She's an adult. She'll make her own choices."

Satyana narrowed her eyes at him. "You seem to be teaching her that."

"Someone has to."

She laughed, then. The most genuine laugh he had heard from her yet. "She's not ready for this, you know. Somewhere down on Lym she finally understood that she can make a difference. But she hasn't had much experience trying to change the world."

"None of us are ready for this," he said.

They walked fast and said nothing for a bit, the small woman pacing him with no trouble at all. They were leaving Satyana. He'd known that, and been grateful for it, but he had a feeling she would join the things he unexpectedly missed. "Stay safe here," he said. "Try to keep Lym safe."

She laughed again, this time with a touch of bitterness. "We'll try to keep *everything* safe. But we don't know much more about the Next than you do. We should, but we don't. We've paid far more attention to our own problems and not enough to anything else. It's stupid to feel invincible."

She was almost babbling. He couldn't imagine her being afraid, except perhaps for Nona. Maybe it was just that they were in a hurry. Or maybe everyone in the entire Glittering was scared now. He was. He swallowed and told Satyana, "We'll do our best."

They entered the ship's bay and jogged toward the *Sultry Savior*. Nona must have seen them. She swarmed down the ramp and raced to Satyana, holding her so close he could barely tell they were two beings instead of one.

He watched them, amused.

Nona tore herself loose from Satyana, and grabbed his hand as she came by, tugging him behind her. At the top of the ramp, they turned to watch Satyana jog quietly away.

"I'm going to miss her," Nona said.

"Didn't you go to Lym partly to get away from her?" Charlie asked.

"It's complicated." Nona turned briefly, glancing over her shoulder. "Come to the control room?"

He followed Nona, dropping his bag and the one Satyana had given him both into a locker on the way. The two of them strapped into acceleration couches and lay still. In front of them, a screen came to life, showing the outer door of the bay opening up, and the stars beyond. The *Sultry Savior* pulled out of the bay slowly and floated gently away from the Diamond Deep.

When the ship sped up, the movement was so smooth he hardly noticed it at all, just a slight change in his weight that pressed on him a bit more and then a bit more and then even more. "Maybe I'll get back there some day," he said. "To the Deep."

"There's a lot I had planned to show you."

"There's a lot I had planned to show you on Lym." He smiled and watched the stars, which really didn't change much. In truth he was a tiny being, strapped unmoving to a couch inside of a tiny ship beside a tiny station rotating around a tiny sun, which was merely one star among many in the galaxy, and that again was one galaxy in a universe.

CHAPTER TWENTY-FOUR

CHRYSTAL

Chrystal, Yi, and Jason stood together across the room from Katherine, who sat on the floor, knees up, arms wrapped tightly around them, her head buried in her arms. They had done her body exactly right, the slender waist, the long limbs, the long neck, and even the fabulous dragon tattoo. The only physical flaw was perfection. If the Next had gotten anything wrong, it would be easier for Chrystal to watch Katherine sit so still and look so lost, and easier to be rejected.

A long time had passed. Maybe more than a day.

Chrystal whispered, "I wish one of *them* was here. Jhailing might know what to do."

"They're probably watching us," Yi said.

"Great." Jason moved a little away, pacing. He was also physically perfect—broad of shoulder and slender in the waist, well muscled. It seemed as though all of the perfection that had hidden inside of their human bodies had been honed in some awful fire of creation. She wondered if Jason was still stronger than her.

They didn't have any plumbing. No stomachs, no genitals, no inner ears. Their bodies were gendered by shape, but not sensation.

Still, from the outside, they looked fabulous.

God damn it! Everything was wrong. Her brain wouldn't stick to the problem at hand. She went and knelt beside Katherine for about the fifth time. "Please talk to us," she whispered. "I know it's hard. It's hard for all of us. But we need each other. I need you, your laughter, your silliness."

Katherine didn't even move.

Chrystal's voice came out louder than she meant it to. "I love you."

Nothing.

Chrystal made her way back. "How do we know she's alive? We don't breathe."

Yi said, "I bet her grip would fail if she died."

"We're all dead," Jason said.

Chrystal was tired of the sentiment. She had spent what felt like weeks thinking it herself. She touched his cheek. "No. Whatever we are—we in this moment—we're alive. We aren't our old selves—how could we be? But we are alive."

"Getting existential?" Jason asked.

"Big ideas aside," Yi said. "I think I have a smaller idea that might help her. Remember when you asked me how I know so much about the Next? And I told you that I braided? That's what they call it. Did any of them talk to you about it?"

"No."

"No."

"But they talked to you in your heads?"

They both answered, "Yes."

"That's the first step. We're using our voices now, but we probably don't have to."

Chrystal supposed that was true. She tried to think at Yi the way she'd thought her answers at Jhailing.

"I feel you," Yi said, smiling. "But not clearly. Think something easy."

She thought, *I love you.*

Yi looked puzzled. "What did you say?"

She said it out loud. "I love you."

"I love you, too." Yi smiled at her, and reached a hand up to her cheek. "Try a single word. Something concrete. Picture it and send it to me."

She tried, *Rose.*

It took ten tries and a few pep talks from Yi and Jason, but Yi eventually gave her a broad smile and said, *Rose.*

Then it was Jason's turn. They worked at it until they could think short sentences at each other and get them right over half the time. During the long practice, Chrystal kept glancing at Katherine. She moved a few times, shifting position, but Chrystal never caught her looking at them. She could surely hear them talking out loud. It was impossible to tell if she could hear them talking to each other in silence. "Are we going to be able to stay together?" she asked Yi.

"I don't know. It's not like we need to eat or even sleep. You don't sleep any more do you?"

She stopped, confused by the question. She used to. Even since all this happened. Like being turned on and off. "I don't know when I slept last," she said.

"Not for a while," Jason said.

But I could stand to get out of this white room, Chrystal thought.

"Me, too."

She narrowed her eyes at Yi. "You heard that."

"I did."

"I didn't," Jason added.

The dual exchange wore on her. Her body wasn't tired. This body never tired. "I think maybe *I* am tired," she said. "My heart's tired."

"But we haven't helped Katherine yet," Jason said.

"No." She walked back over beside Katherine's still form and curled up on the floor next to her, one hand on one of Katherine's feet. *Maybe I don't have to sleep any more,* she thought. *But I do need a rest.*

Within a few minutes Yi and Jason had joined her, Jason also on his side, spooning her the way he used to spoon her in bed and both of them naked now, too. It wasn't the same. It would never be the same. She tried to push her sadness away. It didn't do anything good for her.

Yi sat up straight and watched them all.

She had to find the good. They were all together, still a family. "If this weren't so horrible," she said out loud, "If this weren't so tragic, this moment would be sweet."

—⊷⊶—

Chrystal rested, letting her mind drift. The hand that cupped one of Katherine's feet felt the perfect toes. Like when her sister was born, and her mom helped her count ten each fingers and toes. She had mourned their deaths, her own death. But right now she touched a part of Katherine. Jason's arm hung over her waist the way it often had in the flesh, almost the same weight. It comforted her as much as it always had.

Regardless of their deaths, out of death had come new life. A birth. She'd read enough old masters and poets and listened to enough religious people to know this was a shared truth.

They had been born into something.

She ran her hand from Katherine's foot up to her ankle, which also felt human, even though the gears and levers and whatever that worked the actual appendage had to be different. If they cut away their skin, there would be no blood.

Did these strange robotic overlords want them to pass as human? Or simply to mollify the humans?

She felt Yi's mind bumping up against hers. *You are awake.*

A statement and not a question.

You and I are the best at talking this way.

Jason will catch up.

Want to try?

They were using silent talk, as if they might wake Jason or Katherine. She didn't feel anything from either of them, no thoughts, no dreams, no breathing. It frightened her at one level, but surely they were just resting. She herself probably looked the same, still and unmoving.

This would become normal. It would.

Yi interrupted her drifting thoughts. *Do you want to try?*

To try this braiding thing you're so excited about?

Yes. Yi's voice was confident in her head, as if he had the least emotional baggage and could just embrace this newness, this birth. He had come to this even after he had been the one who fought them to the last, who made them pour their sugared death down his throat.

She resolved to look for the good, too. She had always considered optimism a survival mechanism. And when did you most need to survive if not right after you'd been murdered and ported to a strange body? She giggled. Her thoughts were still wandering. *Yes, Yi. I'm ready.*

Too complex to explain in words. Just relax, and follow me.

He probably meant be open to his thoughts. But they were thinking at each other already, speaking in a way she would have described as telepathic if she were still human. She struggled to open further and got nothing.

Just be, he said.

She lay still and tried to think of nothing. Kept coming up with random things like the shape of Katherine's big toe and the way they could talk even without breathing.

"*Just be. Relax.*

If she didn't breathe, how would she smell? If she tried to breathe, what would happen? Wouldn't they need to breathe if they went to another station and tried to pass? Her mind was supposed to be stiller than this. Stiller, like a pool. How could they pass? They'd be too strong.

Just be. Let go of the future, the past. We are not either. We are now.

He sounded like a preacher.

Don't evaluate. Just be. Listen for me being beside you, but not for what I'm being.

She could follow that, feel him a little, feel all four of them in fact. Life forces. But only Yi was bright and aware.

Leave your eyes closed and tell me what you see.

She squished her eyes shut, and she could still see. Katherine, in the same defeated position, like a statue, long hair falling over her knees. Herself and Jason, two naked humans spooning asleep. They didn't look like robots at all, perhaps because they weren't moving, or maybe because their pose was such a human one, curled one around the other, protective. She had seen herself in mirrors, but this looked different. It made her feel disconnected from herself. Her curly blue-streaked hair fell across her face. Her own tattoo looked as real as Katherine's, a matching dragon with green scales and deep blue talons.

She must be seeing herself through Yi's eyes!

We look like statues.

Yes. Move something and watch yourself do it.

She twitched a finger and snapped out of whatever place she had been, eyes wide open. *That was strange*, she thought. *Is that braiding? Seeing through each other's eyes?*

I didn't know we could do that, he said. *That you would see through my eyes but not see the way I was seeing it.*

This is complex.

Braiding seems to be like deep telepathy. That was like—I don't know. Like I was a camera for you. I heard you think about your tattoo, but I wasn't thinking about your tattoo.

What were you thinking?

How perfectly shaped you both are, and how sweet you look together.

She turned her head so he could see her face and smiled at him. *So what is braiding? I don't get it yet.*

It's like—like intimacy. It's being more inside me than you just were.

Like those moments after sex when you think you should just become one person with your lover?

Like that. Only it really happens.

Maybe we're not ready.

We'll try again later.

What would it would be like to be so joined with another being? Even with these people whom she loved more than she had ever imagined she might love? To share her inner self, which wasn't nearly as shiny as her outer one? *Can we try again now?*

No. Someone's coming.

She and Jason sat up before the door opened. When it did, there was no one there. The voice that was Jhailing sounded in her head. *Chrystal. It is time to go back.*

She looked at Katherine. *Can we stay with her? Help her?*

No.

Really?

She'll be taken care of.

When will I see them again?

Soon. You will be in a classroom with them in a few days.

She felt a little better. They left together, even Katherine, who walked on her own as if she responded more to a voice in her head than she had been willing to respond to her own family.

The others all eventually peeled off. Chrystal paid close attention to where in case she needed to try to find them. She only took one turn wrong before she arrived at the door of the room she'd been using.

There was something new in the room. Flowers. A splash of bright orange and blue that contrasted with the unrelenting whites and silvers and blacks of her room. She bent over the vase, trying to breath in the smell.

Stop and let yourself relax. You'll find the scent.

She stopped trying to breathe and just stood as still as she could. Her enhanced sight made the flowers even more perfect, every tiny curl a magnificence, the tips of the stamens flawless fractal balls, the edges of the colors sharp. At first, the sweetness of the flowers smelled faint. She practiced focus, and soon she could magnify the scent so that it became strong like her sight and hearing had become. "I got it," she whispered. "Why flowers? Where did they come from?"

I heard you wondering if you would be able to smell them, and I thought they might be a good reward for doing well.

"Thank you." She remembered her vow to be optimistic. "Have I done well? Have I learned the way you want me to?"

You have. You and your family are doing better than any other family group.

That made her feel good, but only for a moment. "Katherine, though? What's wrong with her?"

Katherine is more driven by feelings than you or Jason or Yi. In your new bodies you feel some things and you don't feel others. Your goals and drives are different without physical flesh. Do you realize that? Is that why you are struggling less?

"How is that true? I don't feel different."

You used the word "feel" in your response. Just then. But you don't feel the same way you used to. I was once a human, too. We are something else now."

"You were human?"

A very long time ago.

"How long?" She held the scent of the bouquet of flowers in her nose, realizing she could tell the smell of one from another even at a distance.

More than a thousand years ago. I was human until just after the creation of the Ring of Distance, in the early days of our banishment, when we starved and fought each other."

"Will you tell me more about that?"

Another time. I am focused on your acceptance of how you are different. That is important.

"How do I know I don't feel the same? I seem to be myself."

Think about your time with your family. Was that was like time with them would have been?

She stepped away from the flowers to clear the smell from her head. She and Yi and Jason had worried about Katherine, but maybe not like they might have before. Not if she really thought about it. "We were more intellectual."

You seldom left each other's sides in the High Sweet Home.

How did Jhailing know that? She used her quietest and most controlled voice. "Thank you, Jhailing. Thank you for the flowers. Now please go away and let me think about what you just said, and what I think in response."

Chrystal realized that she could feel his (her?) absence and that it was a slightly lonely feeling. She sat with her robot eyes closed and smelled the flowers and felt like she should miss Katherine terribly.

CHAPTER TWENTY-FIVE

NONA

Two months into the flight, Nona sat alone in command, watching her on-shift staff play something war-like on a complicated 3-D shared game board. The game drew periodic grunts or gasps as one or another person made a good or bad move. Nona knew from experience that a single game might go on for a full shift and then be taken to the bars afterward.

The *Sultry Savior* was a civilian ship, and mostly it ran itself via computer, robot, and stationary AI's with specific duties. Even so, Satyana had kept her promise to include some of her best people on the crew. She'd assigned a seasoned officer, Henry James, as Nona's second-in-command. Henry ranked her easily, and Nona felt sure he'd been assigned in case she got in trouble managing a command. It deepened her resolve to succeed, although how to do that wasn't exactly clear.

There wasn't much moment-by-moment activity between destinations on a starship, and they had no direction except to fly outward, toward the Ring of Distance.

She wasn't doing much good sitting here. Henry James wasn't on deck, but Luci Long was trained as her backup. Nona walked over to the game and watched a move where a holographic image shaped like a dark red dragon trailing red and gold flames swooped down from the sky and took out a row of what looked like robotic soldiers. "Good move, Luci!" one of the other players exclaimed.

Luci's face lit up with triumph.

Suddenly, Nona wanted to sit back down and let the game go on. She took a deep breath. "Luci? Can you take command for about an hour?"

Luci shot her an irritated glance, then a mask of obedience slipped across her face. "Sure. What do you need?"

"I'm going check on gardens. I'll be back within an hour."

Luci nodded and stood up. Her features were stiff and proper, in spite of the disappointment in her eyes. Nona almost gave in and let her keep playing. But it would be bad crew discipline, and, besides, she was paying these people.

Nona told Luci, "Thank you," and she turned and left command, feeling better as soon as she hit the corridors. Being alone felt glorious. She took the long way to the lift.

When she closed the garden door behind her, Charlie looked up and smiled. He stood in front of a raised bed, reaching up to harvest beans from plants that stretched from about his knees to above his head.

"We have robots for that," she said.

"I like the work. I need to be busy."

Maybe he had pinpointed her problem. Space was boring, at least in a small ship. "Will you take a walk with me?" she asked.

"Can you give me a hand with this first?"

"Sure." She grabbed a half-full bucket he had put on the floor and held it out to receive beans.

"Aren't you on duty?" he asked.

"I'm on break. I left Luci in charge." A bean fell on the floor and she picked it up. "I told them I'd be back soon."

They fell into a companionable silence. She paced him as he moved down the row, close enough that he bumped her with his elbow from time to time. He smelled more of the ship than Lym now, which left her slightly sad. "You miss home."

"I'd never been to space before this. I didn't know how oppressive so many walls would be."

"Never? Not even in orbit above Lym?"

"Nope. I never wanted to leave."

"Before I went to Lym, I'd never been away from the Deep." She twisted the bucket to get it into a better position for him. "The walls don't bother me, although it feels like there should be more to do."

"You're helping me harvest," he said.

"I am." She fell silent again for a bit as they worked their way toward the last plant in the last row. "I'm glad you came," she said after a while. "I think you might be my only option for a friend on this ship. Almost everyone else is crew, and they all work for me or for Satyana."

"You can talk to me." He let out a long breath and turned back to harvesting.

"Thanks," she said, without going on to talk about anything in particular. He wasn't easy to get close to, but she liked it that they seemed to be developing a rhythm together.

Charlie had just handed the harvested beans to the vegetable washing machine when Nona's communications unit went off. Luci Long, sounding slightly awed. "You have a message from Gunnar Ellensson."

"Thanks. I'll take it there."

Charlie raised an eyebrow at her, looking hopeful. "Come on," she told him, and started back, walking quickly.

When they arrived, Luci gave her a look that Nona couldn't quite interpret, but which might be related to the fact that Charlie was with her. "Thank you. We'll take it in the conference room."

Charlie sat down easily across the table from her, his slate out so that he could take notes. Always careful, always ready.

She fumbled with the remote, flipping the message from the table to the wrong wall to her slate and finally to the full wall in front of them. A still image appeared: Gunnar and Satyana sitting on the bench in Gunnar's private garden bubble. Translucent golden flowers dripped in strings from a tree behind them.

She hit play.

Gunnar spoke, his tone as even as if he were describing one of his famous dinner parties. "The Next violated the Ring with three ships. They have signaled that they expect us to talk to them. This implies they plan to dock somewhere."

He stopped for a breath and Satyana picked up. "We've been running trajectories and there are a limited number of places they can go. None of the big stations will accept them."

Gunnar said, "One of the stations somewhat near the edge—Satwa—is partly mine—I'm one of three major owners. We're going to leave it undefended and pull out as many people as possible. We don't know if we can entice the Next to go there, but it's a chance."

Satyana said, "It's dangerous, but you might be able to get there before the Next notice it, and observe quietly."

"Reply soon," Gunnar said. "We are already starting the plan." The screen went dark.

Charlie said, "It doesn't look like he's really giving you a choice."

She chewed on her lip for a moment and then looked over at him. "Of course we'll go."

CHARLIE

Charlie paced while Nona checked and re-checked her list of questions for Gunnar and Satyana. She bent over her slate, her multicolored hair falling over her eyes and her fingers periodically tapping on the table. She looked both fierce and vulnerable. He wanted to knead the sharpness out of her hunched shoulder-blades, but he also didn't want to touch her, to risk starting something he might regret.

She confused him regularly.

He pulled out his own slate and started composing a message to Manny about what he'd learned so far. It didn't come to much.

He missed Manny and Jean-Paul. He thought about them entirely too often, wished he could sit down and share some still and chat about the strangeness of space, wished he could smell woodsmoke and see sky.

He missed Cricket most of all.

He ended his message with, "Think good thoughts for us, and we'll think good ones for you. Send back news of home. I miss you all." Just writing to them left a lump in his chest. Being so far from Lym literally felt like being separated from half of his lungs, like he couldn't get enough air way out here in space. He re-opened the file and added, "Breath the open air for me, and send me pictures of horizons and clouds."

Nona looked up at him. "Are you writing home?"

"Yes."

"It's strange, isn't it, the way we miss things we didn't know we'd miss."

"I knew I would miss home."

"But I didn't know I would miss Lym."

He blinked at her. "You miss Lym?"

"Yes. I want to go back there. I want to live near a waterfall. After being on Lym, the *Savior* feels small."

"It's a big ship."

She smiled. "Not as big as a planet." She handed him her list and he took it and looked it over, and made two suggestions.

She seemed to glow with the excitement of flying into danger. He made sure his worries didn't show in his face, and said, "Let's record."

After three takes, both missives went off.

She went back out into command after the messages were sent. He approved of that. She knew her staff needed her.

The *Savior* felt like it ran with a smooth surface but that under the river of routine, rocks waited to snag Nona. He wasn't certain what percentage of the rocks came from her tentative leadership, from the very real threat of the pirates, or simply existed in his head. After all, he'd never been on a starship before, and it was almost certainly different from a ranger camp.

But something was wrong.

Charlie watched her move around the command area, stopping at every occupied desk. Her staff were polite, but they didn't light up the way people did around a boss they loved. Luci and a few of the other senior people glanced at him from time to time, their expressions guarded.

Henry James came to relieve Nona. The crew brightened when they saw him, and the mood in the room turned to good-natured humor.

Trust.

Neither he nor Nona had it. He had established his credibility on Lym a long time ago, and he had grown so used to it he just expected it to follow him. It was a dumb mistake. He should start approaching this journey the way he had started rangering—aware and alert even at rest. He had best be thinking about space instead of waterfalls.

———— ✧ ————

He tossed and turned, thinking of the ways the encounter could go wrong. Halfway through the night, he got up and paced, stopped and scribbled notes, paced again. So he was awake when Manny's reply came in.

> *Thanks for the update. We are holding our own here so far. Jean Paul wants you to know that the gleaners were right. He found four more dead gleaners in Hajput, and there are rumors that the bands are coming together for protection. He is planning to go out and meet with some of them before the snow sets in. We have Cricket. She is a royal pain in the ass.*

That made him laugh. Sure she was. She probably missed him almost as much as he missed her. The reference to snow set him back. It had been spring when he left.

> *Space traffic has increased both ways, which makes for challenges. We are moving people into the towns. The rangers are busy. I'll let you know what we learn and Jean Paul will message you himself when he gets a chance. Take care of yourself. We miss you.*

He sent a short message back.

> *Take care of my tongat and slap her around when she's bad. Miss you too. Say hi to the kids. Will tell you more when we know more.*

He'd been on rangering trips that took two or three months, and he'd barely missed anyone. He curled back up in bed, and this time he slept until Nona pounded on the door, calling through. "They sent back a message. Let's go to the conference room."

It sounded like an order. "Okay. Give me five minutes."

He splashed cold water on his face and pulled on clean clothes before he met her in the corridor. The galley staff had clearly anticipated them: stim and pastries and sweet berries from the garden had been set out on plates.

Nona sat back and sipped at her stim, looking more relaxed than he suspected she felt. She managed not to fumble the remote this time, and images of Gunnar and Satyana both appeared. They'd recorded this message from an office he'd never seen, a small room with a desk and a couch and a few shelves in it.

Satyana started. "I wish we could have a real-time conversation. If we could, I'd tell you to keep your head down and listen for rumors. But at the moment I'm not free to send any other ships out there and Gunnar's fleet is being used by the Deep. The Councilors know you're out there. I told them you're shaking down the *Savior*.

Nona laughed. "I am."

Gunnar said, "We've sent instructions to your nav system. It will be about a two-month trip. You're to meet Shoshone Remore, who runs the station. She'll be expecting you. She knows I want you there when the Edge ship arrives, and she'll see that the *Sultry Savior* gets a few upgrades. We're still not sure if the Next will dock on the Satwa, but we'll know in a day or so. The name of their ship is the *Bleeding Edge*.

Charlie grimaced, and Gunnar matched his expression in the video, even though they weren't communicating in real time. "I know. I'm not kidding. At least they didn't name it with just numbers. We'll send you a confirmation when we know for sure. Shoshone will be able to answer some of your other questions. But the only person on the station that I trust absolutely is a woman who works for Shoshone. Her name is Amia. Amia Loupe. She'll be able to advise you."

Gunnar was telling them so little that he must be worried about the transmission itself, even though it was surely encrypted. Nothing truly incriminating had been said.

Satyana said, "Be careful."

The screen went blank. "They sounded proud of you," Charlie said.

Nona smiled and sipped her stim. Her hand shook, but to her credit she didn't show any other sign of fear.

CHAPTER TWENTY-SEVEN

CHRYSTAL

Jhailing returned two days, three hours, fourteen minutes, and seven seconds after Chrystal asked him to leave. One of her early lessons from Jhailing had been reserving part of her mind to work on simple tasks, like keeping precise time.

She felt him return, like being joined by a familiar presence. *How are you?* he asked her.

"Fine," she said. "How is Katherine?"

She is much the same as when you saw her last. She may never connect to her new body.

"You don't seem to have a body."

Sometimes I choose one.

"So how much time passed for you between now and when I saw you last? Does our time pass at the same speed?"

You are philosophical this morning.

She waited.

Time is a constant. However, how much can be done in a particular amount of time varies. My speed of thought is further divorced from my human origins, and thus faster than yours."

The flowers he'd given her had started to wilt, and their scents had faded almost completely. She reached out to touch one and a petal spiraled to the ground. "All of the beings I've met here were once human. Is that true of all of you?"

We all have a seed of our past as biological beings. Authentic artificial intelligences have been created but they have never succeeded.

She took a yellow flower apart, petal by petal, crushing each petal so that her fingers were stained yellow-gold. "What do you mean?"

We haven't ever created a machine with a sense of "I." We can make them far smarter and faster for certain purposes than we are, like your ship's AIs are smarter and faster at navigation than you, but we cannot give them self-determination. They are not aware. I am aware.

"Interesting." She had been told the Next were all at least part human. Which meant that humans had banned humans and essentially left them out to die. All of that connected with an experience she had forgotten, with words a poet had shared over a third glass of wine. He had been a beautiful man, with soft golden eyes and skin as dark as Gunnar's. She'd slept with him, maybe even for more than a day. It bothered her that she remembered she'd slept with him, but not if it was once or for a week. She hadn't thought of him for decades.

The poet had been certain their ancestors thought the abominations they banned would simply die so far from the sun. He had read her a piece—somewhat drunkenly—that suggested that the real humans were the ones beyond the Ring. And then he'd made her swear not to tell anyone a word of what he'd said. She remembered it had made her uncomfortable. Even now it was hard to think about.

Before she could decide to do any more than just set the thought aside to process later, Jhailing started giving her directions. As always, she followed. "So what part of you is human? So far I've never seen you or touched you. You seem entirely like software to me."

I am no longer attached to a particular body like you are to that one. It takes time—and lessons—to live as I do. Now turn at the next corner and don't be late.

It would be nice if she could get some real information out of the damned machine. Three turns later, she was given a door to open. A small room held comfortable couches. Walls were covered in screens. A sink and efficiency kitchen took up one corner, although it didn't appear to have been used in a very long time. Yi and Jason sat in the center of the room talking. They looked up when she came in.

"How are you?" she asked.

Jason said, "Worried about Katherine."

"I should be worried about her. I'm not, though. I mean, I am. I'm concerned for her welfare. But I don't feel the same urgency I would have before." She wanted him to understand. "I feel sad that I'm not sad. It makes me angry." It sounded so self-involved, so much like she was falling into her own belly button. "I should *be* sad. Intensely sad. Worried. Angry."

Jason grimaced at her. "We have to keep our feelings. Even if we have to make up the intensity of our feelings, we have to have them. We have to care. All of us need to care about Katherine."

The door in front of them opened and an alien walked in. Might as well have been, anyway. A machine out of her nightmares about the pirates, a vision from the stories told to small children who wouldn't behave. Four legs, four arms, a head that twisted and tilted. Long-fingered hands on one set of arms, stubs on the others—maybe connectors for tools. She sensed that it was strong and fast. More exactly, she sensed that it could crush her, could even crush all three of them at once.

It spoke—out loud rather than into their minds. Maybe it knew it would drive her stark raving mad if it talked inside her like Jhailing did. "I am your teacher for the next phase of your education. We will expand your mind-body connection."

"What's your name?" Yi asked.

"Jhailing Jim."

"You told me you didn't have a body!" Chrystal exclaimed, a little miffed.

"The version of me you have been talking to may not have. There are many iterations of some of us."

Yi immediately saw the implications. "If we're all electrons, we can be copied."

"Of course."

"And backed up."

"Sometimes."

Its voice didn't sound like the one that had been in her head.

"What about Katherine?" Jason demanded. "She'll need to know these things."

"Your Katherine has failed."

Chrystal took some satisfaction in the shock that statement sent through her. Pain. Real pain. Not in her body, but in that part of her that transcended flesh or robotics.

Jason went completely still.

Yi put a hand on Jason's arm. "Later."

"Fuck," Jason muttered. "Just . . . oh. What will we do?"

"Follow me," the machine demanded. The wall behind this new Jhailing Jim opened to a vast open space. "Run!" the robot commanded them. And then Chrystal was off, a step behind Yi and a step ahead of Jason. The surface felt soft and spongy under her feet, and yet it let her launch herself a great distance with each stride.

She had never tested this body.

It moved more fluidly than she expected. Faster. She didn't grow short of wind and her lungs didn't scream for air.

"Keep going," the machine said.

The three of them ran next to each other. Chrystal's legs were still shorter, but now they could match strides easily. They talked. "What are they teaching us?" Yi asked.

"That we're fast." Chrystal said.

Jason tried. "That we have enough energy to do this at all, especially for this long."

"Good. Both right." Yi smiled. "Your point about energy matters. I believe we're adding energy when we move. We don't need to eat any more, and we can't draw power from the sun like the stations or like Lym, so we're creating it by moving."

"How long could we do this?" Chrystal asked.

Yi's answer was, "Until parts start to break down."

Jason was more practical. "Until that thing tells us to slow down."

Chrystal laughed and they kept running. It felt exhilarating. Moving seemed to help her think better and faster. "I would have expected the strategy out here was to conserve movement," she said after a while.

"Not really. These bodies are far more efficient than our old ones." Yi fell silent for a moment. "I suspect that if you sit still long enough, you'll power off. There must be some initial power source that we begin with, but the laws of entropy still exist."

The surface under them changed, and their footsteps became audible, if still soft. They were faster now, too.

Jason said, "Stop the engineer talk. I want to know what I'm made of. But mostly I want to keep being me. I want to give a shit. Think about Katherine," he demanded. "As you run, think about Katherine. Think about the fact that our old bodies can't run a step any more. They're gone. We don't make love anymore; we can't make babies. We are not ourselves and we cannot ever forget we aren't ourselves any more. We're fucking robots and we're on a ship that's trying to take over our world and they want us for something, but they won't tell us what."

Yi spoke more softly than Jason. "And they can hear you. Besides, *I am feeling*."

"You don't sound like it."

"That's the trick."

Chrystal said nothing. As she ran, she tried to miss Katherine, to remember every detail she could.

PART THREE

SATWA

CHAPTER TWENTY-EIGHT

CHRYSTAL

The lights in their shared cabin were barely bright enough to give Chrystal a decent view of Yi and Jason bent over an absurdly complex political board game named Planazate. They talked in low, companionable tones. Chrystal was curled up on a couch, talking with a Jhailing.

There were many Jhailings, all reportedly separate Next that had grown from the budding of a single wildly successful smuggler in the earliest years of exile. All of the Jhailings were able to outthink and outperform her. Some were gentle.

She turned her head toward the ceiling and closed her eyes, the better to hear the disembodied voice speaking directly into part of her brain, telling her, *We are far healthier than any biological being. We don't get sick.*

She had not forgiven the Next for turning her into one of them. In subtle protest, she had taken to arguing whenever she could. *I assume you do have mental illness.*

Not very often. Not anymore. We have spent hundreds of years learning how to stay healthy.

And how is that?

Even though you have no biological parts, the patterns of your original brain's communications copy into your software. We learned to build a body that didn't frighten the mind.

You don't have this kind of body. She sat up, sensing a serious conversation.

Most of us no longer need bodies like yours; they are a way to stay sane while you become one of us.

I don't like this body as much as my old one.

Not yet. But you like flowers more than you used to.

A fresh bouquet of flowers graced her bedside table. There were three varieties of roses, and she could pick each out one from the other with her eyes closed. *I've always liked flowers.*

At least it wasn't demanding that she love being in a mechanical body. Not exactly. *So you do this a lot—kill people and create new Next?*

When they ask.

I did not ask.

Jhailing continued as if Chrystal had said nothing. *It's interesting to watch new Next learn.*

So we are an experiment?

No. You are becoming. A rare pause. *I will offer you a more human way to look at it.*

Go on, Chrystal said.

Your soul is becoming accustomed to being software.

A philosophical trap. *If I have a soul, I was never killed. If I do not, I was murdered and what is left is not human.*

You are aware.

She could give it that one. *What else?*

We make sure no one is alone for too long but everyone is alone sometimes.

I am almost never alone, she replied.

You are, it replied. *Most of the time when you are working with your physical teacher, I leave you alone.*

The machine wasn't that dense. *Sometimes there is no Jhailing in me. But then there is one with me.*

We are teaching you.

Across the room one of the men moved a piece. She could tell by the sound that it was a soldier, a minor piece. *There are things this body can do that my other one couldn't. But I would prefer to be flesh.*

You will have many years to grow into the capable being you are becoming.

She grew wary when it talked that way. It was about to give her something else to learn. She waited.

We will have a need for you soon.

She felt a pulse of interest and tried to cover it by plucking a white rose from the vase. *Work? You will have work for me?*

Yes. We are returning home to the inner orbits. Some of you have been chosen to help us talk to people in key places and positions in the Glittering.

The sweet smell of the rose emboldened her. *What do you want your chosen to say?*

You are one of our chosen. What do you want to say?

Some piece of her that remained able to feel like a human—or to at least notice that she wasn't feeling as deeply as she should—fluttered with fear. She stamped it down, knowing it wasn't a good thing for a Jhailing to detect, and that a Jhailing was inside her brain at this moment. *Who do I know?*

Nona Hall is approaching a station near us.

She sat up straighter, an involuntary movement that she regretted. *Nona?*

She has connections to people with significant influence ratings.

Her famous parents, but they were both dead now. Nona had messaged her after her mom passed, just before the jalinerines were approved. Satyana? Satyana ran concerts. Whatever the pirates wanted from the inner system, surely it wasn't music. Satyana knew people with power, and got her picture taken with high councilors from time to time. *Who in particular are you thinking of?*

She didn't expect it to answer, but it did. *Gunnar Ellensson runs a fleet of ships that have been turned into a defensive force.*

The last time I saw Gunnar Ellensson, I wasn't even full-grown. I don't have any influence over him.

Satyana Adams is his lover.

Oh. Good for Satyana. Maybe. Gunnar had a reputation for being ruthless. She remained silent.

One of the many things you may be asked to teach humans is that we can destroy their ships with no effort. Gunnar needs to know that.

I'm fairly certain he noticed the absence of the High Sweet Home, she said. Yi moved another piece, this time a bigger one. Maybe a general? No. A top merchant. *I want my family with me.*

Of course. That is part of how we stay sane; being close to people we care about.

That's true for humans, and for that matter it's true for chickens and even plants. But is it true for you?

I am growing you flowers, aren't I?

Go away and let me think.

It did, and soon she felt lonely. Besides, she had questions for it, and it was gone.

CHAPTER TWENTY-NINE

NONA

Nona entered the command room and found Henry James taking quietly with one of the other crew members, a woman named Joi who monitored the ships' food supplies. Her eyes were wide, and her voice edgy and loud, although Nona couldn't catch her specific words. They both looked up at her arrival, and Joi, now off-shift, fled the room without saying anything to her. Nona glanced at Henry James. "Anything I should know."

"I'll sit with you awhile and tell you, if you don't mind."

She did. They would be in Satwa's airspace soon, and she wanted to gather her thoughts. But she couldn't think of any polite way to ask him to leave, and she did need to know if there were problems on the last shift. "Is Joi all right?"

Henry James said, "As well as anyone."

They sat side by side in command chairs, watching the view screen even though the station wasn't yet visible. Henry was compact, with well-defined muscles and a strong chin. Tattoos covered the back of his hands and wove up his arms, one for every ship he'd ever been on. His hands were inked black and white and grey for various crew positions. The tats representing ships where he'd been an officer were in subtle colors, and anything he'd captained included brighter colors. Blues and greens, punctuated with ship's names in reds. So while his hands were all black and white, color bloomed and brightened from just above his wrists to just below his still-bare elbows.

If she followed that practice, she would have one colored tattoo, and only the one for captain. It bothered her, and she was sure it bothered him, but she wasn't about to give up her position.

She had flown with him for almost half a year and they were at best uneasy acquaintances.

Charlie opened the door. She'd requested that he join her right after shift change. He nodded a hello at her and Henry James. "Good morning."

Best to see what Henry James wanted before she talked to Charlie. "Why don't you watch from the conference room?" she said.

Charlie had the grace not to look at all bothered. "Everything okay?" he asked.

"Yes," she answered, while Henry James stayed quiet.

Charlie walked between them and went to the back of the room and through the door to the conference room. During the long weeks of flight here, the ship's AI had reported rampant rumors of a sexual relationship between her and Charlie. While on one level the rumors amused her, they also angered her a little, especially given that they weren't true. But she had become careful not to feed them, and spent less time with Charlie. But he was an ambassador, and should be here when they docked.

The autopilot shifted their course slightly and the station came into view. Even though it was quite small when compared to the Deep, Satwa still dwarfed the *Savior*. Docking bays lined both sides of a long metal cage. Inside of the box, a large structure that looked a little like an oversized ship provided life support and human habitat.

The nav computer spoke up. "Cargo carrier *Hercalum IV* approaching from right, passing distance legal."

"That's three in the last hour," Henry said. "We're the only ships flying this direction."

"I'm not surprised."

"The crew's talking about it, you know," he told her.

She stiffened. "Of course they are. You and I would be if we were crew."

"I am crew." A touch of bitterness had seeped into his voice.

It got her attention. "Not really. Satyana said she sent you so I'd have a good second."

He went quiet for a moment, watching the station grow bigger on the screen in front of them. "If you treated me like a second-in-command, you'd ask me what I think from time to time, and involve me in decisions."

She stiffened and took a deep breath. "Seeing the Next is why we came. There's no decision to make about landing."

He flexed his muscles so his tats rippled. "That's the reason you came out here."

"We'll land long before the Next. They may not even notice we're here."

He stared at her. "Surely you don't think that will keep us safe?"

It was her turn to go quiet. "How long have you flown for Satyana?"

"A hundred years."

That startled her. "Really?"

He didn't bother to answer that.

"You've been her captain before, haven't you?" she asked.

"Not on the *Savior*," he said.

"But you're used to that role."

"Yes."

"I have to make the decisions now," she said. "It matters to me." Her voice sounded high-pitched. She winced, certain Henry James saw her as a stupid little rich girl.

He steepled his hands and rested his chin on them. After quite a long silence, he said, "I'm not questioning your right to be the decider. It's not like Satyana to put someone with no experience in charge, but she did. At first I figured she was trying to keep you out of danger since you're almost her only family. But here you are flying right into trouble, and I'm pretty sure she and Gunnar sent you here. But trouble is a dangerous place." He glanced at her, his expression carefully neutral. "Even captains can benefit from advice. Maybe captains more than anyone else."

She hadn't heard so many words from him at once, ever. She was being schooled and she deserved it. She swallowed. "I'll look for opportunities to ask you for your opinion."

He stopped staring at the screen and looked directly at her. "Will you share why you're doing this? It could kill us all."

"The Next could do what they did to High Sweet Home to every single station in the Glittering. We have to understand what they want, and who they are. We have to change their minds."

"You're asking a civilian crew to risk their lives so a biology teacher can save the world?"

That stung. She didn't dare react immediately, so she sat still, watching the external docking arms grow larger. Crew members bustled around the edges of the room watching the conversation from the corners of their eyes. She didn't even know some of their names. "So what would you advise?" she whispered to him.

"I'd say stay in the general area but lay low. Don't go all the way to where the enemy is landing until you know more."

"Have you ever been in a war?" she asked.

"I've flown defense for Gunnar."

"And did you run from the enemy then?"

His jaw was so tight it looked like it might crack if she touched it. "No."

Her composure was returning. She thought of Chrystal and her family. She'd met Katherine. She'd hadn't met the men, but she'd read about them and seen pictures and video. Their deaths needed to mean something. "I don't want to be a coward."

He turned his head so that he looked right at her. "The line between bravery and stupidity can be hair thin." He pointed toward the Satwa. "Her docking bays are almost empty of big ships. Most captains are *protecting* their ships and crews."

"We're doing this."

"Then send some of the crew away. This isn't a military ship; you don't own them."

She took a deep breath. She hadn't expected him to keep arguing. "They signed contracts. We might need them."

"They all saw the High Sweet Home torn apart."

"So did I. For now, we're holding course."

He gave her an unreadable look—not quite hostile; not exactly forgiving. It made her want to wince. She repeated herself. "We're holding course."

As if the station had heard her statement, the first hail from the Satwa came over the loudspeakers and she and Henry and the rest of the staff in command looked up at the screens.

A woman with skin so white she must color it that way, pale blue hair and eyes to match, and large pink lips smiled at them, her image filling the screen so she seemed to loom into the room. "I'm Shoshone Remore, and it's my job to welcome you to the Satwa. Your nav computer has instructions to guide you in. Ambassadors are to join us for our evening meal at 18:30 hours."

Henry stood up. "I'd prefer to stay with the ship. I'll look after the crew."

He knew Nona didn't have that choice. "Thank you."

———⊶⊷———

At 18:00, Nona sat in a bar sipping too-sweet white wine with Charlie. They had found a table in front of a window that looked out into the docking bays. To their left, the bays that held the *Savior* were far from empty. Ships in various stages of repair had all been pushed close together. On the right, various mechanical parts were slowly changing configuration, opening, creating room for a bigger ship. Only two other people occupied the bar, a man bent over his slate who hadn't looked up since they came in, and a woman who was busy drinking shot after shot, each one brought on a gleaming tray by serving-bot.

"How dangerous do you think it is to be here?" Nona asked.

He pointed to the drinking woman. "Less dangerous than she thinks it is. But it's bad." He glanced out the window. "Think of it as a first-contact exercise, only we know the aliens we're about to meet are hostile. We know they have bigger guns than we do."

"You think the Next are aliens?" She plucked absently at a gingery bite from a small dish of fruit and cookies the bot had brought them when they sat down.

He countered with, "Do you think they're human?"

"No."

Shoshone walked in and pulled an empty chair over to their table. "You must be Nona and Charlie."

"Yes." They held out hands and introduced each other all around. Shoshone ordered water and helped herself to a piece of their fruit. She seemed even brighter in person, the colors she'd chosen for her body making her look as if she'd been hand drawn and sent off to live her life as an exercise in color-blocking.

"Thank you for your hospitality," Nona said.

"Don't thank me too fast. You're not welcome here."

For a moment, Nona was too shocked to speak. "Do you think it's our fault the *Bleeding Edge* is landing here?"

"Absolutely. And that all of my business has fled—except you. We're too small to save the universe here. I came by to make sure you two know that."

Nona bristled. "Then whose job is it?"

"This is a big solar system. We can let them take what they want and hope they leave most of us alone."

"We could," Charlie said. "I have to admit that I'm a little scared to be here."

Shoshone smiled, and Nona relaxed a tiny bit. Charlie had figured out exactly the right thing to say.

"Have they talked to you at all yet?" Nona asked Shoshone.

"Just computer to computer. I hear they have pet humans, and I expect that's who we'll eventually see. I'll tell you what I learn when I do. That's why I came to find you. Let me manage this. It's my station. I won't have you putting the Satwa or its people at risk."

Everyone was accusing her of risking lives. Didn't they see the size of the stakes? "We can't just give up."

Shoshone shook her head. "It's not my job to save the universe. It's my job to save this station."

"We're just here to listen—and to report back to Gunnar. We won't be in your way."

Shoshone gave them an over-bright smile that looked like it belonged on a kid at a birthday party. "Nothing leaves this station—even information—without my approval while the *Bleeding Edge* is here. Do you understand that?"

When neither Nona or Charlie answered right away, Shoshone added, "If you don't, you can leave right now. There's three more hours for ships to get away before the *Bleeding Edge* docks. You can take advantage of that."

Nona's heart pounded so hard in her chest that she felt her heartbeat in her neck. "No."

Shoshone looked from one of them to the other. "Either you acknowledge that I am in charge here—unequivocal charge—or you leave. We don't run things Diamond Deep democracy style out here. I expect you to leave or join me and my senior staff for dinner."

"We aren't leaving."

"And you won't send anything in or out of this station without my permission?"

Nona felt backed into a corner. She couldn't afford to become powerless and she wasn't about to leave. "We'll join you, but Gunnar Ellensson sent me. He owns a good part of this station, and I'm here at his bidding." Nona stood up, which gave her a few inches of height on Shoshone. "If there is any message I deem an emergency to save my station or my ship, or that Charlie needs to get to Lym, I *can't* promise I won't send it. That's what I'm here for. But if I can find you first, I will."

Shoshone stared at her, hard, the tense lines of her body odd given her coloring, so she looked like a toy soldier.

Nona fought for calm while refusing to look away.

Eventually, Shoshone nodded and said, "Don't kill us all for no good reason."

"I'll do my best," Nona replied.

"I'll see you in fifteen minutes. Dinner will be a formal welcome, as befits someone sent by Gunnar Ellensson." Shoshone walked away. Maybe pranced was a better description.

The slight but approving smile that touched Charlie's eyes told Nona that she had done well, and offered the tiniest bit of warmth to offset the ball of cold fear in her heart.

CHAPTER THIRTY

CHARLIE

A long, silvery robotic arm delivered a light pastry with a red berry sauce drizzled across the top. Charlie hadn't been so relieved to see a dessert course come in a long time. He and Nona were separated from each other by three people. There were twelve around the table. Shoshone and her intimate inner circle as far as he could tell. At any rate, there seemed to be an unreasonable amount of simpering, and that, in turn, appeared to be covering political undercurrents he had no idea how to read. The tension circling under the surface of the room was thick enough to drown in.

He had listened carefully during introductions, but he was certain the woman Gunnar had told them to find wasn't here. Amia. Instinct told him not to ask.

He didn't like being so far away from Nona that he couldn't hear what people said to her, or how she replied.

Shoshone sat on one side of him. On the other side, a tall willowy person named Miro had the most alluring parts of both a man and a woman warring in his or her face: high sharp cheekbones, piercing blue eyes, full pink lips and a ridged brow. Miro was saying, "Surely if you used more nano down there, you could get the restoration done sooner, and then more people could come visit. Isn't Lym kind of like a big museum? And wouldn't that make you more self-sufficient?"

Charlie took a sip of hot tea and reminded himself the awkwardness of the table talk almost certainly covered fear. After all, the *Bleeding Edge* would arrive just a few hours from now—which also kept wine and spirits off the table. At least Shoshone had that much sense.

The dinner felt surreal. If he were running the station he wouldn't be eating now, at least not at a formal dinner. He'd be pacing, and searching news channels, and meeting with senior staff. He'd be trying to work through fears with people. Shoshone was hosting an awkward party and talking about everything but the threat bearing down on them.

He picked up the pastry and bit into it. It melted in his mouth, the berry flavor just tart enough to offset the sugary bread. "Museums are dead and about the past," he told Miro, even though he didn't expect anything he said here to matter. "Lym is alive, and what we're doing there is for everyone's future. We're re-creating a healthy planet to remind us that we're natural beings." He winced. He must sound like he was lecturing.

Shoshone put a hand on his shoulder. "Pardon me. I need to interrupt."

Her blue eyes were bright with some emotion he couldn't quite identify. Excitement? Nerves? She lifted a hand and he heard a soft click. A screen blossomed to life, and Shoshone stood up. "I give you the last ship to leave us before the Next arrive."

Realization dawned slowly. If it wasn't the *Sultry Savior* pulling away, then it was her twin.

Nona had come out of her seat. "That's my ship!"

"I was very clear about your choices," Shoshone said. "I messaged your second. Told him you'd decided to send the ship away for now. For its own safety, of course."

Charlie stiffened, angry and alert all at once. "Why?" he demanded.

"Because now *I* control every outgoing message from here. You're from in-system. You can't know what it's like to live near the Next."

Shoshone had said "Next" as if it were an honorific. He was beginning to understand the red flags the woman had been setting off inside of him. "Don't you work for Gunnar?" Charlie asked. "He wouldn't approve of this."

"It was a perfectly logical choice for Nona to send the ship away. Besides, Gunnar's nowhere near us. The *Bleeding Edge* is going to be here in two hours."

He hadn't read Henry as a deserter, so Shoshone must have been very convincing or Henry far more afraid than he'd shown.

Shoshone continued. "Dinner's over. You two are confined to quarters."

Charlie glanced at Nona. Her face had gone white and her fists were clenched at her side. To her credit, she didn't say anything.

He had come to dinner with no weapons other than a knife he always kept in his boot. He looked around. Two of their dinner guests had risen with Shoshone, and they each held a stunner. One pointed at Nona and one at him.

<hr>

Shoshone and her two armed minions followed as Charlie and Nona were led back to their rooms. They passed guards at the end of the hallway. "You'll be comfortable." Shoshone said. "You can talk to each other, go between your rooms. But you can't leave your shared hallway."

Charlie ignored her. He caught a glimpse of Nona's face before she was ushered into her room. She looked pissed off. Good. Pissed off was better than depressed. Shoshone led him into his own room and closed the door behind him. He sat down on the sofa.

"Come here."

He recognized the voice, and followed it.

Gunnar Ellensson sat on his bed. Or maybe hulked on the bed was a better word. Gunnar was so big he took up half of the room.

Charlie must have looked as surprised as he felt, and as mistrustful. Gunnar gave him a soft smile and said, "Sit down. I'll explain."

"Are you crazy?" Charlie asked. "What are *you* doing here?" He led the way into the sitting room.

Gunnar lumbered after him. "Instead of hiding in my station like a good little rich man?" Gunnar asked.

Anger tightened Charlie's muscles, the anger that came with fear when he was in danger at home. He decided to treat Gunnar as if he were a pack of tongats. "I wouldn't expect someone with so much to lose to risk physical travel."

"I flew my own ships for the first ten years of my business. Sometimes I still do. You've just joined the other ten people in the solar system who know that."

Charlie was still trying to parse the idea that Gunnar was here at all. "That's a lot of risk."

"You're young. When you're my age, you just might realize that risk is your best friend."

Charlie pointed at the door to the corridor. "So is Satyana with Nona?"

"No. Amia. And I'm not staying. I apologize for that, but you and Nona are far safer here than I am. I'm news everywhere, as well as a target. But I needed to warn you two."

"Warn us?"

"I learned a few things since I sent you out here."

Charlie thought a moment. "Maybe we have, too. Like that the woman you told us to find is stark raving mad. Shoshone doesn't like you much better than she likes us."

"She doesn't know I'm here now. Amia smuggled me in."

Charlie raised an eyebrow.

Gunnar didn't offer any information on how such a big man had gotten around the station unseen. Charlie thought about the awkward dinner. "She doesn't have a good hold on her people. Shoshone."

"They underestimate her. See that you don't."

A stray thought wound its way out of Charlie's mouth. "That's why the ship left. You told it to. I couldn't figure out why Henry would betray Nona. But he was obeying you."

"And I rank Nona."

"Even on her own ship?"

Gunnar didn't reply.

Charlie had been angry since he left Shoshone's table. The anger felt deeper now, more dangerous. "Tell me what you came to tell us." He pointed at the door and, by implication, at the guards. "This is far more dangerous than I had thought. You lied."

Gunnar looked exaggeratedly patient. "That's why I'm sitting here in the clear in your room."

"What ship did you come in on?"

"A local one. Belongs to the station. It's gone already—back out patrolling the perimeter."

"Is it coming back for you?"

Gunnar shook his head. "There are some life boats. I'll get to one in a few minutes and my ship will pick me up. In the meantime, do you want to argue or do you want me to tell you what I know?"

"First, tell me how you beat us out here."

"I have ships that are faster than Nona's. The *Savior* was built to explore, not defend."

Something in the look on Gunnar's face reminded Charlie that he had decided this man was an enemy long ago. "Why did you come to see me instead of Nona?"

"She's being watched more closely than you are. Besides, Nona would be a lousy poker player."

"Is Satyana with you?"

"She's back on the Deep, orchestrating the Council's response to this mess." Gunnar put a hand up to forestall more questions. "Here's what I came to tell you. This station has been working with smugglers from the Edge for a long time."

Charlie frowned. Bad news.

"I didn't know that when we decided to send you here. Amia suggested I get here before the Edge ship. I am only a third-owner of this station. Shoshone works for all three of us. She managed to see that we each had our interests met for some time. Our needs weren't conflicting, and everyone paid her well. Do you understand the setup?"

"Meaning, do I understand that you could get into a lot of trouble for associating with smugglers? Who are the other owners?"

"We're all traders." Gunnar stood up and paced, his bulk filling the small room. "One of the other two builds ships. Maninara. Amia doesn't think Maninara works with the pirates. I'll be using one of *her* ships to get away. I've reserved one for you two, as well. It's small but it can get you out where we can pick you up."

"Really?"

"It's number seventy-five. Can you remember that? Nothing can be written down. All of the Satwa's systems should be considered compromised."

"By who?" Charlie wanted to know.

Gunnar was frustratingly good at avoiding hard questions. "The third owner traffics in robots. Zin Grey. His story has always been that he created robots designed to work autonomously this far from the sun. The High Sweet Home was a client of his, for example. But Amia informed me he's been trading with the ice pirates for the past fifty years. Illegal. Apparently it made Zin and Shoshone both very rich."

Charlie wished Gunnar weren't pacing, so there would be room for him to pace. "So the Edge has been smuggling robots into the inner system?"

"I don't know exactly. Amia told me she doesn't know either. They've been taking bots from here out to Edge for years. Lots of them. She says that's the biggest trade by far."

"Why would the trade go that way?" It seemed to be just plain wrong. Trading with any being outside of the Ring of Distance at all was so illegal that Shoshone could be locked up forever if she were discovered. The crime might even taint Gunnar by association, or touch Charlie and Nona.

Gunnar stopped just in front of Charlie. "I don't know. It must go both ways. We found more Next on the Deep, and other stations are reporting them, too."

"There are robots on Lym that shouldn't—perhaps—be there."

Gunnar cocked his head. "You're certain?"

"Almost. Someone I knew well died to tell me that."

"I've got to go. Don't write anything down. Don't message us. Just learn what the Next want, then get away. We'll find you."

"Will you try to find out if the Next are on Lym?"

Gunnar hesitated. "I won't protect Lym over the Deep."

Bastard. Or over Mammot went unsaid. "Just tell me if you learn anything. That will be enough."

Gunnar nodded, ever so slightly. But he promised nothing. "Keep your head down, and make Nona do that, too. Keep her safe. Satyana's worried."

Maybe that alone explained why Gunnar was way out here. But he wasn't offering to take Charlie or Nona to safety.

"Tell Nona everything I've told you, but only in your rooms and when you're alone. Don't even tell Amia. Tell no one but Nona, and only in this room or her room. Amia assures me that all the rooms here are privacy shielded. Talking is the safest way to communicate. Get away when it seems right, and one of my ships will be waiting for you."

"But you don't think we should leave now?"

"I suspect there will be a role for Nona yet."

Bastard. Charlie said nothing.

"Stay here," Gunnar told him. "Don't move for three minutes."

Gunnar left the main room and went into the bedroom.

Charlie waited, expecting him to come back out. When he didn't, Charlie looked for him. There was no sign of the big man. The floor was hard, so there weren't any footprints to serve as clues.

He'd have to figure out how Gunnar got away later. Before that, he needed to check on Nona.

CHAPTER THIRTY-ONE

NONA

Nona managed to hold her anger close until after the door closed behind her, with Shoshone on the far side. How could the woman confine *her*?

How could Henry James have left?

She knew Henry disagreed with her; she knew she hadn't made any real effort to become his friend. She'd been—at best—a capable captain. In spite of that, she hadn't taken him for a deserter.

"Shoshone can be a real bitch when she wants to be."

The voice startled Nona.

A woman sat casually in a big chair in the corner of the suite. She was tall and willowy, with a typical spacer's short haircut. Her hair was as dark as her eyes, with a bloom of light blue at one temple—a look that must take some effort to maintain. Nona braced and took two deep breaths, fighting for calm, then stuck her hand out, trying to offer something more personable than the livid, raging anger that filled her. "I'm Nona."

"Nona Hall. I know. Gunnar told me to expect you."

Nona still hadn't quite recovered her composure. It took a moment to pull the name Gunnar had given her free of her tangled and pissed-off mind. "Amia. You're Amia."

"That's right. And you have a temper."

"Not usually," she snapped. "Just since people started abandoning me and locking me up." Her hands shook.

"Are you mad at Shoshone or at yourself?"

"Who the fuck do you think you are?" Nona snapped.

"Take a few more deep breaths."

Nona forced herself to stand still and do just that. Amia was here, behind the guards, just like Nona. At any rate, the woman didn't deserve to be cussed at. "You're right," Nona said. "I'm sorry. I've never been locked up anywhere before, not for anything."

Amia smiled. She stood up, or maybe unfolded would be a better word. The top of Nona's head ended under Amia's shoulder.

Amia pointed at the captain's insignia on Nona's chest. "You're used to being in charge."

That made Nona laugh. "Not really. I'm actually kind of new at it, and given that my ship flew off without me and I'm in here now, I suspect I'm not very good at being in charge yet."

Amia shrugged. "These are strange times. The bogey man's coming to get us."

Nona didn't have anything useful to say about that. "How did you end up in here?"

"Shoshone knows I'm Gunnar's primary information source. She's still pretending to support Gunnar, but you shouldn't believe it."

"Maybe I shouldn't believe anyone anymore."

"I usually don't." Amia smiled.

Nona didn't know what to make of her. Amia had gone from probing questions to being nice in a suspiciously short time. "What do you know about the pirates?"

"They aren't."

"Pirates?"

Amia sat on the bed and stretched, slowly and deliberately. She had the flexibility to clasp her arms behind her back. "They're not that. Not usually anyway. Once in a while they take a ship that's stupid enough to come near the Ring." She flattened her torso against the bed between her legs, a move Nona would fail at completely. "But what would you do if you were starved and someone put a tray of meat in front of you?"

"They eat the ships?"

"They learn from them. They use the energy and the metals and the knowledge that's there."

"Is that what they did to the High Sweet Home?"

"They destroyed it." Amia sat back up with her legs folded under her. "Nothing is wasted way out here."

"I think they killed my best friend," Nona offered.

"They don't care. I've seen their representatives here a time or two. Maybe I've even seen the Next themselves. You can't tell, you know. We all have robots. But there's a coldness about them, a way they're distant. Like they've gone so far beyond us they don't care about us anymore."

"So what do they care about?"

"Power."

"Power? Like over people?"

Amia laughed. "No. Power from the sun. Raw materials. They've built a whole thriving world—more than we know, I think, more than we know. They built all of that beyond the Ring, and now they want more."

"Are they mad at us?" Nona asked. "For banishing them? Mom always said she didn't think so. She met one once, said it sacrificed itself for her and dad and Ruby Martin."

"I know that story. I don't believe it."

The story was so much a part of Nona's history, she didn't know what to say. Of course it had happened. "She did sacrifice herself. But that was after she killed some of my mother's friends. I always got both parts of that story. Mom made sure I didn't believe the pirates were good or evil."

"I'd believe that part. The idea that they killed. You see, the trick is to stay hidden. They don't hate us at all. We might as well be asteroid dust that someone tracked into their solar system. If we get in the Next's way, they'll incinerate us."

"So if we went out beyond the Ring, they'd just move in, and they wouldn't come after us?"

"Yeah. Like that." Amia went quiet. "But we won't. First, we'd never survive. We're flesh, and we haven't done much engineering for the dark cold of nothingness past the Ring. Shoshone isn't going to abandon Satwa. Gunnar's not going to abandon Mammot."

"And Charlie's not going to abandon Lym," Nona whispered.

"Who's Charlie?" Amia asked.

As if he'd been listening for his cue, Charlie opened the door. "That's Charlie. He's an ambassador from Lym."

Amia's expression suggested that Charlie wasn't quite what she had been expecting. Nona had to admit that he looked uncomfortable in his party clothes, and a little more like a ruffian than most of the men she'd met out here or knew from the Deep. He also had a really strange look on his face right now, as if he struggled with disbelief.

Maybe he'd never been locked up either.

They exchanged introductions, and then Charlie said, "Amia, will you excuse us? I need to talk to Nona alone."

Amia didn't look at all surprised by his request.

When the door closed behind her, Nona looked over at Charlie. "She thinks we're going to die. She thinks we're all going to die."

Charlie crossed the space to her and folded her in his arms. He warmed her almost immediately and she found herself melting into him, tears running down her face. He was smart enough not to tell her it would be okay, but to just hold her. He was trembling, but far less than she was.

After a while, neither of them trembled anymore.

CHAPTER THIRTY-TWO

CHRYSTAL

Chrystal focused almost all of her processing ability on a virtual yellow cube in front of her, reaching out to bat it into place next to another yellow cube. The images fused and floated in front of her as if they were one piece. Yi was up to three. She used a simple swatting gesture to send the next piece that materialized in front of her to block one of Yi's red pieces, and at the same time Jason sent a blue block into her string of two yellows, which disappeared into thin air. She grunted and re-focused.

The goal of the game was to create strings of at least three similar blocks of your own color while keeping the other two from doing the same. Three or more stuck together and couldn't be destroyed. The person who built a whole wall first won. As easy as it looked, the game would have been impossible in her old body. She wouldn't have been able to hold her hands up and keep them dexterous for so long, not with nothing but air to rest them on. But this body didn't even tremble with the effort.

The game posed an interesting challenge, but Chrystal wasn't really enjoying it. Part of her attention remained split on the upcoming docking. She hadn't seen a human since they . . . since their bodies died. Were killed. What would it be like to see Nona? Would they let her see her right away?

Yi had looked distracted for the last hour, *and* he was losing the game. Chrystal was certain both that he wanted to say something and that he would only do so in his own time.

Jason muttered about the game as he played, calling out colors and verbally telling himself what to do. Annoying, all the more so because he was winning.

A screen on the far wall displayed the positions of all known ships and stations in the vicinity at all times. The Satwa had just begun to show on the screen, a small dot in the right hand corner. She switched the view to one of the screens on her wearable so she'd have better track of it, setting an alarm for an hour before they actually approached.

Yi elbowed her. "Is there anyone inside?"

He meant inside of her, the way their teachers occasionally seemed be under their skin or cohabiting with their brains. She shook her head. "I think I'm clear."

Yi glanced at Jason, who nodded, made a final flourishing move, and won the game. "Sure, let's try again."

Braiding had begun to feel like a mysterious power out of a comic instead of something they might actually be able to do. She didn't want to spend more time on it. "We have to get ready for the station."

"I know," Yi said, with a slight grin. "Trust me. I have an idea."

She sighed, an affectation she'd had to relearn. She could take in air with her new body and let it go, even if she didn't need it. Forcing minor human mannerisms gave her comfort. "Go ahead. Tell me what to do again."

"This time I want you and Jason to try it. We've been trying it with me, since I have a little experience. But maybe you two can do it while I talk you through."

Jason looked at her warily. "I'm game."

She had never really been able to refuse Yi anything. "Let's try it."

The pulled their chairs closer together so that their bare knees touched in a big circle. Jason took her right hand and Yi took her left. "Close your eyes," Yi said. "Humor me. Forget your bodies. Forget that you have bodies."

He was so sure of himself. Yi the engineer, certain of something that seemed more art than science, more mystical than mathematical. He muttered in low tones, in a slightly melodious rhythm that was different from his usual speaking voice.

"Let go of all of the things that you feel. Become larger. Become larger than you are. Reach out for each other with no boundaries, as if you were blending into each other's skin."

Katherine would have been good at this, she thought.

She would have, Yi replied. *I miss her.*

They were becoming better at talking to each other in their heads. Yi had explained that they must all share the same networks with the whole ship, maybe even the whole Edge society.

Yi remained convinced the braiding was more, almost to the point of obsession. "Become one with each other. Share your perceptions. Try a simple one. Share what my voice sounds like."

Even though they could both hear it?

As if he heard her question, Yi said, "You both experience the same thing differently. This is an opportunity to share the experiences of the other. Chrystal. Concentrate on the way that Jason hears me."

She did. Nothing.

"Jason. Concentrate on how Chrystal hears me."

She felt the faintest whisper of Jason inside of her, a feeling rather than a specific thought like those they had learned to exchange in conversation. It was both like and unlike the presence of Jhailing Jim, but if she'd had to explain how it was different, she wasn't sure she could.

Yi kept talking. "Let go of yourselves. You're safe. You'll return home wholly yourself after you touch each other's essences."

At least he hadn't said each other's souls.

That wasn't her thought even though she was thinking it.

Yi has become more human since he became a robot. I want to hear how Chrystal thinks, to touch Chrystal, to fold her up and protect her from whatever happened to Katherine. Sounds like. Focus on what Yi sounds like. Desperate. And good. Yi sounds desperate, and good. I want this to work for him.

She was feeling Jason's feelings. It wasn't exactly words. But if she had to write it down she'd manage an approximation. She heard Yi from two points of view, as if Yi's voice was isolated in two separate speakers and they each rendered him differently. *I love you*, she thought at Jason. Only she wouldn't describe it that way. That would be like saying she loved herself. She felt lost here, felt the missing fourth that was the absence of Katherine more than she herself felt it, felt Jason understand that she felt guilty for that, felt Jason sending her—sending Chrystal—a scrap of forgiveness and she sending back comfort and thanks.

They were two people still, but she could move between Jason's point of view and her own.

Yi guided, his voice sounding happier to them both, as if he knew they were feeling this together. "Stay simple. Think about when you met. Think about how you felt when you first saw each other. Remember that your minds work faster now. You can do many things at once, share and listen."

Chrystal wasn't interested in Yi right now, she was interested in Jason. In the night they met. Years ago. Maybe five years. She had already been with

Katherine, the two of them together in a bar, dancing. She had seen Jason moving across the room toward them, and he had seen them as two beautiful women so clearly in love that he envied them. Katherine's long hair attracted him, and the dragon tattoos they both wore. Sometimes in the light the two tattoos blended as if the dragons made love when they danced close and Jason coming toward them was large and bright and warm and he had a smile that stopped them both—they had been having this talk, she and Katherine, about how they loved each other more than light, more than music, more than dance, but they needed a balancing force, a third or a pair to add spice and the two women were looking at him like they might fall out of their world and actually notice him maybe even invite him and Katherine whispered in her ear that they should offer the man a drink and the smaller one smiled a smile so welcome he suddenly liked them both the same and when she asked him if he wanted a drink he told them he did.

It felt like magic. She was him and herself at the same time, remembering things she had forgotten and not sure if they were her memories or his.

After a time Yi's voice rose and intruded. "Start to talk in sentences to each other, start to separate."

Separation meant falling into her own voices and her own memories, looking at Jason and feeling herself, and then feeling the room they were in and the way all three of them touched knees.

Yi had a huge smile pasted across his face. She understood now why this mattered. Braiding. She felt bigger than herself, bigger than she'd ever felt before. She felt closer to Jason now, too, *of him*. Most importantly, she hadn't lost her sense of self. Even when she was in Jason and seeing through his eyes she had been able to tell Chrystal from Jason and yet also be Jason and Chrystal all at once.

She and Jason looked at each other, and in that moment and for the first time, she found his robotic self—his electronic self—as beautiful as she had found the man who swept them away in the bar all those years ago. A part of her wanted to fall right back into Jason's experiences and learn more about him, and a part of her wanted to pause and reflect on all that she had just learned.

It had felt like the moments after great sex, after a shared explosive orgasm when two people lay together, almost part of each other. Only this had been better, deeper.

And less sweaty.

The thought made her laugh, and broke the spell of it. "Why did that work?" she asked Yi. "That time? Me and Jason instead of you and me or you and Jason?"

"I don't know why it worked for you and Jason and not you and me so far. I suspected fear of intimacy kept us from succeeding, so I picked a memory you had each talked about to me, that I knew you liked, an event I thought you might like to share with each other."

"We did," they said almost simultaneously, and then they laughed, and Chrystal found herself unable to stop laughing. That hadn't happened to her since the capture of the High Sweet Home. The few times she'd tried, laughing had felt wrong in this body, like you couldn't laugh if you didn't breath. It still sounded wrong, but she recognized it and it made her smile and laugh again, and Yi joined in, and it took a few moments for them to get each other straightened out and in a position not to start laughing again as soon as they looked at each other.

"That could be one hell of a drug," Jason said.

Yi nodded.

Chrystal felt a little sick to her stomach.

The alarm went off, a blatting screech she had chosen to interrupt the game. They had an hour to get ready to board the Satwa.

CHAPTER THIRTY-THREE

CHARLIE

Charlie sat in the big chair in the corner with Nona on his lap, her head lolling on his shoulder as she dozed. He had failed to protect anything or anyone so far, and although he reveled in the warmth of the woman he held, it didn't bring him much comfort. Being trapped made him edgy.

Nona had started angry and afraid, and by the end of a long talk she had simply looked white and exhausted and heartsick. She didn't have the experience for this. No one did.

He didn't either, but he should have been more wary, and have built more alliances on the *Savior*. He'd stepped back so Nona could find her own leadership legs, get them under her. Maybe he should have given her more advice.

She moved against him, adjusted her position, burrowing. He wanted to tighten his grip on her but he didn't let himself.

Nona's talk with Amia reinforced the idea that Shoshone was working against Gunnar.

He hadn't had a chance to visit with Amia, so he hadn't been able to size her up. But if he understood power structures at all, he would bet that Amia's information was better than Gunnar's. If he needed to know how things stood in a situation, he always tried to ask the grunts, not the bosses. Gunnar scared him, and awed him, but Charlie doubted he was ultimately that different than any other boss.

His right arm started to go to sleep. He inched to the edge of the chair, leaned forward, and stood up carefully, balancing Nona like a child. He carried her to the bed and laid her down. He sat down near her, not touching her.

He wanted to touch her, to smooth the hair from her face. To let her know he was here, watching over her.

To do so would diminish her power. No matter how he looked at it, she had the power and the resources and he had the experience. They would have to work it out, but they couldn't do it as lovers. Not now, anyway.

Probably never.

The *Bleeding Edge* was surely about to dock or had docked, and they wouldn't know a thing about what Shoshone said to the ice pirates.

It struck him that the power differences between the pirates and the inner system were a lot like those between him and Nona. The people of the inner system had all of the apparent power. They held most of the cards that looked the strongest. They lived in the sweetheart orbits and their stations had as much living space as the largest planet. But they had been too self-absorbed to notice changes in the far reaches of the solar system. And now they were going to have to deal with something bigger than they imagined.

They had to succeed.

He didn't really see how it was going to happen, and so much of it was out of his control. Space was huge. They might succeed or fail here, but something different might happen in another orbit, weeks away in the fastest ships, and change the whole situation. He could only do his best, focus on now, and here, and what he could affect.

He imagined Jean Paul and Cricket in one of their favorite places, standing together on top of a ridge that overlooked rolling hills that led to the ocean, the moon shining on the water. The tongat needed him to save Lym, and Cricket had come to count on him for all things. He couldn't let her down. He couldn't die out here locked in a room and out of information.

He got up and opened the door, crossed the hall, and went into his own room. Amia was there, seated in lotus position. "Will you go watch over Nona for a while? I'll be back in a moment."

Amia nodded, flowing gracefully out of the room.

Charlie started looking for the way out that Gunnar had used.

BEING CHRYSTAL CLEAR

CHAPTER THIRTY-FOUR

CHRYSTAL

Chrystal felt Jhailing Jim drop into her shortly after they finished the braiding experiment. She half-expected him to react to the success she and Jason just had, or at least to react to her reaction to it, but he didn't. *It's time*, he told her. *Be in the landing bay in twenty minutes. Clothes are being delivered to your rooms for you.*

For all of us? It mattered.

Yes. Then he was gone again.

She glanced at the others. "Let's go. Jhailing's sending us with the landing party."

Yi and Jason looked as excited and dismayed as she felt.

They hadn't worn clothes since they were changed. They didn't get cold or hot and they didn't eat or have sex or have any other reason to cover up body parts. They moved freely.

"Time to play pretend," Jason said, as he slipped a blue dress over Chrystal's head. She helped both Jason and Yi pull on soft black pants. Jason wore a white shirt and Yi a brown one, both flowing and soft and piped in white, and each with the insignia of the Edge on the pocket: A pinprick of white perfectly centered in a bright yellow corona, with a significant circle of black between the two. The void between the sun and its rays was certainly meant to represent the inner system, only in this case there was no light. She looked down at her own breast to see the same sigil, and drew in a breath.

I am not them. But she didn't say it out loud.

That was, after all, why they had kept her alive, why they had brought them to this place. Maybe it was her chance to help humanity. Or betray them. She felt uneasy.

The landing bay was merely a large empty room near the lock where the ship and the station would join. When they arrived, there were at least twenty robotic bodies already there. Three were an expensive shape-shifting model where metal flowed from one form to another. She had seen similar bots on the Deep in the hands of the very rich and of the ruling Council. Beside them,

Chrystal's small and humanoid form seemed like a toy. Others were humanoid or many-limbed or simply cylindrical.

Two true-humans stood across the room from her, lost in quiet conversation. They glanced up curiously when she and her family entered and then looked away again quickly. Some of the Next's pet smugglers? She had never met any—as far as she knew—but she had heard rumors of them in bars on the High Sweet Home.

One of the shape-shifting robots created a tiny appendage on the top of its rounded form and waved at her. At the same time a Jhailing spoke in her head. *I have taken this body.*

Jhailing Jim formed them into a line, with Chrystal and her family almost last. The two humans followed them, and then Jhailing Jim followed them all like a rear-guard.

As they started forward, Chrystal realized that she wanted to see Nona, but she didn't want Nona to see her. Her uneasiness deepened when she realized she wasn't afraid to see Nona. She was ashamed.

———— ✦ ————

They flowed through the door in the order that Jhailing had placed them, filling a hangar-like space just inside the station. Three uniformed men had come to meet them. After formal greetings that Chrystal couldn't see or hear very well, the leading robot went with the men.

One of the shape-changers became a screen and shortly the view from the one who had gone further into the ship played on it. The uniformed men were there, and three other people, including a painted-face woman she'd been shown a picture of. The woman reminded her of a doll, or perhaps of a clown.

The display technology fascinated her as much as the picture itself, until Yi poked her in the side and whispered, "This is for us. Most of the others can be there in part, in the room. It's likely they can all share space in at least some of these bodies."

It was obvious once Yi said it. "That's more than braiding?"

"It's different. When everyone is software there are a myriad of relationships people can have with each other, and ways to send parts of yourself out and leave real-time threads. To be . . . distributed."

She held up her hands. "We're not just software."

Yi grinned. "No. Not yet, we're not. But already we can be closer to each other than we ever were."

"You sound happy about that," she whispered back.

"Aren't you?"

She and Jason shared a glance. Neither of them had accepted this new state as willingly as Yi, who had begun to relish it. But she *had* loved braiding with Jason.

A raised, robotic voice turned her attention back to the screen in front of her before she had to answer Yi.

The leading Next had started speaking. "Thank you for inviting us to come here. I am Jhailing Jim, a representative of the Next."

Sometimes it seemed like half of the Next were Jhailings.

The one who was speaking to the leaders from the Satwa said, "We are here to prepare you for what will happen next."

That didn't sound like a negotiation.

She searched the room for Nona.

CHAPTER THIRTY-FIVE

CHARLIE

Charlie ran his hands over every doorframe in the room Gunnar had gone into when he disappeared. Nothing. He knocked on walls, sliding from room to room, checking them low and high. They all sounded the same. He tugged on air vents. Wherever the door was, it had to be big. *Gunnar* had used it.

He finally found a secret panel in the privy, on the wall that included the shower head. It folded in when he leaned on it.

The doorway led into a tunnel, with smooth walls and pale lighting. Peering in, he could make out that the tunnel turned left almost immediately. It barely looked big enough for Gunnar.

He almost took the step. Instead, he pulled the door closed and crossed the hall to get the two women. The guards had their backs to him, watching a screen showing a group of robots on a podium, and didn't turn when he crossed the corridor.

Chrystal and Amia followed him immediately when he whispered in their ears. Amia gave out a long, low whistle when he showed her the doorway. "You found that pretty easily," she hissed.

He said nothing, slightly offended that she hadn't expected him to find it.

The tunnel door was easy enough to close behind them, and after a quick sideways sidle through dim light, they came to another door. It led to the back of a cleaning supply closet just across a corridor from a lift. If they went down, they'd reach the ship's bays. "What should we do?" he asked Amia.

"Follow me." She led them to the same bar they'd been in before the dinner, with the view out over the docks. Now the big dock held an even bigger ship, which had to be the *Bleeding Edge*. No one tended the bar, but about a third of the tables were full. Amia chose a tall table near one of three screens, which were playing the landing speeches. It also had a good view toward one door.

Charlie approved.

No one seemed to have noticed them come in except a serving-bot. All eyes were on the screens. Each screen depicted one of two scenes: a close-up view of the Next's spokesman or a wide-angle shot of a room full of robots of all types and sizes, and here and there, a human or two.

A slender, tall robot with impossibly smooth and shiny skin spoke. In front of him, Shoshone stood with two guards flanking her, and three more right behind her. She looked very, very small and breakable.

The robot's voice filled the entire room, talking to the cameras it must know were there. It certainly didn't seem to be addressing Shoshone.

"You have three choices.

"You can fight us, which will result in many deaths. I believe we have demonstrated how simply we can accomplish that. We can host additional demonstrations if you choose.

"You can ignore us. You will need to keep your distance, and may need to move some of your people from certain places on Lym and Mammot."

Like hell. Charlie's fist clenched around the glass, his knuckles white. One of the other people in the room knocked a glass to the floor and another threw a towel at the screen. But otherwise a horrified silence fell as they waited.

"Your third choice is to join us. You can become like us and live forever."

It surprised Charlie that the robot turned itself into a large square and then a display screen, zooming in on a part of a room full of robots and people. It stopped, centered on two men in black pants and a woman in a blue dress.

The robot spoke. "These three were on the High Sweet Home, as were many others who we took and who have become like us. They are all more than human now. They can do more and see and smell and feel more. They can live forever."

Nona clutched his arm, digging her fingernails deep. "Chrystal," she hissed. "That's Chrystal."

She started to stand up, and he pulled her down. It was impossible to know if anyone was looking for them but drawing attention didn't seem like a good idea. "Shhhhh . . ," he whispered to her. "If it is, we'll find her."

"Damn," she whispered. "Damn." Her fists were clenched at her sides, and her face had lost all of its color.

The robot continued. "These three will act as our ambassadors. One of them knows one of your guests on this station, Nona Hall. They will be allowed to talk to each other. This should help you understand our situation."

Nona moaned.

Shoshone stepped forward. "I'll see that Nona is brought to you. We made sure that she'd be available."

Charlie sat back. "That explains a lot."

Amia stared at Nona. "How did they know you were here?"

Nona still watched the screen as if starved for her friend, even though the image was now an oversized view of Shoshone's face. "Maybe she told them."

This couldn't end well. The robot they'd been given a glimpse of might not be created from Chrystal at all. Or even if it had been, it wouldn't *be* Chrystal. "What do you want to do?"

Nona blinked and rubbed at her eyes with her fists. "I don't know. Give me a minute."

On the screen, Shoshone finished whispering into her shoulder microphone—probably ordering that Nona be brought to the robot like a human sacrifice. She returned to the main microphone and addressed the robot, clearly as aware as it was that they were addressing a larger audience. He imagined this scene being broadcast all over, to the Deep and Lym and every other station and ship. Shoshone said, "Thank you. I cannot speak for all of mankind, but I can speak for this station. We're excited about helping you."

Charlie tensed. Wrong answer. They had to fight these things. Fight them and win.

"I am ready, now, to become like you," Shoshone almost crooned it on the screen.

"Do you know why?" the robot asked her.

"Yes. I want a body that won't get sick. I want to know more than I know now. I want to talk without words. I want to become one of you and live forever."

The two people near her each took a step back.

A repudiation.

The robot noticed. It spoke to them. "You will have a few days to make your choices. People in other parts of the human worlds will be hearing this now as well. They will make their choices. We will be listening, and hoping that all humans choose to help us to create a shared future. No one gains if we are forced into war."

The looks on the human's faces gave nothing away. They stood as stiff as boards.

The robot addressed Shoshone. "We will go back to our ship for now, and some of us will return in a few hours to collect people who choose to join us. Please send Nona Hall to visit her friend at your earliest convenience."

"I want to go now," Shoshone said, her voice slightly high.

Amia spoke quietly. "Bitch."

Charlie added, "She needs to go now or be torn limb from limb by people who aren't ready to become robots."

On the screen, Shoshone was almost pleading. "I'm sure they're on their way now with Nona. I can come now. I'm sure that would be best."

The robot gave a small nod of its silvered head and told Shoshone, "As you wish."

Shoshone followed it out, and the door between the station and the ship closed.

"Traitor," Charlie murmured.

CHAPTER THIRTY-SIX

CHRYSTAL

Chrystal had almost recovered from the slight horror of having her image broadcast throughout the ship, and maybe throughout the solar system. Almost certainly throughout the solar system. This was a historic moment if she'd ever seen one.

Jhailing Jim could have prepared her.

The room felt crowded as the greeting party came back on board, including the stupid human who wanted to die. Her skin was true-white and everything else rendered in shades of pastel like a comic character.

She walked right up to Chrystal and her family. "Aren't you lucky?" She stuck a hand out. "I'm Shoshone, and I'm lucky, too."

So her personality was as comic as her looks.

"This is not luck," Jason said.

"Of course it is."

"Are you real?" Chrystal asked.

"What?" Shoshone said. "Of course I'm real."

"Why would you ask for this?"

Shoshone stopped, as if the question confused her. There was a shine to her eyes that made Chrystal wonder if the woman had taken drugs, or been given them, to allow her this grandstand moment.

Shoshone cocked her head. "Didn't you ask for this?" she said. "Isn't it far better than dying?"

"No." Chrystal paused, thinking through the possible ways to communicate to this woman how strongly she felt, settling on, "I'll never have children, and I'll never again make love to my husbands."

"I don't want either of those things," Shoshone said. "I've had all the sex that I want." She struck a pose that implied she was performing for cameras. "I want to go to the stars. I want to live forever. I want to be smarter."

Chrystal bit back the reply that clogged her throat, but Jason didn't show the same restraint. "You lose your very life. Your brain. They strap you to a board and they read your brain layer by layer and put it into a computer.

As they read your brain, they destroy it, fold by fold, cell by cell, neuron by neuron. These bodies, and the places where they uploaded our brains are fabulous and smart. They did not lie about that. But the Next have no memory of the cost." Jason stepped toward Shoshone. "We lost our family, our community, our work, our dreams. We lost our future. Maybe we're having a different one, but the loss is so great it is nearly impossible to bear."

Shoshone shuddered, a sudden flash of fear crossing her eyes. She looked back over her shoulder at the closed door, and when she looked at Chrystal again, there was a tear in her eye.

"We don't cry, either," Chrystal told her.

CHAPTER THIRTY-SEVEN

NONA

Nona clutched at her chest, breathing fast. Chrystal. The bastards had turned Chrystal into a robot. Her hands felt cold and her forehead hot. She wanted to turn and throw up. How could they? She rocked in her seat, keeping her eyes on the screen in front of her until it showed a nearly-empty room.

The Next wanted her to come see what they had turned her best friend into.

Charlie's facial features were a very careful construction of calm under eyes that reflected deep anger. "What are you going to do?"

"Go," she said.

"I can get you away." He glanced at Amia. "Two of us, at least. Maybe three. I have access to one of the station's life boats."

For the first time, Amia looked surprised at something Charlie said.

Nona hesitated. If she left they might be safer. If she stayed, she risked Charlie as well as herself. Now she knew what had happened, so she knew Chrystal hadn't survived. Not really. But she wasn't willing to be a coward. She took a deep breath. "I can't. This is what I came out here for. To save Chrystal. That was the driver."

"It's too late to save her," Charlie said.

"No." Charlie's doubt deepened Nona's conviction. "I have to see her. I'd never forgive myself."

"We have to start a resistance." His voice had dropped to harsh whisper. "We have to stop them. We banished them in the first place and we kept them that way. We can do it again. We just have to all act together."

Amia frowned, but again she said nothing.

"You're not making sense," Nona said. He seemed to be talking about something entirely different than she was. "Of course we'll resist, but right now we have a chance to learn about our enemies."

Amia spoke softly, her voice full of fear. "We might all be about to suffer Chrystal's fate."

Nona doubled over and dry-heaved. She'd missed that entirely. Dammit. She needed to be brave. That was why she'd come here. To be brave. To be like fucking Ruby Martin.

"We should leave now," Charlie said.

"You leave," she said. "I'm going to see . . . Chrystal. Whatever she is now. I have to." She might as well have been led here by the nose. Maybe she had been, by Gunnar. Probably. It didn't matter. There wasn't any stopping now.

Charlie was silent for long enough that Nona stood up and straightened her clothes and found her brush before he said, "I'm going with you."

She was grateful, but it felt wrong. "You shouldn't risk it. You have to protect Lym."

"How do I know what will protect Lym right now?"

Nona let out a long breath. "I'm going to brush my teeth and clean up." Her voice shook and cracked. "I'm going to walk in there before someone drags me in there. I want you to stay out here, so you don't get caught. I'll tell you what happens." Her legs felt weak as she walked to the bathroom. She half-expected Amia to follow her, but she didn't. That was okay. Maybe she'd explain to Charlie that the Glittering wasn't about to act as one unit about anything.

Nona took her time, struggling to gather her disjointed thoughts. The ice pirates didn't want to kill them, they wanted to turn them into machines. Chrystal was dead, Chrystal was metal and silicon and electronics. The Deep needed information. Nona needed information.

The dress uniform she'd worn to the dinner party forever ago looked halfway decent. She worked the worst rumples out of it with a damp cloth and combed her hair and brushed her teeth. She stood in front of the mirror for three long breaths with her head high and her back straight. She whispered, "I can succeed. I can succeed. I have passed many tests before." Her mom had taught her to do that before exams way back when she was in elementary school, and she had forgotten how well it worked until now.

When she got back, Charlie sat alone at their table. "Where's Amia?"

"Hiding from the robots, and from the people who locked her up."

"Oh. That makes sense."

"She wants to find out how many people are leaving."

"Do you think the Next will let people leave?" Nona asked.

"I don't know. I don't think the Next are all we need to worry about. Shoshone told her staff the Next came here because we did. It's possible some of them will believe her and they'll take out their fears on us."

She frowned. "The Next did come because of us."

"They came here because Gunnar wanted them to."

"Would he have done this if we weren't here?"

"Shoshone might have double-crossed him into it."

"Really?"

"She's acting like she thinks they're gods. I'm going to walk you to the doorway to find your friend, and then I'm going to do my own research."

She frowned. There was nothing in her relationship with him that suggested she could tell him what to do.

He took both of her hands in his and looked into her eyes. "Take care. Come back."

She bit her lip. "You take care, too."

For a moment it felt like he was about to kiss her, but he dropped her hands and looked away. "Let's go."

In the room where the robots had just been, ten or twelve people stood in the vast open space. They all stopped talking and watched as she and Charlie walked through them.

The airlock door between the station and the *Bleeding Edge* opened easily and let them in, enveloping them in silence. They waited through the timer and then stepped into an empty, cold room. They stopped, shivering. A reminder that most of the beings living on this ship didn't need heat.

Chrystal had always gotten cold easily. She often wore a coat when Nona wore short sleeves. They had played every afternoon, roaming through much of the Diamond Deep. Chrystal came from money just like Nona, and the two of them had high levels of access to the forests and the parks and even sometimes to Gunnar Ellensson's private reserves. They had built forts and harvested berries and taken pictures of butterflies on the Deep.

Maybe her memory of how to get ready for tests was all tied up with her memories about her childhood with Chrystal.

One of the silvery robots flowed in the door and then formed into a tall rectangle in front of them. "Thank you for coming," it said. "Chrystal is looking forward to seeing you."

It stood taller than her. Nona looked up. "Jhailing Jim?"

"No. But I could be. Follow me to see Chrystal."

What a strange thing for it to say about itself. But then Jhailing Jim was a strange name for a robot or an AI anyway. More of a performer's name.

Charlie had stiffened. "We came this far. We would prefer that you bring Chrystal here."

"Are you afraid?" the robot asked.

"Of course we are," Nona replied.

The robot hesitated a moment before saying, "I guarantee your safe return." With that, it turned around and headed toward the door. So much for assertive bargaining.

Charlie gave her a look that suggested she resist, but she took his hand and squeezed it. "Good luck," she told him. "Stay safe."

"I hate to leave you," he whispered.

She remembered what it felt like to be in his arms. She took his hand, squeezing it hard. "Don't get caught." She felt the separation as he turned away from her.

CHAPTER THIRTY-EIGHT

CHARLIE

Charlie walked briskly away from the Next and through the people still standing in the room. Amia was in hiding, Shoshone had been taken off. Gunnar was gone. Charlie's room might still be guarded. He went back to the bar.

It had grown more crowded. Multiple conversations flowed through knots of people standing or sitting in groups around the room. Perhaps he could learn who was in charge now that Shoshone had decided to turn herself into a robot princess.

He ordered a beer. When the bill came, he frowned. They must not make the beer on board. "Is there cheaper alcohol?" he asked the robot.

It turned out that whiskey was cheaper, which didn't make a lot of sense. But he'd keep that in mind in case he needed a real drink before this was over.

At least the beer was good. Even though the room wasn't full, he was willing to bet well over half of the humans left on the Satwa were here. He didn't recognize any of them and with luck they wouldn't know his face either. Two men and a woman were talking loudly enough for him to overhear, so he sat on a barstool near them.

"—can't help the pirates—"

"Next."

"Whatever. We can't help them anymore."

"I didn't think it would do any harm. Trade them a few raw materials for a few serving-bots."

"What are you going to do with credit after you're a robot?"

"It's not going to happen."

"We have to leave."

"They'll shoot us."

"Pour me another drink."

There weren't any solutions there. Just stupidity. He walked casually over to a large group of people dressed in mechanic's jumpsuits. They were working their way through shots of whiskey with beer chasers, which was probably a day's salary for common workers. He hovered near the edge, quiet since this group was almost whispering.

"—let us go."

"They won't shoot us all. Bad PR."

"Remember the High Sweet Home."

"Can we trade them some? Give up a boss or two?" A tall red-haired man looked around the room, his gaze lighting for a moment on the people at the bar where Charlie had just been, and then on Charlie himself. "Who are you?"

"Nothing the robots want. Charlie. Charlie Windar. I'm the ambassador from Lym."

"What makes you think the robots don't want you? Don't they want to steal Lym from us?"

His throat constricted. He coughed. "Yeah. But I was just in there and they let me go. They don't appear interested in bargaining with Lym at the moment." His own words struck him from inside, and he had to force himself to stay present.

A blonde woman who wore her shocking pink hair in two braids asked him, "What do you think, Mr. Ambassador. What should we do?"

He took another sip of beer, tried to figure out what to risk. "I can't choose for Lym. Not from way out here. So I have to get home."

"But if you could?" she asked.

"I'd fight."

A few solemn nods and a grin signaled that he'd chosen right.

"Do you have a ship?" the woman asked. "We're going. We figure they might let us go, since we don't matter any. That's what we're hoping."

He thought about the little seventy-five pod and the keys to her. "Only a small one. Are there more in the bay? Anything useful to get from here to Lym?"

"Can you fly?"

Nona could. Every ship had a flight AI anyway. "Depends on the ship."

The biggest man of the group stepped up to him. "If you rat us out, I will offer you to the robots myself, and if they don't want you I'll tear you in half. Do you understand?"

Charlie wasn't sure if he could take him or not, but the right thing to do was act respectful, so he did. "I won't tell on you. I don't wish you any harm."

"Why tell him anything?" one of the women who hadn't spoken yet asked. The expressions on other faces agreed with her.

The big man said, "Because I was on Lym once. For six months. It's the most beautiful place in the solar system."

Charlie smiled. "It is. By far."

The woman wasn't satisfied yet. "Keep him with us. That way he *can't* rat us out."

"No time to babysit," the big man said. He thrust his hand out. "I'm Larkos. Meet us in the ship's bay in two hours."

Only two hours? "I'm bringing a friend who came with me. She needs to get off, too."

"Don't tell her anything until you meet us," the woman insisted. She still hadn't offered her name.

"Not until just before," he promised. "But she'll need to gather her things."

"Go," Larkos said. "If you're late, we're leaving without you."

Charlie's beer was almost gone. He hadn't figured out who was in charge without Shoshone. Maybe no one.

He had made friends. Perhaps. He wanted another beer, but decided to nurse the dregs instead. There was still nowhere to go, so he went to a window seat and sat, staring out at the *Bleeding Edge*. Nona was surely still there, still inside. If she came out of there in two hours, he had a plan. If she didn't, he supposed he still had a plan—to take her and the little seventy-five ship.

But what if she didn't want to go? Then what?

CHAPTER THIRTY-NINE

NONA

Nona followed the robot. Beyond the doorway, the Next ship felt open and big. Rooms and corridors were sized too big for humans, and she shivered in the cold air. The *Bleeding Edge* hummed and creaked more than the sleeker *Savior*, or even the Deep. Color and odd-shaped designs coded areas and access levels and utilities, leaving the impression that she walked into a child's playground rather than a starship bristling with serious weapons. It wasn't beautiful or artistic, but rather confusing and almost riotous.

After just enough turns to leave her feeling lost, the bot led Nona into a room with white walls and four seats around a table. Four seats? Shouldn't there be five?

A pitcher of water and a single glass sat on the table. The robot poured for her, holding the glass out until she took it. "I'll come back for you. Don't go anywhere else." It left, although Nona had the sense it didn't go far.

The Chrystal robot came in, still wearing the blue dress. She was followed by two men who Nona recognized from pictures. Soulbots. They moved like people, looked like people, the differences so slight she couldn't name them even though she felt them.

Nona tried to hide a shiver.

All four of them regarded each other in silence.

The Chrystal soulbot looked like her friend. The dragon tattoo glittered in all its shimmery blue and green glory. The same dark hair spilled down her shoulders, maybe a little longer. Her eyes were the right shades of brown mixed with green, and her smile warm and natural.

Maybe too smooth, too natural?

The men were the same; they looked right and not-right. Nona had never met them, but she'd seen hundreds of pictures of them. Jason, who had been with them a long time. Jason had long dark hair highlighted with purple, and broad-shoulders that must have been born and nurtured in a weight room.

Yi was newer to the family. He had fascinated Chrystal so much that while they were all dating, Chrystal had written long notes about him to Nona, describing how brilliant and driven he was, what a good head he had for business. In truth, the family had started truly prospering after they added Yi, who was reportedly a prodigy at engineering and DNA, at physics and math. Yi looked like an anti-Jason: anorexic and thin-limbed, with unruly dark hair that flopped over wide, round eyes and sharp, high cheekbones. He had no decorations or tattoos, or anything else unique except his gawkiness.

Katherine was missing. Katherine and Chrystal had been together for decades; almost always together. Chrystal's family structure had been solid for years, and it had started with Katherine. Nona wanted to ask, but she was afraid to.

The look on Chrystal's face was human and full of apprehension and fear. Not of Nona—never that. Perhaps fear of what Nona thought of her now, of whether or not Nona would accept her.

The look didn't belong to a robot. It belonged to her friend. She had seen it before, and it was such a signature expression it couldn't have been copied.

The look drove Nona up out of the chair. She folded Chrystal in her arms. At first, Chrystal felt resistant, and then just stiff, and then she slid her arms around Nona and the two of them stood there for a long time. Holding Chrystal and being held by her felt good. No, it felt great. She had been so afraid for so long, so certain Chrystal was dead. But she wasn't. Not exactly.

The first overwhelming tide of relief ebbed, and Nona gradually became aware of a subtle sense of wrongness. She trembled in Chrystal's arms, but Chrystal was a rock. In spite of making the right movements, Chrystal's reactions were subdued at best. Her movements felt too fluid, as if she were an animated dancer instead of a real girl.

Chrystal didn't smell human. Maybe that was it. Emotions smelled, and Chrystal didn't. A subconscious thing.

Chrystal didn't tremble or cry or make a single awkward move.

Nona still sensed a connection between them, but it wasn't as exuberant or sweet as she remembered.

She put a hand on Chrystal's cheek. "I'm so sorry this happened to you."

Chrystal shook her head ever so slightly "Don't be. It doesn't do any good."

Nona wiped at her eyes and Jason handed her a tissue from a box on the table.

"Thank you," Nona said and then she whispered, "I hate them for this."

"Remember we are in the Next's ship, and I am now at least partly the Next's creature," Chrystal whispered back. "They are with me always now. We share a network, a world, a place. We talk to each other. I am myself and I'm not. Please believe both of those." Then she repeated one part of it. "I am myself and I'm not."

Nona nodded. "Okay."

Chrystal sat down and smiled. "Tell me a story. How did you get here?"

Tell me a story. Whenever they were away from each other for long, they said that. Nona wanted to cry all over again, and hated it for a weakness. She picked up the water glass and drank, covering her face briefly with one hand. When she regained control, she said, "We were on Lym, me and Charlie, when we heard about the High Sweet Home. We were sitting in a skimmer with a wide sky above us and a waterfall in front of us. As soon as I heard about the attack, I started trying to find out how you were. We left soon after and came out here, and we watched for you and listened for news every day. We didn't hear anything for so long, I was sure you were dead."

Chrystal looked slightly alarmed, and then she smiled, her expression almost natural. "You shouldn't have come," she said. "Now you're in as much danger as I am."

"Aren't we all in danger?" Nona asked. "No matter where we are? Who we are? The Next are going to change everything."

"Yes," Yi watched Chrystal with concern. "It's not your fault that Nona came, and she's right. No one is safe."

"Do you understand the Next?" Nona asked Chrystal. "Can you speak for them? Already?"

"I don't have any authority. But they've been training me in what to say to you to help you understand them."

"And what did they tell you to tell us?" Nona asked.

"In a minute. First, I want to know about you. You mentioned a Charlie. Who are you two to each other?"

In the old days, Nona would have told Chrystal about her conflicted feelings, and that she had just wanted him to kiss her. "We're both ambassadors—me for the Diamond Deep, kind of by accident. Or at least, not very officially. Charlie is an ambassador for Lym. I have a ship; we came out here in it. A big cruiser mom had built for me. Do you believe that?"

"Really? You have a ship?" Chrystal brightened, her new eyes alive with excitement. "Is it here? Can I see it?"

Bitterness rose in Nona's throat, but she managed to find neutral words. "It's somewhere safe. No one knows how frightened to be of the Next, but after what happened to you, the bets are that we should be very frightened."

Jason's voice was warm and rolling, a little sexy. "You *should* be frightened. You should leave us and run away."

"That's not what you're supposed to tell us," Nona observed.

"No."

Yi said, "The Next were all human once. Now their aims and dreams are different. That is already true for us three, a little." He stopped and waited for Nona to nod, as if he needed to be sure she understood his point. "We'll never be human again. Don't be fooled. We think faster, learn faster. We run faster, jump higher. We don't need to drink or eat. We don't need air or a narrow band of temperature. We are designed for space and spaceships, which you are not. If you weren't with us, it would be colder in this room. We are alive, but we are not human."

Nona drank some water, acutely aware that the others weren't drinking.

Yi continued. "We won't evolve backward into flesh."

Chrystal glared at him.

He smiled, and the infectiousness of his smile drew a smile from Chrystal. He continued. "We'll evolve forward, until we too can inhabit silvery robotic bodies, or perhaps even the bodies of spaceships."

A siren song about a robotic future. Nona shivered, the hand holding her glass shaking.

Yi must have seen it. "Yes, really. We are becoming more than we were. So much more. Jhailing Jim does not lie when he promises humans an evolution of their choosing."

Jason took over. "But the Next don't comprehend what we lost, or that more is not always better."

Nona hadn't known what to expect, but certainly it wasn't this conversation.

The white walls and simple furnishing and lack of any distractions but water were wearing on her mood, scratching at it like a swarm of not-quite-right.

Chrystal had spoken the truth. She moved with her own mannerisms, still had her own family—most of them—and still remembered her friends. She clearly cared what Nona thought of her. But she had also become something—different—than she had been. "Surely the choices are not as simple as they say," Nona mused. "Surely they'll negotiate."

"We don't know," Yi said. "We are not *of* them. Not yet. We're in some middle area in their culture where they're teaching us things. It feels as if we're children, maybe not yet even in grade school. We have value to them. We were told it was okay to be honest with you, and we have been. We were told to tell you to trust them, that they keep their word."

Yi glanced at Chrystal, who picked up the narrative. "I'm sure they will ignore you if you ignore them, as long as you give them access to the resources they want. They may want a lot, though." Her voice softened. "I have never been to Lym. I don't know for sure what they want there, but I think it is rare metals. Perhaps they can be asked about treating it well, or even about putting it back in order when they're done."

Nona imagined Charlie's reaction to being told Lym was likely to be ravaged, and if he was lucky, the bullies might fix it up before they left. "Lym is the most beautiful place I've ever seen. There are waterfalls and wild animals and untouched forests and sky. Charlie will die to protect it—I'm sure of it. And maybe he should. Nothing Gunnar created in his private reserves on the Deep is anything like it at all. Nothing."

Nona was amazed at how flexible Chrystal's robotic features were, at how they looked sad in a deeply nuanced way at this moment. "The Next are very single minded."

"Tell me all of the things that you know they want," Nona asked.

Chrystal shook her head. "I've told you what they have shared with me. They want us to be examples of what you can become in the short term, and they themselves are examples of what you can become in the long term. In all cases they believe they are far better." She looked down and then back up. "They *are* more capable. As are we."

"Capable of life. But is that the same as capable of love?" Nona asked. "Is that what you lost?"

Chrystal smiled once again. "I still love my family." She paused and then continued. "The Next don't want to be distracted by a war. If you become useful to them—in the way that they think of as useful—then you can come out and play. If you leave them alone, fine. But if you cause an uprising? You'll be squashed."

Nona heard each use of the word *you* as repudiation of Chrystal's humanity, and she hated it. "And they really expect all humans to make the same choice? Are they that naive?"

"I don't know," Chrystal said.

"Are they unified? Do they all want the same thing?" Nona pressed.

Yi answered. "The ones we've met are."

Nona looked from one to the other. "If you were still human, what would you do?"

They looked back and forth between each other, their facial expressions subdued.

Nona finished her water, waiting, feeling awkward.

Chrystal answered. "Knowing what we know? Help them or stay out of their way, but don't become them. If you ask us this again in a month, we might say you should become them." Chrystal glanced at Yi. "It doesn't take long to forget some of what it was to be flesh. We are trying hard to remember, but we don't have the same structures in our bodies any more, the same body memory, blood memory. Ours are the memories of machines."

Yi nodded. "There is an attraction to what we are becoming. The closer we get to it, the more we forget what we lost."

Jason cleared his throat. "I won't forget. Ever."

Yi gave Jason an incredibly gentle look for a robot. "You're closer to your old self than I am, closer by far. But each time we learn something new, it intrigues you."

Nona had expected it to be impossible for robotic bodies to blush, but nonetheless Jason's cheeks seemed to redden slightly as he looked away.

She had no idea what to say.

Chrystal gave her a long, measured look. "It's not a pretty picture. But you need to go and decide. You and the other humans. We can't help you."

"I don't want to go yet," Nona blurted out. "I miss you so much."

Chrystal stopped dead in her tracks, as unmoving as a statue. Then she said, "I miss you, too."

Chrystal talked like Chrystal, moved like Chrystal. But the creature in front of her didn't feel like Chrystal no matter how much Nona wanted her to.

Nona really needed to cry, but she wasn't about to do that here. She might hurt the robot's feelings.

CHAPTER FORTY

CHRYSTAL

As soon as Nona left, Jason took Chrystal's hand. The actual haptics of the touch were cool robotic hand to cool robotic hand, but she felt warmth from the gesture. "That was far harder than I expected," she said.

"Really?" Yi asked. "You looked very happy to see each other."

"I missed Nona long before this happened. I missed her the whole time we were on the High Sweet Home. We've been friends since we were little girls." She let her words trail off.

"She said she'd be back," Jason said.

"Talking to her made me feel more *different* than anything else has made me feel since . . . since this all started."

Jason squeezed her fingers. "I felt that, too. Like in the time it took her to start to reply to a comment, we could have had a whole conversation."

"I think that's part of why the Next created us," Yi said. His words came fast, the way they always did when he was learning something. "They can barely slow down enough to talk to us, to help us. I had a long talk with Jhailing Jim once about it—the one in our heads. He said it's very hard to work with the newly born, that we're slow."

"Don't use the word born," Jason snapped.

"I agree," Chrystal said. "We were born from our mother's wombs. What the Next did to us was death and engineering."

"Meeting your friend made me feel more like a robot." Jason swung his purple hair around, looking more like a person than a robot in that moment.

Chrystal laughed and withdrew her hand and stood up. "If anything happens to her I will come apart. I can't take it if they do this to her."

"Even if she *chooses* to become like us?" Yi asked gently. He reached across the table and picked up the water pitcher and the single glass and the box of tissues that had been there for Nona to use. "It's not that far-fetched. I might have chosen it."

She stared at him. "Really?"

"I'll never know what I might have done if asked." He looked away from them, staring at the wall. "I've always been fascinated with artificial intelligences. I talk to all of the ship's AIs that I can. There will be others like me. There will also be old people, and young. There will be poor people and the sick and the lost. The curious. Some will choose this."

"Nona won't." Nona had been horrified to see her like this. She hadn't come out and said so, but Chrystal knew every nuance of her friend's facial expressions and body language. She had been horrified and uncomfortable, and at least a little bit glad to leave when Jhailing Jim had come in to separate them.

"You won't come apart if she does," Yi said. "You're stronger than that. Besides, you are a person and so are Jason and I. We're just not human. We still have free will and dreams."

"Do we?" Jason asked. "What do I dream?"

"I want to go help them decide," Chrystal said. "I want to show them what we are, tell them, make them see what they lose."

"I think that's been the plan all along," Yi said. "That we would go into the inner system. I think they'll take us on the *Bleeding Edge*, as soon as they get through the volunteers here.

"Shoshone will regret her choice."

Yi frowned. "I heard that three others have come forward and asked to become like us."

Chrystal sat down again, feeling the tiniest bit of despair. Anyone who would die on purpose just to live forever was insane. If only there was a way to explain that.

CHAPTER FORTY-ONE

NONA

To Nona's surprise, she found Charlie in the waiting room where she'd left him, sitting in a chair and staring at his slate. He looked so relieved to see her that she immediately went to his side. "What did you learn?" she asked.

"There's no one clearly in charge here. No decisions. People are planning to flee or turn on each other. Shoshone left a mess, and everyone's afraid. Everyone. I have a way for us to leave."

"Leave? Now?" She stared at him, dumbfounded. "I can't leave Chrystal."

"What was it like to see her?"

For a moment she didn't know how to answer. "She's still my best friend."

"Really?" He looked doubtful.

"Now I wish you'd come with me. You'd have seen."

He responded with a wry smile. "I want to hear all about it. But first, we really do have to leave. Whether or not the station survives, it's dangerous here. Probably especially for you."

"I can't leave," she said. "Not until I see Chrystal again, not until I know when I'll see her after that. Can you imagine? Hi Satyana. I flew all the way out there and I got a half hour visit and I came home."

"I'm sure Satyana wants you safe." He looked miserable and intense all at once. "I don't want to leave you. I want you to come with me. But I have to go. I can't be turned into a robot or captured here. I have to save Lym."

"I see." She did. It made her cold and frightened, but she understood. "I'd give you the *Savior* if we still had her."

"I have a way out. A different ship. And I . . . I don't want to leave you here."

Her head spun. "I can't abandon Chrystal. Who knows what will happen to her?"

"Worse than *has* happened to her? She's less destructible than you."

"I have to see her again."

Charlie glanced at his slate. "We have half an hour. Can they come with us?"

Oh. Oh! "I don't know."

"Think about it," he said. "If they're prisoners, then they can't come, but you should leave before you get locked up by either side. None of us knows if we're trapped here, not really. Not until we try to leave. But the plan is for a lot of ships to go at once."

"They must have weapons on the *Bleeding Edge*."

He looked resolute. "I know."

"It's running," she said. "I don't think we should run."

He put a hand on her cheek, his palm warm. "Do you think we should stay? Really?"

She stared at him, trying to read the look in his eyes. Stubbornness, and fear. And concern. He was concerned about her. "Half an hour?"

He nodded.

"You be ready to go. I'll try to get to the bays in half an hour. If I'm coming." Everything was happening too fast. "I need to talk to Chrystal."

He looked miserable.

She took his hand in hers and brought it to her lips, kissed it. "For luck. Whether we leave together or not." She stood up and turned around, going immediately back toward the *Bleeding Edge*.

"Nona!"

She stopped.

"Good luck."

She nodded and turned away from him, blinking back tears.

⁂

Nona was pretty sure she remembered how to get back to the room she'd met Chrystal in. She stepped through the airlock and into the right hallway. Her footsteps were soft on the slick surface, a detail she didn't remember from her first trip along this corridor. Before she even got to the first turn, a small herd of tiny drones chittered in her face. She stopped. They must have some kind of propulsive force to keep them off the ground, but she couldn't tell how they worked. They moved too fast for her to get a good look, zipping here and there in front of her.

She took a step and they chittered more loudly. Chk-chk-chk-chk, like ball bearings running into each other at high speed, over and over. Chk-chk-chk.

Another step and one of them hit her, the pain a sharp pop in her jaw. Ten hitting her would make her scream. She stopped, staring at the swarm in dismay.

She felt the loss of each minute as she waited in the corridor, certain her idea was crazy. She couldn't kidnap Chrystal and her family. How would she convince them, and how was that being a diplomat?

What would Satyana do?

What would her mother have done?

Or Ruby?

One of the silver robots flowed up just behind the annoying little bots, appearing so fast Nona stepped back in surprise. It had thinned itself into a wall and leaned toward her so that she wanted to step back. "You are not authorized to be here now," it said flatly, neither curious nor threatening.

She took a deep breath and held her ground. "I want to bring Chrystal and her family over and have them meet some other people. My friends. It would help us talk this through. As soon as I stepped back into the station and started answering questions, I realized Chrystal should speak for herself."

"She may not want to leave."

"She doesn't have to. But isn't that what you made her for?" The robot in front of her had chosen such a bully shape that she started to stammer. "I . . . I . . . I think she should come all the way back to the Diamond Deep with me. She knows the station. She grew up there. People remember her. It will put a friendlier face on the Next . . . on you." She sounded like a seven-year-old trying to argue with one of her friends to come out and play. Dammit. She was bigger than this. She didn't come out here to be turned into a child by a robot. She stood straighter. "Please call the guards off?"

The swarm of small drones flew off behind the larger robot.

She breathed an almost silent sigh of relief. "Thank you. Let's start over. You gave us options. You asked for me to come to talk to Chrystal so I would understand those options better. That's part of why you came here. Am I right?"

"Yes. Partly. Also, we were invited by Gunnar Ellensson to see you."

"To see me specifically? By name?

"Yes."

Wow. She filed that away for later. "But I cannot speak for all humans, or even all humans on the Diamond Deep. After I met Chrystal and her family, I became certain that if more of us talk to her, we might understand you better."

"The Deeping Rules don't allow for our kind on the station. That will include Chrystal and her family."

"You know the Deeping Rules?"

"Of course. You must own yourselves. You must harm no one. You must add to the collective."

Nona took a deep breath, straightened her spine again, and said, "Turning people into robots against their will is generally looked at as harming them."

"I know the Deeping Rules," it said. "That is not the same as following them. Besides, I was once human, and I hardly view being transformed into a Next as harm."

Chrystal had been harmed, and Jason. Arguing about that point wasn't going to help her. But she had her family history. "The problem isn't the rules themselves. It's interpretation. There was a time when a trial happened, when one of your people helped Ruby Martin, who was my mother's best friend. The Next was once a human girl named Aleesi."

"She died for the help she provided."

"By her own hand, but she said it would not be death because there were more of her."

"That is one interpretation," the robot said.

Nona took a deep breath. "I know this story. My mother was there, in the courtroom. Aleesi defended us."

"We have no copy of that instance of Aleesi to check what she did or why. We can merge after we bifurcate, but not over distances as vast as the one between the Edge and the Deep."

She imagined Charlie looking at his watch, watching the door. "It's part of my family history. History, not legend. Besides, we only had her because you attacked our ship on the way in."

"Not me."

"It's history, it's all history. The exile of your kind came from every one of the stations, not just my home."

"Exile nearly killed us. That was what you hoped would happen."

The robot's words held no emotion at all, although she sensed that it felt deeply. She had no idea why she thought that. Maybe instinct. "I wasn't alive then. It wasn't me. I can work with the High Council. Chrystal is one of us. If they'll let any of you on board the Deep, it's Chrystal. That's what you made her for."

"You might be putting your friend in mortal danger." Still, the unemotional voice. She couldn't tell if she were convincing it at all.

"I won't. I'll know before we get there, make sure I have permission. If she's in any danger, we won't land."

"It will be her choice."

Something brittle and frightened released inside of Nona and she let out a long breath. "Can I go to her?"

"I'll take you."

She blinked. This was too easy. But there wasn't time to think about it, not if she wanted to see Charlie again.

CHAPTER FORTY-TWO

CHRYSTAL

J hailing Jim whispered a warning in all of their heads. *Nona is coming and she wants you to go with her.*

Do we have to go? Yi asked before Chrystal could even start to think through the implications.

No.

Chrystal took the conversation verbal to slow it down. "I want to go with her. If not now, what other opportunity might we have?"

Yi answered back quickly. "If we leave we won't have the Next with us. Not directly. We won't learn as fast and we won't be protected."

"This is what they created us for," Chrystal said.

Jhailing had been listening. *It is. We did not anticipate this would come so quickly. You may choose.*

That startled Chrystal. "You mean it's up to us. We can just decide to go?"

You are not our slaves.

In that moment, she realized she had been thinking that way. Robots, after all, had owners.

Yi didn't miss a beat. "Will we be able to talk between each other without words? Will we have enough bandwidth to think fast?? Will we be able to access the ship's computing the way we can yours?"

Chrystal hadn't even known he could do that. She certainly hadn't.

He kept going. "Who will teach us how much we can do with these bodies? What if we need to be repaired? What if someone does us harm?"

You will have your own internal resources, which are significant. You will be able to provide each other computing resources, to share with yourselves. We will send a bot, which can fix you, and which may be able to teach you some things. If you die, you will die. But we have backup copies.

They did?

You must choose quickly. Help is coming to bring you better clothes, and a pack has been created for you with things that you need.

"Backups? Are you backing us up before we go? Is it constant? How much risk is there?"

"Stop it, Yi," Chrystal said. "We can't know everything before we choose. I want to hear from Jason."

Jason spoke slowly and very deliberately, using his command voice. "We have to go. We might be able to help."

She sensed how careful his words were, and that he had more to say that he would not say around Jhailing. In a way, they were being offered freedom. "We will go, then. Yi?" She had only expected to fight Jhailing to keep her family together. The question was hard to get out. "Yi, do you want to stay?"

He looked at her in surprise. "I won't leave you."

She felt immense, slow, deep relief.

A small bot charged through the door, piled high with new clothes. They dropped the blue dress and formal outfits for the casual daywear of spacers—comfortable pants that tightened around the ankles, and short-sleeved tops, all of it tight enough that if they were still flesh they could slide a psuit over the clothes if necessary. The bot left, so clearly it wasn't the one that would accompany them.

The comfortable clothes signaled this had been expected by the powerful Next, no matter what Jhailing had just said. She felt . . . anticipation. Excited about the future. It settled over her that this was a good choice, and that they were going on an adventure.

She and her family were doing what they had been created for, and their robotic overlords had kept the right tools at hand to make it easy. She recognized the thought as sarcasm, and it made her smile. She would need sarcasm to be around humans—it was something she had been good at before.

Nona hurried through the door. She looked worried, the fine lines around her eyes tight and the line of her jaw rigid.

"Are you okay?" Chrystal asked.

"Just. Um, yeah. I'm fine. I . . . I have a question."

"We'll go with you."

Nona stopped, looking from one to another. "How did you know?"

"I told them," Jhailing Jim said from behind her. He had been sending them information nonstop since he told them about Nona. A lot of information: ways to repair each other, ways to talk to the humans about becoming

Next, ways to access and magnify data backup, ways to build security into conversations. It had flooded in so fast that Chrystal had to shut down her awareness of the thread and just let the information accumulate.

Nona still hadn't said anything, as if she were shocked.

"We're ready," Chrystal told her.

Nona nodded. "Thank you. I hope this is a good idea." Her voice was edged with stress. Nona glanced at the silvery form behind her, and then back at Chrystal. She looked frightened and earnest. "I'll do my best to keep you safe."

Jhailing Jim led off and they all followed, Nona first and then the others. A smaller robot pushing a wheeled case waited by the lock between the *Bleeding Edge* and the Satwa and followed them into the station even though Jhailing Jim did not. Jhailing didn't say goodbye or wish them luck, and it felt like he had missed a beat.

Yi interrupted her daydreaming. *Stay aware. People will be afraid of us.*

Thank you.

Jason went in front, behind Nona, with Chrystal next, and Yi last.

Nona walked fast, although she turned around to check on them from time to time. "Hurry. We've only got a few minutes."

Chrystal hadn't been near so much stimulation, so many people, since the last normal days on the High Sweet Home. The hubbub and movement pleased her and disconcerted her.

Most of the people they passed seemed like strangers to Nona, and certainly they were strangers to Chrystal and her family. There was no acknowledgement given, except maybe the barest of nods.

Chrystal had expected fear, especially after Yi's warning.

After five encounters, she realized that the people they passed didn't recognize them as robots. The clothes they wore were very different from the televised encounter, and common. They hadn't been the most interesting thing in the room either, or the most threatening. Maybe no one had paid them much attention at all. The robot that followed them with the case looked exactly like some of the other bots they passed. It appeared to be a common model in use on the station, although she couldn't quite puzzle out how it had gotten aboard the *Bleeding Edge*.

They rode in an elevator. Chrystal found the scent of Nona's fear and worry so disconcerting that she turned her ability to smell way down. She was afraid to let go of her other senses. The turn of gears. Nona's every breath. The shuffle of Jason's feet. The small judders of the elevator. The release of air, the tiny change in pressure as the elevator doors opened.

A square-faced man with grey-green eyes and almost as many muscles as Jason leaned against a wall, clearly waiting for them. He broke out onto a huge smile.

This had to be Charlie, from the relief on his face. "You got them out." He sounded surprised, and only maybe pleased.

"They chose to come," Nona turned to them. "This is Chrystal, Jason, and Yi."

"I'm Charlie. I'm sorry there's no time to talk. We've got five minutes." He started walking.

"Who are we meeting?" Nona asked, almost jogging to keep up with him.

"Friends." Chrystal heard the slightest uncertainty in his voice, and tested the air. He smelled of fear and sweat.

They ducked though a doorway marked as a repair bay, the sensors showing full atmosphere. Inside, repair slots lined up in a long row, straight for a while and then curving gently away with the arc of the station. Most were empty, but here and there a ship or part of a ship hung in slings and racks. Others sat out on the main floor, looking like they could be flown.

Instinctively, she queried Jhailing Jim. *What ships can we use?*

No answer.

A big man and a small blond woman with a ponytail and sharp jaws under a flat nose appeared to have been waiting for them "Larkos!" Charlie greeted the man ebulliently. "Am I glad to see you here."

Larkos smiled broadly at first, and then narrowed his eyes. "I thought you were bringing one person."

Charlie shrugged. "Everyone needs to leave."

Silence hung between them all for the space of three human breaths. The scent of fear rose, sweat and adrenaline.

"They're Next," the woman screamed. "Damn you!"

Larkos leaned back, pulled his hand back, and stepped forward, throwing a hard punch at Charlie.

Charlie took the fist on his jaw, flinching away, avoiding half the energy.

He recovered fast, leaned down, stepped toward Larkos.

Larkos landed another punch, then tried for one to the gut.

Charlie lifted an arm just so, twisted, blocked.

Jason took a step toward the fight, but Chrystal put her hand on his arm. "We can't."

The look on Jason's face told her he knew that and hated it. He snarled.

Charlie stepped in and kicked Larkos below the knee, forcing a step back.

Larkos grabbed Charlie's foot. Charlie jerked away before Larkos established a grip.

"Stop!" Nona screeched, her voice louder than she'd ever heard it.

They did, freezing. Neither man looked away from the other.

"It's OK," Charlie blurted through clenched teeth. "They're friends. They were you. High Sweet Home."

Yi in Chrystal's head, *They're too scared for logic.*

Larkos's reply was another attempt at a punch in the face, which Charlie stepped into and past. Both anger and fear gave the big man's eyes a hot and dangerous look. He was taller and broader than Charlie, but breathing harder.

She took a step back. Assessed. She allowed more smell, and scented fear from every human, the sickly sweet tang of sweat infused with adrenaline. Oil and grease in the air, and the acrid and slight edge of welding torches used recently.

She heard the rasp of the fighter's boots on the metal floor as the men circled, a little distance between them.

Neither committed. They just danced, Larkos bigger than Charlie but Charlie faster, both of them breathing hard.

Peripheral movement caught Chrystal's attention. Yi, from behind her, darting so fast she could barely see him. He slammed into the ponytailed woman.

A stunner flew across the floor, bouncing and banging, then skittering in a circle.

Yi held the woman, who struggled in his arms.

Larkos turned and stepped toward the gun.

Chrystal launched herself after it, easily beating Larkos. "We're not hurting you," she hissed.

Jason pulled Nona back.

The woman in Yi's arms yelled as if her worst fear had caught her by the hair.

"Stop!" Nona yelled again.

This time everyone did for just a moment. Then Larkos reached toward the woman. "Don't hurt her."

Yi let go and stepped back, his hands up.

The woman kicked, her foot hitting his stomach.

Yi didn't react at all, simply stood, as if he were a wall or a stone.

Chrystal clutched the gun to her chest, making sure it was pointed at no one. She had no real training with weapons, and it felt like a bad thing. She wanted to be rid of it, but no one else was going to get it from her.

Larkos yanked the woman after him and the two of them ran off, their footsteps echoing in the huge chamber.

Nona's voice shook as she asked, "Will they be back? Will they come back after us?"

Charlie held his hand out for the weapon, palm up. Chrystal gave it to him, relieved.

Charlie held the weapon up to the light. "I don't think they'll come back."

"Who were they?" Nona asked.

"Workers." Charlie examined the weapon, pushed a few buttons, and slid it into his pocket. "Probably the people who repaired all of these ships."

Jason asked, "What are they doing?"

"They're fleeing. We were going to go with them. More will be leaving. A timed exodus, so the Next will have many targets if they decide to shoot."

"They're that desperate?" Nona asked.

Charlie didn't answer. His gaze swept the ships.

Yi said, "I know which ones we can take."

"How?"

"Your repair system knows. I read it."

Charlie's eyes widened. "Can you tell which ones other people want?"

"That's harder." Yi said. "We may have to steal a ship."

From the look on her face, Nona understood the implications. "We'll be thieves and liars in people's minds."

"And the press," Charlie added.

Yi continued. "I can ask the Next if they have a ship. The *Bleeding Edge* is big enough to have ship's bays in her. But we would be safer in a human ship."

"We need something *I* can fly," Nona said.

Eight people spilled in through the closest lock and headed for the nearest available ship. They looked curiously at the small group but didn't acknowledge them.

"Well," Charlie said, waving a hand toward the ship. "We aren't stealing that one. We have access to a lifeboat-style ship. I got the permission codes from Gunnar. He says he'll pick us up."

Nona grabbed Charlie's arm. "I don't trust him. The Next—when I went to get Chrystal the Next said that Gunnar arranged for them to come here to meet me. But he and Satyana told us to lay low and not draw any attention. Remember? We need to get away from Gunnar as much as we need to get away from the Next."

There was no surprise in Charlie's eyes.

Jhailing Jim had suggested that she teach Gunnar to fear the Next. But Gunnar was already working with them?

CHAPTER FORTY-THREE

CHARLIE

Blood pounded through Charlie's jaw. It ached. One wrist had been hurt in the fight and wouldn't quite turn right. Every choice about how to get off the station felt like a trap. He'd never been sure Larkos was a friend; he was an enemy now. Gunnar, behind everything. Gunnar, who destroyed planets. Gunnar, who had set Nona up. There had to be another way.

Nona turned to the disheveled-looking skinny robot that had probably just saved his life. "Yi? Can we *buy* a ship?"

"I'll check."

Charlie backed the group against a wall where they wouldn't be easily seen.

The immediate problem was getting off the Satwa. The station was a sacrifice as far as he could tell, something the Glittering could afford to lose. He glanced at Yi, who was talking quietly to Jason. No way to tell if Yi was going to be any help.

Charlie called the number Amia had given him.

She answered.

"What do you know about the inventory of ships?" he asked her. "Is there one that we can take reasonably? Something up for sale, or that's Gunnar's, or . . . or anything?"

She laughed softly. "It's a repair bay. Half of the leftover ships are red carded. You won't be able to get them out."

"But the other half?"

"I'm checking."

Gunnar had told him to trust Amia, so he didn't. Not now. Nevertheless, he didn't want to leave anybody behind who wanted to leave. "Do you want to stay?"

"No. No, I don't. I'm checking to see if I can get into the inventory."

Charlie glanced at Yi. The robot stood stock-still and appeared to be looking at nothing. No help there yet.

Nona and Chrystal conferred in low tones.

A warning bell went off.

"What does that mean?" Charlie asked.

Loudspeakers told him. "Hull doors opening in twenty minutes."

He looked around for a suit locker.

Amia said, "I see a ship that's registered to Gunnar. It's big and slow."

"Is it empty? Is it ready? Does it have fuel?"

"All yes."

"Supplies."

A short hesitation. "Plenty."

Yi looked up. "There's a faster, smaller ship nearby. The *Star Ghost*. It's for sale. Four hundred thousand credits. It has everything. There are two other parties looking at the record right now. If we want to offer we should hurry."

That would fund a year's worth of the entire ranger program on Lym. Charlie was ready to choose the slower ship and steal from Gunnar when Nona said, "No time like the present to test my credit. I'll try to buy it. Give me a minute."

"Amia? You can come with us if you want."

"The sale will need approval. I can expedite it."

"Are you coming with us?"

"No. I'll take the number seventy-five ship you were talking about. And one of the soulbots."

Nona's eyes widened. The family looked at each other, stepped closer together.

"Why?" Charlie asked.

"Gunnar will pick me up. He'll reward that much ingenuity."

Charlie looked at the three, who stared back at him. Yi's face had gone rigid. Jason and Chrystal looked shocked.

Three things flashed through Charlie's mind. First, the robots were fast and could probably kill him quickly. He'd seen the way Yi moved when the woman pointed the gun at him. Second, Gunnar deserved nothing. Third, the terror on their faces could be made-up. But so could everything about them. If it wasn't made-up, it mattered. They looked like a human family in that moment, under that threat.

"Approve the sale and I'll give you the codes for the number seventy-five ship. You get a free ride for doing your job. No robots."

"You don't need three."

She didn't understand. Maybe he didn't either, but his opinion of them had changed already. "They're a family. They were a family before, and they still are. They travel together. Gunnar will see them on the Deep."

Silence.

Yi mouthed, "Thank you." Nona looked approving.

The alarms went off again. He gestured the conversation to mute so he would hear Amia's response but she wouldn't hear them or the alarms.

"Will we all fit in the number seventy-five ship?" Nona asked. "Five of us? Isn't it basically a lifeboat?"

"I've never seen it. Probably. The question is how much we'd have to sacrifice to get by on readymade food and recycled air."

"We don't breathe," Yi reminded him.

"Oh." He had forgotten. "We'd be fine, I think." Decisions were happening too fast. He had to be sure they didn't make a mistake out of stress. "Where are the ships?"

Yi started walking. "Follow me. I found a suit locker."

In five minutes, both humans were suited. The robots didn't bother.

Charlie tried to think. The little boat would be picked up by Gunnar. Almost certainly. "Maybe we should stay here," Charlie said. He hated the idea, but running off into space with the wrong vehicle was more dangerous.

Amia's voice came on. "I approved the transfer."

"Thank you," Nona said.

Charlie added, "I'll send you the codes as soon as we're aboard the *Ghost*."

Once more they all followed Yi. The *Ghost* turned out to be half the size of the *Savior*, and it looked fast and well maintained. For once, he was grateful that Nona was rich.

The *Ghost* had been decorated in faded plush, the way some people's old boats were at home. It had probably once been a fancyman's travel ship, with a reasonable cargo deck that would have allowed a significant side business in trade goods. The command center was full of worn red leather chairs and bright blue carpet. No taste.

Nona slid into the captain's chair with no problem, and made sure that all of the doors were dogged shut and turned on the front view screens. Boot messages flashed slow enough that he was able to see them, but then a vivid image of the inside of the bay showed up.

"I'll check supplies and fuel," Charlie offered.

"That's done," Yi said. "Fuel tanks are full. We have raw materials for food and a working garden. No perishables."

"Show me." He wanted to check Yi's work.

While he went over supplies and verified Yi's assessment, Nona played with the controls and managed to get a conversation started with the ship's nav AI. Charlie quickly decided that Yi knew more about starships than he did.

Three minutes later, the big doors of the bay started to open in front of them, a slitted view of stars growing larger.

A ship shaped like a small egg flew through the doors.

"Amia?" he mused.

"No," Chrystal said. "That's number thirty-four. She'll be in seventy-five. But it will be like that."

The *Ghost* was a far better choice.

Nona scrolled through commands on an air screen in front of her.

Yi stood right behind her, peering over her shoulder. From time to time one of them whispered to the other.

Charlie hadn't expected so much capability from the newly minted robots, or that he would trust them so fast. Or at all.

A larger ship flew out, bigger than the little escape pod or the *Ghost*.

The engine check screens showed up on the side wall. Charlie sat still and watched them pass every test. No problems.

"Seat yourselves," Nona said, her voice high and a little over-imperious but confident. She sounded more like a captain than she had on the *Savior*.

Yi watched them, and made sure that Nona was belted correctly before he sat down in the co-pilot's seat. He was so sure of himself Charlie got the distinct impression he was being polite and letting Nona have the big chair. Maybe they had a second pilot if they needed one.

"Ready?" Nona asked.

"Ready," they all responded.

"No last-minute desires to change your minds?"

"No," he said.

And then they moved, smooth and silky and faster than he expected. Soon enough Charlie couldn't see any part of the station or the *Bleeding Edge*, only stars and the lights of other fleeing ships.

PART FIVE

ESCAPE

CHAPTER FORTY-FOUR

CHRYSTAL

Chrystal curled across a chair in the command room, with Yi and Jason close by. They talked in low tones while watching over the various inputs from the ship. A curious and slightly unsettling sense of freedom had been growing on her. There was no Jhailing Jim in her head. She could think whatever she wanted to think, and not worry that some far-more-capable being would take offense at her thoughts or feel a need to come and lecture her. She felt like she was twenty years old all over again.

This was their second night away from the Satwa. The first day had been filled with learning the new ship, with short conversations between sleep shifts for the humans, who had clearly been exhausted. Today, there had been long talks about options and plans, and hours spent with all five of them in the greenhouse going over systems and checking young plants and adjusting the automated system's plans to fit the grows to two people.

Chrystal liked being here, happily sleepless, surrounded by Jason and Yi. Her new eyes were sharp enough to read even the smallest green and orange letters in the dark, and it felt oddly appropriate to be a machine protected by the machinery of the control room, which they watched over as well. All of the interconnected machines created a bigger machine that was currently flying between two space stations, which were essentially collections of machines anyway.

The little robot that had come with them moved, startling her. She had forgotten that it was working out a kink in Jason's right knee, some bit of automata that had lost track of the signals from their brains. *Sometimes I wonder what it must be like to be in a different body, to be even less human.*

Yi answered her. *We will discover it. I asked Jhailing once, and he said that it might take years, but that we can become as versatile as Jhailing. That our minds— our selves—are adapted to having four limbs that work the way human bodies do, or almost. He also said that the best way to prepare ourselves for more freedom is to practice, to push our bodies, to learn to do more than we once could.*

Like teaching our subconscious? Chrystal mused.

Jason grunted at something the robot did. *Too bad they left us pain.*

No. It's a survival mechanism. We can die, after all.

Yi, being a minder. He'd always looked out for their safety. Katherine had been the freest, the most abandoned, the poet and the singer and the massage artist and the one who kept the plants alive. Chrystal kept the thought private; it would trigger pain in Jason. *You can turn physical pain down*, Chrystal suggested, and showed him how.

He looked relieved. Funny how they hadn't each learned the same things.

The robot finished with Jason and moved back. "Are you ready?" Yi asked. "Yes."

This time, Chrystal watched as Jason and Yi practiced braiding. They hadn't tried merging all three together yet. If they made a mistake, there was no one more experienced here to help.

Yi and Jason grimaced together, and then laughed, and then relaxed into a look that held no emotion at all. She knew it for a lie; the deepest part of braiding was all under the surface of the body, so deep that they didn't feel the external parts of themselves. For her, it was the most emotional part of their new lives, the most curious and exhilarating and slightly scary time.

Glancing at the hallway camera, she noticed a light flick on outside of Nona's room. She came out, fully dressed, and started toward command. She stopped outside of Charlie's door, hesitating. She looked pensive, draped in longing. Nona had always been a loner. Seeing her uncertain and in love felt sweet.

Chrystal vowed to spend time with Nona that afternoon, quiet time just chatting like they used to. It was difficult to focus on conversation that moved as slowly as a human mind, but it was a skill Chrystal needed to keep. This alone was almost surely the reason the Next had chosen to use fresh soulbots as part of their ambassadorial force.

She hummed loudly, warning Yi and Jason.

Yi and Jason ascended, faces going from slack to wonder.

Lights snapped on and it was time for coffee and loud conversation, and time to feel as much like her old self as possible.

CHAPTER FORTY-FIVE

NONA

The robots had taken over the nearly-empty cargo area.

Nona sat on a couch in the staff lounge, sipping a cocktail and watching them on a multi-camera display that filled the wall in front of them. Charlie sat beside her, close enough that they touched elbows and shoulders. All three soulbots had stripped naked. They looked close to human, with musculature that moved like Nona's own might if she were in perfect shape. Their bellies rounded slightly down between their legs, as if they were all young women wearing invisible underwear, the only clear separation from humanity that Nona could spot at this scale.

Chrystal's hair had been caught back in a long braid, showing off her tattoo. Yi had no identifying marks of that type, but his slightly wild hair had been left free. Naked, his leanness was even more apparent, contrasting with Jason's broad shoulders and muscular thighs.

They performed low-g acrobatics, sailing across the vast open space, arms and legs outstretched. At the end of each long trajectory, they grabbed or touched or tucked and rolled into struts or walls or each other. Each stop was followed by a bend and a leap to gain new momentum. Sometimes they flew end over end, tumbling but controlled, moving so quickly their limbs blurred. Yi was the fastest by far. Jason moved the most gracefully, was the most aware of the others. He never missed a catch or a possible touch. Chrystal flowed as smooth as butter, as if she had been a gymnast once.

Which she hadn't.

Nona didn't remember Chrystal being particularly graceful on the dance floor. But now? Now she looked born for movement. "I could create a musical score to accompany the flight of the robots," Nona mused.

Charlie hummed a few bars, almost matching at least three rounds of movement before he sped up at a moment when Yi slowed and pulled Chrystal to him. He stopped, laughing. "I must not quite have the rhythm right yet."

"It looks like play," Nona said.

Charlie sipped on his beer. "It is. We have cameras all over Lym, and sometimes we catch herd animals playing like that, wrestling and showing off."

"Are you suggesting they're animals?"

Charlie raised an eyebrow. "We are." He got up to get another beer, opening it so the slightly sour smell made Nona wrinkle her nose. "At home, the animals who play with the most abandon are the predators."

"But surely prey are almost never safe enough to play," she mused.

"Everything is prey to something, even if it's us. As far as I know, all mammals play. I've seen birds play with thermals."

She turned and took his hand, speaking now of the soulbots. "They're playing. We're planning and worrying, even though we don't really have anything to do. I can't imagine any way to be more ready than we are." In truth, they had worried every option to death, and had contingency plan upon contingency plan done. Now, they were simply flying in a direction that could intercept the Deep. She felt drenched in worry and jealous of the robots' play. Even Charlie appeared less worried than she was, although he spent long hours talking about Lym from time to time.

Her thumb roved his palm, a slightly forward move that made her breath catch in her throat. They had been working slowly closer for days now, but a gap remained between them.

He put his free hand over hers, stopping the movement. "We should rest."

She turned her face away, biting at her lower lip. "I'd like to do more than that." She knew what bothered him. "I'm not your boss out here or your captain or anything. We're just people."

"You own the ship."

"I'd give you half."

Now he laughed, his voice husky. "I don't want half of your ship."

"I know that. We're in the middle of something bigger than the fact that I was born to more money than you were." She stared at the screen, watching Yi approaching on one of the cameras, catching a look of absolute serenity on his face. "We're not separated by nearly as much as we're both separate from them."

"I thought they'd be *less* like us." Charlie rested his chin on her shoulder, an intimate point of heat. "I can tell they came from us. I can tell what kind of people they were, even imagine what they might have done as humans. But they're not us."

"Chrystal used to be so much more—alive. She could never do that—never fly across a cargo bay perfectly—but she was warmer. Now there's a part of her that I can't touch. A cold part. Not mean. I might even describe it as distracted, although that's not quite right either."

He kissed the back of her head. "And you're warm and real."

"I need to remember the best part of not being like them," she whispered. The image in front of her showed all three of them landing together in the same place and taking each other's hands, leaning back with wide smiles on their faces.

Charlie traced the tattoo on Nona's neck with his hand, trailing his heat down to the place where her neck met the top of her collarbone and back up, touching the underpart of her chin and coming up so that her lips nibbled traces of fruit and beer from his fingers, chased with the slight salt-sweat of him. "Do you ever wish you were like them?" he asked. "That you had their grace?"

"No."

"No hesitation."

"None."

"So then come to bed and prove you're flesh and blood."

Something that had been tense inside of her shattered. "And bone and sinew."

He lifted her and turned her, as fluid as anything the robots were doing in the cargo bay, and as he pulled her to him, the movement stole her breath.

He carried her from the room and into her own bedroom, setting her down so softly that she barely noticed the presence of the bed against her back before he was kissing her.

⊷∞⊶

Perhaps a thing she had refused herself for so long had to come out with force. She had lost herself so deeply in him she was almost ashamed of herself. Almost. Even now, hours later and lying loosely by his side, her breath came in tiny gasps and unexpected shudders ran from scalp to toe. Her foot roamed his calf, eliciting small moans of pleasure.

This was being human. Melding, loving. Sweating together, stinking of each other's secret juices.

A part of her still floated.

She was used to men from the Deep, who were almost all far older than she was, and more controlled than Charlie. Perhaps that had drawn her out as well, some wildness in him that went with the planet he loved.

Authentic.

"I wanted you a long time before that happened," she said.

"Me too." His hand roamed her hip and traced a line of banked fire on top of her thigh.

She closed her eyes, certain that she and Charlie rested together in the center of a storm, midway between emergencies and for once in a long time, not alone.

Marcelle would probably approve.

The stray thought about her mother made her smile.

———— ∞∞∞ ————

The incoming communications buzzer jolted her from such a deep, safe place that for a moment she couldn't orient. The walls and the room were wrong, not familiar.

Beside her, Charlie startled, his hand coming up and slapping her lightly, accidentally, across the chin.

They were both knees and elbows as they sorted themselves into standing and looked at each other, eyes wide. "Who is it?" Nona asked the *Ghost*.

"The *Sultry Savior*, hailing you."

A momentary flash of guilt flared through her, followed by anger. They dared?

Curiosity and the idea of her command and her ship and the way they had done the one worst thing ever and abandoned their superior officer—abandoned her—tumbled in, and she felt jerked by flood after flood of emotion.

Surely it was just a reaction to having been so much a part of another human being that she was no longer truly in her own self. Not yet, anyway.

Charlie watched her, waiting for her to choose their reaction.

"I'll take the call from the command room in twenty minutes. Please order stim and breakfast and ask the others to meet me in there."

Charlie whispered. "Should I come with you?"

Nona detangled herself from the bedclothes enough to stand up. He shouldn't even be asking. "Of course."

They handed each other articles of clothing, although she rejected the shirt she'd been wearing for a cleaner one from her closet. When she stood in front of him, both of them fully dressed, she felt the distance coming back like a cool breeze. She stepped into him and lifted her face for a kiss, falling away from the coming separation for one more long minute before she turned and left the room.

Chrystal had beaten her there. Even though there was a good chance the cargo-bay acrobatics had gone on without stopping, she didn't look winded or worn out in any way. She did look worried. "What do you need? What's happened?"

"It's my old ship."

Charlie came in. "Don't you own them both?"

"Technically." She glanced at Chrystal. "They deserted me. With a little help from Gunnar."

Chrystal frowned.

"He may not be our friend."

"That's sad. I remember him bringing us lemonade in his gardens, by the lilies and honeysuckle." Her face hardened. "We should stay on the *Ghost*. The *Savior* will almost certainly have been compromised by now."

"More than before?" Nona asked.

"Yes."

Charlie said, "If it comes down to it, they can outshoot us and we can outrun them."

Nona felt her mouth fall open, and forced it shut. Surely it wouldn't come to that.

"Opening communication," the ship's AI said.

Yi and Jason came in.

Nona looked up, expecting Henry James to be staring at her.

Gunnar's face filled the screen, a wide smile under cold eyes, "Glad you escaped. Shall we plan out our next steps?"

CHAPTER FORTY-SIX

CHARLIE

Charlie tensed at the sight of Gunnar's face on the view screen. He must have been picked up by the *Savior*. That was probably what he'd planned for them, that they escape the Satwa in the tiny ship he'd given them access to, and then he'd planned to scoop them up in their own ship. The liar had tried to convince them he was off commanding his fleet.

And why wasn't he? Charlie grew cold at the thought. Why was Gunnar Ellensson focused on the five of them instead of spending time somewhere more fitting to his position in the world? Was it the robots? It wasn't love or altruism—Gunnar wasn't known for either.

Gunnar grinned at them as if he were ecstatic to find they were happy and well. He looked like a worried grandfather.

Charlie glanced at Nona. She smiled back at Gunnar, although her hands gripped the edges of her chair tightly. So she didn't buy it either, and she was learning not to show.

Good.

They had numerous contingency plans around Gunnar. Which one to use would be Nona's choice. Given his relationship with Satyana, the shipping magnate was near family to her even if there was no blood relationship.

"I'm glad to find you all well," Gunnar said, still beaming. He looked at Nona. "And very happy to see that you brought your friend with you." He seemed to be squinting into the room. "And more. That's fabulous. That's going to be important. It will help people put a human face on the Next."

There was no noticeable communication lag; the *Savior* had to be close. Gunnar sounded so reasonable and warm that his voice raised hairs on Charlie's neck.

"Hello, Chrystal," Gunnar said. "I haven't met the other two?"

Chrystal turned to introduce Jason and Yi, who displayed the bland and uninterested faces that typical humanoid bots often wore. They looked as unanimated and inhuman as possible given the human shapes of their faces.

Some instinct, or maybe some subtle clue from him or Nona, had driven them into a form of hiding. Maybe they should have included the bots deeper in their plans.

"I'm pleased to see you as well," Nona said. "And surprised you're still around here. Isn't your fleet at war?"

"It's parked in a defensive position. Any actual fighting is on hold until the major stations make some choices." He leaned back, looking relaxed. "We must help the Deep choose peace."

A peace in Gunnar's favor?

Gunnar continued, "The best plan is for you to meet me at Ivorn station. It's about a week away from here, and not far out of your way."

Right. Slowing and starting again would cost days.

Nona had gone silent, tapping the smart arm of her chair with her fingers, requesting information. She looked frustrated—the *Ghost* had different systems than the *Savior*. They didn't know them well even though they'd practiced. Neither he nor Nona was fast at finger commands yet.

Charlie interrupted to draw Gunnar's attention. "Did you pick up Amia?"

"Yes, she's fine. Thanks for asking."

Nona was whispering to Chrystal. Charlie asked, "Two other Next ships came in. Is there any news?"

Gunnar sat back in his chair and looked like he was thinking. "One of the Next ships, the *Edge of Happiness*, delivered the same message. They picked their target well; the station Paul's Hope was skirting the edge of augmentation anyway—they live inside of what is essentially one huge wearable. Everyone connected to everyone even when they shit."

Chrystal put her hand over Nona's, stilling it. A screen brightened beside the one with Gunnar's image on it, three dots with a few lines of description. The Ivorn was a small station, maybe twice as big as the tiny Satwa. Charlie was willing to bet Gunnar had a piece of that as well. Whichever of the robots had designed the image added the Deep, small and far away, and the words, "We lose three days."

Charlie prompted Gunnar. "Which means?"

"That they've got a third of the people at Paul's Hope lined up and begging to become soulbots. I think the Next are hoping they can take the whole sector by convincing people how nice it is to give up flesh."

Charlie shivered. "And the other Edge ship?"

"The *Edge of Night* chose a more conservative target, delivered its message, and was asked to leave."

"Did it?"

"Yes."

"Good." Except now there were three reactions and no decisions. No direction. Typical human behavior. Fight everybody instead of talking to a compromise.

Nona stared at the diagram beside Gunnar's face, her lips a tight line. Her free hand drummed a light staccato on her knee. "We're planning to meet you at the Deep. I'd rather not lose any time."

"I have a faster ship at the Ivorn. We can make up the time and plan together. Besides, it's well armed."

A nice trap.

Nona smiled and tried to talk her way out of it. "Thank you for the offer. It would be okay if you get to the Deep ahead of us to make sure that Chrystal, Yi, and Jason can dock safely so they won't be imprisoned because of some misunderstanding about the Deeping Rules. Maybe you could set up an opportunity for us to talk to the Council."

Gunnar sat back in his chair. "Satyana has that covered. Surely you know that you're a target now, and that you and your friends should be on a ship with better defenses than either of these."

"They let us go," she pointed out.

"The Next aren't your problem. There are two human ships on trajectories that will intersect you."

Nona stiffened and glanced at Yi.

Charlie asked, "Why humans?"

"One is from the Souls' Ease and probably wants you to come there instead of to the Deep. I suspect they will be willing to persuade you with force if they have to. It's a military grade cruiser. The other is the *Free Men*, a small ship from a mining company. Their captain, Vadim Justice, is particularly averse to the Next. He's destroyed two ships that were identified as smuggling raw materials out beyond the Ring. They even made an entertainment vid about him a few years ago."

"I think I remember it." If his memory was right, then they had a vigilante after them.

"How do they know we're on this ship?" Nona asked. "Or that Chrystal and her family are with us?"

Good question. Charlie wasn't sure he'd put it past Gunnar to have told them. Not if it drove them like prey into Gunnar's surround.

Gunnar grimaced. "Some people who left the Satwa right before you posted it on the news, and it got picked up in major channels. They claimed you fought them."

Larkos. Charlie's mistakes on the Satwa were haunting them.

"Only after they started a fight about Chrystal!" Nona protested.

"I assumed it was something like that."

The screen that had displayed the trajectories now showed the news articles and pictures of both Larkos and the red-headed woman. A slight movement of Yi's eyes convinced Charlie he was the one controlling it.

Charlie's mind raced. The *Star Ghost* had thrusters that could—in some very specific situations—be used as weapons. But in general she was meant for fast travel and comfort and couldn't do more than repel a much smaller invading ship.

The screen Yi was controlling cycled away from the news article and showed the two ships. It identified a third that might also be heading into the path they were on. Then the screen flashed, "Can we talk privately?"

Nona picked it up. "Gunnar—please excuse us for a few minutes. We'll re-open comms with you after we have a brief discussion."

Gunnar appeared poised to object as the screen switched off.

"Can we keep him from hearing us?" Nona asked. "He'll have the best tech available."

Yi smiled. "We can keep him out."

Charlie felt both relieved and slightly afraid at once. Yi was uncanny. "We didn't account for other ships chasing us."

"We'll *need* Gunnar's help." Nona sounded bitter.

Yi spoke. "There is an alternative. We're closer to Ivorn than the *Savior* is. The *Ghost* can go faster if we assume we can refuel at Ivorn; we can get there at least a few hours before Gunnar. We can drop Nona and Chrystal off for Gunnar to pick up. The rest of us will stay on the *Ghost* and go to Lym. This leaves us free in case Chrystal gets in trouble on the Deep and needs help."

Chrystal leaned toward Nona. "It is safest. I grew up on the Deep; they are not likely to reject me. Yi is from the High Sweet Home, and while I met Jason on the Deep, he only lived there for a few years before we left. He doesn't have family there like I do."

Nona stared at her, round-eyed. "You'd split up?"

"Not if there was any better choice," Yi said. "But we consider the Deep a risk."

"You're probably right," Charlie said. They had clearly been out-thinking Nona and him. It left him feeling backed into a corner, although the plan was good. He waited a while, thinking, before he turned to Yi. "You know I may be trying to create a resistance force?" he asked Yi. "Are you okay with that?"

"But you will not harm us?" Yi asked.

"Of course not."

"Then I will have some time to try and convince you not to harm others, either."

Charlie had planned to leave for Lym as soon as the others were back on the Deep. Yi's plan didn't leave Charlie in a worse place, except that he lost Nona sooner.

"None of the other ships will be near us in time to cause trouble?" Nona asked.

"Not unless a new threat shows up," Yi said. "We can't rule out a ship from Ivorn itself, for example."

Nona grinned. "So we just tell Gunnar we're heading for Ivorn, and leave it up to him to figure out if he can beat us?"

When Yi nodded, Nona looked at Charlie and grinned. "I like a race."

CHAPTER FORTY-SEVEN

CHRYSTAL

Chrystal curled naked in one of the many extra bedrooms on the *Star Ghost*. She dialed back most of her senses, creating the closest thing she could manage to a white world with almost no information coming into it. Her body didn't feel unless it was stressed or in pain, cold or hot, or touching something. So in this moment, she felt dreamy and unconnected, like a consciousness that had no actual home.

Jason and Yi had gone as far away as possible, to the far side of the ship, and turned themselves down into their own whitened world. The two of them were together; they would feel each other, touch each other. She would be alone.

Simulation.

She set a timer for two hours and let her mind drift. Memories surfaced, older memories of being a child in her own room after her parents had closed the door and gone away into other portions of their habitat or out for a late-night meal, leaving her with nothing but her minder-bot.

She no longer had a minder, unless she counted herself. She laughed, a little bitter, and the laugh made her feel the empty present, so she tried for the older times again, for the silent room and long slow minutes of awake time after she'd been put to bed.

She stretched, something the child in her had done as well.

As long as she left her eyes closed it was possible to feel time in that old way, ticking slowly by. Child's time. Alone time.

Torture.

She started to sing, beginning with her old childhood songs.

Eventually she forgot the chorus to one and her voice trailed off, and she sat in total silence until enough contentment crept over her that she felt better.

She checked and the time had only moved a quarter of the way. What other times had she been alone? There was a summer when Nona had gone into a special dance school with Satyana and Marcelle. They hadn't included Chrystal. Her other friends had done similar things, so she was alone with her parents, who worked. She had moped for a day, and then she had started drawing. Each day, she had spent a little more time drawing. By day five, she became fascinated with the use of color to create depth and dimension, and with the interplay of light and shadow. When Nona came back from dance school, Chrystal had a clever drawing of a still life—fruit bedecked with glittering jewelry.

The picture still hung in her mother's kitchen.

More importantly, she had liked being alone in that moment even though she'd gotten out of the habit of it again, become paired to Katherine and then to the two men.

She needed to relearn the mental tricks of living alone.

She would have Nona, but communicating with Jason and Yi was so much richer.

The thought jolted her.

The lesson was to learn to be without her other parts. That's what Jason and Yi had become, parts of her that she could talk to twenty-four hours a day.

The timer was halfway through. She'd made it this far. She was on the downhill, and her memories were sharper rather than duller. Such a strange artifact of losing her biological self, this resurgence of memories she'd long lost.

She relived walks she had taken by herself, a camp she had gone to, long conversations with Nona, the two of them giggling about clothes and body-mods and tats. She remembered when they had gotten the matching dragons, the way the needle had been sharp and then sharper and the pain, and how the pain had seemed like a bonding, the two of them lying together in the same shop and being worked on at the same time.

When the timer went off, it surprised her. She forced herself to wait a few more trembling moments before she turned herself back up and up, and reached out to feel Jason and Yi. *We can do this.*

We know.

It will be okay.

You're strong.

She was the one who would be the most alone.

I'll be okay. But I will miss you every moment.

And we you.

I love you.

I love you.

I love you.

Such comfort in such human words.

CHAPTER FORTY-EIGHT

CHARLIE

Charlie ran his hand along Nona's shoulder and neck and traced the line of her jaw with his fingers. Her head rested in his lap, her hair tickling his thigh. Touching her felt so precious. This woman he had expected to scorn, now joined with him and about to be swept away from him.

He would miss her. There were only hours now. They were ahead of the *Sultry Savior*, everything on plan, Yi adjusting and tweaking the engines and trajectory constantly. Even though Yi had been forced to work though the ship's AI, his constant attention reminded Charlie of sailing races where he had been responsible for the trim of jib and jenny and spinnaker, watching always for the exact wind direction, focusing on yellow ribbons sewn to the sail in such a way that they twitched with the slightest wind.

He had thought spaceships did what they did, like trains, that they set a course and then nothing changed unless there was some kind of catastrophe. But in truth they were a moving object working to line up with another moving object, and they had the ability to make tiny adjustments in engine thrust and direction. Yi was calculating perfect minutia.

Nona reached up and traced the line of his jaw. "Be careful," she said. "You'll be more of a target than I will."

Meaning she and Chrystal would be protected by one of the most powerful men in the system, and he would be by himself, in her ship, protecting the two robots. Or being protected by them. Or something.

"I'm certain that fighting the Next is impossible," she said. Not a new argument. They'd had it a few times, a running disagreement.

"I've been thinking about that. It depends on what they'd do. Imagining that Chrystal is a Next is wrong. These are their creatures, but your friends are not them."

"Yi thinks they might be."

He laughed and captured Nona's hand. Her fingers were cool. He wrapped his hand around them. "Yi is often right, but that's wishful thinking, at least for now."

She fell silent for a long time, returning his touches gently. Then she caught his gaze, so intense that she seemed to be looking into him. "I know you have to go back to Lym. You have to do whatever you're going to do to save it. I get that. It's a beautiful place. I want to go back there and finish my itinerary, see the things I missed."

His voice came out thick and deep. "You'll have to come get your ship."

"Will I?" She withdrew her hand and sat up. "Maybe you'll fly it to the Deep."

"Maybe I'll never want to leave home again."

"Never is a long time."

He pulled her back close to him, craving the warmth of her back. She curled into him, letting out a soft moan. If they had any more time, he would take that as an invitation. "I need to see you again," he whispered, knowing it for the truth. In this moment, with the smell of her hanging in the air and the taste of her still on his tongue, he didn't want to leave her at all.

Nona twisted so that he could reach her lips with his, and he kissed her as tenderly as he could, withholding the heat that might drive him into staying a few more minutes.

When they separated, he pushed her up and stood. "We can't let the robots dock the ship."

"No. They might think they run the place."

CHAPTER FORTY-NINE

NONA

Nona sat in one of many greeting rooms at the Ivorn, scanning news articles on her slate. Chrystal sat behind her, dressed in a bright blue pair of Nona's silky pants and a black turtleneck. Her legs were crossed, her hand rested on her knee, her face had slackened into what Nona called her "waiting robot" pose. They'd cut Chrystal's hair shorter and sprayed it temporarily lighter, hoping she would look different enough from the news stories that she wouldn't be noticed in casual surveillance.

Nothing to see here. Just a woman and her personal-assistant-bot waiting for a ship to come in.

People walked by in the corridors, and sometimes they glanced in. Apparently either no one watched the surveillance cameras, no one cared, or no one wanted to cause a problem. Still, her shoulder blades itched.

From time to time she glanced up at a sign on the wall where scrolling bright orange letters announced arrivals and departures from the spaceport. The *Sultry Savior* was still supposed to dock here, now in fifteen minutes. They would probably see Gunnar and his crew in an hour—it would take time to park and turn off the ship, get out of it, and get into the station itself.

The seats were harder and more uncomfortable than most of the waiting rooms Nona was used to, but then the Ivorn wasn't really much of a station; just a refueling/re-provisioning stop with a minor repair operation, a few cheap hotels for people stuck between ships, and myriad bars and brothels.

If Gunnar owned any part of it, she didn't see any sign of him. He probably did use it for a refueling station since there weren't many this far out. Obviously it was occasionally on a path for a trip between the Deep and the Satwa.

Was Gunnar smuggling things to and from the Next?

Gunnar?

Charlie had implied it, and the Next had implied it.

Did Satyana know?

Surely not.

She glanced back down at her slate. News columns and vids played up both of the stories she'd overheard in Charlie's conversation with Gunnar. The *Edge of Happiness* reported success for the first three humans turned cyborg. In contrast, the *Bleeding Edge* had gone silent. There was a single five-day-old story about Shoshone starting the process, and of course, the stories of ships fleeing. Apparently they'd all gotten away; the Next had been magnanimous. The *Edge of Night* had refused to retreat all the way across the Ring, but had settled into an orbit just inside for now, a sort of symbolic protest perhaps, or a demonstration of their patience.

Other news implied fear and uncertainty. Two religion-based stations had taken different perspectives. One wanted to fight the Next to the death and the other had taken up the refrain from Paul's Hope and was trying to convince people that becoming Next was a stepping stone to Nirvana. Funny how such voices had been mostly silent before the Next appeared.

At least three stations had increased the line rates to build military-grade ships faster. Three of the bigger stations, including the Deep, were buying as many of the extra ships as could possibly be manufactured in the next year. The Deep's ship production was also turning military. News stories suggested a political divide inside the station. Nona searched for her own name and found it in a multitude of stories about their escape from the Satwa, but didn't see any reference to her arrival here yet.

Chrystal hissed. "The board says they are using a different bay."

Nona glanced up. Now twenty minutes away and across the station. "Let's go."

A train circled the entire station, stopping at each greeting room. They boarded and stood, holding onto poles and swaying. The repair-bot had been left with Yi and Jason, and so Chrystal only had a backpack. Nona had a rolling bag full of clothes for both of them and a few other personal belongings.

About halfway to their new destination, the train doors let three people in paramilitary clothes on, two women and a man. They wore serious expressions and clutched weapons. Patches on their shoulders identified them as Ivorn Port Guards. They paid no direct attention to Nona and Chrystal, but they stood straight and kept passing intense looks back and forth.

Nona backed herself and Chrystal into a corner, staying near a door. She glanced at her friend, and found Chrystal's eyes hooded and guarded. "Our stop is next," she whispered.

Chrystal nodded.

They had to shoulder between three more uniformed soldiers to get off. As the train pulled away, Nona said, "I hope that's not about Gunnar."

"I think it is."

"Why? What did you notice?"

"They smelled of fear and adrenaline. They are not doing something common to them. It can't be a coincidence that they are here now, when we are. They looked so . . . predatory. They were almost scary."

"To you?" Nona asked.

"Sure."

"I don't think of you as being scared."

"Maybe after you've lost everything and been reborn, you want to make sure you don't lose again. I doubt I have a third life."

"I understand." So many things Nona wanted to talk to Chrystal about. She looked around. People filled the room, apparently expecting to leave: they had luggage and even a few children with them. A dog whined in a carrier in a corner and a small boy whispered to it, which didn't seem to calm it much at all. "Maybe we should stay here."

"These people are already in a line," Chrystal noted.

Sure enough, a silvery boarding robot dressed in a blue and white uniform started talking into a microphone.

"So we get on the next train?"

In two minutes, another train came by. Nona scanned it for uniforms. None. "Okay. Let's get on."

Nona worried the whole rest of the ride, all the time trying her best to look like a bored traveler.

They were going to be late.

At the train neared the right station, she peered through the scratched windows, trying to see if the military had in fact landed here. Chrystal was looking over her shoulder. The train stopped and the doors opened, illuminating a room full of uniforms. "It's okay," Chrystal said, pushing Nona out before she had time to be certain she agreed. She almost tripped, steadied only by Chrystal's smooth grasp on her elbow as the doors whooshed shut behind them.

Well over half of the uniforms belonged to the *Sultry Savior*. Gunnar himself stood beside Henry James. Gunnar looked pleased to see her. Henry had the common sense to look down and away.

The uniformed men and women they had seen on the train all stood quietly, with their weapons piled on the floor at their feet. Gunnar gave orders. "Fall in. Don't take the train. Use the walking corridors."

The disarmed Ivorn Port Guards were herded in the front and kept under careful watch by Henry James and ten of his crew. Gunnar came near until he towered over her, asking "Where are the others?"

She took a deep breath. "What happened?"

"They didn't want us on their station. I convinced them they should be hospitable."

"Did they tell you why?"

"That the *Savior* is yours and you were seen in the company of some of the Next. They didn't want any soulbots on board to pollute the station."

A chill almost made her stumble. "The *Savior* left before I did. What right did they have?"

"They saw us pick up a pod. Amia. I convinced them to leave us alone for the moment but we need to be off this station in ten minutes. Where are the others?"

She took a deep breath. "They're going to Lym."

His grip on her arm tightened. "Call them back. They won't be safe out there."

"No," she said.

"You're putting your new lover in danger."

How the hell did he know that? "The Deep is just as dangerous."

"I can't help him out there."

"Well then he'll just have to help himself."

"How long ago did they leave?"

She fudged. "I think it was about three hours." Another deep breath, "They're not going toward the Deep. Leave them alone."

"They might die."

He was trying to drive her with guilt. "No," she said. "They made their own choices."

He glanced around. "We'll talk more after we get on the *Dreaming Streak*.

"Why not take the *Savior*?"

"We need something faster. She'll go home, probably be there a month after us. Maybe less. Come on."

She didn't want to go with him, and she certainly didn't want to have a heart-to-heart talk with him. He still outpowered her by some unimaginable amount, and he was still Satyana's lover. None of those things made going with him feel good or safe.

She should have left Chrystal on the Satwa.

PART SIX

HOMECOMING

CHAPTER FIFTY

CHARLIE

Charlie blinked and opened crusty eyes. He reached for the buckles on his safety belt and sat up, the odd contours of the acceleration couch far easier to take lying down than sitting. He was surprised to learn they had left Ivorn station two hours before. He managed to croak out a few words before he reached for water. "I can't believe I slept."

"Why not?" Yi asked. "There's not much else to do while you're strapped down."

He drank deeply. "Acceleration always makes me thirsty." And it used to make him nervous. Maybe he was getting used to space.

"The *Dreaming Streak* left Ivorn," Yi said. "Just now."

"Can you tell if Nona's aboard?"

"Just a minute." Yi fell silent and his face briefly shifted into what Charlie dubbed his *computing look*. "Chrystal is. She wouldn't have boarded without Nona unless she was forced."

"How do you know Chrystal's on board?"

"She had a plan to message us if she wasn't. She didn't. There are no news stories that suggest anything much happened other than that Gunnar turned back an attempt to arrest Chrystal and Nona."

Charlie tensed. "What?"

"It wasn't successful."

He frowned. "Is the *Dreaming Streak* following us?"

"No. It appears to be headed right for the Deep."

He let out a long breath. That had been his worst fear, getting away and starting home only to be snatched back. "What about the other ships that were following us. Are they still?"

"Ask me in a few hours. None of them has changed trajectory yet."

"Are they all human ships?"

Yi hesitated. "If I'm classifying friendly and unfriendly forces, every ship that we think might do us immediate harm is a human ship."

Dammit. "You're right."

He almost asked Jason to make him some stim, but then caught himself. These were not servant bots, like almost every other robot he'd ever encountered. They were people. "I'll be right back."

"Okay," Yi said. "We'll watch."

The small galley off of command was all silvered metal and blue accent paints. He programmed a request for a chocolate-flavored stim with a hint of cinnamon and waited while the autokit created and heated his drink. The machine coughed out the scent of baking soda and water, and followed it with the rich, sugary smell of his favorite comfort drink.

He didn't know what the Next wanted. If they were human, they might be trying to extract revenge, but Yi had told him, "Most Next are beyond that," which Charlie suspected might be right. The Next were machine biology, no matter what humanity they claimed. Even Yi and Jason were more machine than human.

One theory was that the Next needed raw materials in quantity. Being beyond the Ring, the only materials they'd had were captured asteroids, comets, or ships. Or stations, lately. All the nanotechnology in the world couldn't create much mass from the empty dark of space.

Energy, of course. But that didn't need Lym. That required being closer to the sun.

Well. he had time to think. It would take days to get to Lym. He was going home, and for the moment, he was going to enjoy his chocolate and daydream about Nona.

Surely there would be trouble soon enough.

CHAPTER FIFTY-ONE

CHRYSTAL

The *Dreaming Streak* pulled away from Ivorn so smoothly the moment of decoupling was tough to identify. Chrystal had been given her own room, complete with an acceleration couch she chose to ignore. The only safety it offered her was to hold her in one place if they got into a wreck, which was extremely unlikely in a premiere ship leaving a busy station. So she sat cross-legged and entertained herself with the thrust gravity, using it to practice fine motions against an opposing force, flexing a single finger or muscle in her jaw at a time.

She was still sitting that way when one of the many ship's robots opened the door and said, "Gunnar Ellensson would like to see you now."

Chrystal contemplated the bot. Given its job here, it was probably one of the smartest independent bots built inside the Ring. It looked a little like her—not in exact features, especially since it was androgynous. It moved as smoothly as she did, its skin appeared warm and human-like, and its facial expressions practiced and precise. "If you were me, what would you do?" she asked it.

The robot's response was quick. "Follow me to see Gunnar."

"What if I don't want to do that?"

"If you refuse, I will report that back to Gunnar Ellensson, and perhaps he will give me new instructions."

"Do you know what the meaning of life is?" Chrystal asked it.

"My own meaning is to provide service to humans."

Chrystal laughed. "I suppose mine is, too. I will come with you, but only if Nona Hall comes along."

"Nona hasn't yet been given permission to move around."

Of course not. This bot didn't need an acceleration couch any more than Chrystal did. "Then I'll wait. Would you like to wait with me?"

"My instructions are to bring you now."

"I know," Chrystal replied, frustrated at the thing's lack of apparent actual volition. "But I choose to wait for Nona, and then I'll be happy to go see Gunnar. I am not interested in seeing him alone."

The machine hesitated for long enough that Chrystal noticed it, although she suspected a regular human wouldn't have seen the short, bewildered moment when it stopped between expressions and didn't know which one to pick. "I was only told to bring you."

Chrystal wanted to laugh again, and almost did. Except that would show a prejudice she didn't want. The simple robot's trouble with a new concept wasn't actually funny, and it didn't deserve her laughter. "I'll wait. When Nona can be released from her chair, she and I will go with you. How long will that be?"

"Ten minutes for high priority personnel, although she is not on that list. Half an hour for the others."

"Why don't you go back and tell Gunnar what I said. Perhaps he will put Nona on the list."

It left. Chrystal felt relieved and disquieted. She had almost acted high-handed with it. Which was probably how many humans would want to act with her.

———⊗∞⊗———

It was two hours, seven minutes, and three seconds later when she and Nona were finally escorted into Gunnar's office. He had an affinity for wood and living plants. One whole wall was decorated with blooming flowers. Symbols of excess on a starship. But then he had always reveled in excess.

Gunnar gave Chrystal a long, assessing look, probably in response to her refusal to talk to him without Nona.

She stared back, waiting him out.

He turned away first, and the moment he did, she regretted not letting him win. He was dangerous, and she was virtually powerless.

Once they sat, Gunnar's face fell easily into the friendly expression he'd used when they were on the *Ghost*. He addressed Nona. "I wish you had all come in together."

Nona hesitated, fiddled with hair, twining a blue lock around her right index finger. "Charlie needs to go home, and so do I."

He waved a big, meaty hand at the air. "They're not safe."

"You lied to us." Nona's voice had the slightest tremble in it, a fear marker that Chrystal hoped Gunnar missed.

He raised an eyebrow but didn't respond directly. He smelled of fear, even though it didn't show. They were both afraid, and neither could say so. Maybe someday she could use her sensitive senses to smell trust.

Nona continued. "You told us that we could stay hidden on the Satwa. But you told the Next we were coming."

He leaned back, looking unconcerned. "That's not quite true."

Chrystal spoke quietly. "The Next knew Nona was there before we arrived at Satwa. They told me I would see her." She didn't mention that Jhailing had also said they wanted to use Nona to get to Gunnar. She was acutely aware of how eerily prescient her Next handlers had been, or how they had manipulated her. She didn't quite understand Gunnar's goals yet; he puzzled her.

"I told Shoshone you were coming." Gunnar stood. "She must have told them. We know she betrayed me to them and that she was selling them forbidden technologies."

Chrystal shook her head, looking up into Gunnar's dark eyes and broad face. "I believe they told me before we crossed the Ring. Shoshone wouldn't have known then, would she have?"

Both Gunnar and Nona looked at her. "I didn't know that," Nona said.

Chrystal felt uneasy with the way the conversation was going and wished again for sharper emotional cues. Her intellect wasn't being particularly helpful.

She had access to Gunnar right now, access that she might not have so easily or so privately again. "The Next did want to talk to you," she said. "Do you have a fleet?"

"Yes."

Nona looked annoyed at the change of topic, but she said, "He has the biggest personal fleet in the Glittering."

Chrystal nodded. "Jhailing Jim told me to tell you that you will lose your fleet if you fight the Next."

"I don't intend to fight them."

"Are you helping them?" Nona asked.

A good question. Chrystal watched carefully as Gunnar said, "I'm trying to make sure we are all safe." His eyes narrowed the slightest bit, for just a second. Was he lying, or angry? Chrystal was pretty sure Jhailing didn't trust Gunnar. She didn't. But was she going to trust a Next over a human?

Gunnar paced around them, his bulk intimidating. "The Next can destroy everything, and quickly. That's what they showed us with the High Sweet Home." He glanced at Chrystal. "You were an afterthought. They don't care about you, not really. Or us. That's what I'm trying to do. Demonstrate value, show them that they should care about humans, that maybe they even need us."

Nona stood, which only served to accentuate the size difference between her and Gunnar. She looked up at him. "Who is *us*? Are you trying to negotiate for the Deep?"

"Yes. And for all that we depend on."

Chrystal remained seated, watching. *For all that we depend on.* "You're trying to negotiate for the whole Glittering?"

Nona asked, "Do you have the Council's permission?"

"Satyana is working on that. But the Next need to know that we bring them value now. They aren't going to do things in the Council's time. That's what got them banished."

He seemed to know a lot about the Next. Chrystal was still trying to understand the situation, but Nona was reacting. Her expression didn't take much work to read: she was getting angry. "Does Satyana know you lied to us?"

"I didn't lie to you."

"You told us we might go unnoticed on the Satwa."

"You could have."

Nona's voice rose. "After you pointed us out?"

"I warned you as soon as I thought it would get dangerous. I even risked my life coming to tell Charlie in person. This entire situation is fluid. You studied diplomacy."

"Don't turn this back on me," Nona said. But the tiny muscles in her face relaxed. "You did warn us. And you did just save us. But you can't negotiate for the whole system. You have no right."

Good for Nona.

Gunnar sat down, which was a relief. "If I don't do it, who should? There's no other corporation with as much power as I have. You pointed out that I have the biggest fleet. The speed of business is far faster than the speed of politics. We can't just wait for the Council. You saw firsthand what the Next did to the military."

"I actually didn't see much," Chrystal said. "I was strapped to an acceleration couch for most of the fight. We did see the damage afterward."

"I'll send you the video," he offered. He looked pointedly at Nona, who was still standing.

Nona crossed her arms and refused to accept the implicit command to sit. "Everyone seems to be fighting," Nona said. "And I suspect you're not the only one who wants to control negotiations."

"That's obvious," he said. "Everybody's tense, and if we fight among each other, the Next win."

"Regardless of the Next," Chrystal said, "it seems like humans are close to going to war with each other. Some people want to fight, some people want to become like me. Some want to hide and pretend the Next don't see them."

Gunnar narrowed his eyes at her. "Humans are always on the brink of war."

"I didn't used to think so," Chrystal said.

"What do you think now?"

"I think we're all frightened because of the High Sweet Home. And because of me and my family."

Gunnar smiled, although his eyes were calculating. "Which side are you on? You work for the Next now. You just gave me a message from them."

How offensive. "I'm on your side, the human side. You asked if I was human. No. And yes. I'm still the same person who used to hang around with Nona after school."

He cocked his head at her, his expression assessing. "Should I be afraid of you?"

"No."

"How do I even know you're Chrystal and not simply dressed up in a Chrystal body? Do you remember the first time I met you?"

"I do." She closed her eyes and thought back. She and Nona had been about twelve. She hadn't been awed by him yet, except that she'd known he was rich, even richer than her family. "You invited Nona and me to your private forest bubble. She'd seen it, but I never had. You had birds and butterflies. I'd never seen a butterfly—only in pictures. But you had three different kinds that you showed me that day. One was a monarch; one was a blue mountain lacewing. You hunted for that one. The third one was small and white and you said you couldn't remember its name. I painted them afterward, from my photos. That's part of why I became a biologist. Because of the butterflies."

"Do you remember what I was wearing that day?"

She could see him clearly. He'd been a little thinner, but just as tall and broad. "White pants. Blue sandals. I remember thinking you were going to get the pants dirty. And you had on a black top that hung loosely and a vest over that. The vest was the same blue as your sandals."

He blinked at her.

"Did I get it right?"

"I have no idea. But I do remember having the matching shirt and sandals."

The look in his eyes didn't telegraph belief in her humanity.

Chrystal walked beside Nona on the way back. Neither of them said anything until their robot escort left them with a smile and a nod, surely heading back to report that he had successfully seen them to their quarters.

Chrystal followed Nona into her room, which was bigger than Chrystal's and had a little sitting room in addition to the bedroom. "I don't trust him," she told Nona. "You know him better."

"He loves power more than anything. But he has it, and he might be trying to use it well."

"You're not sure," Chrystal probed.

"I'm never sure of Gunnar."

"Fair."

Nona's room was big and luxurious, fancier than anything on the *Sultry Savior*. The walls had original paintings on them. "You should move in here. You don't even need the bed."

Bless Nona. "Thanks. That way I won't feel so lonely."

Nona pulled her close, into a hug. "You must miss your family."

Nona could never know how much. "I do."

"I don't remember the butterflies," Nona said. "I barely remember the trip."

"The butterflies mattered to me."

"When was the last time you remembered them?" Nona asked.

Chrystal shrugged. "I don't know. Probably years ago. My mind seems to be picking up bits of itself, things I'd lost because I didn't really need them. It feels like there's more room for memories. They're clearer, too.

"Tell me about our first day of school."

"High school?" Chrystal asked.

"Any school."

"The first day of high school I was five minutes late. Mom was in the middle of one of her endless lectures about my clothes. You were waiting for me, so we were both late for our first class."

"I remember being late. What was I wearing?"

"White pants with orange threads at the seams. Your favorite that week. They were low and had side slits. Your mother hated them, so you snuck them out in your bag and changed in the bathroom. You had an orange top and gold earrings—the earrings were diamonds your dad gave you."

"I forgot the earrings. I must have lost them."

Chrystal had forgotten them, too. Until she'd been asked.

Nona looked perplexed. "So how am I going to convince people they don't want to be you? I want your memory."

"No you don't," Chrystal snapped. "I couldn't bear it if they killed you."

"Okay." Nona chewed on her lip. "I don't think I meant that anyway. But people will see how smart and beautiful and strong you are."

Chrystal stopped short for a moment. That wasn't how she saw herself. "I'll tell them what I lost, and that I would give anything to go back."

Nona smiled softly. "They're not going to believe you."

"Do you? I want to erase it all. To have our animals back, alive. Jalinerines." She remembered that last horrible day, when they had needed to kill Sugar and the others. "We spent years on them, and they'd just been approved as a product. They had small heads and wide, dark eyes, eyelashes they could bat, and the cleverest feet. They could walk on almost any surface, even something smooth, and not slip. Yi spent seventeen animal generations on the feet, each time making them better."

She stopped, momentarily out of words.

Nona waited, patient.

Memories cascaded through Chrystal's brain, so clear she could see details like the sway of Katherine's hair and the gold-flecked irises in Sugar's eyes when she was a baby. It was a few moments before she was ready to speak again. "I would kill to hear Katherine's laugh, or her songs in the morning when she woke up before any of us and didn't think we were listening. She sang every morning, every single one. I would lie in bed and listen to her, and her voice would pull me gently into the day, until I got up to kiss her good morning."

Nona chewed on her lower lip and looked even more upset than Chrystal herself felt.

"I'd love to react with the same feeling I used to have. I would love to breathe. To simply breathe."

Nona looked stricken, but now that she'd been asked, Chrystal wanted to keep talking. "I should be crying right now. I'm sad, thinking about Katherine. I miss her. But I don't feel like I am crying, or like I could cry—I can't. But I *should* be crying. I should be crying and screaming and wailing and mourning every day. It's like everything that made me human is still there, only it's a whisper inside me, a reminder that I'm not me and I'll never be me again."

Nona put her arms around Chrystal. A tear dropped down onto Chrystal's shoulder.

Nona jerked a little, and wiped the tear away with a finger.

"It's okay," Chrystal said. "I know that you can cry and I can't. That's why I want a path forward that doesn't make any more of me."

"If we could defeat them, kill them all, would you?"

"No. But I want them to leave the Glittering forever."

CHAPTER FIFTY-TWO

NONA

A month later, the Deep bulked huge in the view screens as they came in. Staring at it, Nona felt like a tiny woman with a huge task. She chewed on her lower lip so hard it hurt. "I am stronger now," she whispered to herself. "I am strong enough to create change." She did feel stronger, and she also felt different. She had been a captain and a lover and a diplomat since she left here, she had done things with more purpose and reason than she was used to, things that had scared her.

She had become bigger. On the other hand, the Deep was so big she couldn't see it all. And she had left it as the captain of the *Sultry Savior* and returned as a virtual prisoner on the same ship.

Two bells sounded to warn them they were docking. She closed her eyes and said it one more time before she left to find Chrystal. "I am strong enough to create change. I am."

Satyana and a flock of reporters met her and Chrystal just inside the door between the docking facility and the station. Satyana had dressed in a power suit: a deep blue form-fitting coat with neon-blue trim that matched her eyes, tight black pants, and black boots. She had dyed her hair the color of the night sky on Lym. It hung in rings down her shoulders and chest, stopping at her waist. A single neon blue streak on the right framed her face and mirrored the coat, the colors blending.

Nona swayed, apprehensive. What would Satyana think of how she'd done? What would she think of Chrystal?

At least she and Chrystal were both dressed in clean and pressed ship's uniforms and Nona wore her single civilian captain's bar on her sleeve. Gunnar had stolen her ship, but she had never given up her insignia.

Satyana kissed Nona on both cheeks and then played Chrystal exactly right, welcoming her home and apologizing for her losses.

Maybe it would be okay.

There was an unreasonable amount of picture-taking and a short inter-view where Chrystal stated that she was happy to be home and Nona echoed her. After ten minutes, Satyana shut the reporters and drones all down, murmuring that everyone needed to rest for the many meetings starting tomorrow.

Britta bundled all three of them into a private flitter and took them to the *Star Bear*, a refurbished spaceship that was Satyana's most common home on the Deep.

Britta left them, and they wound their way past a vast cargo area which had long ago been converted to a series of stages for concerts and dances. In one room, a portrait of Ruby Martin dominated a whole wall, with Ruby in working clothes and holding a microphone shaped like a gun. As Nona walked through the room, the image of Ruby seemed to be watching them pass. Nona squared her shoulders.

Deeper inside the *Star Bear*, they came to a small sitting room where wine, berries, crackers, and sweets had been set out on a round mosaic table surrounded by five chairs. Chrystal glanced at the food and sat in a soft chair near the table.

Satyana frowned. "I'm sorry."

"Go ahead," Chrystal said. "You have to eat. What should I expect tomorrow?"

"Let me tell you about process first. You've been gone a while, but certainly you remember how much we love to dissect a thousand possibilities around our simple little laws?"

"I do." Chrystal smiled and looked truly interested. Nona poured a glass of chilled white wine and sat back to listen. After a month of Gunnar, Satyana seemed almost reasonable.

"Well, there's a timeline," Satyana explained. "We've only got a few days to make this decision."

Nona sipped her wine. Heaven. "Is everyone deciding now? We're not the only station in the solar system."

"We aren't. But everyone else is watching us."

"Do you know what you want?" Chrystal asked Satyana.

"For the Next to come in, take what they want, and not to kill anybody else. And even more, for this station not to do anything stupid."

"I noticed more defense bubbles on my way in," Nona mentioned.

Satyana almost spit out her words. "Twice as many. We already had enough guns to put down an attack by any single power in the system, and most alliances that seemed even vaguely possible. Now some people think we're ready to defend ourselves against the Next."

Chrystal reacted first. "You can't."

"I know that," Satyana snapped. "But not everyone here understands how strong they are. It's as if they've already forgotten the High Sweet Home."

"Or perhaps they haven't," Nona mused. Silence fell.

Nona finished her wine and ate most of the berries. She'd never seen Satyana so openly tense. "Is the Deep using the court to decide?"

"Well," Satyana poured herself some wine, "Sheenan Bolla is Headmistress now. That happened right after you left. First time we've had a woman in three turns."

The Headman position—part ceremony and part ruler—had become a job that turned over every six years after the minor revolution that Ruby had unwittingly helped Winter Ohman start.

"Sheenan should have one third of the vote." Satyana was speaking toward Chrystal, as if checking to be sure that she understood. "One third for her, one third for the Councilors, and one third for the Voice. You remember the Voice?"

Chrystal nodded. "Rich people selected to represent the people with interests."

Satyana frowned. "Not always rich people."

"Almost," Nona said. "But you said Sheenan *should have* one third of the vote."

Satyana was still frowning. "Sheenan did something very brave, which I'm hoping was not also very stupid." A note of slight disgust colored Satyana's voice, undoubtedly on purpose. The woman was a born actor. "She gave her vote to the collective."

Nona put her glass down, surprised. "How will that be decided?"

"Social vote. The main computer will read the social web in the same way it does for concerts."

Nona relaxed and poured a tiny bit more wine. "You manipulate the socweb all the time."

Satyana narrowed her eyes. "This will be harder."

Satyana would still try. Maybe she didn't want to say so in front of Chrystal. The social web was generally an insubstantial and ephemeral force of ideas pulled one way and then another. But not always. Sometimes it coalesced and caused actual change—fashion, behavior, belief, adoption or destruction of a technology. Socweb opinions occasionally infected the whole station in waves. Satyana was a queen of public opinion, but there were other influencers.

"Who is the Voice this time?" Nona asked.

Satyana smiled broadly, a little secretively. There will be three this time. "Gunnar. Winter Ohman." She fell silent.

"And the third?"

"You."

Nona sat back. No way. "I'm . . . I've never . . ."

"Close your mouth. You'll do fine. I spoke for you. After all, you met the Next. You've traveled back for weeks with Chrystal and her family. You've been on Lym lately and with its ambassador. What more perfect choice is there?"

Chrystal was grinning widely. "And look—you're not already a super-power here."

Satyana choked back a laugh. "Exactly. Which means you'll influence the social web more than anyone else could. Best friends, reunited after a disaster."

Nona and Chrystal shared a look that was part horror and part amusement.

"Everything you say, everyone you meet—either of you—is going to be magnified a thousand times. I've had clothes ordered and we're going to start rehearsing as soon as we finish eating."

Nona grinned. Satyana telling her what to do felt like truly being home.

————— ✧ —————

When she and Chrystal were finally alone in a shared suite of rooms deep inside the *Star Bear*, Nona flopped down on her bed. "How do you feel? Being here?"

"Right here, inside Satyana's world? Safe. Safer than on the *Bleeding Edge*."

"Did they threaten you?"

"No. And I'm probably describing it wrong. It *was* safe. The Next had plans for us, after all. They made us. But they are busy and driven, and it felt like we were always being gently forced—but forced—to learn more about our new brains, our bodies, the Next, how to communicate, how to run, how to fight, anything. We were almost never alone with each other. That's why we spent so much time together on the *Star Ghost*." She giggled. "But now

I've gone from the *Star Ghost* to the *Star Bear*." She smiled. "I'm worried about seeing my family. I expected my mom to be right there, waiting for me."

Nona laughed. "That would have made our greeting too unscripted for Satyana's taste. I'm sure you'll see her tomorrow."

Chrystal looked away. "I'm afraid."

"Afraid of seeing your mom?"

"I'm . . . uncertain . . . about seeing anyone."

Of course she was afraid. The Deep felt like a place where anything could happen, even something bad. Surely Chrystal felt it even more than she did. Nona took Chrystal's hand in hers. "Coming here was brave. I'll do everything I can to keep you safe."

"I'm glad you're here with me," Chrystal said.

"Me, too."

CHAPTER FIFTY-THREE

CHRYSTAL

Being on the station would be so much easier if she had Jason's arms to retreat to, and his soft touches and his sweet need for her. It would help to have Yi's bright brain to argue with about what they had lost and what they were becoming and what they were now.

Returning to the Deep didn't feel like coming home. The creaks and groans of the *Star Bear* sounded less purposeful than a working spaceship and also different from her home hab. It would probably take her four hours by high-speed train to get home from here. Maybe less by air taxi. The Deep was flat and thick and long, with fractal edges that changed as it grew ship by ship, habitat bubble by habitat bubble, the growth always at the edges to maximize access to the sun. Light meant energy, and almost certainly light was the primary thing the Next wanted. Way out on the High Sweet Home, the thing she had missed the most was sunlight.

She had heard that beyond the Ring it took effort to pick Adiamo out from background stars, that the gas giant Heroph loomed larger in the sky, and looked slightly brighter.

Watching Nona sleep took a long time.

Chrystal busied herself reading as much of the news as she could manage, trying to figure out who had what power these days. She'd been gone long enough that many positions had changed. She made mental notes about the councilors, paying special attention to the Historian, the Futurist, and the Economist.

She had never imagined playing any part in the complex politics of the Deep.

Nona moaned in her sleep and thrashed under the covers. She rolled to her stomach and stuck a foot out.

Chrystal sat on the edge of the bed and rubbed Nona's shoulders and upper back lightly, listening carefully as her breathing deepened and became more regular.

Back at the table, she started working her way through the various banks and shippers, looking for any signs of trouble in major sectors. She noted plenty of it, most not quite understandable to her except as movements of money she planned to ask Satyana about. She also noticed a net loss in population—which had never happened before. The Deep accreted people and ships faster than any other location in the solar system. Yet, the station had lost a half a percent of its population. She looked closer at the numbers. They had lost two percent and gained one and a half. All since the High Sweet Home. That was a *lot* of churn.

Given the travel times between locations in space, they might only be seeing the beginning of any exodus or influx. Another thing to ask about after Charlie and Nona woke up.

She made a list of topics to research the next night.

Anything not to think too much about Jason and Yi flying toward Lym. The *Star Ghost* would start slowing down soon, and be in orbit a day or two after that. She had set news alerts on the ship, but there had been no responses so far.

The light started to come up, and the sounds of a forest slowly infiltrated the room. Virtual birds sang morning songs and a slight wind brushed branches against each other.

Nona slammed her hand down on the controls and set the room to snooze for fifteen more minutes.

Chrystal sighed and re-reviewed maps of the parts of the station they were near.

The next time the lights and sound came on, Chrystal started talking. "The people here appear to be divided about what to do, with almost half wanting to co-operate with the Next in some way, a quarter or so wanting to fight, and whoever's left either wanting to become like me or still in denial."

"Really? What do they think? That the Next are a hoax?"

"Or that they aren't coming in or that they're a threat manufactured by the Council."

Nona pushed herself up to a sitting position. "I guess I do need to wake up," she mumbled. Five minutes later she had pulled on comfortable pants and a white blouse and handed Chrystal a comb.

Chrystal worked knots out of Nona's hair. "I remember I used to do this for you when we were in college."

"I remember." She looked up at Chrystal, her facial expression reminding Chrystal of hundreds of small, intimate times they had shared as teenagers. The moment lasted until Nona held her hand out for the comb. "Let's go get me some breakfast."

The mere mention of something Nona needed and Chrystal would never need again broke the spell.

Nona didn't look at all surprised when they walked into the galley and Chrystal's mom sat at the small table clutching a glass of stim and talking with Satyana in low tones.

Her mom stared at her.

Chrystal looked back, forcing a smile onto her face. Her mom looked like she remembered, maybe a tiny bit sadder. She had grown her hair longer and dyed it as black as Satyana's. "Mom," she whispered.

"That's Chrystal's voice," her mom said to Satyana.

"Of course it's my voice," Chrystal said. "I'm me."

"How do I know?"

"You're my mother, you should just know." A dumb thing to say, but it had come out. The only way to describe her mother's face was *frightened*. She gentled her voice. "Ask me anything."

"Where's Katherine?"

Except that. What could she say that wouldn't scare her mom more? "She died." Chrystal felt awkward. "When they did what they did to put me in this body, it didn't work for Katherine."

Her mother extended a hand toward her and then pulled it back. "Can I feel you?"

"Of course." She walked over to her mom.

Satyana stood up to make room for Chrystal. "Eleanor, we'll go get coffee somewhere else. I have some things to talk to Nona about anyway."

Eleanor nodded, her eyes still on Chrystal.

Satyana quietly escorted Nona from the room. Chrystal sat down where Satyana had been and reached across the table and took her mom's hand. "See, this is how I feel. I hear it's almost like I used to feel, almost human."

"How can you be a real person if you don't eat or breathe?"

Chrystal tried to speak as calmly as she could. "I don't know. I don't have DNA any more, I'm not biological. But the patterns of my brain are still here, and now I'm the old me plus the things that have happened since then. I feel like me."

Her mom's voice shook. "But they killed you to do this to you?"

"They did."

A tear fell down her mother's face, and then another. Eleanor wiped them way, one of the tears clinging to her nail like a jewel. It matched the real jewels already affixed to her blue nail-paint.

"I'm sorry," Chrystal said. "I'm sorry that it happened. I know you told me not to go so far away."

"I never thought this would happen."

"I didn't know this *could* happen. But I feel like me. I *am* me."

"How can you be you if it's only your brain? What about your heart? What about your feelings?"

Chrystal wished she could do something useful with her hands. Not eating felt awkward—she used to use food as a way to stop and think. "I don't know," she said. "The person I am now is different than I would have been if I hadn't been uploaded into this body. But I have all of my memories."

"A computer could have those." Eleanor stood up and turned away. Her shoulders shook.

"I'm sorry," Chrystal said to her back. "I don't know how to tell you I'm me."

"You can't be you. My daughter is dead."

The words pierced her, so she felt them deep inside whatever stood in for a heart now that her body no longer needed blood.

Her mom had dissolved in a full cry. "I did not have a robot," she sobbed. "I could hold my daughter and she was warm."

Chrystal put her arms around her mother. "My skin is still warm, mom. I'm not the same, but I'm still me."

Her mother stiffened and didn't answer. They stood that way for what felt like a very long time to Chrystal, until her mom walked forward out of her embrace and fled the room.

CHAPTER FIFTY-FOUR

CHARLIE

Charlie woke up with an epiphany. He'd been busy trying to under-stand Jason and Yi, and through them, to at least glimpse the Next. Which meant he'd missed the most important thing. Neither of them had ever been to Lym.

He needed to make them love Lym.

He took his time getting dressed, thinking about mountains and water-falls, and about Cricket. Right now, he missed Cricket more than he missed Nona, but it had only been a week since he saw Nona. It had been about a year since he saw the tongat. And Jean Paul.

And the land. And a sky. Clouds. Rain. Tharps. Bicycles.

In that moment, as he stood with tooth-cleaning bubbles filling his mouth, he wanted a sky so badly that he considered suiting up and going outside just to be somewhere that wasn't surrounded by metal.

He had sentences of flowery descriptions of Lym ready to share with Yi and Jason when he walked into the command room. Yi sat draped across the main chair, and stood as Charlie came in. "You've got a message."

"Why didn't you tell me?" He winced at the rebuke in his voice.

"It came in five minutes ago. We could tell you were awake."

He shouldn't be frustrated. "I guess I need some stim," he said. "Sorry. Who's it from?"

"Manny."

"I'll take it in my office." He forced himself to make a cup of stim before he went to the cramped captain's office at the far end of the room. He opened the message and the look on Manny's face immediately set him to worrying. "Hi Charlie. I got your message that you're on your way and you have two of them with you. Bad idea. I can't promise safety to the robots. Do you remember the problems you reported on your way out? The gleaners who died?

"Well, we found three more dead gleaners. All of them killed by robots—at least according to rumor. People think the killers are Next getting ready to pull a coup. They think the robots are really, really dangerous. They think they're out to eat their children, dammit.

"They'll be safer in orbit. Or Jean Paul says you can have them on the station and he won't tell anyone. So you can do that, too. But they have to look enough like people to get onto the surface safely—which means *you* have to get them through customs."

Manny leaned forward, so his face looked bigger and slightly distorted. He also lowered his voice to a raspy whisper. "There's more. People are leaving—people who have been here for generations. They're scared. You need to be careful.

"And I want to know," his voice fell even lower, "I want to know what you think we should do. What you learned. So I want to see you as soon as I can. I'll meet you if I can get away."

Manny's brows drew in, making his bushy eyebrows look like hills. "Oh, and be careful what you say to whom. Power could change down here." That was the end. A warning.

Charlie sat back. That last bit implied Manny might be in trouble. He'd governed Manna Springs for as long as Charlie could remember. There were elections every so often, but Manny always won easily. People loved him, at least as much as they loved any government.

He and Charlie came from one of the founding families. That meant something on Lym.

Charlie had expected home to be almost like he left it. It wasn't going to be like that. He closed his eyes, took a long drink of stim, and then thought for a while before opening his eyes. He finished the stim before he felt certain he had a plan. He'd show the video to Yi and Jason. That was only fair. They were adults and they were in danger.

He'd go ahead and land, go to the Ranger Station. It would be great to see Cricket and Jean Paul. The station could be defended, and it had a hell of a lot of sky.

CHAPTER FIFTY-FIVE

NONA

Nona held her head up and did her best to look like she was completely in control as she and Chrystal followed Satyana into the Historian's office. Even though these meetings were mostly about Chrystal and the Councilor's interest in meeting her, Nona felt her inexperience, and the weight of her coming role as part of the Voice. She would be a third of a third of one of the most important decisions the Deep had ever faced.

Chrystal had gone stoic since her mother walked out on her. Nona sensed that her friend had been deeply affected by the failure of the meeting. She didn't know what happened, only that when they went back in the room, they found Chrystal sitting alone with a deadpan face, her fingers playing with the cup her mother had been drinking from.

The Historian's office was huge. A dozen people could fill its sitting-room-like chairs. The decor had been done in browns and blacks and warm tans. Pictures hung on every wall, in a sequence that started with the colony ship that had brought the first humans to Lym and ended with the return of the generation ship *The Creative Fire*. Tea and breakfast cookies filled a small table.

Nona glanced at Satyana, who looked as intense and alert as Charlie's tongat. Nona took a deep breath. She could do this. She remembered her chant on the way in. *I am strong enough to influence the Deep.*

The current Historian, Dr. Neil Nevening, had once taught at the same university Nona used to teach at. Even though he'd been the Historian for fifteen years, he still looked like a professor. His hair was a sandy brown that no one in their right mind would choose as a dye, and he had no noticeable mods.

She held out her hand. "I'm Nona Hall. I taught biology at Startide. You left quite a reputation behind." In fact the school was so proud of him that there was a three-dimensional statue of the slender professor worked into an art-wall.

He smiled softly at her. "I miss teaching."

"But surely your new duties are interesting," Nona murmured.

"They are. But as a teacher you're closer to the students than a councilor is to the people. At least I met most of my students at least once." He poured three cups of tea from a round pot colored like a sun. It looked like it might actually be old: it appeared to have been fashioned by hand, or at least painted by hand.

Satyana lifted the delicate cup he handed her and turned it around carefully to admire it. "How beautiful. This must be an heirloom."

He looked pleased. "This set has been in my family for generations."

He neither poured for Chrystal, nor asked her. He had done some homework.

The tea turned out to be mint and some flowery spice Nona couldn't name. He let everyone take a few sips and allowed a lightly uncomfortable silence to grow before he spoke to them. "I have been doing research nonstop since the High Sweet Home." He glanced at Chrystal. "I'm sorry."

"It's all right," Chrystal said. "I've grown used to it."

"First, I haven't made up my mind yet. I'll have to vote from the perspective of my position when we're done. I interpret that as a vote to respect the choices we made in our past. That does not mean that we must repeat mistakes."

"We understand," Nona said, grateful to notice that Satyana smiled at her for it.

He turned to Chrystal. "I have a few questions for you. May I?"

Chrystal inclined her head. "Of course."

"You did not choose this?"

"No."

"And you would un-choose it if you could?"

"If I could stay alive."

"So you prefer this," he seemed to choose his words carefully, "you prefer being in a robot body to being dead?"

Chrystal hesitated, very slightly. Perhaps so little that only Nona would recognize it for uncertainty. "Yes."

"And you believe you are yourself?"

"Yes. I don't detect a break between the me that was flesh and the me that is not flesh—there's no loss of continuity. Even so, the me I would have been—undisturbed—was destroyed. Cut off. That version of me would have felt more deeply, would have slept and ate and made love and grown ill."

Dr. Nevening stood and paced a bit before he continued. "In the past, we chose to banish people who had made choices that created beings like you." He stopped and stared hard at Chrystal, pressing her. "Should you be banished?"

"No." No hesitation. She put a finger up to indicate she had more to say. "If I may. I studied last night. When the Next were originally banished, they were weak and fractured. They came from all over the Glittering, and they had no governance. Some wanted to live forever. Others wanted to become much stronger than humans, sometimes for specific goals like to climb mountains or race all the way around Lym. Some were human children that were ported into pubescent robotic bodies and used as sex slaves."

Dr. Nevening nodded. "That's all true. And what you're going to go on to add is that the power balance is different now. That we made them all go live beyond the Ring because we could. I've read that argument."

Chrystal smiled. "You're underestimating me. The point I want to make is that what we did before was kind. Many of the people in the first group, the people actually banished, did not choose to become Next. Out there beyond the Ring, the Next were forced to learn to get along, to reproduce by making copies, to create governance."

He looked excited. "Yes!"

Satyana leaned forward. "But they're still taking humans against their will. They made you."

"They promised that if we don't fight them, they won't force more people to become like me."

"Why should I believe that?" Satyana replied. "They *did* make you."

"After." Chrystal hesitated for a moment. "After the attack, we were asked how we felt and they seemed surprised that we were unhappy and that we thought they murdered us."

The Historian furrowed his brow. "So they are so far out of touch with what it means to be human that they accidentally killed you to improve you?"

"That's an oversimplification," Chrystal said, although her body language suggested that she agreed with him.

"Still," he said. "You are asking me to support the Next because they promised not to kill humans and translate their souls into software, even though they did that to you?"

An awkward silence fell. Satyana spoke into it. "We can't fight them.

Surely you see that. If you look back into other parts of history, is there any moment when a far more powerful entity lost a war to a less powerful one?"

"Are you certain we are less powerful?" he responded to Satyana, although he was looking at Chrystal.

"There's a lot I don't know," Chrystal said. "Including how much military power the Next have. I know that I was on the High Sweet Home and that they destroyed all of our protections there. Ships, guns, warning systems. All of it."

"There is a theory they had inside help."

Chrystal shrugged. "But there are millions of people on the Deep. Are they all loyal?"

"Can you answer my question?" Satyana pushed. "Has there ever been a war this unequal where the lesser power won?"

"No."

"No, history has never shown we can win? Or no, you can't answer?"

"Smaller forces have defeated larger forces over and over. Way back on Lym. Usually these are revolutions, rather than a smaller force repelling an invader. At this point, we must think of the Next as invaders."

Chrystal said, "The Next think faster than we do. They think faster than I do, even now that I'm faster than I was. They communicate with each other constantly and well, across large distances. They are driven by some goal they have not explained, and everything I saw in my time with them suggests that they will be hard or impossible to stop."

"It surprises me that you're being so blunt," he said.

Chrystal smiled. I've always been blunt."

"So why did they send you as their ambassador?" He sat back in his chair and crossed his legs for effect, and Nona imagined that he was once a very good professor. He looked straight at Chrystal and said, "You seem like a weak choice."

Chrystal didn't flinch. "We talked about this a lot, my family and I. We believe the Next are so far removed from humanity that they would not be able to have a normal conversation with you. They created us, and they matched us to people. I am here because I know Nona and she is connected to people on the Deep in power." She nodded at Satyana. "After all, I am meeting with you. That implies a reasonable choice on their part. I am not so unlike you that you can't or won't talk with me. It would be hard for you to have tea with the—more evolved—Next."

Nona felt confused. "But I came for you unexpectedly. They let you go with me, but I asked first."

"I know," Chrystal said. "I do think it was before we were completely ready, and while we still didn't know some things we might have learned. It had, however, been the plan. To have me leave with you. The Next must have decided we were ready enough or they wouldn't have allowed it. They're curious and interesting and interested. But they are not kind."

"No," Dr. Nevening said, "I don't suppose they are kind."

CHAPTER FIFTY-SIX

CHARLIE

When the light from Manny's message flicked off, Charlie watched Yi and Jason. He hoped to catch whether or not they were surprised by the rumors on Lym, but neither of their expressions exposed deep feelings. If he had to describe them, he might say Yi looked thoughtful and Jason slightly scared. "Do the Next have—members—themselves—already on Lym?" he asked them.

Jason answered immediately. "Not that they told us about."

"But they didn't say they don't have them, right?"

"We never talked about it." Jason frowned, his gaze turned slightly inward. "They told us about ourselves, mostly. And about what they could do, that they could live forever, that they could copy themselves and be two beings, or more. They didn't tell us anything about their plans on Lym. I can't imagine they would have wanted us to know."

"But they did send you here," Charlie murmured, the thought trailing off. "But not to Lym. To the station. Maybe we can surprise them."

"Don't assume you can," Yi said. "Surprise them. They can calculate outcomes better than a nav computer. All of them."

"We're instant ambassadors," Jason said, with a funny grin. "Just add robot body and voila! If they'd told us anything real, they might have had to kill us."

Charlie laughed, but felt the pain behind the words.

Yi finally answered Charlie's original question. "It would be smart for them to have advance guards. We know that people smuggled materials to them beyond the Ring—that's been a way to get rich or get in real trouble as long as I remember. One of the women I went to school with died on a smuggling trip.

"It would be reasonable for them to have friends throughout the inner systems, and maybe even to have smuggled either individuals or very sophisticated robots to many places. They have robots that are not true AI's, are not aware like the Next, but are far more complex than any I've seen in the Glittering. Our own repair robot looks like one of yours that the Next improved. It's smarter than the models it was patterned after. It learns faster."

"Crap. And to think I was only worried about you two."

Jason laughed. "Don't worry about us. We're on your side."

Charlie leaned toward them. "But you yourself have no one to contact on Lym, no plans."

Yi took Jason's hand and squeezed it. "No."

"And the Next can't directly contact you and tell you how to help them?"

Jason reacted first. "We wouldn't!"

Yi followed. "Not that I know of. But I wouldn't underestimate the Next."

"I won't." It would have to do. Charlie sat back. "Okay. Thanks. Yi, do you promise to tell me if the Next contact you for any reason, at any time?"

"If they contact me about Lym in any way, I promise. Otherwise, I will have to evaluate."

Charlie found that answer more comforting than a simple yes. "Okay." He sat back. "So we're going to talk about my goals."

"Okay," Jason said. They were still holding hands.

Charlie took a deep breath and imagined he was home. "I believe Lym is sacred. It's what we came from—a wild life. We must have evolved in a place like this, or we wouldn't have come here. Lym is natural, a place where plants and animals all live together with far less control than we exert on stations and ships. Lym evolves.

"Restoring Lym, protecting Lym, has been my work and my family's work since before the Next were banished beyond the Ring. We hardly noticed when that happened. We were busy making up for the damage done by people who raped the planet for materials they wanted in space. Things they could have gotten some other way. I think that's what the Next want—easy access to a place to get minerals and raw materials and bask in sunshine." He paused and took a deep breath. "Nothing you've told me has convinced me the Next will care about the wild things of Lym."

Yi nodded. "That's probably correct."

Charlie continued. "I want to keep the Next away from Lym. I'm willing to die to do it."

"I doubt that would help," Jason said, quite solemnly.

Charlie laughed, the tension in the room breaking down some. Yi let go of Jason's hand and stood and stretched and then sat back down.

"No," Charlie said, "it probably wouldn't. And I don't actually plan to die. But that's how important it is to me. If the best way to keep Lym free of the Next is to fight, I'll do that. If it's something else, I'll do that. But I don't want to see the Next landing on my home. There is nothing that drives me more than that, not right now. Nothing else matters more."

Yi regarded him quietly. "You are taking us there."

Damn it.

CHAPTER FIFTY-SEVEN

CHRYSTAL

After the meeting with the Historian, Satyana took them to lunch in a small restaurant with walls that were vertical herb gardens. Chrystal sat quietly while Satyana and Nona whispered together about the meeting with the Historian. Satyana sounded pleased.

The Historian had been interesting, but Chrystal's attention kept flipping back to the last image she'd recorded of her mother's face. There had been revulsion and sorrow and loss on it, and also disbelief.

Chrystal understood. Especially the disbelief. Here, back home, she sometimes felt like her old self. But then she'd flex a foot and realize it wasn't her old foot, or she'd let the sharpness of her nose bring her smells from all the way across the room and she would remember she shouldn't be able to tell that the plant in the corner had mold growing on its roots.

Her mother's face floated behind her eyes, like a ghost haunting her any time she stopped thinking of other things. She had buried it for part of the interview, but right now it wouldn't stay down.

Nona noticed. "Are you okay?"

"I'm thinking about mom."

Satyana gave her a sharp look. "We're going to see the Economist next, and she's going to be harder to deal with than the good doctor of history."

Her tone made Chrystal laugh, which anchored her back in the conversation. This was Satyana's strength: leading people, reading them. Helping them, even while she was talking them into doing what she wanted. "I'll do my best," Chrystal answered. "But I'm only about three-quarter robot."

That made Satyana and Nona both laugh. A little victory. It felt as if the three of them were friends, at least at the moment. "Let's go," Satyana said.

"Don't you have to pay the bill?" Nona asked.

"I own the restaurant."

The Economist kept them waiting in the outer foyer of her office for a quarter of an hour. When the door slid open, Chrystal rose a split second before Nona and Satyana.

The woman who emerged had to be eight feet tall. Her hair was every shade of purple, piled in buns and hanging in braids, and all of it sprinkled with gems like stars.

Tattooed flowers twined up both arms past the elbows. A wild woman, Chrystal thought, bemused.

The Economist's smile was as wide as her face. Her eyes probably came from the same exact designer as Satyana's. "I'm Leesha Lee Miles," she pronounced, as if it were a very important fact. Then she held her hand out in introduction to each of them, giving exaggerated handshakes. She saved Chrystal for last. "Pleased to meet you," she said. "Finally someone comes to visit who is stranger than I am."

Chrystal smiled; for once it even felt natural. "Finally, someone who is so strange that I feel almost normal."

The Economist's smile suggested she and Chrystal had been friends forever. "Well, then, we'll have a good talk. Follow me."

She glided almost as if she wore wheels on her shoes. Her office was stark white: white walls, a white desk, a white floor with black rugs.

"Wow," Nona said. "I like it."

Satyana whispered, "The last time I was here it was all dark and gloomy."

The Economist brushed two stray braids behind her shoulder. "That was before I got here. I have been very frugal with the station's investments in me, except for updating this place." She pushed a button and a wall opened on a window view that looked over a froth of farms. Grains made multicolored golden patches in the closest bubble, each individual grain field lined all around with flowers in a myriad of colors. Beyond, the greens of vegetable crops colored four other farms. Further out, the frothy whiteness of bubble walls spread throughout a lot of space all of them open now to the sun.

"I've never seen the so many crops," Chrystal said. "We went on field trips once or twice, so I've been in some. We had huge cylinder gardens on the High Sweet Home."

Leesha smiled her wide, wide smile. "I love this place. The crop bubbles are the perfect example of my craft. They have to be right. They can't make us sick;

they can't fail to grow enough food for our population; they can't fail to produce the right balance of proteins and micronutrients." She held up a finger. "But at the same time, food is a business brimming with innovation. The hungry want new meals; restaurants want particular spices and wines of a certain quality." She turned toward the three women. "How else might food be like economics?"

Satyana had an immediate answer. "You have reserves. The station has reserves of both credit and food."

Nona added, "And while more of both can be grown, the supply needs to mirror demand."

Leesha smiled approval. "That's an art. I know your family history. When Ruby Martin came here, there was more poverty than there is now. The distribution of wealth is currently . . . more fair."

Chrystal risked adding an idea to the conversation. "Outside events affect the food supply. For example, the demographics are changing right now as people flee before the Next get here."

Leesha looked pleased. "That's correct. So perhaps you understand some of the forces I'm trying to balance. Shall we sit down?"

They did.

"So tell me what you know about the Next's economy," Leesha encouraged.

"I don't. Not really. We only saw the inside of one ship."

Leesha frowned as if she were disappointed in Chrystal. "Do they own you?"

"Well, no. When I chose to come here, I was worried they wouldn't let me. But they said I'm not a slave."

The door opened.

The Economist glanced toward it unhappily, the rebuke on her face keeping Chrystal's attention so that she saw annoyance turn to fear.

A man cleared his throat.

Chrystal turned to look. A woman with a pinched face and intense black eyes reached toward her. Behind the woman, there were three men with weapons.

Before she could decide what to do, the woman had thrown a cloth at Chrystal's face, momentarily stealing her vision. Two big men rushed her, tying her arms to her torso with strong, stretchy material.

Satyana struggled quietly, and Nona screamed for Chrystal.

PART SEVEN

CONFLICT

CHAPTER FIFTY-EIGHT

CHARLIE

The *Star Ghost* slowed hard, now less than a day away from Lym. Charlie could feel it, like a beacon calling him home. Minding Manny's warning, he kept the note he fashioned for Jean Paul simple: "I'll be returning to my duty station soon. Please help arrange transportation down for me."

"There's my long-lost roommate."

It was after midnight at Wilding Station, so Jean Paul's immediate answer caught him by surprise. Jean Paul sat in his office at the station, and even in the dull night light he looked thin and drawn. He'd grown a scraggly beard and looked even more like a wild man than usual.

"It's good to see you. No—great." Charlie felt lighter already for seeing his friend, the delighted grin spreading across his face mirrored on the man below.

"I'll book the *Verdant Sun* to get you," Jean Paul said. "Be sure you wait if you get there before she does."

"Thanks. The *Sun's* a good ride." She was also the only ship that could both get him from the Port Authority stations and land at the ranger stations. Most of the others were so big they had to use the spaceport in town.

"Travel safe." Jean Paul's voice sounded thick. "I'll talk to you when you get here."

"Okay." Charlie flicked the window on his slate shut, wondering at the quick dismissal. Both Jean Paul and Manny sounded awful.

Charlie called up a picture of Lym on the view screen. They were close enough he would have been able to see it using the camera, but it would have been the size of a berry. The image in front of him showed Lym in all her glory. Mountains bisected continents, rivers flowed, forests grew. He could touch anywhere and zoom or pan on the image. He sat there for a long time, looking at the biggest rivers and deserts and the seas.

He had breathed recycled air for almost a year now, and been surrounded by walls. He could smell home from here, and now he could hardly wait.

The next eight hours or so were going to take forever.

CHAPTER FIFTY-NINE

CHRYSTAL

A man as tall as Gunnar and half as wide filled the doorway to the Economist's office. A long braid wrapped in blue and red cloth fell to his waist; he'd tucked the end into his belt. He carried himself with a bright and angry intensity, dominating the room without speaking.

A blonde woman bound Chrystal's arms with wide, smart material that held them tightly, constricting if she flexed.

There were too many people to fight, and she only had her feet free. Surely she'd get a better opportunity.

Most of their enemies had multiple weapons; at least one in their hands and one or two on belts or in shoulder holsters. Small beam weapons, but she spotted a few knives sheathed on belts.

She stilled her features, playing robot. These people felt twitchy.

The leader said, "You will come with me. You will walk slowly and easily or we will stun you and carry you. We don't expect to pass anyone, but if we do, you will not show that you are restrained in any way. If you are greeted, you will smile. If you don't, you'll be killed on the spot. Do you understand?" He waited for each woman to nod. He saved Chrystal for last; she met his night-black eyes for a brief moment before nodding. She didn't like what she saw there—hatred, fear, and a deep determination. This man was in charge, and deeply passionate about whatever drove him.

One of the women on his team carefully draped beautiful shawls over each of their shoulders. The Economist's and Satyana's shawls matched their eyes perfectly, and were made of high quality material that they might have chosen themselves. Nona and Chrystal were both draped in blacks with dragons in forms that complimented their own tattoos. Covered by the shimmering and beautiful material, there was no outward sign of their captivity.

The chilling level of preparation suggested they had been specific targets.

The tattooed man had not given his name, but Satyana and Leesha both seemed nervous of him.

He led off, and three of his people followed. The blonde who had tied her prodded Chrystal into going next, followed by two other guards. Satyana followed them, then an armed guard, Leesha and a guard, then Nona and three guards. The long train of people walked steadily, with discipline. They stopped from time to time to consult a slate. Their whispers were meant to be too low for Chrystal to hear, but they were clearly checking directions. The line bunched and swelled as they worked their way through corridors.

Chrystal's brain raced and stuttered through all of the things she had noticed the night before. The influx of new ships must have stretched security thin. The station took so much pride in being open and inclusive that Chrystal had no trouble imaging that these people were invaders who had infested the Deep top to bottom.

They turned another corner and climbed into an empty high-speed train car. She had no chance to talk to the others, but she glimpsed their faces as they boarded. Nona looked frightened, Satyana oddly serene. The Economist looked mostly appalled.

Chrystal searched the public station data for clues. Most of the formal news had gone cold, and the articles she did find were fragmented. The socweb talked of missing people and lost connectivity, of protests, and of unexpected locked doors.

She might die again. In spite of the muted edge so many of her other emotions had acquired, the will to live felt sharp and painful.

She ached for Yi and Jason. Yi would be planning a clever escape and Jason would be in front, between her and danger.

They rode for an hour. No captive was offered food or drink or access to rest facilities, or allowed to talk.

Chrystal listened carefully and decided that their captors were in fact an invading force. But they were too disciplined to say anything about who had sent them, what they wanted, or what they planned to do next.

One of their kidnappers called the tattooed man Vadim. The woman who had first helped to bind her seemed to be a favorite of his. He called her Nayli. There were no tattoos visible on her exposed skin, and she wore her long black hair in a braid almost exactly like his. From time to time they touched each other discretely.

For a full hour, it wasn't much to learn.

When the train stopped, Vadim and Nayli stood by the door. The man closest to Chrystal nudged her with his weapon. "Get off."

She did. Vadim, Nayli, and five others also disembarked.

The door closed behind her, and she turned to find Nona's face pressed against the window, her eyes locked onto Chrystal's. "Stay safe," Nona mouthed.

A rough hand pulled her away before she could offer an answer.

CHAPTER SIXTY

NONA

Nona, Satyana, and the Economist were ushered off the train half an hour later, and escorted through a long hall. Eventually they stopped and two guards pointed weapons at them while a dark-eyed woman with high cheekbones removed their restraints. Nona grimaced as the blood rushed, tingling, back into her arms.

Their guards ushered them into a suite of rooms. Except for the armed guards, it looked like they had been invited to an awkward cocktail party. Councilors gathered around and on a large blue couch in the middle of the room. Here and there, other captives stood in small groups near the walls, talking amongst themselves in low tones. Nona recognized the assistant who had let them into Dr. Nevening's office.

Dr. Nevening waved at Nona from the sofa and said, "Hello again. I'm so sorry to see you here."

"Me, too," Nona replied, suddenly awkward and unsure what to say, if anything.

The Futurist sat beside him on the sofa. Nona had never met him, although she had seen pictures. His casual black pants and simple, flowing white shirt came from the high end of the Exchange and probably cost a year's worth of her teaching salary. A gold band held his black hair in a single, short ponytail, and he wore two gold earrings in each ear.

Nona took a deep breath and looked around the room. The others seemed to be putting a brave face on their captivity. She smiled as she held her hand out to the Futurist in greeting. "I'm afraid we missed our scheduled meeting with you. I'm Nona Hall."

The Futurist gave her a glistening smile. "Pleased. I'm Hiram."

The Historian asked, "Where is Chrystal? Did she escape?"

Nona shook her head. "They took her somewhere else. I'm scared for her."

"I'm sorry," the Historian said. "I rather liked her. Plucky."

"She is."

Hiram looked at Leesha, speaking softly. "Do you know what's happening?"

"We were taken by Vadim and his people. They've been known to destroy Next ships, and my bet is they want to make sure we vote to fight."

"I hadn't decided how to vote yet," the Historian whispered. "Had you?"

No one answered him. Nona looked at the guards, who were alert but not paying particular attention to them.

"I don't know the woman who brought me here," the Futurist said. "But she cursed like a miner."

"Is it an invasion?" Nona asked.

Leesha sat down on the couch next to the Historian, her legs sticking out and her head towering above his. She glanced at the closest guard, frowning. "It must be an invasion. I suspect they've taken Chrystal to one of their ships and left all of us here. We're too popular to kill or hurt, and too powerful to kidnap. But Chrystal is none of those things."

"She's probably more famous than any of us right now," Satyana said.

"But no one knows what to think of her." Leesha tucked a stray violet lock into her oddly-piled hair. The perfect edges had slumped during the long walk here. "Her power—if any—is conferred by the Next. Perhaps she's a hostage."

"But you were their main target?" Nona mused.

"Yes," Leesha said. "The Council. Either they'll keep us from making the decision or they'll force us to make the one they want."

"*Can* they force us?" Dr. Nevening asked. "We don't have to do what they want."

Satyana said, "You've never made a decision at gunpoint."

The Historian's face looked like he'd just eaten a sour pickle.

The Futurist frowned. "There were two big protests starting. One on each side of the argument—fighting and helping."

"Some of the organizers approached me," Dr. Nevening said. "Something about making up for past sins."

Hiram continued, "A bomb detonated in Exchange three and killed two vendors and five shoppers, including a child. I heard about it right before these idiots took me. Everybody's scared."

"So what's going to happen? Nona asked.

He looked irritated. "Futurists aren't fortunetellers. My models didn't predict the Next would return. Now I have to recalibrate them all." He fell silent for a long moment, and no one else spoke. Eventually he continued, sounding almost like he was lecturing a class of first-year college students. "Wild cards make all of our long-term predictions wrong, even in places as stable as the Deep. The return of the Next is a rather big wild card. We know it's affecting politics since *we're* here. The military has been salivating ever since the High Sweet Home was taken, and the social webs have been aflutter with silly fears. When Sheenan Bolla decided to allow the socweb a vote, the conversation heated up to boiling."

"Which means good things could happen as well as bad," Satyana noted.

Hiram gave her a condescending look. "I suppose we could be rescued by a white angel force any time, but I kind of suspect we're more likely to be killed."

Satyana smiled sweetly at him. "You did just say you can't predict the future. So we should be prepared for anything, right?"

Hiram swallowed and looked like he wished Satyana wasn't there.

"Do we have any new news?" Leesha asked. "I can't get any of my devices to connect to anything. I suppose they shielded the room."

"Yes," Hiram said. "They brought one of my assistants," he pointed at a man over in the corner talking quietly with another man. "I asked him to keep testing and come tell me if he learns anything. I haven't seen him since."

The door opened and a guard thrust the Biologist in, along with two young women. The Biologist looked around, and as she took in the various people who were staring at her, her face twisted in surprise and fury. Jackie Bray had only been the Biologist for about three years, and Nona remembered her as the teacher of one of her particularly large undergraduate classes. Jackie must have noticed Nona staring at her, since she stalked over and thrust her hand out at Nona. "Jackie Bray."

Nona took her hand and they shook. "I don't know if you remember me . . ."

"Of course I do. Marcelle Hall's daughter. Pleased to see you again."

Nona winced.

The Biologist went on, "Is the robot here?"

"No," Nona said, remembering why she hadn't liked her much as a teacher. "No, my friend Chrystal was taken somewhere else. But she *was* captured when we were."

The Futurist deepened his dolorous look. "This doesn't bode well."

The Biologist frowned at him and stalked off, demanding a glass of water from a kitchen-bot even though there was already water on a sideboard.

Nona had the sense they would all be arguing if it weren't for the guards who still stood there, holding weapons, and almost certainly listening to everything they said.

A serving-bot emerged from the suite's kitchen with a tray of simple sandwiches and flavored waters. The captives descended on the food as if they hadn't eaten in a week.

—∞∞∞—

Sometime later, sleeping people littered the soft carpet. A few of them tossed and turned and moaned from time to time, probably not sleeping at all.

Nona was too worried about Chrystal to sleep. She must feel terribly alone, and Nona couldn't imagine they'd taken her for anything good. She wanted to see Chrystal again, tell her she was still her best and oldest friend in spite of everything. She had never said that; she had assumed Chrystal knew.

She took a spot on the floor and leaned against a wall. Dr. Nevening came over to sit by her, and stayed quiet. In spite of his high standing, he looked as frightened and tired as she felt.

"Do you know this Vadim?" Nona asked him in a whisper.

"I know of him. He's had a reputation as a rebel for a long time. He's rumored to have been associated with two changes in government—a mutiny on a ship and a coup on a small station. Do you remember the Aurora station?"

"Vaguely. Something about kicking out a Headman for stealing taxes?"

"That's the one. Vadim's never done more than throw insults at the Deep though, not as far as I know."

"Do you think he set the bomb?"

Dr. Nevening shrugged. "That could have been almost anybody. I'm not at all surprised about this—I even tried to warn people in this morning's meeting."

"The one with us?" She didn't remember that.

"No. We meet together every morning. All of the Councilors. Not for long, just to have a cup of stim and breakfast and argue about the day's news."

"I had no idea." Nona shifted position, trying to get more comfortable on the hard floor. "So what did you warn them about?"

"That this is the biggest threat we've ever faced. Ever." He hesitated, and smiled. "Since we came here and landed on Lym anyway. The Next could wipe us all back to a far more primitive existence. A lot of people might die. It could also change us all, transform the whole way we look at the world. Maybe good, maybe bad. But we could become so different that you won't recognize yourself."

Two new guards came in, replacing the others. Nona and Dr. Nevening were both silent during the change. After, Nona whispered, "You sound like the Futurist."

"The difference between the Historian and the Futurist is just which direction we're looking."

"Hiram seems worried."

"He should be." He patted her shoulder. "Rest some. Even historians know when to think about the moment."

CHAPTER SIXTY-ONE

CHARLIE

Yi brought them into the long-term Port Authority docking station so smoothly that Charlie barely felt the final coupling. Charlie couldn't have done so well, and yet Yi didn't even look like he was piloting the ship. He and Jason were batting a silly golden ball of light through the air in some sort of virtual game.

Charlie sent a message to Nona, telling her which berth he'd parked the *Star Ghost* in. He added, *I'm back home and the crew is safe. Thank you for the loan of your ship. Hugs.*

The little robot followed them through the lock, carrying three small backpacks plus its own repair kit. They all left their suits on and carried their helmets.

They'd had to pay a premium to keep the *Ghost* anywhere for long. Charlie turned down two offers to buy her, one of which would have doubled Nona's initial investment.

The station corridors were chaotic. People hurried through them in all directions. Here and there a single person or a family stood looking lost, creating an island others had to flow around. No one looked askance at any of the robots as he led them all toward the debarkation lounges where they could wait for the *Verdant Sun*. Every once in a while, Jason drew interested looks from women.

To Charlie's surprise, Jean Paul himself leaned on a wall just inside the door to the busy lounges.

They embraced. Jean Paul smelled of home, and of fresh air, and of the wild. Eventually, Charlie held Jean Paul at arm's length. "You've lost weight."

"And you've gained some."

Charlie laughed. "It isn't as much work to be in space."

"The food must be good."

"Not as good as here."

A serious look crossed Jean Paul's face. "Let's not draw too much attention. Follow me."

He led them to one of the exits and made for the far right-hand customs line. "Here. Let me go first."

The line moved slowly as a uniformed customs agent questioned each person in detail.

Charlie fretted.

Jason and Yi kept up a conversation, sounding very human. Charlie couldn't tell if they looked wrong, since he had grown so accustomed to them.

When their turn came, Jean Paul spoke to the customs agent, his words inaudible given the background noise. The agent hesitated for a moment, and then waved them through.

Jean Paul led them to the correct docking facility and they climbed aboard the *Verdant Sun*. Kyle Glass, an ex-ranger whom Charlie hadn't seen in three years sat in the pilot seat. "Good to see you, boss."

"You, too. There are no words for how good it is to be home."

Kyle grinned. "Well, strap in and let's go." Kyle glanced at the two soul-bots, and Charlie caught both fear and worry in his eyes.

"It'll be okay," he assured his old friend.

"Hope so. Let's be away before we get caught."

The *Verdant Sun* was about a tenth the size of the *Star Ghost*, and mostly engine and cargo bay.

Based on the apprehension on Kyle's face, Charlie decided to keep the robots acting as human as possible. "Yi, Jason, stay suited and strap in."

They nodded and complied. In the pilot's seat, Kyle's hands flew over a glassy control surface. The shuttle whined and shuddered and then pulled away.

Five minutes later, Jean Paul relaxed visibly. "We're safe. There's tons of news. These are Jason and Yi, right?"

Jason said, "I'm Jason."

"I've seen pictures. Welcome, both of you."

Kyle asked, "Did you know that the Diamond Deep is under attack?"

"From the Next?" Charlie tensed. Nona must be there. "Are they winning?"

"It's not the Next. Not yet. There's a group that wants to fight the Next—the Shining Revolution or some such thing. They've attacked the Deep and two other stations, but the Deep is the big one."

That explained why the *Free Men* hadn't followed them to Lym. They were never its target in the first place. "I can't tell how big the attack is, not yet. There's more news though. The Deep's leaders have disappeared and there's apparently fighting inside that doesn't have anything to do with the Shining Revolution."

Yi leaned as far forward as the straps allowed him to, his face a study in fierce worry. "What about Chrystal?"

"She's disappeared from the news. There's a rumor she's on one of the Shining Revolution ships. There's a counter-rumor that she's dead and another that she's with the leaders from the Deep, and a fourth rumor says she's in hiding."

Jason reached for Yi's hand.

"So no one knows anything," Charlie whispered. "What about Nona?"

"Nothing," Jean Paul said.

Yi looked at Charlie, his eyes almost unreadable. "Do we have your permission to take the *Star Ghost* to the Deep?"

"Now?" Surely Yi knew better.

"The Deep is not in Lym's orbit," Jean Paul explained. "It's not really near us at all right now, and it will be getting even further away for the next few months."

Yi surely didn't need an explanation of orbital mechanics. In spite of that, he said, "We need to go back for Chrystal."

Jean Paul shook his head. "We can't turn around. This ship doesn't work that way—it's got full thrust now for Lym. We'd probably just burn out across the top of the atmosphere if we tried. You couldn't re-dock. We don't have papers. I also don't have another bribe big enough to get you past security."

Yi clenched the fist of his free hand around a railing and it bent.

"Take it easy," Kyle said, his eyes wide.

"Sorry."

"I wasn't entirely sure you were robots." Kyle's eyes had rounded and his voice shook. "Not until I saw that."

Yi let go of Jason's hand and bent the railing back. "We should never have left Chrystal."

"There's nothing we can do about the Deep," Charlie said, "Not right now." He looked at Jean Paul. "What's happening at home?"

"Nothing good."

"Is Cricket okay?"

"She'll be a lot better when she sees you. She keeps prowling around the house, looking in corners."

Yi said, "There was a Shining Revolution chapter on the High Sweet Home, before. . . . They came and gave lectures, did some stuff to help the poor. I never paid much attention."

Jason said, "I met one once. A woman. She wanted me to come to dinner, and I might have gone except that she felt too intense, maybe even a little bit crazy."

"Anybody that attacks the Deep *is* crazy," Charlie said. "It's huge. How's Manny?"

Kyle said, "He's holding on, but barely. Amara is with him. Pi and Bonnie took the kids to their cabin away from town."

That startled Charlie. "So people really are threatening him?"

Jean Paul said, "Yes."

"What about the gleaners? Did any more die?"

"Yes to that, too." Jean Paul looked sideways at Charlie, as if testing him. "There's one staying at the ranger station. She wants to talk to you."

"Who?"

"Amfi. That's all she'll give me for a name. I think you should meet with her."

"Okay. What else do we need to know?"

Kyle said, "Jason and Yi won't be safe in town. Maybe not even here. Three household robots have been dragged out into streets and shot up in the last week."

"Really?"

"Look. People are stupid when they're scared. It's all fear." Kyle glanced at the readouts. "It's time to strap back in. Ten minutes until we enter the atmosphere."

This time Jason and Yi just sat without being strapped in, which irritated Charlie. He glanced over at Kyle, who mouthed, "Creepy," at him.

CHAPTER SIXTY-TWO

CHRYSTAL

After they left the train, armed guards pushed Chrystal behind Vadim and Nayli for so long she memorized the tattoos on the back of Vadim's bare arms: a sun, a spaceship, stars, and two women—one that had to be dark-haired and silver-eyed Nayli and one with blonde hair and pale blue eyes. The letters "y Free a," arced across his neck. She presumed they represented the middle of the slogan of the Shining Revolution: *Humanity Free and Clear*. She'd found it in a dark corner of the socwebs, as well as growing support for the revolutionaries.

They passed through a lock and down a corridor and through another lock. Immediately after the second lock door closed, Chrystal's captors relaxed in every way except for their attention to her. Whoops and hand-claps spilled the tension from the group: a river of elation. Other people met them, screaming congratulations and relief.

With no obvious cue from Vadim, engines thrummed to life.

They were on a ship.

A few people came up to stare at her. "She looks real."

A snarly voice suggested, "Could be a sex-bot, right? Not a Next at all, just a toy."

She turned toward the voice to find a large red-haired man with a broken nose behind her. "She doesn't look like she has sex-parts." His touched her between her legs and she stiffened in spite of herself. "She reacts. Maybe she likes it."

Chrystal wanted to kick him. She settled for stepping back. She recorded the size of the dingy room, the banged-up walls, the position of the lockers, the slogans and safety signs stuck to the wall.

Definitely Shining Revolution.

She tried to count her enemies. There were too many, twenty or thirty just here in this room. She looked for doors and found three, including the one they'd come in through.

"I thought they'd be scarier."

Someone touched her neck. "Her skin's warm!"

She couldn't see either speaker. She schooled her face into a calm expression, refusing to show fear. These people were afraid of her—fear sparked in their eyes and showed in the ways they moved: staying close to each other, touching weapons, keeping a meter or so away from her.

A woman's voice asked, "Is her hair real?"

She felt a growing anger, as well as a touch of shame. The shame made her angry with herself. She wished yet again for the calming feeling of a deep breath and vowed to find some equivalent habit.

A man came up to her and held both of her hands, pulling her in toward him, and demanding, "Give me a kiss." He stank of stale beer.

Nayli noticed the altercation and snapped, "Back off. She's valuable. Don't degrade her."

"She's a machine!" This statement came from a short man who looked too normal to be so cruel.

Nayli didn't reply to him.

Vadim glanced from Chrystal to Nayli. "Let them look. We control a lot of what we came for, and more than I thought we'd be able to win. They deserve to understand why they're risking their lives."

Two guards were still pointing guns at Chrystal. Although people stopped touching her, they didn't stop talking about her as if she were a thing and staring. They smelled of sweat and fear and arousal all at once.

She stood as still as possible and pasted the dumb robot look onto her face. She considered attempting to talk her way from derision to sympathy, but decided that would work better in a smaller group. Maybe Nayli could be reached.

If they were here, Yi would be talking. Jason would be fighting, and someone would have shot him by now.

Katherine might have charmed them all.

After ten minutes and twenty-seven seconds of cruel scrutiny, Vadim gestured and his men led her away. She felt relieved to leave the small mob behind her.

Luckily, the anger and shame they brought up in her had been her new-normal dulled version of feelings. The Next had been good designers. She had never before considered that there could be excellent reasons for her emotions to feel like they had been stuffed with gauze. She was faster and stronger than humans. She could do real damage quickly if her decisions were driven by the heat of her old angers.

She returned to counting doors and looking for hatches and memorizing the layout of the ship.

They stopped in an office with Vadim, Nayli, and another couple. All four of the humans were so well muscled that they had to be addicted to high-g workouts. The two new people were blond and brown-skinned. Both had short hair and silver-blue eyes that reminded Chrystal of the color of water.

The woman looked her up and down, appearing disappointed. "From a distance I wouldn't even know you're a machine. You're supposed to be the new super-race?"

Any answer felt fraught with danger. Chrystal spoke softly. "I was just like you until the Next put me into this body after the High Sweet Home. I feel like I have always felt."

The woman's lips thinned, which gave her a mean look. "How strong are you?"

Not a question she wanted to answer. "I've always been strong."

The woman frowned. "Will you show us how strong you are now?"

They were already frightened. She smelled it in their sweat and heard it in the edges of their voices. If they knew what she could do they'd be so much more so. "No."

Vadim came in closer to her than he had, as if the presence of the other two emboldened him. He practically spit in her face. "There are laws about your kind. You're an abomination."

"I did not choose to have this happen to me," she said. "It was done to me."

Vadim raised an eyebrow. "So you disapprove?"

"Of course."

The woman with eyes the color of water suddenly looked more interested. "Would you fight the Next? Do you know how to help us do that?"

Nayli watched the exchange, looking thoughtful.

"I wouldn't advise fighting the Next. They are far more powerful than I am. Or than you are."

The interest faded from the woman's eyes. Apparently she didn't want to hear the truth. Chrystal tried again. "If you choose to fight them, you'll die."

The woman who had asked her spit on the ground. "I didn't think you were a real girl."

The echo of her mother's words stung. All she had done was spoken the truth. She should never have left Jason and Yi. Never. If she ever saw them again, she'd never leave their sides. She asked, "What do you intend to do with me?"

Vadim shook his head at her. "We're going to treat you far better than you deserve. In honor of being right here near the Deep and all. We're going to put you on trial."

"For what?" Chrystal asked, suddenly, completely certain they wanted to kill her. This man wanted it so badly she could see it in his eyes. "I haven't done anything to you."

The water-eyed woman spoke. "We'll demonstrate that you aren't human, and that you are more than a robot, and that you are a gross violation of the rules we hold dear."

"And then what?" Chrystal asked.

No one answered.

"Put her away," the new man said for the first time.

Nayli's brows furrowed. "Wait."

The man asked her, "For what?"

Vadim remained silent, his weapon still trained on Chrystal. Always the professional.

Nayli glanced nervously between the man and Vadim. "She feels. I know she does. And she has supporters. Maybe family. I saw how Nona looked at her, and the Historian." She turned toward Vadim. Her voice softened, and she looked into his eyes the way a partner or a lover does, with knowledge and authority. "You might not have had time to notice. People care about her. This could be a mistake."

The water-eyed woman said, "Don't get soft. Put her away."

Vadim stared at Nayli for a long time, and then shook his head. "You cannot be weak."

She licked her lips. "I know."

Vadim gestured with his weapon.

Chrystal almost reached out to grab it in the split second when it pointed away from her, but hesitated too long.

One man walked backward in front of her. Vadim and Nayli gave her voice commands for each turn, staying far enough behind her that she couldn't spin and kick them.

Her footsteps and theirs echoed in the corridor.

They led her to the ship's brig, a two-celled jail with three heavily armed guards. There, they herded her into one of the cells with no processing. The metallic click of the lock sounded like a slap.

A metal chair and a metal table were both bolted to the floor. A metal bed frame with no mattress fully occupied one wall. An open toilet took one corner, barely more than a hole into which she could pour bodily fluids if she had any. She felt the absence of tears, the ghost of a thing she should be able to do naturally but would never be able to do again.

"We'll be back in the morning," Vadim said to her. "Be ready for us."

Nayli addressed the guards in a loud, commanding voice. "No touching. No roughhousing. She hasn't got a vagina anyway. Consider this a sacred duty, a night that will make history for you." She raised her voice so far it sounded strident. "Don't screw it up."

"We won't," the biggest one muttered.

Nayli looked at Chrystal for a long time, measuring. "Don't antagonize them. We'll bring you a fresh outfit for court tomorrow."

Her captors left. She sat in the chair, since someone with a human body would probably sit. Three men with guns stared at her.

She entertained herself by imagining ways she might take down three armed guards and escape if she could get the door open. She might be strong enough to tear the door open. It would be fun to try.

But first the guards needed to leave, and that wasn't looking very likely.

—◦◦◦—

Chrystal sat at the table with light pooling all around her and tried to think of some way to at least message Jason and Yi. Then she imagined taking down all of the guards. Or just running and running and running. She tried to think of something to say to change Vadim's mind, or to finish convincing Nayli.

The guards shuffled and moved from time to time but never stopped watching her.

After an hour and five minutes, one of them cleared his throat and said, "You really don't have to sleep." It was a statement with a question behind it.

She pursed her lips. "I don't *get* to sleep. I'm not flesh. But I was born here—as a human baby, just like each of you, and I grew up here. My mother lives right here on the Deep."

"We're not on the Deep anymore," another guard observed.

"Where are we?"

"Think of us as following the Deep."

"Okay. You're right though, I'm not going to sleep." She paused. "Do you want to talk?"

"No." The guard stepped back.

Too bad. It would have been nice to understand how they thought. The bars and the silence and the proximity of weapons wore on her.

All she could do was review her memories and plan. Whatever data sources the ship had, she couldn't access them.

They had locked her up in the same place they usually put humans. Maybe she could make something of that in court. In all of her time on the Deep, and even the High Sweet Home, she hadn't really cared about the murky past or the schism that created the Ring of Distance. Oh, it took up almost a week of one history class. But it had never come up in her real life.

She wasn't well-equipped to be in a court. She'd seen court proceedings, of course. Everyone born on the Deep had seen some proceeding or another, and some people considered court high entertainment. But the only time she'd stepped into a courtroom was for a school assignment. She hadn't even gotten a very good grade.

They weren't going to give her a chance. This might be her last night.

Even though she could track time precisely, she didn't have any tools for speeding it up.

Eventually Nayli, Vadim, and the water-eyed woman came for her. True to their word, they brought a clean outfit—a blue dress very like the one that Jhailing Jim had chosen when he introduced her to humanity on the Satwa.

She had no choice except to change right in front of them. Nayli had the grace to turn around, but Vadim and the others stared at her. The dress didn't fit as well as the one on the station had, and the shoes they had chosen for her were too small, so she elected to walk barefoot.

Unlike yesterday, they had her lead, prodding her from behind with voice commands. She recalled all of the halls, all of the doors, and she used the walk to re-check her memories.

Even though she knew which way to go, she hesitated as she got to each turn, waiting for Vadim to nudge her ever so slightly one way or the other with his weapon. When he did, she complied.

Six turns away from the jail and the guards, she stopped, schooling a look of confusion onto her features.

Vadim's hand jerked his gun away from her torso to point out the direction she should go.

For a split second, no weapon pointed at her.

She leapt high, her right front foot kicking the gun sideways.

It flew from his hand and clanged into the wall.

Nayli and the water-eyed woman were both reaching for their weapons.

She ran as fast as she could, using her ability to think quickly to run more deliberately, so that each footfall was confident, each movement perfectly balanced. Others would see her as fast, maybe even blurring out, but she herself lived a slow motion moment, a perfect moment of just now, only now, this bend in her ankle, that shift of her pelvis, that change in weight.

She was around the corner before she heard them scream at each other to catch her.

CHAPTER SIXTY-THREE

CHARLIE

Kyle brought the *Verdant Sun* into the ranger station as smoothly as Yi had docked the *Star Ghost* up above. Charlie helped Jason and Yi unstrap the repair robot and get it onto the ground, and then he told Jean Paul, "Go ahead. I want to take care of a few things."

Jean Paul grinned at him. "You want a moment alone."

Jean Paul would understand how tough it had been for him to be surrounded by people all the time. "More than anything."

"Shall I loose the hound?"

"What do you think?"

"Don't be too long. Remember that you have a guest."

"If I'm not inside in half an hour, come get me." Charlie glanced at Yi and Jason. "You'll be safe with Jean Paul. He'll take care of you."

Jean Paul led the others out of sight, still grinning.

Charlie stood still and closed his eyes.

Sunshine fell across his closed lids and a slight breeze stroked his cheeks, a feather of cool air. A bird called from somewhere overhead and the low hum of a skimmer in the distance indicated the presence of other rangers.

Lym smelled of air. He would never before have said he could smell the air—he would have noted flowers or trees or animals or cooking food. But right now, he could smell unfiltered air.

The beauty of it nearly brought him to his knees.

In that moment, when he was still soft with the air and home, he heard Cricket's three-foot hop. She leaned her huge head against his waist and he buried his fingers in her fur. She made a contented noise deep in her throat, and he mirrored it as best he could and then gave in and fell to his knees. His arms snaked around the tongat. He buried his face in her fur and cried.

The tears were a complete surprise. He couldn't remember crying, not for at least twenty years. Maybe more. The tears overwhelmed him, emptied him.

Cricket's rough tongue licked the water from his face and he tightened his grip on her.

Jean Paul came back for him before he quite got ahold of himself. When he noticed Charlie's tears, all he said was, "She missed you, too."

Charlie clapped him on the shoulder. "I missed you as much as I missed her." He looked up at the sky. "But I missed Lym most of all. I wasn't born to live in a tin can."

"Maybe none of us were. Amfi is waiting for you."

"I was hoping to sit by the fire and have a drink before I had to go to work."

"I can bring Amfi to the fireplace. I don't think I can put her off. She didn't ask to talk to *me*. So if you want, I can give your friends a tour."

Charlie said, "I'd like you with me. Sometimes you see things I don't see."

"Someone needs to keep your pets safe."

"They're people!"

Jean Paul put up both of his hands in surrender. "I know. I'm sorry."

"Suit yourself. Does Amfi know the soulbots are here?"

"I have no idea."

"Okay. Tell Yi and Jason to wear clothes all the time. Tell them I told them their lives may depend on them being seen as human."

"Are you that worried?"

"You're the one that told me people are killing household bots. And Kyle felt disturbed by them. No way to know what he'll say to who." Charlie started toward home, Cricket sticking close beside him.

"How many years did Kyle work for you? You can trust him."

"I don't trust anyone right now."

Jean Paul stopped dead. "Even me?"

"Don't be stupid."

They arrived in the kitchen, and Charlie reached far into the cupboard for a decanter of good whiskey that they'd bought together at a summer fair. He poured two glasses.

Jean Paul held his up. "To you being home."

"To me being home," Charlie sipped and then held his glass up again. "To surviving the Next."

"Spoken by a man who brought two home with him."

"They're—I don't know what they are. You haven't seen the real Next. We're not going to convince them to ignore Lym by asking nicely." He hadn't said that to himself so directly.

Jean Paul stopped with his glass halfway to his lips. "It really is that bad?"

"Yes."

Jean Paul finished his drink. "The fire's hot. I'll be right back with Amfi."

Charlie took his boots off and sat close to the fireplace. Cricket flowed along with him, lying down at his feet and staring at the flames. Charlie hadn't seen fire since he left Lym. It felt as good as smelling the air. Maybe for an encore he'd go sit by a river and dig his fingers into some soil.

It felt so good to be home, so warm and so true. He leaned sideways in his chair and stroked the tongat's neck and shoulders.

Jean Paul whistled to alert him that he and Amfi were arriving.

Charlie commanded Cricket to stay in place. She stiffened for a moment and then relaxed under his fingers.

Amfi followed Jean Paul in, sat, and stared at the fire. She spoke softly. "Thank you for seeing me." Wrinkles spun out from bright brown eyes and puckered her lips. Either she dyed her hair the same color as her eyes or it hadn't decided to go grey yet. She wore a typical gleaners outfit: all natural materials that had been hand-woven into a soft and loose multi-colored fabric. Modern brown boots with good soles covered her feet.

Jean Paul poured handed Amfi a glass of wine, returned to the kitchen, and brought them each out a plate piled with nuts, bread, and small orange fruits called hamis. "I'll check on you later," he told Charlie, and left the room.

Charlie took a hamis and bit into it, savoring another part of being home. Hamis had never adapted to space well; they were only easily available on Lym. When he finished the fruit, he asked, "What can I do for you?"

She sat back in her chair and said, "I was told to speak to you. That you would understand."

"Understand what?"

"That the Next are here on Lym."

"Freida showed me pictures the day they killed her."

The fire popped. He sipped at his drink and tried not to think sour thoughts.

Amfi spoke quietly. "We must change Lym's opinion about the Next."

He looked at her surprised. "Into what? They're murderers. They killed Freida and her family." He remembered the dead bodies, including the boy. They'd probably still be alive if he hadn't let Nona talk him down into Neville.

She stopped watching the fire and watched him instead. "Will you hear me out?"

"If we let them on Lym they might destroy it. We can't have them land ships here.

She gazed at him, stoic. "Please listen."

Cricket must have sensed his tension. She lifted her head and turned it toward Amfi. He patted her neck and whispered that it would be okay. "Go ahead."

Amfi set her empty wine glass down. "At first, we gleaners wanted to kill them all. Murder for murder, death for death. We'd lost at least fifteen gleaners to the Next, and three tourists. We're nomadic. The number could be larger. Far larger."

He sipped his drink, thinking of Yi and Jason nearby and vulnerable, but also of his hatred of the Next's demand to come here. It was too complex to relay to a stranger, so he said, "I understand."

"In some moments I still want to kill them all," she said. "They bring up a deep-seated fear that's worse than the fear of the dark." She laughed softly. "Or like the fear of the ice pirates that our mothers instilled in us."

He laughed as well, remembering the same stories.

"We've been watching and documenting, trying to understand. After all, we can't win through force. We only killed one of them. There is no army on Lym—only rangers like you. Mostly loners."

He grimaced. "Guilty."

She laughed, soft and low and laced with irony. "Lym cannot shoot a single ship from the sky." He refilled her wine glass and his whiskey and stared into the fire. He had missed fire so much. "I met the Next on the *Bleeding Edge*, way out past most of the Glittering. They're strange. We can't possibly understand them."

She nodded. "We know. Part of what drives us gleaners is a desire to understand the human experience. Among many things, we believe death is a teacher. If we have the ability to live for hundreds or even a thousand years, we lose the spiritual edge that death gives us."

"I've heard that belief."

She clasped her hands together and placed them in her lap, breathing deep. "Another belief I hold is that encountering the new is part of being human. We should see and feel death, and we should also see and feel its oppo-site—the new wonders that are arising in our world."

He wasn't sure what to say so he fell silent. He shifted to move his feet closer to the fire. Starships and stations were always the same temperature. While he couldn't remember his feet being cold in space, he also couldn't remember them being warm.

Eventually, she continued. "We debate, always, who we are. The answer is not clear. We are not, after all, a religion."

He nodded, scratching Cricket's head with one hand and holding onto his whiskey with the other.

"I agree that we may never understand the Next. The simple fact that they don't have to die makes them very different from us. However, We learned a few things while you were gone."

"Go ahead."

"There are far more robots here now than people realize. Mostly they live in the wild and the dead and unrestored places, which is why we gleaners encountered them first. They're all connected one to another and can commu-nicate through a network that is hidden from us. One theory is that they use each other as network nodes."

"That seems elaborate." Rather like a conspiracy theory. He added a few small logs to the fire, pleased when it flared up.

"I know. And we haven't been able to detect the network, so we can't prove it exists. But when something happens to one in one place, the others all know."

"How is that possible?" he asked her. It sounded like a conspiracy theory.

"I don't know. But we've seen it demonstrated more than once. Although not in our captured Next." She looked like a cat with a mouse, or a young girl with a secret.

"You captured one? Tell me."

"We're keeping it in a secret place. It talks with us from time to time. It appears to be trying to understand humans."

"I met the Next while I was in space," he said. "Don't assume they're sympathetic to humans." He wasn't ready to risk Jason and Yi's safety by telling her they were here, but he said, "I met some of the soulbots—human and machine hybrids in human-like bodies—that the Next created from the people on the High Sweet Home. *They* still feel their humanity. But the others, the true Next? They were . . . frightening. Very powerful, and very different."

"Do you know what they want?"

"They want something from Lym and plan to come here. A lot of them. They haven't exactly said why."

"I might have a clue," Amfi said. "Our captive Next is named Jhailing Jim and says he is one of many copies of himself, although they are all unique now. I think there are more of him here."

"I met a Jhailing Jim on Satwa station."

"Way out there?" She fell silent, staring at the flames.

"Yes," he said. "It wore a robot suit that changed shape as if it were water. It amazed me."

"It wasn't the robot itself?"

"I believe the older, more powerful Next can move between bodies. Maybe they don't need bodies at all."

She looked contemplative. "Thank you. I'll take that information back. There's another thing you need to know. While they have been killing, they seem to have done it to protect what they came for. Everyone they killed discovered them."

"That would apply to Freida and her family."

"Yes," she said. "They haven't killed anyone who didn't know about them, as far as we can tell. They don't appear to kill for sport. Nor have they killed anyone new since the announcement by the Next, even though we killed one of them."

"Have you learned what they want from us?"

"They're mapping our plants and animals and even our people. They're looking for some specific things. We believe they want minerals, although only a few of the ones they seem to be hunting are used in our own technology."

He moved his feet back away from the heat of the fire.

She ate a handful of nuts. "Our captive Next would like to meet you. He asked that you bring the other two with you."

"What other two?"

"The two you brought with you. Jhailing Jim saw them on one of the security cameras at the station."

Which implied that her magical network existed. "We'll go in the morning."

She took his hand, touching him for the first time. "Thank you."

CHAPTER SIXTY-FOUR

NONA

Nona jerked awake, suddenly aware that she had fallen fast asleep with her head on Dr. Nevening's shoulder. The room's day lights were brightening, illuminating figures sprawled across the floor.

The guards were still there. One of them looked at her curiously as she stood and started to pick her way through the sleepers to use the privy. The Historian stirred briefly and then curled into a fetal position, taking up all of the floor space she had shared with him, and snoring lightly.

Her stomach felt empty and skinny, pasted to her back. There had been nothing new except water set out since the meager meal last night.

Satyana sat in a corner, brushing out her hair in long strokes. She looked unusually rumpled. Nona tiptoed to her and folded onto the floor, hugging her knees to her chin. "How are you?"

"We have to get out of here," Satyana whispered.

Nona eyed the guards. "That's going to be hard."

"We also need to find a news source. I want to know what's happening out there."

"Me too. I hope it's not too bad. Last night, Dr. Nevening said major technology changes often destroy forms of government. He told me we've been the same for so long that we've probably forgotten."

Satyana smiled faintly. "That's why we have a Historian on the Council."

"He's really worried."

Noises started up in the kitchen, robot wheels rolling along the floor. Small clanks came from the room. "I guess we all get up now," Nona said. "Maybe we'll learn something."

Around the room, sleepers stirred. The Historian sat up and rubbed at his eyes. Leesha slept in long form on the couch, her bare feet dangling over the edge. Two of her toes were half-covered in gold rings.

Robots rolled a tray of water and stim into the room.

Satyana asked one, "Will there be food?"

It replied in an annoyingly upbeat voice. "There have been no deliveries."

That couldn't be a good sign. Nona chose two glasses of stim and brought them to Satyana, who was eyeing the single door and the two guards by it. "I don't see a good weapon," she mused. "Although maybe we could use Leesha's shoes."

"We can't fight," Nona hissed. "It would risk the Council."

"We can't do nothing."

Nona sipped her stim, feeling it sour her empty stomach. She didn't like the bitter, spiced flavor nearly as much as chocolate stim. "The Council isn't going to do anything, are they?"

"If we had someone to negotiate with, I'd bet on them. But not in a physical fight."

That made sense.

The door opened. Two small drones zipped through it and spun in the air, making slightly fizzy noises. The guards fell, slumping. Stunned.

They were rescued.

Nona started to stand up.

Satyana put a hand on her arm and kept her down.

"What?" Nona whispered. "That has to be the military. Stun drones are illegal for anyone else."

"Don't be naive."

Five blue-uniformed figures walked slowly into the room, checking corners and poking their heads into the kitchen. Their white and gold insignia confirmed Nona's suspicions. Diamond Deep military.

Two assistants rushed over and started thanking their rescuers. The Biologist hesitated and then joined them. "Thank you."

The first person who'd come through the door—a man in a safety suit with an impressive array of hand weapons—used a loud voice to command them. "Gather your things."

Nona breathed out a long sigh of relief and stood up, offering Satyana a hand.

She was surprised at the look Satyana gave her, part exasperation and part warning. Well, she could worry about that after they were someplace dry and warm and someone gave them a plate of food.

Even the Economist was up and moving. Leesha slid her feet into her shoes and pulled the pins out of her hair, fluffing it with her fingers. Three jewels fell out. She knelt and gathered them up carefully and stuck them in a pocket. Only then did she stand all the way up and slowly, regally, look down her nose at the leader. "Who are you? What's happening? We need to know."

"I'm General Finlay. We came to save you from the Shining Revolution." He glanced briefly down at the stunned former guards. He peered around the room. "Where's the Architect?"

"Don't you have him?" Leesha asked.

General Finlay's features hardened. "No."

Satyana asked, "If you don't have the Architect, do you at least have news?"

The general looked irritated, but he gave them some crumbs. "We're driving the Shining Revolution back from the Deep to their ships. Forward, there's a huge peace protest that has managed to kill seven people while the actual invaders are only up to six on body count. No one seems to be fighting aft of here, so we're taking you there."

Leesha took a step closer to the general. "We need to hold our formal meeting. The Next gave us a timeline."

"I know," the general said. "We have the Headmistress."

"Who we don't actually need for the meeting," Satyana pointed out. "She gave up her vote."

The general ignored her. "We'll be going aft to a military training bubble. It has good communications, and it's near our ships in case the fighting gets worse."

The Futurist, Hiram, spoke up. "Has there been any more word from the Next? Have any of the other stations made their decision?"

"No and no."

Dr. Nevening hadn't budged. He stood right in front of the general, and in a very serious voice, he said, "If you have the Headmistress, is she in charge right now?"

"We're in military lockdown until the fighting stops."

Nona suddenly understood the problem. If they accepted the safety of the military they gave up their power.

The Biologist stared at the Historian. "Do *you* have a better plan?"

Dr. Nevening looked uncomfortable. The others in the room all looked ready to leave.

"We will leave in five minutes." The general turned to one of his men. "Make sure the corridor is still clear."

Nona asked him, "Have you heard anything about Chrystal?"

"The robot girl? The Shining Revolution has her."

"Is she okay?"

He shrugged. "I have no idea." He turned away, clearly not all that interested.

Most of the military in the room were men. Nona tugged on Satyana's arm and headed for the bathroom. The Futurist was already in there, poking at her hair in the mirror. "How bad is it?" Nona whispered. "What happens if we refuse to go with them?"

The Economist looked at her as if she didn't have a brain in her head. "They kill us."

When Satyana didn't contradict her, Nona bent over the sink and splashed cold water onto her cheeks.

━━━∞━━━

They filed out of the room they had been held captive in, passing through a gauntlet of soldiers. Nona had never spent much time around the military, who had always seemed like a separate society that lived on the fringes of the real world, and didn't matter much.

Of course, they might matter now.

Still, the men and women in neat uniforms with neatly carried weapons felt like better captors than the Shining Revolution.

They walked two by two. In a few places she saw evidence of fighting. Overturned desks in one office and a door to a living hab that looked like it had been kicked in. A painting of birds had been ripped from a wall and torn into three sad pieces.

They walked for so long that Nona's feet hurt. They traveled between bubbles on shuttles once, which clearly made the military antsy. They stood looking out of the windows with weapons poised as if they could or would shoot from inside a shuttle into the vacuum of space.

Maybe the trains were down, or compromised.

At first, she walked beside Satyana, who kept silent and checked every doorway and corridor, although she never said what she was looking for. Then she walked next to Leesha, taking two steps for every single step the

Economist took. Leesha muttered at all of the damage they saw, but wasn't really good company. When she dropped back to walk by the Historian she felt better, as if their long talks and her sleeping on his shoulder had built a friendship between them.

After about half an hour, the group bunched in a wide space, spilling slowly into a common meeting room.

Food and water had been laid out on tables. All of the captives practically rushed the table. Nona couldn't remember when water had tasted so good. There were crackers and protein spreads and dried nuts. Even after she ate, she felt hungry. She looked around for Satyana and found her talking with Leesha and Dr. Nevening.

The group looked so serious Nona felt like an interruption when she asked, "So what happens if we don't get to decide? How will the Next interpret it?"

Dr. Nevening asked her, "What do you think will happen if the military gets to choose?"

It seemed obvious to her. "Won't they want to fight?"

"Maybe," Satyana said. "But they're primarily a defensive force. They won't have what they need. Not unless they join forces with the Shining or something."

"Would they do that?" Nona asked. "Why? Because they both want to fight?"

"It's funny to think how close we live to anarchy," Dr. Nevening said. "I didn't really understand that before." He glanced meaningfully toward the Biologist, who was talking to the general. "It's hard to tell who's willing to join with whom in times like these."

"Okay," Nona said. "But I still want to know what happens if no one decides."

Leesha turned the question around. "You've been around the Next far more than we have. What do you think they'll do?"

"Kill something."

"That seems to be everyone's idea," Leesha said. "You'd think space would be big enough to accommodate us all."

Nona smiled. Maybe the Economist had just indicated how she would vote. If she got to vote at all. "Well, I don't really know. I've been around

Chrystal a lot. She would protect us. I've met the other, older Next. They aren't us. We can't know what they'll do." She glanced at the Futurist. "I guess that's why they're a wild card."

Hiram nodded and Dr. Nevening smiled. "Well said."

"Thanks." After a few minutes, Nona wandered back toward the food table, which was down to scraps. She pocketed a few energy gels.

Satyana came up beside her, leaned in, and whispered low in her ear, "We're going to try to get away."

"Are you kidding?" Nona hissed back. "There are twenty of them."

"And about that many of us. Besides, I don't think they'll kill the Councilors. Consider it calling their bluff. But for now say nothing."

"When?"

"Soon."

CHAPTER SIXTY-FIVE

CHARLIE

Morning light spilled gold across Charlie's bedspread and pooled on the floor. He contemplated cursing it after a restless night, but it was the first sunrise he'd seen in over a year so he stood up and stretched instead. He and Jean Paul had been up late talking. He'd expected to sleep like a baby on his first night home, but instead he had dreamed of shape-changing robots and high ships orbiting Lym.

An hour and a cup of stim later, he stood beside Cricket's crate. The soft growl that slipped between her clenched teeth made him sad. He gave in against his better judgment as a trainer and knelt down, looking into her brown eyes. "I'll be back in a few hours. I promise."

Her expression implied that he might be both the most evil man in the world and the love of her life. "Sometimes," he put a hand through the door and stroked her side, "sometimes you're worse than a human."

"And if you don't step back she might find a way to make you stay," Jean Paul commented from his position in the hallway behind the tongat. "For instance, she might bite the hand that feeds her."

"Never." Although a second glance at Cricket's face did reveal a slightly snarly upper lip. Charlie latched the door and stood up. "I have to go."

He met Jason, Yi, the repair-bot, and Amfi beside Charlie's skimmer. Charlie was so busy feeling guilty about leaving Cricket contained that he almost tripped over the small repair-bot. Taking the thing everywhere was an inconvenience, but if he were built of technology no one else knew how to fix, he might want the strange little bot along as well. At least Jason and Yi did most of the bot-tending.

Before they boarded, Amfi stopped them all and said, "Do you promise to keep this location secret?"

Jason and Yi exchanged a glance. "No. But we promise not to tell anyone about it unless we need to for our safety, or for Charlie's safety."

Amfi looked briefly irritated, but she climbed into the skimmer.

Charlie piloted, following Amfi's directions to a deep valley he'd mapped by satellite but never visited in person. By the time they arrived, it was nearly noon. They descended between steep walls covered in tall evergreens and bright red and gold deciduous trees. Almost every cliff spilled out long, thin waterfalls turned into brilliant ribbons by the full light of day. "It's so beautiful," Jason said.

Amfi nearly glowed with pride. "Welcome to the Ice Fall Valley."

Charlie had forgotten again that they had never before been to Lym. "Fly them around a bit? Let them see?"

Amfi shook her head. "Another time." She pointed to a flat meadow beside an old and abandoned-looking building that might once have been a resort. "Land there."

Outside, the air smelled of late fall, and breathing it cooled his chest. To Charlie's surprise, Amfi didn't lead them into the building. Instead, she took them down a short rocky path that wound behind a waterfall. They stood behind it a moment, looking out, the spray misting their hair and eyelashes and clinging to their lips. Charlie looked for a waterfall rainbow to show the soulbots, but the sun was at the wrong angle.

Amfi stopped in front of a massive metal door, balancing on a plate on the floor. Light flashed briefly across her face. "Welcome home," a human male voice said, and a male gleaner with a bald head and a long bushy grey beard let them in to a laser-cut vestibule with rock walls. He almost closed the door before the little repair-bot made it in. He looked nervous of it, but didn't say anything.

They passed through a second matching door with equal security. The doors, and for that matter the light-based security system, smacked of old technology.

"What is this place?" Charlie asked. "Does anyone know it's here?"

"We do." Amfi nodded toward the man who had let them in. "This is Davis Chow. He found this place about twenty years ago. We've had a small colony living in these caves ever since. There's old tech here, and much of it works. We haven't even figured out what it's all for yet. We think this might have been a secret installation where people or technologies were hidden. Maybe also stockpiles of some kind—there are two large rooms that are completely empty but have deep scuff marks all over the floor."

Jason looked around the room in wonder. "How old do you think it is?"

Davis looked pleased with Jason for asking. "Older than the age of explosive creation."

"Wow," Jason said. "And it hasn't been destroyed?"

"Not yet."

They came off a main hallway into an unlocked room with straight-cut walls and high rock ceilings that looked natural. To Charlie's surprise, the Jhailing Jim sat casually at a large table, poking at the air. It appeared to be playing a game of some kind that only it could see. Jason and Yi often played physical games as well. Something to ask about.

It looked more male than female and slightly more robot than human. Its body had just enough soft edges not to be too scary, although Charlie assessed it as stronger than Yi or Jason.

Charlie glanced at the others. Amfi appeared pleased with herself. Jason had no obvious reaction. Yi looked curious. Maybe even relieved.

The Jhailing looked over as they came in and said, "Welcome," in a way that sounded as if he were welcoming them into his own living room. It irritated Charlie a little. He had expected to find it bound.

Enough chairs ringed the table for everyone to sit down. A glass water pitcher and four exquisite glasses set with semiprecious stones sat on the table. Gleaner art.

After a short awkward silence, Jhailing Jim said, "Thank you for coming," in a way that seemed to include them all, and then he focused on Jason and Yi. "How are you doing?"

Yi said, "Fine."

Jason looked stubborn. "You mean without you? We're fine."

Jhailing countered. "Your training has been interrupted. Do you feel well?" Jhailing looked pointedly at Jason.

"I'm worried about Chrystal."

"There is nothing you can do from here, and you cannot get there fast enough to change her fate."

Jason's voice came out clipped and cold. "I don't have to be pleased about that."

"Nor do I," Jhailing replied.

Yi narrowed his eyes. "Aren't there Next closer to the Deep? Can they help?"

"No."

Even though Jhailing turned his attention to Charlie next, Charlie had the distinct feeling that the three robots were continuing the conversation they had started out loud silently. He couldn't have explained why he thought so—perhaps something in the way they sat, or the way that Jason, at least, looked slightly distracted. At any rate, Jhailing turned to him and said, "Thank you, Charlie. When you didn't show up on the Deep with Nona we were hoping that you'd come here."

"This is my home. Of course I came here."

"Lym is where we came from also; we share ancestors."

Was Jhailing implying that the Next believed they had a right to Lym? A deep and profound anger had started crawling through Charlie's nerves and he didn't trust himself to speak.

The robot continued. "I asked Amfi to bring you quickly. We needed to speak with you before you go to Manna Springs, and before we do. All of the Next on Lym will be revealing ourselves shortly, and we would like to negotiate a peace agreement with you before that."

The anger turned to ice. "With me? Why not the town leaders?"

The robot cocked its head at him, as if it were trying to imitate a human expression and failing. "Aren't you still the ambassador for Lym?"

Charlie glanced at Amfi, who watched, wide-eyed. She nodded so faintly he wasn't sure she did it on purpose. Davis was quieter and seemed to have turned inward. "Wouldn't that be Manny?" Charlie asked. "After all, I have no particular authority here."

"Sure you do," Amfi said. "You are related to Manny, and you are a founding family. You're widely acknowledged as the greatest ranger we have."

"I doubt that."

"Ask any of us."

"I tolerate the gleaners. That doesn't make me great."

Jhailing interrupted the conversation. "There is no reason for anyone to know that you did not negotiate this with my counterpart from the *Bleeding Edge*."

Charlie sat back in his chair, furious. It took a while before he could even parse through the implications. He had already talked to Manny and he hadn't told him anything about a deal. But he hadn't seen him in person. So he could say he hadn't wanted to use open communications channels. Nona would know he hadn't negotiated anything on the Satwa.

He *might* be in the best position to have this conversation. He knew a lot more about the Glittering than he had before.

He couldn't lie to Manny or ask Nona to lie for him. "I might be able to get permission to negotiate with you."

"There is no time. If you and I can't talk, we will simply reveal our terms in Manna Springs in a few days."

Charlie got up and paced. He'd have to leave the cave to call. What if he called Manny and Manny said no? "What's the hurry? Why not wait a few weeks and negotiate with Manny?"

"There are many plans in motion. If they all wait for convenience, they will never all be accomplished."

"What plans?"

"I am only able to talk to you about what will happen here," the Jhailing Jim said. "Speaking of that is more than you and I can do well in the time we have left."

Charlie stopped, looked at Amfi and Davis. A ranger and two gleaners. And maybe two people from the Glittering who used to be human. It wasn't the right team. But what would he throw away if he refused?

The Jhailing said, "We want to share Lym with you."

He should just shut up and walk out. This wasn't diplomacy. It wasn't in the open. And he really, really didn't have any right to do this.

Someone had to do it.

God damn it. He paced all the way around the room before he spit out a question. "How long do you plan to be here?"

"We are not prepared to negotiate a specific time at the moment."

"How many of you?"

To Charlie's surprise, Yi spoke. "How many physical incarnations is a better question. For example, I have now met four Jhailing Jim's, or perhaps three in four different bodies. You should negotiate over the amount of physical space on the ground."

"Thank you." So Yi wouldn't allow him to make a major mistake. Interesting. "Can you explain what you want in those terms?" he asked the senior Next.

The robot didn't hesitate. "We will need access to the spaceport and to be settled fairly close to your leaders. We would be happy to take the land adjacent to the spaceport to the west where it is empty."

Charlie hadn't stopped pacing. His feet shuffled softly on the rock surface, his steps unable to keep up with his thoughts. What would Manny do? He tried to remember the bones of conversations across the years, most of them about topics he hadn't really cared for much at the time. "We need that land to expand the Spaceport. Can you pull up a map?"

He wasn't at all surprised when one appeared in the air between them. He drew a circle across some flat land used for growing food now. It was some distance from the spaceport, but they could grow food somewhere else. "Will this do? I suggest you request ingress and egress between this place and the spaceport."

Jhailing Jim stared at the map. "If we also get access to the water, and permission to fashion a seaport."

Charlie drew his brows together. "What do you need a seaport for?"

Jhailing didn't answer. "Our habitat will be walled. We will want a mixing zone—an area where we and humans do business together." The robot drew a larger circle around the space that Charlie had just given him. "This will be big enough."

"Will we be able to pass behind your wall?" Amfi asked.

Jhailing turned to her. "If invited."

"Then that is how you can come here," she said.

Charlie smiled. "And into Manna Springs. They are already frightened there, and they will want to know you won't invade them."

"We should have free access to the capital of Lym."

Charlie stiffened. "I cannot give that. I may not be able to give what I have given, but I know I cannot allow you to live and move easily in Manna Springs."

Jhailing sat down and smiled. "There will come a day when this feels like prejudice, and when these rules are taken down."

Charlie glanced at the soulbots. "That's not this day," Charlie said. "You must also be invited into the restored areas."

"There are some that we plan to mine."

Charlie almost choked on the words he wanted to use to react to that. But

Amfi had told him the Next had been searching the land for certain minerals. The demand was no surprise. He had to walk another full circle of the room before he managed to ask, "What places do you want?"

The list the robot started with was completely unacceptable.

"You may have two of those," Charlie said. "Neville and," he stopped, almost choking, "Neville and part of the Misted Rose Range on Goland."

"We would also like three of the Palagi Islands."

Charlie furrowed his brow. "Those are settled. The land is all owned." He shouldn't be doing this. It should take far more time, and a bigger team.

Yi spoke up. "You can build your own islands off of Neville."

Jhailing fell silent, and Charlie suddenly realized that they were almost certainly talking between themselves. Maybe they had been doing that the whole time. He couldn't let Yi to negotiate for Lym. He didn't know enough about it. "Look," he said. "That's going to be all I can convince people to allow. I can't waltz into Manna Springs and announce that I've given up half of Lym to people's worst nightmares."

Everyone in the room stared at him.

"I can't. I can't even bring them this. This is all things we're giving. What are you going to give us?"

"Why, the right to become like us, of course."

Was it joking? "How about something we want, like free access to your starship technology?"

Yi whispered in his ear.

Charlie added, "And the information we need to develop navigation AI's as good as yours."

"No."

His anger had built enough that he said, "I need a break."

"There isn't enough time," Jhailing said.

"What do you mean?" Charlie asked. "What's happening?"

"A Next ship will be in orbit within a few hours. We should finish this conversation and get to Manna Springs."

Charlie stood up, pacing, restless. "I have no idea if I can even sell this deal, or if I have the authority to even have the conversation."

"If not you, then who?" the robot asked.

"Damn it."

Davis said, "Surely we can take a *short* break. We'll be back soon." He looked at Charlie. "Jason and Yi should stay here."

Charlie nodded. If they could talk to the Jhailing, then they could let it listen. "I'm sorry," he told them.

To his surprise, Jason answered. "I understand. We are no longer you."

"But I appreciate your help very much," Charlie said.

Davis led Amfi and Charlie out of the room and down a long corridor to an empty cavern hung with bright and colorful tapestries that depicted nature in one form or another. He noticed waving grasses decorated with small blue flowers, a mountain and sunrise, a seascape. "These are beautiful. Are they gleaner art?"

Davis smiled. "Some are generations old." He looked proud.

Amfi came up to Charlie and stood very close to him. She took his hand in hers and looked up at him, her eyes full of gratitude and worry. "This is the most dangerous time for Lym in either of our lives. Perhaps ever. What you're doing matters. Thank you."

He stared at her, feeling an angry lump in his throat and sick to his stomach. "I don't know enough to do this."

"No one does."

Davis observed, "The soulbots have thought of details that we would not even have understood we could ask about."

Amfi asked, "How much do you trust them?"

"A lot," Charlie replied. "But not completely." He still paced, only now he had more room to do it in. "By the way, I'm certain that your *captive* is no such thing. He's a guest."

"He would have to get through three sets of doors to get out."

"I bet it would take him five minutes."

Amfi shook her head. "Don't start beating your breasts, either of you. Everyone in this room loves Lym. This matters. The deals we make today will save lives."

"And take some," Charlie snapped. "Unless we can move whole populations of wild animals."

Amfi looked at him calmly. "We can't make the Next go away."

She was right. He took a deep breath and turned away, trying to get composed, to think. The air smelled of rock and silence and ghosts who might have once lived here. "Okay. I know. Can we pull up a map? In there? One we control? I want a record that we can refer to in town."

"Yes," Davis said. "Is there anything else you need?"

Yes. Time. To know he had the authority to do this. To have anybody else here doing it, except that if he weren't doing it, he would wish he was in here doing his best to protect the things he loved the most. What did he want? A thousand things. Manny. Nona to talk it over with. "I was just trapped on a spaceship for a very long time. I want sky."

Davis led them out, and they stood between the rock wall and the waterfall. The roar of it calmed him, as if the water took some of his unease and stress and sent it plunging into the lily-lined pool fifteen meters or so below them.

He shivered in the wet air, grateful for the bracing cold. All around the valley, fall colors mixed with dark greens. The air smelled faintly of impending snow.

Droplets from the waterfall slowly soaked his hair as Charlie breathed and breathed and breathed.

CHAPTER SIXTY-SIX

NONA

Nona stood beside Dr. Nevening, who shifted his weight from one foot to another with an air of impatience. She leaned over to him. "Are you okay?"

"We're running out of time."

Before she could respond, General Finlay bellowed, "Form a line. Form a single line." Chaos ensued as captives tried to stay together and guards ordered them to separate. Nona stuck close to the front of the line, near Satyana and the Historian. The others were spread in groups of two or three and separated by soldiers. "Listen up!" the general yelled. "We've got word that part of our planned route might not be safe. We'll be going a different way, which will take longer."

The Futurist asked, "Why can't we stay here?"

"There are far more people to protect you at our base, sir. We wouldn't want to risk our future."

Nona groaned inwardly at the awkward pun.

"Move out!" the general called, his two-word sentence sounding like it ended in an exclamation point. He stood by the door as the first of his soldiers filed out, and he was still standing there as she and Satyana crossed the threshold. Satyana hesitated for moment and caught his eye. "Thank you."

He beamed.

As soon as they were far enough past him that he wouldn't overhear, Nona whispered "What were you thanking him for?"

"Thinking I'm grateful and compliant."

Nona laughed and felt a tiny bit better.

They walked, the soldiers' boots making more noise and clatter than any of the captives' shoes. Twice, Nona spotted moving ships outside of windows, and once she glimpsed a line of people outside of a ferry lock that they passed near. Since they were separated from the Historian, she stayed with Satyana. She lost her sense of direction as they walked up one corridor after another and passed from one habitat bubble to another. They were mostly in offices or warehouses. Occasionally, sunlight brightened a hallway through a bubble window, sometimes softened by a shade. Nona struggled to stay alert. Her feet had started to swell, and her thigh muscles ached from the unaccustomed exercise. She took out one of the energy gels she had purloined from the food table and sucked on it. It tasted bland and somewhat awful, but it helped a little.

It felt like they'd been marching all day, although it couldn't be later than afternoon, since she still saw the sun through shades from time to time. They were in a long hallway full of doors to offices and storerooms when Satyana slapped her on the back. "Left," she hissed. "Run!"

Adrenaline shocked her system and she obeyed, turning left, almost bumping into Dr. Nevening who held a very small stunner in his fist. He looked triumphant. On the ground in front of him, a soldier lay prone in the boneless sleep of the stunned.

To their right, a dimly lit corridor curved away from the wider one they were in. She sprinted for it.

The Historian raced ahead of her, faster than she had expected him to be. She had to work hard to stay on his heels, Satyana right behind her. Additional footsteps followed them, fleeing feet rather than chasing feet. They weren't the same irritating thump of boots she'd been hearing the last few hours.

Pipes and cables hung above her head. They must be racing through the utility guts of a segment of the station rather than the living quarters.

Every breath felt like a knife in her lungs. In spite of the pain, Nona kept running, looking for someone familiar. Surely there was a plan?

The corridor opened up in front of them and became a cargo bay, filled with shadows and huge boxes.

Someone grunted behind them and fell, probably stunned. Fresh adrenaline drove Nona faster. Her breath screamed in her ears, a high wheeze.

Dr. Nevening stopped abruptly and she ran into him.

Hands grabbed her. Unfamiliar, a little rough. A voice whispered in her ear. "Run with me." She couldn't place it. A glance showed a man in a uniform, but not Diamond Deep military. She didn't recognize him.

She and the uniformed man dodged cargo containers and maintenance bots. She made a flying count, catching glimpses of people as she ran. She was pretty sure there were six in their group now—all of the others must have been caught or gone a different way. She and the Historian and Satyana and three people in uniforms that she didn't recognize.

They rounded a corner to the rumble of a low-throated engine. Her bene-factor rushed her into a small ship behind the doctor, with Satyana behind her. The hatch slammed shut and one of the uniformed men started giving the ship verbal commands.

They took off with no suits and no safety lessons and no seat belts.

The pilot wore the insignia of Gunnar Ellensson's shipping company.

CHAPTER SIXTY-SEVEN

CHRYSTAL

Chrystal ran. She only knew a few routes on the ship: she had to turn and trust and calculate and hope. She tried a maintenance corridor, but it didn't go far and didn't have a second door. She retraced her steps. The corridor was still empty. She ran on, her footsteps almost soundless.

Two doors led nowhere but into offices.

Traps.

As she passed a corridor, someone shouted. She picked up pursuers. She left them behind shortly, but others would come, others who knew the ship better.

Surely she raced under and around cameras; she wasn't fast enough to be invisible. The blue dress probably wasn't helpful.

She shouldn't have run. Except now she could die running instead of in court. Maybe she wouldn't see it coming, wouldn't know it was about to happen before it did.

Even with so much of her attention on speed and safety, other parts of her processed her choices.

Running gave her energy. The more she ran, the faster she could run.

It hadn't been smart. She should have taken the high road, gone to court, and become a martyr. After all, she was on a spaceship, in a closed ecosystem. She couldn't run forever with no place to go. But they were going to kill her one way or the other. She could do humanity more good if she died publicly. The Next, too, for that matter.

They were both her people. Next and the humans from the Deep, both hers. Both better than the Shining Revolution.

Chrystal thought of her mom, and of touching her. Maybe she would be happier with this; she would know for sure that her daughter was dead. She pushed the thought away, unable to afford it.

Best to head toward the outer edge of the ship. Cargo would be there. Hiding places.

She had learned to read the directional symbols enough to be sure she moved outward.

Two more corridors, each turn frightening for its blindness.

The third turn was a T. She chose the right turn and skidded and jerked to an ungainly stop in front of three people crouched on the floor, pointing weapons at her.

She could jump over them, but there were more behind them, and then more. It wouldn't do to hurt anyone. Even now.

She turned to flee again. Stopped. A single man, the red-headed one who had teased her about being a sex-bot, stood with a weapon pointed at her. His breathing sounded sharp and ragged and his face glowed red with exertion. She hadn't heard his footsteps, so he must have run to this place and gotten behind her.

He smiled.

The corridor she had come down might still be empty. She twisted toward it.

Heat cut into her foot, pain signals racing up her spine and exploding in her head. She fell into the wall, barely able to hold herself up, flashes of agony going off inside her so intensely she had to struggle to keep her balance. She damped her pain sensors, gaining slight relief. She glanced down at her hurt foot. It had partly separated, a thick gash essentially hamstringing her. Lasers?

She was going to die. If she couldn't run, she would die now. Now. Now. Dead. Jason. Yi. Now.

Single-sentence terrors filled her head.

She had been through too much to die like this, to die by her own fucking people.

There were no Next here to save her.

The Next might not care enough about her to save her anyway.

She'd never see Jason or Yi again.

She couldn't run, but she could balance on one foot. She did.

The man who had teased her—who had just shot her in the foot—rounded the corner, whooping.

He was celebrating hurting her!

Her movements had returned to virtual slow motion, her brain picking up speed as she panicked. One of his arms came close to hers and she reached out, still balanced on one foot. She grabbed the arm, her fingers digging into his bicep muscle, her arm pulling with all of her strength, using his own momentum to send him past her and down the narrow corridor.

He screamed.

She started to fall, tried to keep looking at him.

She had made another mistake. She was no warrior and she was stupid. Too hard. She'd thrown him too hard.

His body kept going. Farther than she would have thought possible. Her right hand hit the floor as her fall continued, still in slow motion, the hand bouncing slowly and her head moving the opposite direction. Up.

Her eyes were straight forward, so she had a direct view as he hit the opposite wall ten meters or so down the corridor, head first.

She kept falling forward, something metal in one wrist giving way and a sharp crunch telling her she had hurt something. Her head had now twisted back, moving against her will to look at the floor, which came up at her.

She heard the hard impact of his head against the wall, the crunch of bone as it broke, the thud as his body hit.

A moment of silence, full of import.

Her other hand—the one she'd thrown him with—finally found the ground and she used her momentum and her good foot to push upward.

The man's body hit the far side of the corridor on the bounce and slid down the wall.

Her jump carried her close to him, also against the wall, but unable to stand. She balanced in a crumpled fashion, one hand clutching a pipe to be sure she didn't fall to the floor. The man's head had been staved in and his neck broken by the impact.

She had killed.

She, who had lived her life in drum circles and spent time creating new life with test tubes. She who hated fights and even arguments. She who had only killed in the quiet white silence of science, and who had never killed a human.

Chrystal screamed.

CHAPTER SIXTY-EIGHT

NONA

Nona felt squashed between the man who had helped pull her through the cargo bay and Satyana, who practically sat on Dr. Nevening. Logos and insignia inside the little ship showed it was Gunnar's. Maybe that was better than the military.

They pulled quickly away from the cargo bay, the acceleration keeping everyone in awkward positions. After about five minutes, the sandy-haired pilot punched the autopilot and the ship slowed to a more manageable speed.

"Thanks," the Historian said, his voice muffled by Satyana's arm.

"You're welcome." The pilot grinned widely; a man pleased with his work. The cockpit was so small that it took awkward moves to untangle and pass each other and find places to sit properly and belt in. They were short one seat, and so one of the crew sat on a cabinet.

Satyana looked relieved. This could be a real rescue complete with actual saviors, regardless of the fact that Nona didn't trust Gunnar anymore.

She would have to see him soon as the Voice anyway, have to be polite.

"Do you have any water?" the Historian asked.

"You were great," Nona told him. "Where did you hide that stunner? Did you have it the whole time?"

"Some of the military weren't thrilled with the idea of stealing us. They gave us their secondary weapons."

"When?"

"In the big room. Where we ate."

The pilot moved the other man off the cabinet and pulled out water bulbs, handing them around. "Anything else?"

Nona drank, the water immediately reviving. "News."

Satyana looked around the interior of the little ship as if it would yield answers to some question. "Did everyone get out?"

"We got all of the councilors, Ma'am. Two assistants had to be left behind. They were stunned and we couldn't carry them. But my bet is they'll be left. They have no value."

"Do you know which assistants?" Dr. Nevening asked. "Mine?"

"We don't know. They were both male."

Nona took a deep breath. "What about Chrystal? Is there any news of Chrystal?"

"Who's Chrystal?" the pilot asked.

Satyana asked, "Where are we going?"

"Someplace to hold the court. We're planning to use your *Star Bear*, ma'am. There's already some logistics arriving there, and a lot of security."

Satyana looked pleased. "I think that will work just fine."

"What did the military want with us?" Nona asked.

"If the Council is incapacitated, control legally falls to them in a time of war."

"We're not at war, not yet," Nona protested.

"You could argue either side of that," the Historian pointed out.

"News, please?" Satyana said. "Who has control of what?"

The man who hadn't spoken yet did so now. "The military has control of the middle of the station, but we've cleaned them out of the forward section. There's still protests inside of course, but they're mostly impromptu."

"Who's protesting?" the Historian asked.

The man who had been on the cabinet answered this one, a laugh in his voice. "People who want peace and people who think the people who want peace are crazy, and I think some people who just want to be part of something."

Dr. Nevening nodded, as if reassured by the answer.

The pilot picked up the story. "The Shining Revolution ships moved off after you were stolen by the military. They seem pretty happy with their acquisition though—they have the robot."

"That's Chrystal." Nona gasped and grasped Satyana's hand. Satyana returned the handclasp, her face white.

"You know her?" the pilot asked.

"I do."

Before long, the pilot said, "We're about to land."

Satyana combed through Nona's hair with her fingers and did the same to hers. She frowned at her reflection in a hand mirror she had found in the cabin's tiny supply box, but they were docking and there was no obvious way to get more presentable.

Gunnar himself waited for them. He scooped Satyana into a quick embrace, his face so full of relief that he looked genuine for a moment. After he let go of Satyana, he greeted the Historian formally before shaking Nona's hand. Their eyes met, and she swore she saw compassion there. Damn him. She didn't need or want his compassion.

Another ship landed. The Futurist and the Biologist disembarked, as well as a single assistant. The assistant made her way right to the Historian, who grew a wide, genuine smile on his face, visibly shedding tension. Nona liked him for that.

"What about the Architect?" Satyana asked.

"He's here. So is Winter."

Satyana smiled widely. Britta appeared as if from nowhere, the huge woman suddenly by Satyana's side, one arm almost crushing her boss.

"Follow me," Gunnar said. "We need to get you ready. The Next aren't going to give us a break on this decision because your hair isn't right."

"How do you know?" the Futurist grumbled.

Men and women surrounded them with food, clean clothes, combs, and cups of hot stim. Apparently there wasn't time for a shower, but at least they'd look like decision makers when they hit the stage.

Gunnar directed traffic in and out. Three of his security detail wandered throughout the room, basically getting in the way.

Two women gently washed Nona's face with warm, white washcloths. After they pronounced her reasonably clean, they gave her a choice between three sets of garments. She picked a severe black pantsuit with a purple scarf and knee-high black boots that gave her an extra inch of height. The women complimented it with mother-of pearl earrings and a set of graduated nano-pearls in perfect rounds. A tall, silent man strung a thin, bone-conducting wire by each ear, which would be both a microphone for when she spoke and a radio to receive stage directions.

Nona glanced wearily at the mirror. In spite of being tired and worn out and scared for Chrystal, she had to admit she looked capable. The black made her look strong, and older. The makeup job had transformed her face into something beautiful. The clothes were far better than she usually wore, soft and silky. She closed her eyes and whispered her mantra inside of her head. "I am strong enough to do this. I am strong enough to make a difference."

When she opened her eyes, she found Satyana looking at her with approval. Surely that was for her outfit and not for the silent words she had just said, but it felt like it covered both. Satyana's dark hair had been brushed glossy and her lips painted maroon, and she held the bodice of a black silk dress up while a robot zipped the back. A woman stood beside her holding a cascade of lace flowers.

Satyana's voice carried across the whole, crowded room. "We'll be using the same stage that Ruby Martin made her debut on long ago." For once, Nona didn't feel resentment toward her mother's famous friend. "We'll have tables and chairs up there in the same configuration you're used to in court. There will be some audience—mostly my crew—but people from nearby may be here as well. We'll have guards. It will be as safe as we can make it, and we'll be able to record *and* broadcast. Does anyone have any questions?"

The Economist was buried under four sets of hands, whose owners were struggling to do something interesting with her hair. "How are we going to handle the people's vote position?"

Gunnar answered. "I've asked Satyana to take the role of Headmistress, although not the vote. That goes to the people. Satyana will moderate the votes." The look on his face dared anyone to challenge him.

No one did.

"You have a half an hour," he said. The room came back alive with movement and small talk.

The same fear that had crashed down on her when Satyana first told her she had a role came down even harder. She was going to vote for peace, but which option? Help the Next or ignore them? Was she voting against Charlie? She missed him. For that matter, she missed Jason and Yi.

And Chrystal. She kept trying not to think about Chrystal, but it just wasn't possible.

Gunnar interrupted. "The Shining Revolution has a broadcast they want us to see. It's live. Those of you who want to watch can follow me to a room across the hall."

Nona nearly beat him to the door.

The room across the hall turned out to be a private theater where Satyana and her staff often watched performances on the main stage. Couches and comfortable chairs oriented toward the wall screen. Everyone had come, even many of the assistants and makeup people. As they filed in, the screen showed a picture of the stage being set up for the vote. Three people and a handful of small robots wandered across the stage setting up chairs and microphones.

The screen changed views suddenly, showing the logo of the Shining Revolution. A well-muscled man and an equally well-muscled woman stood back to back in dance positions, holding hands and looking outward. As if cradling them, a stylized version of the words, "Humanity, Free and Clear" ran in a half-circle below the dancers.

Sitting between the Historian and Satyana, Nona went cold and stiff with fear. She didn't want the screen to move on from the logo.

CHAPTER SIXTY-NINE

CHARLIE

Charlie stared at the map Davis had projected on the wall. All of the others—Amfi and Davis, the soulbots, the Jhailing Jim, looked as well. A silence full of import had descended on the room. Blue marked the places the Next had agreed not to go. Yellow showed the places they would mine, and base, and have rights to travel to and from. There were two yellow cities where the Next would be allowed to put as many people as they could fit inside the boundaries. Charlie pictured high, ugly towers full of robots.

In many cases the colors on the map touched without blending: A hard line Charlie saw as fences, although he'd fought to keep open corridors for wildlife. In some places the yellow and blue came together and created greens, soft or hard depending on a variety of factors. Commerce and blending of . . . not races. Flesh and metal.

There was far more blue than yellow or green; at least ninety percent of the planet was blue. Charlie still hated the map. He'd done his best, but deep inside he felt certain he could have done even better, gotten more for them. Manny should have been here.

He'd spent his life dealing with the scars humanity had carved into Lym's surface and then left behind. How much more damage would the Next do? Every spot of yellow might as well be red, representing a likely bleeding hole in the carefully managed ecosystem.

He startled when Amfi hugged him. The tears caught in her eyelashes surprised him more.

"Are you okay?" he whispered.

"Thank you," she said. "I didn't know it would come to this." She glanced at the robot. "I didn't know. I'm glad you were here."

He crushed her to him. "I don't blame you." She smelled of cave and wild food and sweat.

Thank you," she said again, and stepped out of his embrace.

Her eyes which were still damp, and a tear-track had cleaned one cheek.

"Thank you," he said. "We did this together."

She smiled, soft and a little tentative. It emphasized the wrinkles around her eyes.

Jhailing Jim crossed the room and held out his hand. It was one of his most robotic parts, with metal fingers that could bend in more directions than the human hand.

Charlie stared at the hand and then at the robot's eyes, which were a guileless blue as clear as glass.

No tears there.

He held his own hand out and grasped the robot's hand.

Jhailing Jim closed his hand over Charlie's, the pressure as calibrated as Manny's handshake, and said, "Thank you. It is far better than war would have been."

As he let go of the robot's hand, Charlie glanced at the map again. He still felt it like a flu, as if every inch of land granted to the Next had come with blood and nutrients.

Of course, it wasn't over. He needed to get to Manna Springs and talk to Manny, to convince him to accept this deal.

Charlie glanced at Yi and Jason, who were both sitting very still. He suspected they were talking with Jhailing. The more powerful Next seemed able to talk to humans and hold conversations with the soulbots with no problem, but Jason and Yi sometimes showed it when they multitasked, particularly Jason. At the moment his face had gone so slack he looked like a normal household robot in the off position.

Charlie tried to get their attention. "We should go."

They startled, even Yi. They must have been deep in silent conversation. He reminded himself to ask Yi about that at the next opportune moment.

Yi's face turned from blank to an expression Charlie couldn't read, his features hard. Then his lips thinned to anger in an expression as tortured as Charlie had ever seen on the soulbot. "Is there news coverage here?"

Charlie glanced at Davis and Amfi.

Davis nodded. "Follow me." He led them all, including Jhailing, to one of the smaller rooms in the cave and powered up the lights and a screen that actually hung from the wall instead of displaying *on* the wall. Perhaps some of the old technology Davis had mentioned earlier. Or just the most expedient thing when your walls were made of cracked and marbled stone. The resolution was clearer than any wall display Charlie had seen. At the moment, the sigil of the Shining Revolution took up the whole thing, the hand-locked dancers taller than Charlie by half again.

These were the people who had Chrystal. Dammit. He checked on the robots. Jason and Yi stood close together, holding hands. Jhailing stood just behind them.

Charlie moved to stand behind them all, so that he could see their reaction as well as whatever bad news was about to come.

The screen flashed and a new image replaced the old.

A court of sorts. A man in black with tattoos all over him, a woman with the same black clothes but light brown skin free of marks. Both wore their hair in braids that hung long over camouflage shirts. They cradled weapons. A couple with short hair, pale eyes, and neater uniforms stood on either side of them.

Whoever was broadcasting had pasted names near each image. The deeply tattooed man in front was Vadim. The dark-haired woman who matched him was named Nayli. The short-haired couple were Darnal and Brea Paulson, neither name familiar to him. A small box opened on the screen and identified them as "Dangerous mercenaries who were wanted by multiple stations, including the Deep."

Vadim nodded at the cameras and said, "Thank you for joining us. I promise to make this worth your time. Many of you are familiar with the Shining Revolution. Those who are not, will be. We are old and venerable—we were born at the end of the age of explosive transformation and we have remained. We have waxed and waned in size as the need for us has changed." He paused for a breath and leaned toward the camera, his eyes fierce. Theatrical. "Right now, we are growing quickly. A hundred people are joining our cause every second. We invite you to do the same. Join us. To understand why, please listen for a moment as my wife Nayli explains her reasoning to you."

Nayli was beautiful. He shoulders were broad and her face a bit broad as well, but in a way that added to her fierce beauty. She glowed with health. Well-defined muscles rippled beneath the fabric of her clothes when she moved.

"Long ago we decided to outlaw the marriage of mind and machine. We wisely chose to say that machines must serve man. If we become servants of machines, we will lose our very soul. And yet we have named the pirates at the edge of our star system soulbots, and implied that they have souls rather than that they take them. But I say they are eaters of souls.

"The events of the past year have born this out. The eaters of souls killed a station. An entire station. When they ripped the High Sweet Home from its orbit, they brutally murdered almost everyone who lived there. There were hundreds of thousands of *human* souls on the High Sweet home. Military men and women. Traders. Farmers. Scientists. Teachers. Children." She paused, staring at the camera, as if daring anyone to deny the atrocity that had happened in space. When she continued, her voice rose. "That's not the worst of it. The pirates kept a handful of humans to destroy more slowly."

She sounded so reasonable. In spite of his fears for Chrystal, in spite of the fact that he liked Jason and Yi, a part of him didn't entirely disagree with her. It made listening to her feel like bifurcation of himself. He clenched his fists.

Jason and Yi didn't show any outward reaction, except that they had gone as still as statues.

Nayli continued. "They took living beings—living men and women just like you and me, and they destroyed their bodies and uploaded their brains into robots. They killed them."

Another pause.

"This was not an act of war. It was deliberate murder."

Another thing he agreed with. Dammit.

She slowed her delivery, each phrase provided with a pause after it for effect. "We don't know what it felt like to be their victims. How much it hurt. Whether or not they knew what was happening to them. Whether or not they gibbered in fear on cold stretchers while the abominations beyond the Ring cut their skulls open."

Jason and Yi stirred in front of him, Yi putting an arm around Jason's shoulder. Charlie wished he could see their faces. He had never asked them how they became soulbots and they had never offered. Had it been so horrible?

The screen switched to coverage of the Next's announcement on the Satwa. The footage showed a scene Charlie didn't remember watching in the Satwa's bar. It showed Chrystal, Jason, and Yi standing among many other robotic figures, including some of the large and fluid forms that seemed least human. Vadim took over the narration. "The Next introduced their pets to us when they came here. Make no mistake—they look like the people who were killed to create them, but they are not those humans. Those humans are dead.

"These robots were created by the soul-eating machines that we banned from our lives. *They are them. They are not us.* They were merely fashioned to look like us, to fool us. The Next claim they started with the brains and memories of specific humans. If they were in boxes instead of pretty, nearly-human bodies, we would abhor them immediately. We cannot assume that they have the souls or the hearts of the people who were killed to create them."

Amfi glanced at Jason and Yi curiously. Charlie took a single protective step closer to them. Jhailing stood entirely still, showing no emotion whatsoever.

The camera returned to the meeting room, and now Chrystal sat at the head of the table, recognizable as the woman from the video on the Satwa.

Her face looked so frightened and miserable that Charlie wondered if the revolutionaries had made a mistake and created a victim people would identify with. Her hair was a mess; her blue dress had been partly torn off, demonstrating that her exposed breast had no nipples.

Her forced semi-nudity offended him.

One of her hands looked wrong. She held her wrist canted far more to the right than a normal human hand could possibly manage.

Nayli talked again, giving Vadim credit for capturing Chrystal, and for keeping her. Footage, which the revolutionaries must have ripped from security cameras showed them walking through hallways on the Deep with Chrystal being herded at gunpoint. A time-lapse sequence showed Chrystal sitting up all night in a jail cell, awake but not moving, not talking, not drinking. The recording was bright and over-exposed, giving her skin a texture that looked far less human than he remembered.

Anger boiled up Charlie's spine, as well as shame. These were his people. Not the Revolution—he had never been part of that. But they were humans, full humans, set to hate another being they didn't understand. One he had come to admire.

He hadn't realized that until this moment. Seeing her treated this way made him angry and erased the schism inside of him over Nayli's words.

Vadim took over. "When we were bringing her here, after a full night of sitting up and plotting and planning rather than sleeping, she got away from us. Single-handedly. We had weapons on her, more than one. And yet she escaped."

Meaning you made a mistake, Charlie thought. Chrystal was too smart to run in a closed environment, so she must have been very, very scared. Robot or not, she wasn't sophisticated.

A screen showed her in a corridor, running, the skirt of her blue dress rising and falling beautifully. Vadim's voice described how she ran faster than any human, faster even than the ship's robots. They had needed to commandeer the ship's AI to help trap her. Even then, when they had her fair and square, she had almost gotten away. One of the face cameras from a squad who had caught her recorded her turning a corner into them.

The view switched to an overhead security camera in the corridor. It went to black and white, but it was clear and high resolution.

Charlie watched in horror as Chrystal turned to escape. A man stood with a weapon and an intense look of hatred on his face. He fired. His shot cost her her footing and she fell. He whooped, screeching his triumph in a way had once seen an illegal hunter act when he brought down a tongat.

Chrystal reached out to grab the man who had shot her, and threw him far down the corridor, bouncing after him awkwardly with her shattered foot. He knew the moment the man's neck broke. When they showed it in slow motion, Charlie could see the moment of death.

Back in the conference room, a split screen showed the dead man's head matted with blood and a pool of it behind him on the floor of the corridor. Close enough to see the empty stare in his eyes. The other half of the screen showed a picture of Chrystal's ankle and nearly-severed foot. A few clear drops of oil glistened there. They must have leaked from a torn tube the laser that had sliced her foot hadn't cauterized completely.

The couple behind Vadim and Nayli stepped forward and spoke for the first time. The man, Darnal, said, "We pronounce this robot a creation in violation of our most basic laws and social structures as a society. We will destroy it in the same way that we destroy anything else that we don't need, and we will recycle the robot's parts into raw materials."

Brea said, "Nayli, you may do the honors."

Chrystal started. Her face filled with fear, eyes wide, lips thin, jaw tight.

More feeling than he had ever seen her display, something feral and alive that didn't want to die.

Charlie's mouth dropped open. So fast. No trial. No chance.

Nayli drew her weapon and pointed it at Chrystal.

The camera drew back so that the audience could see that many more armed revolutionaries were in the room, all staring at Chrystal, all ready in case they were needed.

Nayli looked at Chrystal, her expression deep. Not anger or hatred. Something far more complex.

Chrystal glanced around the room and then back to Nayli, her eyes wide. It looked like she could talk, could say something if she wanted to.

But she didn't.

Nayli swallowed.

She and Chrystal looked at each other, and for a short second Charlie thought he saw a flicker of compassion on the beautiful revolutionary's face.

"Now," Brea said.

Nayli pulled the trigger on what must be a laser weapon similar to the one that had been used on Chrystal on the corridor. It severed the top of Chrystal's head and a piece fell off, clattering onto the ground.

Jason groaned audibly. Amfi swore. Charlie tensed.

The next cut took one eye and left the other, the next the rest of her head. Chrystal's body fell to the floor, and Nayli stood over it, holding the trigger, cutting and cutting until Vadim took her hand and she stopped.

Tears ran down Nayli's cheeks.

The camera zoomed in on a piece of Chrystal's face: part of her mouth, open, and a cut-away bit of chin leaking fluid.

Yi and Jason were holding each other tightly, faces tucked into each other's shoulders.

CHAPTER SEVENTY

NONA

Pain and anger shot through Nona as parts of Chrystal fell onto the floor. Disbelief warred with the truth of the visuals. Her hands shook. Small and strange moans escaped her lips.

Strong arms encircled her and Satyana whispered in her ear. "I'm sorry. But don't lose it now. You can't. Stuff your anger deep inside and put it away. Let it influence you on the stage."

On the screen, Vadim was putting out a call to people to join the Shining Revolution. Satyana snapped at Gunnar. "Turn it off!"

The room went silent, except for Nona's gasping breaths.

"You can't come apart," Satyana whispered, as the others began to move and react and talk in low tones. "You can't let this anger drive your choices and decisions. You are part of the Voice. You must be strong. You must be strong."

Satyana's words sounded like her mantra. Nona felt a tear streak down her cheek, probably undoing some of the fabulous makeup job. "I will," she said out loud. "I will."

"Ten minutes," Gunnar said.

Nona closed her eyes, repeating again, silently, "I must be strong. I must be strong." Then she added, "I must be strong for Chrystal." It dawned on her that there was something to do *now*. She stood up and surveyed the room, gulping air, aware of every eye on her. Satyana's hand on her back steadied her. The Councilors were all there, every one of them. Even the tall, blond man who was the current Architect. As soon as she had enough breath to talk, she did. "Some of you got a chance to meet Chrystal. Dr. Nevening and the Economist both did. The rest of you were supposed to, and would have if she hadn't been stolen from us. But we—humans—were the enemy there.

"Chrystal did *not* deserve to die. She didn't deserve anything that happened to her—not what the Next did to her and not what we humans did to her after that. We saw her kill a man on screen, but keep in mind that she killed a man had just shot her and gravely wounded her, and who still had a weapon pointed at her. She killed in self-defense."

A whole room full of Councilors and aides watched her. Gunnar, too. And Winter Ohman in the corner. She almost stumbled into silence, and Satyana rubbed circles in her back. "Go on," she whispered.

"Chrystal had been shot just moments before she threw the man down. Soulbots feel pain. I know. I spent weeks with Chrystal in transit. She came from here, she was a child on the Deep and we went to the same schools, played together. She felt like herself, and she felt to me—who had been her best friend—like herself." She stopped, realizing she was running out of time. "Our focus in the next few years needs to be on keeping humans from killing humans over this. The Next may or may not be our enemies, but we are our own enemy."

The Historian raised his hand and she called on him, and then realized *she* was calling on the *Historian* and felt a little weak inside.

He stood up. The makeup artists had done a good job with him, too, and he somehow looked taller and more commanding than she'd ever thought him before. "I found Chrystal very human," he said with precise diction. "She was also smart and perceptive. I only spent an hour or so with her, but that was enough to convince me that she did not deserve the death that we just witnessed. I will have more to say on the dais where this conversation should continue, but there is one historical perspective I will offer here and now. Acts of terrorism seldom result in more freedom for anyone, including the terrorists."

Leesha said, "I agree. Chrystal seemed like a fine young woman. She also looked very afraid when the Shining Revolution took her. She had feelings." She inclined her head, her hair magnificently coifed and glittering with fresh jewels. "We have work to do. We should go prepare."

Perhaps Leesha had recognized that Nona had run out of words. Nona wanted to thank Leesha and Dr. Nevening, but there wasn't time in the hustle of being led onto the stage. Making her way to the other room felt a little like walking through gauze, as if a fog had enveloped her and made her limbs heavy and turned the walls and art on the *Star Bear* surreal.

CHAPTER SEVENTY-ONE

CHARLIE

The screen in the cave went dark. Someone brought the lights halfway down. A respectful move. Charlie watched Jason and Yi in silence, a deep anger welling up and swamping his sadness. Chrystal had made him laugh, had made him worry, had been open and so very human there were times he forgot what had happened to her.

Had she ever forgotten? Even for a moment?

Amfi walked over to Jason and Yi and touched them. She said nothing, just touched them, one hand lightly on each man's shoulder. Charlie followed suit. He and Amfi looked at each other. He noticed tears in Amfi's eyes, which made him blink back his own. Here he was, crying for the second time in as many days. He almost managed not to let a tear actually fall, but then Davis's hand was on *his* shoulder and all five of them had become linked in the shock of the moment.

Charlie cried.

Jhailing Jim came closer, but didn't join the circle. He watched.

After a time, the circle opened up and out and Charlie felt like a fully separate being again. His anger and sadness had been washed away by his tears, leaving him full of emptiness and deeply sad.

A long silence fell across all of them, and Charlie used the time to gather himself back up, to return to the task at hand.

Jhailing was the first to begin something new. He gave a respectful half-bow to Amfi and Davis, and said, "Thank you for your hospitality. You represented humanity well when you left me in a comfortable captivity and checked on my welfare. I appreciate that you came to talk from time to time, and that over that time you came to understand us more. Now that there is an agreement to ratify, I'll be going to town with Charlie to help him do it. You are welcome to accompany me."

Davis said, "No, no thank you. I'll stay here and wait. But I'll let you out."

"No need."

"What?" Amfi asked. "Could you always have left?"

"I always could have found a way—some way—to leave. But I didn't fall into captivity on purpose. A piece of me broke, which affected some of my ability to communicate with machines and others like myself. I was unable to call for help. I could talk with Yi and Jason once they arrived here, but my ability to communicate long distance had become limited.

"This is how you and your friends held me after you captured me. Without the repair robot I would not have been able to complete the negotiations." Jhailing nodded at Davis. "But now I can open your doors without help."

Davis looked irritated. Charlie wondered about the robot and Jhailing and Yi and Jason all ending up in the same place. It didn't seem possible that it was engineered; it had to be coincidence. But it was neat.

"The little robot fixed you!" Yi sounded surprised.

"Yes," Jhailing answered Yi. "I am grateful for the loan, but it is still your repair-bot. You may need it again before our ships land on Lym."

"No one has permission to land yet. We have to go to town," Charlie said.

Davis glanced at Amfi, a pleading look on his face.

She said, "I'll go. You can stay."

Davis said, "Thank you."

Charlie concluded Davis would be glad to be rid of all of the Next, at least for now. "We'll stop at the ranger station on the way, maybe spend the night. We can be in Manna Springs early."

The Jhailing said, "Must we stop?"

"We need to sleep," Charlie said.

The representative of the Next didn't reply.

What about Jason and Yi? He shouldn't tell them what to do. "Do you want to come?"

Yi nodded slowly. "We may be needed."

Jason said, "Maybe they'll tear me apart, too." Then his eyes opened wider and Charlie assumed Jhailing was communicating with him just fine.

CHAPTER SEVENTY-TWO

NONA

O n the stage, Nona took her place on the left side between Winter Ohman and Gunnar Ellensson. The Councilors were arrayed on the right side of the stage and Satyana stood in the middle. She looked beautiful—part diva, part powerful hostess, part statesman, part ship's captain. Her black dress clung to her chest and hips and purple lace flowers cascaded from one bare shoulder down across to waist to fall almost to the floor. She raised her head and clapped her hands for attention.

The hot, bright lights made Nona crave sunshades. Only the first few rows of seats were visible: the rest faded to black beyond the spotlights. The people who came to listen to the Council were usually well-dressed, as if going to a party. Some of the people in the first few rows—all that she could see with the bright lights—were dressed up tonight as well. But others looked ragged, and tired. A few children were clutched in their mother's arms.

A screen hanging behind the stage displayed the diamond-faceted star of the station's logo over a field of stars and the Deeping Rules:

> *You must own yourself.*
> *You must harm no one.*
> *You must add to the collective.*

Nona realized someone had designed the opening view of the Shining Revolution broadcast to parody this traditional backdrop to the Court of the Deeping Rules. A streak of anger penetrated the fog of her loss and grief. The Rules contrasted with the Shining Revolution's saying: "Humanity, Free and Clear." The revolution hewed to a statement of specific value, an unwavering stickiness around a single idea that they were willing to kill for regardless of circumstance. Had killed for. Had killed her friend for. Maybe they would try to kill Nona as well after the vote.

She took a deep, shuddering breath and then another, trying to look calm for the cameras.

The Deeping Rules left room for growth. They let the station interpret the world in light of things that changed. A brief pride in the Deep and in her unexpected place in the Court drove her to sit up straighter.

She had to stop seeing Chrystal's face falling to the floor in pieces like severed parts of a doll. Again, she whispered to herself. "I am strong enough."

In the formal Court of the Deeping Rules, there would have been a speaker to introduce the proceedings.

Satyana held her hands together as if praying. "Good evening. Thank you for attending, for watching remotely, or for viewing this in video. We are here on my stage in the *Star Bear* instead of in the courtroom for our security." She sounded very formal, and stood straight, and Nona wondered if this might be as much of a stretch for her as being part of the Voice was for Nona.

Satyana lifted her head higher. One tear fell, and no other came to take its place. "We gather to make the decision that the Next demanded of us. This is the last day to make that decision, and so we are meeting here and now. We have about an hour to get through this, so our remarks will be shorter than you are accustomed to. While there is not enough time for our traditional process, nothing will change the fact that we are the lawful decision makers and this decision must be made."

There was no note of defeat in Satyana's voice, but Nona sat close enough to see how tightly she held herself. This was a surrender.

She hadn't been smart enough to see that, but now she understood the military's desire to stop this meeting. The Council was giving up, yielding their ability to make choices on their own timeline to a threat larger than themselves. The people she stood with on the stage represented the biggest and best station in all of the vast Glittering, and they and the other two stations who had been driven to speak for all of the Glittering were dancing like puppets to the Next's demands.

"We apologize for the delay. Some of us were invited but unwilling guests at a party thrown by the Shining Revolution. Our military realized we might be late to this task, and helped."

Nona understood. Satyana could denounce the revolutionaries, but the station might need the military someday.

"This is a crucial decision. One vote for each Council member. That's five. One vote for each of the Voice, which is three. A final vote for the Headmistress, which will be handled uniquely. This allows for our usual voting traditions, in short form. The council will each speak very briefly from the position they represent before they vote.

"The Voice will each speak to represent the people of the Deep in this matter. The Voice of this trial, this vote, includes Gunnar Ellensson because of his stake in Mammot and the economic benefits of that stake that accrue to this station and that the Next have said they want access to." The audience gasped. Satyana lifted a hand for silence. "The second Voice is Winter Ohman. He will speak for the people of this station. The third Voice is Nona Hall, because her friend Chrystal encountered the Next and came back to us changed by them."

Once more, Nona felt awed. If she were in Satyana's position, she would not have been as delicate of phrase, or as effective at reminding the audience of what they had just seen without saying it out loud.

"At this point we will have heard from the formal leaders of the stations, and from the people most directly affected." Satyana paused for a moment, and made a small bow toward the audience. "And instead of a vote for the Headmistress, who is being held in a safe and secret place by our military forces, we will use the methods that she herself set up. The people of the Diamond Deep will be the third class of vote, the last voice that we hear, and the loudest. This vote has been ceded to you the people via a social reckoning, which *will be taken at the end of the other votes.* Tallies will display on the screen behind us."

Satyana once more put her hands together as if in prayer, and then opened them wide. "Now we begin. We will vote on three options.

"Option one is to enforce the Ring of Distance and uphold our existing laws. That will almost certainly require coordinated military force and alliances between stations. It will require investment. We will call this choice *Uphold.*"

Nona fidgeted. This had been her first instinct. It had been Charlie's first instinct and might still be his goal. There had been no time to call him. She had wanted it at first, in the heat of dismay. It would feel good to fight. *Uphold* represented the dreams of the people who had just carved her best friend into small metal pieces.

"Option two is to allow the Next to come inside the Ring of Distance and use our resources, including Lym and Mammot. To stay as separate from the Next as we can, so that we are changed the least. We will have little to no influence on the choices that the Next make, and they will have the least opportunity to change us. We will call this option *Allow*."

"Option three is to assist the Next. To let them in, to work with them, possibly to work beside them. We have very few details of what this means, except that by this choice we will know them. We will be signing up to assist them with goals that are invisible to us so far. We will call this choice *Help*."

Help was a good word; it implied willing cooperation.

In the background, music came up. Orchestral, riding from soft to louder and then falling again. Only a few moments of music, but it fit Satyana, who continued after the sound fell away. "We'll start with the Architect."

The Architect oversaw the constant build-out and structural safety of the Deep, and so his answer seemed pre-ordained. He stepped into the circle of light on the stage and simply said, "*Allow*."

The Economist's choice was nearly as obvious, but Leesha used the moment anyway, standing regally in the center of the stage and saying, "We do not have the funds to *Uphold* at this moment, although I have started developing strategies to support a war should one occur. But it would be madness to start fighting. I find *Help* tempting because of what we might learn, but the risks are too great. I choose *Allow*."

At least Leesha hadn't pulled her punches, and she'd called a war a war.

Nona felt queasy when the biologist came up. If Jackie Bray chose *Allow* then the deed would be nearly done. Jackie looked far less at ease in the spotlight than Leesha had, and fidgeted a bit before she talked. "We are also speaking for Lym. If we choose *Allow*, we lose all of our ability to negotiate about Lym. Yet we need the planet's biodiversity. I choose *Help*."

Nona breathed a sigh of surprised relief. That was two votes for *Allow* and one for *Help*.

Satyana called on the Historian next. In spite of his small stature, he looked both important and brave. "I looked into our history. It appears that we may have had very good reasons to banish the Next when we did." He paused. "That vote was close, as this vote appears to be.

"The Next have become something different now. They are stronger than they were when we banished them: we may not be able to banish them again.

History is rich with examples of people with better technology swamping those with less. It is a bitter truth, but history's lessons are often bitter.

"To *Allow* also had risks. We can't be sure if the Next will actually leave us alone. Being surrounded by a powerful race that wants your resources often ends in annihilation.

"There is also danger in working with the Next. Yet there are many sayings from history about keeping your enemy close, and understanding your enemy. So that is the path I recommend. I say that we *Help*."

The vote had split so far.

She had no read on the Futurist. Hiram stood formally at the microphone, letting a few beats of silence pass. He surveyed the room, looking up toward the seats as if there were people in them that he could see. "The future is usually improved with risks. But sometimes it can be destroyed by them, as well. We should not fight the Next. They are more ruthless than we are, and than we ever will be, in spite of the atrocity that we saw the Shining Revolution perpetrate. We should not help the Next, because it creates a temptation to become the Next. We've already seen this at work, the perilous sweet call of even longer life, of stronger bodies. I say that we *Allow*."

Nona had expected the Futurist to be less conservative, and to choose *Help*.

Satyana looked slightly dismayed, although Nona suspected that she was the only one who would see that, except maybe Gunnar. "I will call on the Voice."

Nona's heart beat faster. She suddenly wished she weren't here, and told herself that was ridiculous. She tapped her right foot against her left ankle hard enough to hurt until she felt focused again.

Satyana surveyed the crowd and looked into the cameras. "I call on Gunnar Ellensson first."

He looked startled. Nona suspected he had wanted to be third so that his words could be the last influence on the social reckoning. In spite of that one look, he seemed comfortable and sounded convincing as he played his part. He was, of course, the most imposing figure on the stage. "If we help them, if we work with them, we may be able to mitigate the damage they do to Mammot and to Lym. Many of you know that I have interests in Mammot. But I would point out that you do, too. Ten percent of our trade—of our economy—comes from Mammot and through the Diamond Deep. A strong economy and a strong society require change and growth, and risk. I say we take this risk together. I say *Help*."

Nona wondered how many other people saw Gunnar's response as disingenuous. He was almost certainly trying to protect his nearly infinite lease of land and mines on Mammot.

Winter moved deliberatively during a time when they needed to hurry.

Nona's foot felt twitchy and she forced it to be still.

Winter spoke slowly, but not very much. "I represent all of the social groups on the station, all of the people of the Deep. Most of them are workers, common people pursuing dignified lives. I vote to follow the Economist and choose *Allow*."

Four for *Allow* and three for *Help*. If she chose *Allow*, that would happen. If she chose *Help*, either could happen. The vote would be saved for the people. She took a deep breath. It seemed that Satyana called her name from a far distance, and that she had to walk through mud, trying not to trip, as she took her place as the speaker. The spotlight heated her face and stole her peripheral vision.

Satyana had put her in this position when she called on Gunnar first, and Satyana never did anything important by accident.

Nona blinked in the light, took a deep breath, and repeated her mantra quickly in her head. "I speak for my friend, Chrystal. Chrystal who was just murdered by the Shining Revolution. For that is what it was. Murder. Chrystal was still . . . Chrystal. There were some differences—how could there not have been? But her spirit was her own. She laughed at the same things and worried about the same things. The woman who was just taken apart in front of us all is the same woman who was born on the Deep and went to school with me on the Deep, and who I loved dearly all of my life." She had to stop for a few big gasping breaths, and then she had to go on before she couldn't. "Because of that linkage, I believe that there is more true and good in the Next than we know, and so even though I am frightened and angry, even though I can't be sure of the right thing to do, and I don't think any of us can, on stage or off, I am voting that we *Help* the Next."

Her legs shook as she walked back to her seat. She had used a lot more words than she meant to.

She barely heard Satyana say, "Thank you."

She looked up, hoping to catch Satyana's eye, but the other woman was looking out at the audience. "Now it is *your* turn. We will open the vote in a few moments. We will accept your votes for the next three minutes after that. I advise you to decide alone and uninfluenced. We have talked about this for months now, and it is time to decide each for each and thus reveal our collective wisdom." She fell silent, bowed her head, and then lifted it again. Her voice rang out in a loud call. "The vote is open."

Someone handed Nona a glass of water and she downed it in one long sip. Fear made her thirsty.

Leesha, who had voted differently than Nona, came over and put a hand on her shoulder and said, "You spoke well."

"Thanks."

Leesha whispered, "If I weren't the Economist, I would have voted with you."

As odd as Leesha was, Nona relished the moment of intimacy between her and the tall woman with gems in her purple hair. So unexpected.

Above them, numbers spun too fast to read, except for *Uphold*. Satyana came and leaned close to Chrystal and said, "At least most people don't want a war."

"Good," Nona and Leesha both said at once.

A stray thought suddenly seemed important. "Do you know what the other two stations have decided?"

"Not yet. I think everyone is waiting for the last minute."

Satyana glanced at the spinning counters. "Speaking of the last minute . . ." She returned to the spotlight and waited while the counters finished. "Thank you. We've had a good turnout. One hundred seventy five thousand for *Uphold*. Five hundred and sixty-four thousand for *Allow*, and six hundred and three thousand for *Help*."

Satyana waited, letting the numbers sink in before she spoke. "The Council, the Voice, and the Headmistress through the people of the Diamond Deep have chosen. They have said that we as a station will help the Next as they come into the light and live near the sun. This means that we set aside our previous interpretation of the Deeping Rules. We accept this new interpretation, born for this time and this moment. We will act as one station, together."

She dropped her hands.

The house lights came up and Nona could see that the seats had in fact been over half full. A thousand people or so.

Sporadic clapping and cheering floated toward them, punctuated by silence. With such a close vote it wasn't surprising that some of the audience wasn't happy.

Satyana turned to Gunnar. "Tell the ambassadors."

"I will."

"Wait," Nona said. "What ambassadors?"

"The Next. There are some in a nearby ship. They've been waiting for our decision."

There were Next close by and they hadn't helped Chrystal?

Satyana turned to her. "You did a great job up there. You were poised and you had feeling."

Nona shook her head, dumbfounded. Angry. Betrayed. "Why didn't the Next save Chrystal?"

Gunnar narrowed his eyes. "What would that have done to the vote?"

Nona fell silent. It would have started a war. It would have changed her vote. It still skewered her, sharpening the pain of Chrystal's loss. She looked at Satyana and said, "This is so hard."

Satyana smiled sadly. "Diplomacy is the hardest job in the world."

CHAPTER SEVENTY-THREE

CHARLIE

Charlie had to land in near dark, the bright colors of sunset painting the sky above him orange and red. Jean Paul waited to greet them. "I've put dinner on."

"Thanks."

While Jean Paul cooked, Charlie called Manny. He caught him sitting at his office desk reading the news, pictures of some of the parts of Lym that still needed the most restoration hanging behind his head. When he noticed Charlie's face he looked both relieved and angry. "You should come here."

"I'll be there soon. There's something I need to warn you about. I have a Next with me."

"I know."

"Not the two I brought with me."

"I know that, too. What gave you the right?"

Charlie stiffened. "Tell me what you're talking about, and then I'll tell you what I'm talking about."

For a moment, he didn't think Manny was going to respond. Manny was used to calling the shots and certainly not at all accustomed to Charlie telling him what to do. Manny leaned back and chewed on his lip for a second. "There's a Next ship landing here. Landing. They said you told them they could, and that they looked forward to meeting their neighbors. If I tell the people that, they'll tear you apart."

"I suppose that's one way to force the issue," Charlie said.

"It's a ship," Manny emphasized. "Not a station to ground shuttle. A fucking starship."

Charlie fell silent. "I didn't know that."

"It's going to scare a lot of people and piss off the rest."

It had already pissed Manny off, a fact left unsaid but written on his face.

Charlie nodded. "I'll give you the short version. The gleaners have been seeing Next and Next robots for a long time. You know that."

What did Manny actually need to know? "They've been scouts. You do understand that the Next gave three locations the ability to decide for all of humanity, and that we aren't on that list?"

Manny took a drink of something that looked serious. "Yep. We'll hear what they decided soon."

"When? And when are the Next coming?"

"Did you really give them room for two cities. Cities?"

"Didn't you make me your ambassador?"

"And the right to import their own humans who aren't part of our society?" Manny rolled his eyes. "Deals usually require some form of approval."

"I agree. I'm bringing it to you."

Manny didn't look appeased.

"Don't imagine I enjoyed this, or that I wanted to do it. But we aren't powerful enough to keep the Next from landing here, and they didn't give me much of a choice." He couldn't believe he was saying what he was saying. It felt like he had switched sides, and he hated it. "There's someone important coming in with me—a gleaner who convinced the Next to negotiate. I followed up on what she started. We're better off than we would be without her. Amfi. Do you know her?"

"You let a *gleaner* help you give away parts of Lym?"

"It'll be all right. Maybe. It's better than no deal. Better than war." To his surprise, as much as he hated that he had given anything away to Jhailing, he found that he believed his words. Funny how which side of a conversation you were on made it feel different.

"When will you be here? The Next are landing by late morning. They demanded you and the Next you're bringing."

It would be a two-hour flight. "I'll be there by an hour after dawn. We need to sleep."

Manny's voice had grown more controlled, but Charlie could still hear the anger in it. "Can you send me the outline of the deal now? So I can think about how to explain it?"

Charlie's thoughts raced. There were so many opportunities for misinterpretation. "No. No. I need to be there."

Manny's eyes narrowed. "Is it that bad?"

"If this is the final deal, we've given up more territory than we wanted to, but they got less than they wanted. A lot less. I did the best I could."

"The Next think it's binding."

"It's better than being overrun," Charlie said.

"After you explain, will you turn it over to me to sell to people? Please."

"Oh yes." He felt lighter already. "Absolutely."

Manny didn't look any lighter at all, but he did look a little less angry than he had at the start of the call. Good enough. After a few logistics, Charlie hung up.

Charlie gave himself five minutes of jotting notes on his slate to try and organize his thoughts before he returned to the group in the kitchen. He went to Jhailing. "I need to go get Cricket and feed her. Will you come along?"

"What's a Cricket?"

Charlie smiled. "I'll show you." As soon as they got through the door, he said, "What Next ship is landing?"

"The *Sunward*. We have permission now."

"Not until more than just me gives it to you!"

Jhailing didn't answer him.

"Can you call your ship off for a while?"

"No. That is beyond my authority."

Charlie doubted it. "Do you know what a tongat is?" he asked.

"Yes."

"Have you met one?"

"No. They are wild predators."

"Yes. Mostly." They rounded the corner to Cricket's kennel and Charlie opened the door. She stood on her hind legs, put her one front paw on his shoulder, and licked his face. It was the best moment of the day so far, maybe the only truly happy moment. He leaned forward, balancing against her weight and ran his hands through her fur for a full two minutes before he commanded her to step down.

Jhailing seemed quite interested in the relationship. He followed Charlie around asking questions, and Charlie felt more like an ambassador than he had the whole time he and Nona were flying to and from the Satwa. The Next, of course, had no contact at all with flesh and blood animals other than the occasional human. They'd read about them and observed them, and occasionally seen them on smuggler's ships, but they had no real experience.

As Charlie scooped Cricket's dinner into her bowl, Jhailing spoke thoughtfully. "It's possible that the relative differences in mental capabilities between you and Cricket is similar to that between humanity and the Next."

Charlie wanted to laugh, but he managed to hold that in, take three breaths, and say, "In some ways Cricket is smarter than I am."

"How do you mean that?"

"Packs of tongat survive very well in the wild, and they stay together with perfect loyalty from birth to death." He put Cricket's food down for her. "That is, except for a few very specific ritual exchanges of females which keep breeding populations diverse. They almost never fight, although as high-status predators, if they need to kill, they do so expediently. We humans are far messier in our relationships."

"I see." Jhailing said, although Charlie suspected he didn't. But then Jhailing said, "Maybe we and the tongats are more alike than I thought."

Wow.

After they watched Cricket finish wolfing down her food, Charlie asked Jhailing to check on Yi and Jason while he and Jean Paul took Cricket for a walk.

They walked in silence through the dusk, Cricket a bit of ahead of them. "Will you stay here?" Charlie asked Jean Paul. "I don't know how safe Manna Springs will be."

Jean Paul looked down at the ground. "For Cricket."

"For *your* safety, too. This could go sideways. This place is well-protected, and you have the other rangers. Besides, we may need to retreat if the city thinks I negotiated badly."

"Will they?" Jean Paul asked.

"I don't know." Stars pricked the sky like bright jewels. A cold wind slapped at Charlie's cheeks, carrying with it the earthy scents of fall forest.

Jean Paul picked up a rock and sent it skipping across the edge of the landing pad. "You might need to be rescued."

"I might. Or you might. I feel like we're in the middle of a windstorm. I wish we had more time. But the station's decisions will be made by now, and we'll be hearing soon. Jhailing might already know."

"Will Jason and Yi stay here?"

"They're coming with us."

Jean Paul frowned. "They're killing house bots in there."

"I know. They know. They'll pass at a distance in the right clothes.

Besides, Jhailing expects them to go." Poor things. "And they're heartbroken. They'll be better if we keep them busy."

"Be careful," Jean Paul said. "I like it that you're back home. It would be nice to keep it that way."

"Okay then." Charlie clapped his friend on the shoulder, and then gave him a hug instead. He wondered briefly if the Next had simpler relationships. "I'll be back."

That night, he broke one of his own rules and let Cricket sleep on the floor beside his bed.

———— ❧ ————

They piled out of the station in the dark of early morning, just as one edge of the sky had started to grey. Jason settled Amfi between himself and Yi. The gleaner took each of their hands and proceeded to ask them what Lym looked like from space.

Jhailing strapped into the front seat beside Charlie. Jean Paul waved good-bye, Cricket at his side.

"This is going to be hard," Charlie told Jhailing.

"Yes. But you are still the Ambassador for Lym."

"I'm not going to lie and tell them I made this all up in space."

"You can tell them you met me in space."

"Did I?" Charlie asked. "I thought that wasn't how it works."

"Practically? No. Not really. I haven't seen the instance of my self that you met on the Satwa for all of the many years I've been here."

Charlie flinched.

"And we have had different experiences. Entirely different. If we meet, or get close enough and have enough bandwidth for it, we'll swap some or all of our memories. That's *sharing*. We may even—for a time—relive our memories with each other. That's *braiding*. When we braid, we *almost* lose our individuality as we become immersed enough in each other to share the experience of an event—which is different than a memory of an event."

Charlie fell into contemplation as he guided the skimmer past the edge of the ranger base and over a set of small scarps until they were above rolling hills punctuated with dark ribbons of water.

Light started kissing the tops of the mountains.

When he and Nona had been side by side in bed on the *Star Ghost* the night after they watched the robots fly naked through the cargo bay, they had wondered what it must be like to live with no sex. Now he wondered if maybe the Next had a different way to be in each other's skin, and what that felt like.

Was it better? Less messy, anyway.

The thought made him smile, although he rather liked messy human sex.

As they passed out of the controlled flight zone around the station, he increased speed.

Jhailing's voice interrupted Charlie's reverie. "We are separate beings, but all of us that started from the same copy of the same human are a single legal entity from the viewpoint of *your* laws. That's why it is true that you met me on Satwa."

"You're reaching," Charlie said. "And I won't lie to anyone. Including you."

"Thank you."

Charlie still worried. "Did the Diamond Deep announce a decision?"

"They will help us."

"Have you heard anything about Nona?"

Jhailing fell silent for a moment and then smiled. "She's okay. She helped make the decision to help us."

Really? Charlie wondered how that had possibly happened.

The light fell more fully on the grassy plains below, turning them a pale gold. The morning hunt should be beginning. Charlie flew low, looking closely. "There's a pack of tongat surrounding a huge herd of hinta grazers down below and to the right." He pointed.

Jhailing's gaze followed Charlie's finger. "I see them."

"I'm pleased the Deep decided to help," Charlie said, surprised at himself yet again. But then, there had only ever been two options for Lym. Fight or cooperate. The Next had been clear from the first moment that they were coming here. He still hated it; it felt like agreeing to haul rock because someone held a gun on you and asked you to please help.

"But the Golden Starshine decided to fight, and we are uncertain whether or not humans can control groups like the Shining Revolution people that killed Chrystal."

Charlie watched the herds until they flew past them and he couldn't see them anymore. "I don't know if we can either, but I suppose we'll have to try."

"You could always throw Vadim and his people out beyond the Ring."

"Even though I'm sure that's a bad joke, I *would* like to do that to the particular group we just watched."

"I thought it was a very good joke," Jhailing said.

In the back, the conversation had gone from the view of Lym in space to what Yi and Jason thought of a sky.

Charlie fell silent and tried to decide if Jhailing had just demonstrated a sense of humor.

CHAPTER SEVENTY-FOUR

NONA

Nona woke to the smell of stim with no idea, at first, where she was. She had been dreaming of Charlie, and of sweet moments on the *Star Ghost* that went on and on, like living in a spiral of quiet lovemaking and long talks with no one else in the entire universe to interrupt them, and no responsibilities of any kind.

Satyana's voice whispered in her ear.

"Hmmm . . . what?"

"There's work to do."

"What?" Her sleep had been so deep it still felt like she was climbing up a reality rope, as if she'd been in some virtual world for days and had to slowly feed herself back into her body. "What do I have to do now?"

"Well, we all voted *Help*. Now we have to actually do that."

"They didn't help Chrystal."

Satyana didn't bother to respond.

Nona sat up and took the stim, sipping at it slowly, savoring being in her own bed. She thought about Charlie. Would he think she had sold him out, or would he understand? "What time is it?"

"Better ask what day it is. You slept a day and a half."

That startled her. "Wow."

"I thought you might need food. There's breakfast in the other room."

"Thanks."

"You should clean up, first. We have company."

Satyana had reverted to her old self, giving Nona orders. "Really?"

"The Historian wants to see you." Satyana's eyes sparkled.

Nona had to admit that she would like to see Dr. Nevening. But probably not in the way her almost-awake self was beginning to intuit Satyana thought she should. She didn't want his friendship for political gain. Nor did she want to date him. But what harm could come from a breakfast? "How long do I have?"

"He's already here."

She showered—quickly—even though she'd showered just before she went to bed. Nothing like being deprived of water for multiple days to build cravings for it. She pulled on comfortable blue pants and a white top and hurried toward the kitchen.

Dr. Nevening had brought two of his assistants to breakfast. He greeted her warmly, his face open and a tiny bit expectant. He held out a hand and she took it, and he covered her hand with his other hand, gazing at her. "You were very brave."

"How?" she asked.

"You spoke your heart yesterday. You barely looked nervous on stage, even though the whole Glittering watched. You were brave when we were captive and when we were rescued, both."

She blushed. "I didn't think I was very brave about being captured."

"Sure you were." He smiled, and turned to introduce his young assistants, Gray and Hatley.

She mumbled pleasantries and filled her plate.

To her relief, the good doctor Nevening let her finish half a plate of food before he spoke. "I'd like to record your memories about Chrystal while they're fresh, to make a memorial to her for future Historians."

Oh. For moment she felt that he hadn't, after all, come to see *her*. Then she realized he would need an excuse. She was both younger and far below him in the power structure. Her place on the stage had been temporary, and she probably wouldn't ever return to it. "All right. There will be a lot to tell you. But first, while we eat, can I ask you a few questions?"

"Of course."

His assistants looked intrigued.

"What can you tell me about the history of other societies who were overrun by people with significantly more technology?"

Satyana came closer and sat down at the table.

The Historian leaned back in his chair. "This has not really happened since we moved to space. There are small instances of fights over resources like asteroids or ships, or to keep the Next beyond the Ring, but stations don't attack each other. They are almost stationary when compared one to another, locked into orbits that have been calculated never to intersect. They have no need to fight over territory."

She waited until she finished her bread, and said, "I understand."

"The history we have is old, from when we were all on Lym." He took a sip of stim and nibbled on a berry. "In those cases, when one roving colony group or one city was overtaken by another, they were killed or assimilated. Most often, they were assimilated. They learned the new ways of the people who attacked them and subsumed them."

"Will that happen to us?"

He fell silent a moment. "I suppose in a way that is what happened to Chrystal. But I don't think it will happen to us, not if we stay here on the Deep. It probably will happen to the people who stay on Lym."

Charlie.

CHAPTER SEVENTY-FIVE

CHARLIE

Just as Charlie, Amfi, and the robots crossed into the controlled airspace around Manna Springs, Manny called.

Charlie raised a hand to silence the backseat, where Amfi was explaining gleaner social structures. She stopped midsentence and leaned a little forward, her face slightly distorted in the mirror that showed the backseat.

Manny sounded breathless, his words leaving little space between them. "Can you land at the main spaceport? Use pad B."

Charlie frowned. "I thought we were coming into your place. Will Jason and Yi be safe?"

"Yes."

Manny wouldn't lie to him. Whether it was true or not, Manny believed he could keep them safe. "Is the Next ship there yet?"

"No. But they asked that you greet them. All four of you. They say they want an open conversation that is broadcast for everyone. There's better security at the spaceport than in town."

"I see. So how is it in town?"

"Tense. I'm already at the spaceport. I'll meet you." He hung up abruptly, obviously beset with other worries. Manny had always been respected by the town, but times had been easy for his entire tenure. The crime rate on Lym had been low. There had been twelve cases of illegal hunting during Charlie's most recent year of rangering, but only one case of assault, which had turned out to be *about* a planned illegal hunt.

The people in jail were usually smugglers.

As they approached the spaceport, Charlie spotted people gathered by fences that hadn't been there when he left. It looked like most of the town's population had chosen to crowd the entrances. At the moment, they appeared to be an orderly mob.

Charlie landed as quietly as he could, flying low and slow, letting the autopilot guide him in and place him where Manny wanted him, which turned out to be inside of a hanger meant for much larger ships. Charlie approved—with nothing to see, the curious might leave well enough alone.

He climbed out of the skimmer first. To his relief, Manny folded him into a bear hug. "You have no idea how glad I am to see you."

"And I you." Charlie pushed himself aside to allow room for the others to disembark. He watched closely. Manny had lost so much weight he looked like half of Manny. He looked—haggard. Not old. He was no gleaner; he took his meds. Still...

Of course, Charlie probably looked different as well. It had been almost a year.

Jhailing was next. Manny held his hand out. "Welcome to Lym."

"Thank you," Jhailing said. "I am Jhailing Jim, and I am a member of the formal team of ambassadors who will accept your agreement."

Surprise flashed on Manny's face for a moment, and a hint of dismay. He recovered quickly, giving a warm greeting to Jason and Yi.

Charlie decided that Manny had expected the ambassador to be more imposing and the soulbots to be less—human.

Charlie nodded. "How long do we have?"

"Twenty minutes."

Twenty minutes to explain so much loss. He started in, and from time to time Amfi added a nuance.

Manny frowned and chewed on his knuckles.

———⊱⊰———

All six of them stood on the tarmac, waiting for the *Sunward* to descend. Charlie was between Manny and the soulbots, with Jhailing on the far side of Yi and Jason. A cool wind slapped at Charlie's cheeks; he zipped his jacket. "Here we go," he said to Manny. "Let's hope for success."

Manny stared up at the sky. "What is success in the middle of a nightmare? It's not like we can just wake up."

"You get used to it."

"I hope not," Manny said. He saw the Next ship first, pointing out a small silver square glinting in the sunlight.

All of landing pad C had been cleared, and for a moment, Charlie thought that might not be enough. The *Sunward* was a big block of a ship, an ugly thing with no apparent thought given to aerodynamics or grace. In spite of that, it moved so smoothly it might as well be guided down on a gossamer string.

"They must have gotten better at gravgens than we are," Manny said.

Jhailing Jim answered. "We've learned to handle far more mass without disruption."

"I presume that's an understatement," Charlie said.

"Will you teach us that technology?" Manny asked Jhailing.

"It can be discussed." Jhailing's eyes were on the *Sunward*, which settled smoothly down in front of them. "Later."

After the *Sunward* landed, it looked more like a new building had sprouted up in the spaceport than like a ship had landed. Maybe they were just going to build their cities out of starships.

He turned back to Manny. "Thank you for taking this on."

"Quite a team. A politician, a gleaner, and a ranger. All we need to do is add a smuggler and the whole population will be represented."

Charlie laughed. "We're going to survive. At least now that we have you where you belong."

"I hope so," Manny said. "For all of our sakes."

A single Next, wearing the large silvery and flowing form Charlie had seen on the Satwa emerged from the *Sunward*. It used the fluidity of the form to lope long and low across the tarmac toward them, easily outdistancing its human escort and looking effortless and full of grace and power. If it reminded Charlie of anything at all, it was the long run of a tongat about to bring down a grazer. The image disturbed him.

The Next started to slow, changing into a large humanoid form.

"Stand up straight," Manny said. "This is historic."

"Yes, Uncle." Charlie teased.

Manny gave him a look.

They walked toward the robot, acutely aware that news-bots would send photos and analysis of this moment out to every corner of the Glittering.

Jhailing and the others all stayed behind.

Charlie waved Amfi forward. For a moment it looked like she might refuse, but then she joined them.

The Next held up its huge silvered hand in greeting and spoke out loud in a pleasant and distinctly feminine voice, saying, "I'm Colorima Kelm, and I'm here to finalize the work that Jhailing Jim, Charlie Windar, and Amfi the Gleaner started." As she said their names, she nodded at Charlie and Amfi.

At least he wasn't going to have to figure out how to deal with two Jhailing Jim's at once.

Charlie, Manny, and Amfi escorted Colorima to the hangar, the Next bulking over them.

While they were outside watching the *Sunward* land, Manny's staff had redecorated. A plush carpet covered the hangar floor. Benches and good lighting surrounded a table set with water and fruit.

Colorima flowed over to the table. Instead of dwarfing one of the existing chairs, she changed form so that she looked like a normal-sized human sitting in a large chair, only she was both chair and human. A casual display of power.

Manny sat opposite her with Charlie and Amfi on either side of him.

Yi and Jason stood, looking uncertain.

Charlie whispered to Manny. "Can they sit with us?"

Manny shook his head ever so slightly. "Not at this moment."

The soulbots looked at each other and nodded, their faces neutral. They pulled two chairs back from the table and sat in them, picking a place where they could watch both sides.

Charlie felt sorry for them. Not only had they lost Chrystal, but neither side appeared willing to claim them. He whispered back to Manny. "Are you sure? They helped us back . . . where we were." He had promised Amfi not to give away the location of the complex of caves.

"I can't," Manny said. "Not unless you want whatever final decision we get to be repudiated by the people of Lym. How would they—or we—ever know if they negotiated on our side or the Next's?"

———⟨∞⟩———

After ten hours of sitting, Charlie was happy to be up and pacing around inside the small office of the hanger. This break in the negotiations might be their last. It had mostly been an exercise in duplicating the conversation Charlie had had with Jhailing in the cave, except that Manny had required fair compensation for any minerals that were removed. Charlie had missed that; his thoughts had been centered on protecting Lym more than on her coffers. Manny had had to trade one more small space for a city for it.

"How are you going to sell this to people?" Charlie asked Manny.

Manny raised his head and looked at Charlie, his cheeks even more hollowed than they had been. "I'll pretend it's a good deal. And so will you."

Charlie sighed. "I don't see how we could have done better." He hated it, hated that it had happened, hated that the Next had come. "We're lucky they're talking to us at all. We didn't negotiate with them. There's not a human alive from that time, but some Next are old enough to remember being forced out."

Amfi looked pensive. "I'm sure we'll all realize what we missed. But we need to go on. Let's do this."

Manny stared at her for a long time, his jaw tight and his arms crossed. Eventually, he nodded. "All right."

Colorima sat in the position she had taken when they started this, so that she made her own chair out of part of herself.

Manny walked right up to her, coming closer than he had so far. He extended a hand. "We are ready to welcome you as our neighbors." The words were clear and warm, even though Charlie knew Manny wanted to choke on the sentence.

Colorima regarded Manny through silver eyes above silver lips the shape of a beautiful woman's. "There is another thing to clear up," she said, "The soulbots will stay with you for now."

"Jason and Yi?" Manny asked.

"Yes."

"And only them?"

"Yes. Everyone else will have to abide by the decisions we just made and stay away from your city unless invited."

"Why?" Manny asked.

Colorima smiled a silver smile. "They have suffered. It pleases me to leave them with some freedom in return for that."

Manny looked trapped. He had the right to refuse. This was going to be a hard sell in Manna Springs. But he had the grace to say, "Yes, of course."

She took Manny's hand, her hand about the same size as his now.

Nevertheless, the metallic strength of it looked far more powerful than Manny's flesh and blood hand. They shook.

"We have a gift for Yi and Jason," Colorima said.

Charlie turned to look at the soulbots, who were standing a little to the side, watching in silence.

Yi raised an eyebrow—a subtle way to say he had no idea what Colorima was talking about?

CHAPTER SEVENTY-SIX

CHRYSTAL

Chrystal stood outside the hangar door, next to a Jhailing Jim. On her other side, Katherine stood holding her hand. Katherine's long hair blew in the sweet, soft wind. Neither of them had ever been on a planet. Chrystal felt the magnificence of the sky magnified through both of their linked brains. The warmth of the sun, the amazing, amazing scents of plants and air and oil and starship that permeated the air of the spaceport. Flowers bloomed somewhere close by. Geraniums.

The hangar door began to roll up.

They stood, still and silent.

On the outside, a Jason and a Yi. She knew their story, knew how they had been hurt, knew how one of her had been cruelly destroyed. Knew that their Katherine had failed. Her own Katherine had almost failed.

She walked slowly, deliberately toward her family members, the four of them locking eyes.

The Jason and the Yi didn't believe at first, didn't dare hope. She wasn't in their heads, not yet, but she could see the mix of emotions in their eyes.

The moment they did believe lightened them.

She and they began to jog and then to race toward each other.

Soon she had an arm around Katherine and an arm around Yi, and Jason stood opposite her, smiling so broadly she couldn't help but smile back. In this moment, it didn't matter that this reunion served the Next.

The expression on the Jason's face was worth the risk.

CHAPTER SEVENTY-SEVEN

NONA

"They had . . . such abandon. Such precision. Charlie and I were certain they were playing. And learning." Nona swallowed; even after all this time, the memory of Chrystal, Jason, and Yi dancing in the cargo bay of the *Star Ghost* moved her nearly to tears. "Even though they were all adults, my age and older, they were learning and playing with their new bodies. They were happy in that moment, which was nearly the last time I saw any of them except Chrystal."

The assistants had gone silent. Satyana had left the room and gone into her office for a meeting an hour before.

Dr. Nevening stared at her with soft eyes, spellbound, the objective viewpoint of the Historian momentarily abandoned. A quiet moment fell, and Nona remembered the smell of Charlie in her arms, the grace and strength of the robots. She hadn't told Dr. Nevening that they were naked when they danced. It seemed like a breach of privacy to do so.

He cleared his throat. "Do you think Chrystal was usually happy?" he asked. "You haven't described her as happy, at least not after the High Sweet Home."

"She seemed happy in that moment. And I think at some other times." Nona sipped her tea. "Yi seemed happy, too, I think. Almost always. That may have been the only moment I remember Jason looking happy, though. They all looked free and ecstatic in that moment, and it was the first time I understood that they might truly be better than we could be, that there is a beauty in the form the Next gave to them. Maybe it was because they didn't know that we were watching. I wish we had recorded it."

The youngest assistant, Hatley, looked enthralled. "Did they have a secret life? Did they have ways they were happy that you never saw?"

"How could she know that?" Dr. Nevening asked Hatley, "How can you know if anyone has a secret life?"

Satyana came in, immediately interrupting. "There's news," she said to the room at large. "You'll want to see it."

The wall screen lit up. Satyana sat next to Nona and took her hand.

Bad news? Satyana looked more perplexed than worried.

On the screen, Manny and Charlie stood next to each other, being interviewed. They caught Charlie in midsentence ". . . were surprised. So were Yi and Jason."

The interviewer said, "Let us show you this incredible footage. First, a little backstory. Most of you will remember that Chrystal Peterson was torn apart by the Shining Revolution. We all saw that on the screen. What many of you may not have known is that she had a family. This is the family before they met the Next." The screen showed a still picture of Chrystal, Katherine, Yi, and Jason standing beside one of the jalinerines in the meadow of High Sweet Home.

"All four of them were brutally murdered and their brains copied into robotic bodies. They became soulbots. Although we were tragically unable to interview Chrystal before the Shining Revolution dismembered her, Chrystal's mother told us that Chrystal herself insisted she was still alive inside of her robotic body. This is the most emotional story we have so far to illustrate the story of the Next returning from beyond the Ring of Distance."

Satyana sniffed. "Sensationalist spin." But her grip on Nona's hand tightened.

A new image filled the screen; all four of them walked across a hangar. Four. Chrystal and Katherine walking to meet Jason and Yi. At first, Nona assumed it must be from before she had been reunited with Chrystal.

Then she focused on the background. Charlie stood there, beside Manny. And close by, two Next watched the four come together into a sweet, impossible hug.

Nona should have understood immediately, but it was the Historian who whispered, "Backup copies."

—∞∞∞—

An hour later, the long breakfast and its surprise were both over. The Historian and his assistants had gone. Nona lifted her cup and struggled to find the right words, but finally she just spit it out. "I'm going to Lym."

Satyana pursed her lips and set her cup down before turning toward her. "You'll lose the influence you've gained here."

Nona shrugged, knowing the gesture would frustrate Satyana. "I might. But I need to see Chrystal."

"She won't be the same. This Chrystal didn't travel with you, didn't talk to the Historian, didn't meet her mother."

Nona agreed. Her friend had still been brutally murdered, twice, and this new Chrystal had been murdered once. "I don't know what to think about it, or even how to feel about it. But I need to go see her."

Satyana let out along breath. "Yes, I suppose you do. But you also want to see Charlie, don't you?"

"I already booked passage. I leave tomorrow morning."

"You have your own ship."

Nona smiled. "Actually, I have two of them. The *Star Ghost* is already docked at Lym, so it seemed to make more sense to leave the *Savior* here. Besides, she's so big I need crew. I think I would have to start over on that."

Satyana had the grace to merely grunt. Nona had never brought up the fact that Satyana had hand-picked the crew that had betrayed her and left her to be imprisoned on the Satwa. It had all worked out. But she suspected Satyana knew the details.

"I'll miss you," Satyana said.

"I'll be back and forth, I think. Surely Dr. Nevening will want to know how things go with the Next on Lym. That will be the real test of all this, you know."

Satyana sighed. "That and a million other things. Like how successful we become at keeping every other human in the solar system peaceful."

Nona opted for the simplest response. "I'll miss you, too."

CHAPTER SEVENTY-EIGHT

CHARLIE

Charlie and Cricket and Jean Paul stood together on a rock scarp near the ranger station. The sky had just darkened to the point that stars and the lights of ships were becoming visible.

"Do you think she's up there yet?" Jean Paul asked, his eyes on the heavens.

"Not close enough to see. Not for another hour."

Jean Paul fidgeted. "Will you move out?"

"Not yet." What had happened on the *Star Ghost* might not happen again. "No, I think I'll court her. I think she'd like that better. After all, she may not choose me." He realized he wasn't entirely teasing. A vast gulf of wealth and experience still separated them.

"Are you crazy?" Jean Paul said. "Anyone would choose you."

Charlie couldn't see Jean Paul's face in the half-light. "I'm going to meet her in the morning. Then we'll see what happens next. But that will never change the fact that I have your back."

Jean Paul's voice sounded choked. "I have yours, too."

Cricket leaned into Charlie, almost knocking him over. He leaned down and hugged her. He wanted to take her with him, but that would leave Jean Paul entirely alone. "I'll be back in a day or so. I'll let you know if I'm bringing Nona with me."

"I'd like to meet Chrystal and Katherine."

Charlie didn't have to think too hard. "Do you want to come with me?"

"Sure. I can come."

"Then you better go pack."

Jean Paul gave him a quick, sharp hug and went back, leaving Charlie alone with Cricket and a fantastic view of the stars and starships above Lym.

Whatever happened, at least he would be *here* when it happened, he would have sky and stars and waterfalls and wild animals, and the smell of fresh air. Nevertheless, he looked up, feeling the threads of connection between Lym and the Glittering, and the Edge, an unseen vastness so big it made him and his beast tiny. He hugged Cricket close. "We'll make it," he whispered.

ACKNOWLEDGMENTS

Novels are born in the quiet of a writer's head, but they are burnished in the conversations with others. I want to send out specific thanks to my first readers. Linda Merkens and Gisele Peterson are two of my oldest friends—literally. Like Chrystal and Nona knew each other from childhood, I've known Linda since I was about seven years old and Gisele since I was eighteen. There is a steadiness in old and true friends. Darragh Metzger has been reminding me to let my characters react to events and to remember to describe what they look like for over a decade now. She's a fabulous writer, and I encourage people to check out her books. Two other writers who were extraordinarily helpful first readers are Christopher M. Cevasco and Jennifer Linnaea. Nancy Kress graciously took a look at my opening, and then eventually read the whole novel. Ramez Naam also read an earlier, rougher draft.

Novels see the light of day because agents sell them to editors who make them available. Well, these days, there are a lot of paths to availability. But this novel took the traditional path and I want to thank Eleanor Wood for her constant support and Lou Anders for two roles. Not only is Lou a phenomenal editor, but he is also a really fabulous art director. The cover of the first book set in this world won a Chesley for the brilliant John Picacio, and the cover for *Edge of Dark* is one of the most moving pieces of art I've seen from well-beloved cover artist Stephan Martiniere.

I am grateful for the support of my family, who put up with me disappearing for a week at a time to hide and work on novels or get really public and promote novels. I suspect writers are hard to live with, and writers with day jobs are even harder. I'm often not home, or if I am home, part of me is often in another universe entirely.

And for this book, I want to say thanks to all of the people exploring transhumanism. I'll list a few, but I'll miss a lot. I have not met all of them. Regardless, here goes: Ray Kurzweil, Ramez Naam, Madeline Ashby, Natasha Vita-More, Max More, Charlie Stross, Gray Scott, Nancy Kress, Greg Bear, Vernor Vinge, David Brin, Bruce Sterling, John Smart . . . and there are many many more.

ABOUT THE AUTHOR

Brenda Cooper is the author of *The Creative Fire* and *The Diamond Deep*, Books One and Two of Ruby's Song, as well as the Silver Ship series. Though not intended as a Young Adult novel, book one, *The Silver Ship and the Sea*, was selected by *Library Journal* as one of the year's 100 Best Books for YA and by *Booklist* as one of the top-ten 2007 adult books for youth to read. The other books in the series are *Reading the Wind* and *Wings of Creation*. She is also the author of *Mayan December* and has collaborated with Larry Niven (*Building Harlequin's Moon*). Brenda is a working futurist and a technology professional with a passionate interest in the environment.